HUNTING SEASON

Also by P. T. Deutermann

Train Man

Zero Option

Sweepers

Official Privilege

The Edge of Honor

Scorpion in the Sea

P. T. Deutermann

HUNTING

a novel

SEASON

ST. MARTIN'S PRESS
NEW YORK

HUNTING SEASON. Copyright © 2001 by P. T. Deutermann. All rights reserved. Printed in the United States of America. No part of this book may be used or reproduced in any manner whatsoever without written permission except in the case of brief quotations embodied in critical articles or reviews. For information, address St. Martin's Press, 175 Fifth Avenue, New York, N.Y. 10010.

www.stmartins.com

Design by Kathryn Parise

LIBRARY OF CONGRESS CATALOGING-IN-PUBLICATION DATA

Deutermann, Peter T.
    Hunting season : a novel / P. T. Deutermann.
      p. cm.
    ISBN 0-312-26979-X
    1. Intelligence officers—Fiction. 2. Fathers and daughters—Fiction. 3. Washington (D.C.)—Fiction. 4. Missing persons—Fiction. 5. West Virginia—Fiction. I. Title

PS3554.E887 H86 2001
813'.54—dc21   00-045959

First Edition: February 2001

10 9 8 7 6 5 4 3 2 1

This book is dedicated to the fond hope that, one fine day, the U.S. Department of Justice will once again represent the epitome of public integrity within the government of the United States.

ACKNOWLEDGMENTS

I would like to express my appreciation to the Federal Bureau of Investigation and the Bureau of Alcohol, Tobacco and Firearms, whose Web sites and public information agencies were most helpful in writing this book. Thanks as well to my editor, George Witte, and my agent, Nick Ellison, for their usual fine professional help.

HUNTING SEASON

1

Rip and Tommy hit the leg traps at the same time. Rip yelled and pitched headfirst into the small stream. Tommy grunted, lurched sideways, and then he, too, slipped over the bank. Lynn, a few steps behind them, stopped in her tracks, her arms windmilling to recover her balance. The grass along the stream was high enough that she couldn't see what was holding the two boys' legs at such an odd angle while they flopped in the shallow water. Whatever it was, it was hurting them a lot. Rip was on his back in the water, groaning and sobbing as he tried to sit up. Tommy was white-faced and tight-lipped, his right leg pointing diagonally up as he struggled against the weight of his backpack.

"My God!" Lynn exclaimed. "What happened?"

"Something's got my leg," Tommy said between clenched teeth. "I think it's a trap of some kind. Help me."

Lynn shrugged out of her backpack, knelt down, and pushed aside the grass. What she found made her swallow hard. "Stop moving," she said. "Let me see how bad this is."

Rip had stopped crying. As Lynn looked over at him, his eyes were rolling backward as he subsided into the brook. Lynn swore and jumped over Tommy's trapped leg to get to Rip. She splashed through the stream and snatched Rip's face up out of the water. He began to choke and splutter, then yelled in pain. She heaved and pulled until his back was partially supported by the opposite bank. Then she eased him out of his backpack straps, tugged the sodden bundle off his back, and threw it up on the bank. A vicious metallic-snapping sound cracked in the grass. She froze. Oh Jesus, she thought. She stood up very slowly, then tramped back through the icy water to Tommy, being very careful about where she put her feet.

"I can't feel my foot," Tommy whispered.

Lynn knelt down. "That's probably a good thing, Tommy," she said, trying to keep up a good front. She was supposed to be the strong one, but her throat was dry and her hands were shaking. She picked up a small stick and pushed aside the wet grass to expose the trap. It was two feet wide and gunmetal gray. It consisted of a heavy base that had been chained to some kind of heavy ground screw. The two snapping arms were solid steel bars, and they had Tommy's leg just above the ankle. There was some bleeding on both sides of his leg, and the fabric of his jeans was indented at least an inch into his flesh. The skin below the jaws of the trap was already purple. She swallowed again as he groaned. She tried not to avert her eyes.

"Can you get it off?" he asked. His voice was cracking and beads of sweat stood on his forehead. Lynn reached gingerly for the two solid bars and tried to pry them apart, but it was like pulling on the edge of a building: The only thing that moved was Tommy's leg, and he shouted in pain. Rip was still blubbering behind them, and suddenly Lynn wanted to yell at him, to make him shut up. It had been Rip's idea to sneak onto the abandoned base. She was very scared.

"I can't move it," she said. Just then, there was a thump and rumble of thunder to the west; the afternoon storm clouds that had made them hurry down toward the creek, away from the tall trees, were still coming. Tommy closed his eyes, sighed, and lay back on his pack.

"Let me see if I can find something to pry it open," she said. She stood up and looked around. They were in a small clearing. The streambed ran down an east-west gully that wound between two broad hills covered in dense forest. Across the stream and up the other side of the gully was another stand of trees, through which she thought she could see a smoke-stack and the top of some kind of building. The sky above the hills behind them was darkening fast, and a flicker of lightning gleamed wickedly at her from within coiling clouds. Tommy tried again to get out of the stream but couldn't manage it. She helped him get his pack all the way off, and then she repositioned his upper body against the opposite bank, the pack under his neck. There was a chunky stick a few feet downstream, which she lifted and then used to beat down all the grass on either side of the creek between the two boys. She found no more traps, although she went no farther than Tommy's backpack. Then the stick broke.

She told them not to move and then retraced her steps up the side of the gully to the edge of the forest, which was about thirty feet back from the creek. Another crack of thunder boomed along the face of the low hills to the west, and the sky seemed to darken again. The forest ahead of her stirred uneasily, as if the trees knew what was coming. She began working a two-inch-thick limb off a pine tree, when she saw a curtain of gray rain sweep down the gully, pursued by another clap of thunder. Her raingear was rolled up on top of her pack, but she kept working the branch, twisting it back and forth, swearing at it under her breath as it became slippery and her hands grew sticky with pine pitch. Finally, she got it off and then ran back to where Tommy was sitting awkwardly on the side of the stream, one hand under him. The pain in his eyes nearly broke her heart. Rip appeared to have fainted again. His chin was down on his chest, but at least he was well out of the water.

She took out her camping knife and whittled frantically on the blunt end of the branch, trying to form a wedge point. The rain came down hard and cold, but at least there was no more lightning. And then a single brilliant blue-white bolt punched out an ear-clenching blast that made her scream and drop the knife and the branch. Her ball cap fell off into the stream. The bolt vaporized the top of a nearby tree, showering the gully with flaming embers and enveloping them in a pungent fog of crackling ozone. A bolus of fire flared briefly at the top of the tree, then disappeared in a new roar of rain. She scrambled around, trying to find her knife. Finally, she saw it in the creek, retrieved it, and went back to hacking at the end of the branch. She glanced over at Tommy, but his eyes were closed and the rain was running into his partially opened lips. The rain was so heavy, she almost couldn't see Rip.

When she had the base of the limb cleaned off and shaped into a wedge, she knelt back down by Tommy's leg. She cut the fabric back away from his ankle. She was appalled at the swollen purple mess that had been his lower leg. She didn't know how she would be able to wedge the limb into the space between the snapping arms without hurting him. She looked up at Tommy's face. His eyes were open now.

"Just do it," he said, his voice barely audible above the noise of the rain. "Get it off me."

She nodded and pushed the wedge end of the six-foot-long branch between the two steel jaws as close to the hinge joint as she could get. Then she stood up and planted her right foot in the stream, which she noticed was deeper now, coming up to the tops of her boots. She put her left foot on the base plate and then leaned slowly against the branch. Tommy groaned as the trap moved, but the arms did not budge. Not one inch. She relaxed and then tried again, positioning her hands for maximum leverage. She thought she saw the arms move fractionally, but without her hat, the rain was in her eyes, and then the branch snapped cleanly in two just above the trap and she went tumbling into the grass below where Tommy was trapped. She swore aloud and then realized her cheek was touching metal.

She gasped, commanding every muscle in her body to freeze. Taking tiny breaths of air, she tried to see through the individual blades of wet grass.

"What's the matter?" Tommy called through the rain.

"There's another one. Wait a minute."

She finally mustered the courage to push some of the high grass aside. Her head was on the base plate, her cheek actually touching one of the snapping arms. But not the trigger, a flat spoon-shaped piece of metal between the arms, which she could just see. Moving very carefully, she pulled her head away from the trap and then sat up in the grass. She reached for the broken branch, stood up, and then jammed it furiously into the trap, which slammed shut hard enough to break the pine branch into two additional pieces and sting her hand. She swore and hurried back to Tommy, who was trying to pull himself higher up on the bank. The water was rising, really rising, as all the rain upstream began to invade the gully. Tommy's free leg was completely out of sight, and the water was swirling around his hips. Rip was still passed out, but his lower body was quickly disappearing from sight. She looked at Tommy and found him staring at her face. The rain kept coming, plastering her short hair to her skull. He knew.

"Tommy, what do I do? I can't open that damn thing."

"See if you can move the chain."

She examined the chain, whose links were at least a quarter-inch thick. The chain was about a foot long. The links on both the base plate and the ground screw were solid, welded in place. She jammed the broken end of the pine branch into the screw eye and tried to turn it, but the chain immediately tightened against Tommy's leg and he groaned. A lightning stroke threw the trees on the far side of the gully into stark relief. She saw the building again.

"There's a building beyond those trees," she said. "I'm going to go see if I can get help."

"Rip said this place has been shut down for twenty years," Tommy said. "There isn't going to be anyone there."

"There might be a metal bar or something," she said, looking upstream. There was an ominous noise coming from the far western end of the ravine, a sound of something substantial, moving. "Tommy, we don't have much time."

"Okay, go. Go! Jesus Christ, this hurts."

She checked Rip one more time, but he was still fading in and out. The water was swirling around his waist now. She started to step out of the streambed, then wondered if there were more traps on the opposite bank. She grabbed a stick and beat the grass in front of her, but nothing happened. She reached the far side of the gully and glanced back through the driving rain. The creek, which had originally been maybe two feet across, was now almost ten feet wide and becoming a menacing, foaming coil of muddy brown water. Tommy was clutching at a tuft of grass to stay upright. Rip was leaning like a drunk against the bank, his left arm undulating in the current. The rumbling sound that came from behind the trees upstream was more pronounced. She peered through the trees ahead but could no longer see the building. She couldn't bring herself to leave the boys, so she started screaming for help, knowing it was probably hopeless. There wouldn't be anyone there. The boys were going to drown. She yelled again and again, then gave up and climbed back down to Tommy, being careful to stay in her own tracks.

The water was up to his lower chest now, and he had managed to pull his free leg underneath him so he could kneel and get his face higher. She waded out to him, feeling the force of the current. The stream had spread out in the gully to fifteen feet, submerging the traps and all the grass.

"Something's coming," Tommy said, looking upstream. The rain began to let up, and Lynn felt a surge of hope. But the noise from upstream was definitely still there. Then she saw lights in the trees across the gully.

"Oh my God! Look!" she said to Tommy, and then she stood up. "Over here! Help! Hurry, they're trapped in the water!"

Two dark figures were coming through the trees from the direction of the building, their flashlights bobbing in the gloom. The rain was definitely letting up, but the water was still rising. She called again, waving her arms, wondering if she should get out her own flashlight. Then the larger of the two men apparently saw her. He was tall and had a black beard. He put his arm out in a signal for the other man to halt behind him, which he did.

"Over here," she yelled again. Why were they stopping? The rumbling noise from upstream was gaining strength; she imagined she could feel the ground trembling under the water. There was a sound like the rattle of individual boulders and rocks audible above the water noise. She yelled and waved her arms again. The tall, black-bearded man stepped down to the edge of the flooding gully. He was wearing a long rain slicker that came all the way to his boots. His bearded face was partially covered by a large black hat. He looked at her and then upstream. The rain began to intensify.

"Tommy's trapped," she called out. "So's Rip. Please, can you help me get them out?"

The tall man was about fifteen feet from her now, and the water rose up to the hem of his slicker. Tommy coughed and then groaned in pain as the current shifted him sideways. The water covered his shirt pockets, and he was shivering uncontrollably. Behind him, Rip, wild-eyed and wide-awake now, sputtered something as the water came up to his neck. She still could not see the big man's face under his large mountain man–style hat.

He came forward again, steadying himself against the current. When he reached her, he put out a hand and motioned for her to take it. She was trying to decide what to do when a roaring noise erupted upstream. As she turned to look, a five-foot-high wall of brown water and debris came sweeping around the bend.

She screamed at the sight of it, knowing what was about to happen. Then he had her by the forearm and was pulling her back toward the tree line. She screamed again, something about Tommy, but the grip on her arm was like a vise and she was literally being dragged by her heels through the water and up the slope. He pulled her the last few feet out of the water as the flash flood roared by, filling the air with the smell of mud and the sound of cracking rocks. She put up a hand to see through the rain, to find Tommy and Rip, but they had disappeared. The surge front was followed by a second, swelling tide, this one as much mud as debris-choked water. It rapidly filled the gully all the way to the tree lines on both sides. There were bushes and small trees sailing by in the rumbling water, but the boys were now five feet down and lost forever. She felt sick.

The big man did not relax his grip. "Take her to the nitro building," he said in a cold, commanding voice. "Full restraint. Then we'll come back for the bodies."

"There'll be a vehicle somewhere," the other man said. She could not tear her eyes away from the brown river sweeping by them, which only a few minutes ago had been a small brook.

"Yes, we'll need to find that, too. And their backpacks. Take her, now."

Take her? Lynn thought. Take me where? Who are these men? She started to ask them what was going on, when the tall man pulled her arms behind her and held them.

"Hey!" she yelled, but then a second set of hands pulled a wet length of fabric across her eyes. Then some kind of gag was taped across her mouth. She tried to struggle, but the man behind her lifted her pinned elbows, causing a lancing pain in her upper back. She gave a muffled yell of pain and stopped fighting.

"Be still," the tall man ordered. She could feel him bending close. His body gave off a scent of wet canvas and leather and something else, some kind of chemical smell. "You should not have come here," he said, his voice ominous above the rumble of the flooded stream. "You should never have come here."

Special Agent Janet Carter checked herself out in the ladies' room mirror before going back to her office. She was still smarting over a remark she had overheard that morning down in the deli next to the Roanoke federal building. A new agent, fresh in from the Academy, had asked another agent about her while standing in the coffee line, unaware that Janet was sitting on the other side of the register, just out of sight. She was the only female agent in the Roanoke office, so when the new guy started talking about the cute little redhead in the Violent Crimes Squad, she had naturally paid attention. Then the other guy answering: "Don't let that little-girl face fool you; she's thirty-something, going on forty, has eight years in the Bureau, and she doesn't date other agents. You figure it out."

Figure out what? she thought. Was he saying I'm a lesbian because I won't date other agents? Is that what they think? Or that I'm too old for the newbie? She examined her "little-girl face." Red hair, bright green eyes, okay, a couple of wrinkles here and there, but nothing substantial. Firm chin, healthy skin. So she looked younger than her thirty-seven years—and what was wrong with that? She worked out three, four times a week and was in better shape generally than some of her male coworkers, if the annual physical-fitness test proved anything. There was nothing wrong with the old bod, either. Which was why the newbie had been asking, right? So relax. They're just guys flapping their jaws. In general, she liked the Roanoke crew, and they liked her.

She sighed and went back to her office. There were four cubicles in their office. One, belonging to Larry Talbot, the squad's supervisor, was slightly larger than the others. The other three were Bureau-issue identical. Each contained a computer workstation, a single chair, and some file cabinets over and under the computer table. It was a four-person squad, with one semipermanent, budget-cut vacancy. The other worker bee in the squad was Billy Smith, who was generally conceded to be RIP, as in retired in place. The RIP designation was a little unfair to Billy, who had a serious blood-pressure problem, for which he would take a pill upon arrival in the office. It would promptly put him to sleep at his desk for an hour or so, and then he would wake up and do paperwork throughout the rest of the morning, until lunch, at which time he would take his next pill and slip back under again. He'd come down from some obscure Washington assignment three years ago and supposedly had two years to go until he was eligible for retirement. Larry Talbot had worked a deal: Billy would do the bulk of the squad's routine paperwork, while Larry and Janet would do the legwork. Everyone figured the Bureau was simply looking the other way until Billy could take his retirement and go away. His repertoire of dark two-liner jokes had become notorious in the office, especially when he could catch someone off guard, as he had Janet when he asked her what it meant that the post office flag was at half-mast: They were hiring. Between those little bombs and handling all the squad's paperwork, Billy had found a home.

She sat down at her desk, checked E-mail, and grunted. Larry Talbot had left her a message: Today was the day they went out to tell Mr. Kreiss that they were sending the missing college kids' case up to Washington. She was supposed to meet Talbot in the parking garage at nine o'clock. She looked at her watch. She barely had time to finish her coffee. She thought about that guy's remark. Figure it out, huh? As she remembered, the guy talking to the newbie was a married man. She'd go figure him out all right. Maybe drop a dime, speculate to his wife about the guy's sudden interest in redheads. Make his home life a little more interesting. But then she just laughed. Not her style.

2

Edwin Kreiss waited in the doorway as the FBI car from the Roanoke office ground up the winding drive from the county road down below. He knew why the Bureau was coming: They were going to call off their search. It had been almost three weeks since the kids had vanished, and neither the Bureau nor the local cops had come up with one single clue as to what had happened. No bodies, no sign of foul play, no abandoned vehicles, no credit-card receipts, no phone tips, no witnesses, no sightings, and not the first idea of even where to look for them. His daughter, Lynn, and her two friends, Rip and Tommy, had vanished.

Kreiss frankly did not care too much about the two boys, but Lynn was his only child. Had been his only child? He was determined to keep her memory in the present tense, even as he now lived with the sensation of a cold iron ball lodged permanently in his stomach. It had been there since that first call from the university's campus security office. And here was the world's greatest law-enforcement organization coming to tell him they were going to just give up. Special Agent Talbot, who had called that morning, hadn't been willing to come right out and say that, not on the phone, anyway. But Kreiss, a retired FBI agent himself, knew the drill: They had reached that point in their investigation where some budget-conscious supervisor was asking pointed questions, especially since there were no indications of a crime.

Kreiss watched the dark four-door Ford sedan swing into the clearing in front of his cabin and stop. He recognized the two agents who had been working the case as they got out, a man and a woman. *Special* agents, Kreiss reminded himself. We were always special agents in the Bureau. Larry Talbot, the head of the Violent Crimes Squad, was dressed in a conservative business suit and was completely bald. He was heavyset, to the point of almost being fat, which in Kreiss's day would have been very unusual at the Bureau. Special Agent Janet Carter was considerably younger than Talbot. She appeared to be in her early thirties, with a good figure and a pretty but somewhat girlish face, which Kreiss thought would make it difficult for people to take her seriously as a law-enforcement agent. Her red hair glinted in the sunlight. He stood motionless in the doorway, his face a patient mask, waiting for them. He and the other parents had met with these two several times over the past three weeks. Talbot had been patiently professional and considerate in his dealings with the parents, but Kreiss had the impression that the woman, Carter, had been frustrated by the case and was increasingly anxious to go do something else. He also sensed that she either did not like him or suspected him somehow in the disappearance of his daughter.

Kreiss's prefab log cabin crouched below the eastern crest of Pearl's Mountain, a 3,700-foot knob that was twenty-six miles west of Blacksburg, in southwest Appalachian Virginia. The mountain's gnarled eastern face rose up out of an open meadow three hundred yards behind the cabin. The sheer rock cliff was dotted with scrub trees and a few glistening weeps that left mossy bright green trails down the crumbling rock. The meadow behind the cabin was the only open ground; otherwise, the hill's flanks fell away into dense forest in all directions. Two hundred feet below the cabin, a vigorous creek, called Hangman's Run, worked relentlessly, wearing down the ancient rock in a deep ravine. A narrow county road paralleled the creek. There was a stubby wooden bridge across the creek, leading into Kreiss's drive.

The two agents walked across the leafy yard without speaking as they approached the wooden steps leading up onto the porch. "Mr. Kreiss?" Talbot said. "Special Agent Larry Talbot; this is Special Agent Janet Carter."

"Yes, I remember," Kreiss said. "Come in."

He opened the screen door. Talbot always reintroduced himself and his partner every time they met, and he was always politely formal—using *sir* a lot. If Talbot knew Kreiss had been with the Bureau, he gave no sign of it. Kreiss kept his own tone neutral; he would be polite, but not friendly, not if they were giving up.

"Thank you, sir," Talbot said. Kreiss led them to chairs in the lodge room, an expansive area that encompassed the cabin's living room, dining room, and kitchen. Talbot sat on the edge of his chair, his briefcase on his knees. Carter was somewhat more relaxed, both arms on the chair and her nice legs carefully crossed. Kreiss sat down in an oak rocker by the stone fireplace, crossed his arms over his chest, and tried not to scowl.

"Well," Talbot began, glancing over at his partner as if making sure of her moral support. "As I think you know, the investigation to date has come up empty. Frankly, I've never seen one quite like this: We usually have *something*, some piece of evidence, a witness, or at least a working theory. But this one . . ."

Kreiss looked from Carter to Talbot. "What are the Bureau's intentions?" he asked.

Talbot took a deep breath. "We've consulted with the other two families. Our basic problem remains: There's no indication of a criminal act. And absent evidence of—"

"They've been gone without a trace for three weeks," Kreiss interrupted. "I should think it would be *hard* to disappear without a trace in this day and age, Mr. Talbot. Really hard."

He stared right at Talbot. Carter was looking at her shoes, her expression blank. "I'll accept what you say about there being no evidence," Kreiss continued. "But there's also no evidence that they just went off the grid voluntarily, either."

"Yes, sir, we acknowledge that," Talbot said. "But they're college kids, and the three of them were known to be, um, close."

Close doesn't quite describe it, Kreiss thought. Those three kids had been joined at the hip in some kind of weird triangular relationship since late freshman year. Tommy and Lynn, his daughter, had been the boy-girl pair, and Rip, the strange one, had been like some kind of eccentric electron, orbiting around the other two.

"We've interviewed everyone we could find on the campus who knew them," Talbot continued. "Professors, TAs, other students. None of them could give us anything specific, except for two of their classmates, who were pretty sure they had gone camping somewhere. But nobody had any idea of where or for how long. Plus, it was spring break, which leaves almost an entire week where no one would have expected to see them. Sir, they could be literally anywhere."

"And the campus cops—the Blacksburg cops?"

"We've had full cooperation from local law. University, city, and county. We've pulled all the usual strings: their telephone records, E-mail accounts, bank accounts, credit cards, school schedules, even their library cards. Nothing." He took a deep breath. "I guess what we're here to say is that we have to forward this case into the Missing Persons Division now."

"Missing Persons."

"Yes, sir. Until we get some indication—anything at all, mind you— that they didn't just take off for an extended, I don't know, road trip of some kind."

"And just leave college? Three successful engineering students in their senior year?"

"Sir, it has happened before. College kids get a wild hair and take off to save the whales or the rain forest or some damn thing."

Kreiss frowned, shook his head, and got up. He walked to a front window, trying to control his temper. He stood with his back to them, not wanting them to see the anger in his face.

"That's not my take on it, Mr. Talbot. My daughter and I had become pretty close, especially after her mother was killed."

"Yes, sir, in the airplane accident. Our condolences, sir."

Kreiss blinked. Talbot was letting him know they'd run his background, too. Standard procedure, of course: When kids disappeared, you checked the parents, hard. So they had to know he was ex-FBI. He wondered how much they knew about the circumstances of his sudden retirement. Talbot might; the woman was too young. Unless they'd gone back to Washington to ask around.

"Thank you," Kreiss said. "But my point is that Lynn would have told me if she was going to leave school. Hell, she'd have hit me up for money."

"Would she, sir?" Talbot said. "We understood she received quite a bit of money from the airline's settlement."

Kreiss, surprised, turned around to face them. He had forgotten about the settlement. He remembered his former wife's lawyer contacting Lynn about it, but he had made her deal with it, whatever it was. So far, the money had covered all her college and living expenses, but he still gave her an allowance.

The woman had her notebook open and was writing something in it. He felt he had to say something. "My daughter was a responsible young adult, Mr. Talbot. So was Tommy Vining. Rip was . . . from Mars, somewhere. But they would not just leave school. That's something I *know*. I think they went camping, just like those two kids said, and something happened. Something bad."

"Yes, sir, that's one possibility. It's just that there's no—"

"All right, all right. So what happens now? You just close it and file it?"

"Not at all, sir," Talbot protested. "You know that. It becomes a federal missing persons case, and they don't get closed until the persons get found." He hesitated. "One way or another." He paused again, as if regretting he had put it that way. "As I think you'll recall, sir, there are literally thousands of missing persons cases active at the Bureau. And that's at the federal level. We don't even hear about some of the local cases."

"How comforting."

"I know it's not, Mr. Kreiss. But our MP Division has one big advantage: They get to screen every Bureau case—every active case—for any possible links: names, credit-card numbers, evidence tags, telephone numbers. They've even developed special software for this, to screen the Bureau's databases and alert for links to any missing person in the country."

"What did the other parents say when you told them this?"

Talbot sighed. "Um, they were dismayed, of course, but I think they understood. It's just that there isn't—"

"Yes, you keep saying that. Any of them going to take up a search on their own?"

"Is that what you're considering, Mr. Kreiss?" Carter asked. It was the first time she had spoken at this meeting. Now that he thought of it, he had rarely heard her speak. Kreiss looked at her for a moment, and he was surprised when their eyes locked. There was a hint of challenge in her expression that surprised him.

"Absolutely not," he answered calmly, continuing to hold her gaze. "Civilians get into police business, they usually screw things up."

"But you're not exactly a civilian, are you, Mr. Kreiss?" she said.

Kreiss hesitated, wondering just what she meant by that. "I am now, Agent Carter," he said softly. "I am now."

Talbot cleared his throat. "Um—" he began, but Carter cut him off.

"What I think Special Agent Talbot was about to say is that we ran a check on you, sir. We always check out the parents when kids go missing. And of course we knew that you had been a senior FBI agent. But your service and personnel records have been sealed. The few people we did talk to would only say that you had been an unusually effective"—she looked at her notes—"hunter. That was the term that kept coming up, sir."

Time to cut this line of conversation right off, Kreiss thought. He let his face assume a cold mask that he had not used for years. He saw her blink and shift slightly in her chair. He walked over to stand in front of her, forcing her to look up at him. "What else did these *few* people have to say, Agent Carter?" he asked, speaking through partially clenched teeth.

"Actually, nothing," she said, her voice catching. Talbot, beginning to look alarmed, shifted in his chair.

Kreiss, arms still folded across his chest, bent forward to bring his face closer to hers. "Do you have some questions for me that pertain to this case, Agent Carter?"

"Not at the moment, sir," she replied, her chin up defiantly. "But if we do, we'll certainly ask them."

She was trying for bluster, Kreiss decided, but even she knew it wasn't working. He inflated his chest and stared down into her eyes while widening his own and then allowing them to go slightly out of focus. He felt her recoil in the chair. Talbot cleared his throat from across the room to break the tension. Kreiss straightened up, exhaled quietly, and went back to sit down in the rocking chair. "My specialty at the Bureau was not in missing persons," he said. "I was a senior supervisor in the Counterintelligence Division, Far Eastern section."

Carter had recovered herself by now and cleared her throat audibly. "Yes, sir," she said. "So what you said earlier pertains absolutely: Do not go solo on this, please. You find something, think of something, hear something, please call us. We can bring a whole lot more assets to bear on a fragment than you can."

"Even though you're giving up on this case?"

"Sir, we're not giving up," Talbot protested. "The case remains in the Roanoke office's jurisdiction even when it goes up to national Missing Persons at headquarters. We can pull it back and reopen anytime we want. But Janet's right: It really complicates things if someone's been messing around in the meantime."

Kreiss continued to look across the room at Carter. "Absolutely," he said, rearranging his face into as benign an expression as he could muster. For a moment there, he had wanted to swat her pretty little head right through the front window. He was pretty sure she had sensed that impulse; the color in her cheeks was still high.

"Well," Talbot said, fingering his collar as he got up. "Let me assure you again, sir, the Bureau is definitely not giving up, especially with the child of an ex-agent. The matter is simply moving into, um, another process, if you will. If something comes up, anything at all, pass it on to either one of us and we'll get it into the right channels. I believe you have our cards?"

"I do," Kreiss said, also getting up. "I think you're entirely wrong about this," he told Talbot, ignoring Carter now.

Talbot gave him a sympathetic look before replying. "Yes, sir. But until we get some indication that something bad has happened to your daughter and her friends, I'm afraid our hands are somewhat tied. It's basically a resource problem. You were in the Bureau, Mr. Kreiss, you know how it is."

"I know how it *was*, Mr. Talbot," Kreiss said, clearly implying that *his* Bureau would not be giving up. He followed them to the front door. The agents said their good-byes and went down to their car.

Kreiss stood in the doorway, watching them go. He had fixed himself in emotional neutral ever since the kids went missing. He had cooperated with the university cops, then the local cops, and then the federal investigation, giving them whatever they wanted, patiently answering questions, letting them search her room here in the cabin, agreeing to go over anything and everything they came up with. He had attended painfully emotional meetings with the other parents, and then more meetings with Lynn's student friends and acquaintances. He had endured two brainstorming sessions with a Bureau psychologist that aimed at seeing if anyone could remember anything at all that might indicate where the kids had been going. All of which had produced nothing.

Some of Lynn's schoolmates had been a bit snotty to the cops, but that was not unusual for college kids. Engineering students at Virginia Tech considered themselves to be several cuts above the average American college kid. Perhaps they are, he thought: Lynn certainly had been. He noticed again that his thinking about Lynn was shifting into the past tense when he wasn't noticing. But there was no excuse for the students to be rude to the law-enforcement people, given the circumstances. And there had been one redheaded kid in particular who seemed to go out of his way to be rude. Kreiss had decided that either he had been grandstanding or he knew something.

Give all the cops their due, he thought wearily as the Feds drove off. They hadn't just sloughed it off. They had tried. But the colder the trail became, the more he'd become convinced that they would eventually shop it to Missing Persons and go chase real bad guys doing real crimes. The Bureau had budgets, priorities, and more problems on its plate than time in a year to work them. Missing persons cases often dragged on for years, while an agent's annual performance evaluations, especially in the statistics-driven Bureau, were based on that fiscal year's results: case closings, arrests, convictions. Fair enough. And they had been considerate enough to drive all the way up here to tell him face-to-face, even if the young woman had been snippy. So, thank you very much, Special Agents Talbot and Carter. He let out a long breath to displace the iron ball in his stomach as he closed the door. In a way, he was almost relieved at their decision. Now he could do it his way.

Talbot navigated the car down the winding drive toward the wooden bridge at the bottom of Kreiss's property. Janet checked her cell phone, but there was still no signal down here in the hollows.

"I hate doing that," Talbot said as he turned the car back out onto the narrow county road. "Telling them we're giving up. Parents always feel Missing Persons is a brush-off."

"We do what we have to," Janet said. "Personally, I still think the kids just ran off. Happens all the time, college kids these days. They have it too easy, that's all."

"I thought for a minute he was going to blow up back there. Did you see his face when you started talking about his background? Scary."

Janet did not answer. She fiddled with her seat belt as Talbot took the car through a series of tight switchbacks. The road was climbing, but the woods came down close to the road, casting a greenish light on everything. She'd seen it all right. It had taken everything she had to come back at him, and even then, her voice had broken. She'd never seen anyone's face get that threatening, especially when the person was a big guy like Kreiss, with those lineman's shoulders and that craggy face. Talbot had said Kreiss was probably in his mid-fifties, although his gray-white hair and lined face made him look older. He appeared to be keeping the lid on a lot of energy, she thought, and he was certainly able to project that power. She had actually been afraid of him for a moment, when he'd trained those flinty eyes at her with that slightly detached, off-center look a dog exhibits just before it bites you.

"You know," Talbot was saying, "like if I had some bad guys covered in a room, he'd be the guy I'd watch."

"I suppose," she said as nonchalantly as she could, trying to dismiss the fact that Kreiss had unsettled her. Get off it, Larry, she thought.

"I mean, I wouldn't want him on my trail, either. Especially if what Farnsworth said was true."

Their boss, Farnsworth, knew this guy? "What?" she said.

"Kreiss was apparently something special. One of those guys they could barely keep a handle on. Lone wolf type. I've heard that the Foreign Counterintelligence people get that way, sometimes. You know, all that cloak-and-dagger stuff, especially if they get involved with those weirdos across the river in Langley."

"Special how?" Ted Farnsworth was the Resident Agent in Roanoke. Janet couldn't see a homeboy like Farnsworth consorting with the FCI crowd.

"He didn't elaborate, but he was shaking his head a lot. Supposedly, Kreiss spent a lot of time apart from the normal Bureau organization. Then something happened and he got forced out. I think they reorganized FCI after he left to make sure there was no more of that lone wolf shit."

"I've never heard of Bureau assets being used that way. It would give away our biggest advantage—we come in hordes."

Talbot concentrated on navigating the next set of hairpin turns. "Yeah, well," he said. "Farnsworth said Kreiss got involved with the Agency's sweepers, who supposedly are all lone wolves."

" 'Sweepers'? What do they do?"

"They're a group of man-hunting specialists in the Agency Counter-espionage Division. They're supposedly called in when one of their *own* clandestine operatives gets sideways with the Agency. Farnsworth said they were 'retrieval' specialists. Supersecret, very bad, et cetera, et cetera."

Janet winced when Talbot went wide on a blind curve. "Never heard of them," she said. "Sounds like another one of those Agency legends—you know, ghost-polishing for the benefit of the rest of us mere LE types."

Talbot looked sideways at her before returning his attention to the winding road. "I'm not so sure of that. But anyhow, this was four, five years ago. Farnsworth said he was at the Washington field office when Kreiss was stashed over at headquarters, so this is all nineteenth hand. But, basically, I was relieved when Kreiss said he'd stay out of this case."

Janet snorted.

"What?" Talbot said.

She turned to look at him. "There is no way in hell that guy's going to stay out of it. Didn't you pick up on that back there?"

Talbot seemed surprised. "No. Actually, I didn't detect that. I think he's just pissed off. Besides, whatever he used to do at the Bureau, he's retired now. He's a parent, that's all. I think he's just a guy who screwed up at the end of his career, got kicked out, moved down here to be near his kid, and now she's gone missing, and here's the Bureau backing out. He's old, for Chrissakes."

"I think you're wrong," she said, shaking her head. "And he's not that old."

Talbot laughed. "Hey, you attracted to that guy or something?"

"Oh, for God's sake, Larry," she said, looking away, afraid of what her face might reveal. It hadn't exactly been attraction. She'd been scared and embarrassed. Eight years in the bureau and some veteran stares her down.

"Well, just remember, Janet, there's still no evidence of a crime here. You know RA Farnsworth's rules: no crime, no time. He's right: We shop it to Missing Persons and move on. Hey, where do you want to stop for lunch?"

Janet shrugged and continued to stare out the side window. Gnarly-barked mossy pines, some of them enveloped in strangling vines, stared indifferently back at her. They were going down now, but another steep hill filled the windshield in front of them. It didn't take a huge leap of her imagination to visualize Edwin Kreiss slipping out of that cabin and disappearing into the woods. Her heart had almost jumped out of her chest when he had loomed over her like a tiger examining its next meal. She had never had such a powerfully frightening reaction to a man in all her life. "Wherever," she said. "I'm not that hungry."

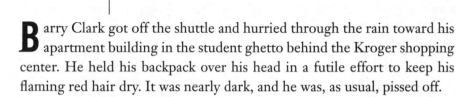

3

Barry Clark got off the shuttle and hurried through the rain toward his apartment building in the student ghetto behind the Kroger shopping center. He held his backpack over his head in a futile effort to keep his flaming red hair dry. It was nearly dark, and he was, as usual, pissed off.

He reached his ground-floor apartment, checked the battered mailbox cluster, which always got wet when it rained—stupid, dumb damn place to put the damn mailboxes, anyway, mailmen getting lazier and lazier—and then went into the concrete hallway, which stank of fried foods, cat piss, and laundry soap in about equal proportions. A single bulb threw minimal light on the trash accumulated in the hallway corners. He unlocked the flimsy door to his apartment, pushed aside some of the junk and litter that filled his so-called living room, and closed the door behind him. The curtains were drawn to discourage campus thieves, and with the wet gray evening outside, the room was dark and gloomy, perfectly matching his mood. He dumped his wet backpack onto the floor and hit the light switch, which produced absolutely nothing. He swore out loud. The breakers in the kitchen power panel were probably wet again. Jesus! Would nothing go right on this miserable day?

He ran a hand through his mop of hair and was starting across the room when a very large figure with no head rose up out of a chair and hit him high on the right side of his chest, just inside his right shoulder, so hard that he staggered sideways. The pain was incredible and he almost stopped breathing. Then the headless figure delivered another stunning punch, this one to the same point on his left side. Almost without realizing it, Barry began sinking to his knees, then squatted back on his haunches on the floor, eyes teary, trying to make a sound but only managing a whimper. His arms were paralyzed right down to his fingertips, and the pain was making him sick. When he opened his eyes, the figure was not visible, but then he sensed that some *thing* was behind him. He tried to turn around, but it wasn't possible with his frozen arms, and then a viselike hand gripped him by his hair and lifted him straight up to his feet. It hurt like hell, but what really scared him was that the man was able to do that with one hand: Barry weighed over 160. The headless man frogmarched him over to the interior living room wall and pushed him back down to the floor, onto his knees, pressing Barry's face to the wall before letting go. When Barry's head came off the wall, the hand pushed his face back against it, hard enough to mash his nose and start a small nosebleed. Even Barry, who wasn't into following orders, understood: Don't move. He stopped moving.

The fire in his upper arms threatened to envelop him. He tried to understand what he had seen: a large dark figure in a full-length coat, black gloves, and no fuckin' head! Reviewing the image scared him again, and then a very large polished chrome blade flashed up along the right side of his face, its edge resting casually one millimeter from his right eyeball. He flinched automatically, ducking his head away, but that iron hand came back and pushed his nose up against the wall again, where a dark blotch now bloomed. The man pressed the edge of the blade against Barry's right cheekbone and he felt a sting on his skin. He began to tremble uncontrollably. He wanted to say something, but he couldn't figure out what was happening to him, and besides, his throat was dry as paper.

"We can make this long or short. Your call." The man's voice was a hoarse, accentless whisper.

Barry tried again to say something, but he managed only another croak. He felt the man's body settling down behind him, a huge presence, what felt like a knee pressing in against his back. That knife blade had not moved. He suddenly felt an extreme urge to urinate. The pain in his shoulders was getting worse, much worse.

"Here it is, sonny," the man whispered. "I want to know where Lynn Kreiss and her friends went camping."

Barry blinked in the semidarkness. Lynn Kreiss? Who *was* this fucker? He'd been all over this with the cops. He had blown them off, of course. Barry Clark didn't give cops of any variety the time of fuckin' day, not after all the hassle they gave him with traffic stops and parking tickets. He had also feigned total ignorance because Rip had made him swear not to tell anyone, but then that knife did move and there was a sudden cold draft on his skin as the man sliced open the back of Barry's shirt from waist to collar. As Barry was trying to assimilate this development, the man took him by the hair again, hoisting him all the way up on his toes. This time, Barry yelled with the pain. And then that huge knife pressed for an instant against the small of his back, its cold steel tugging once at his belt line, and then his jeans and underwear were sliding down his thighs. He looked down and saw the tip of that brilliant blade projecting from between his naked legs. He struggled, then stopped when he felt a stinging sensation on the bottom of his scrotum. He made a squeaking noise and went even higher on his toes, teetering almost out of balance, managing to stay upright only because of the man's grip on his hair.

"Talk to me, wipe," the man whispered again. "Where did they go?"

Barry was shaking all over now. This giant bastard was going to cut him in half! "Okay! *Okay!* Jesus *Christ*, man! Don't! Rip said they were going to break into someplace called Site R. I don't know what that is. *Please*, man!"

Barry felt the knife turning between his legs, the edge of the blade scraping against his inner thigh, and then it was withdrawn, its dull edge pressing pointedly into his genitals. The grip on his hair relaxed. As Barry sagged back down onto his feet, something tapped him behind his right ear and he sagged to the floor. He felt almost grateful as he slipped into unconsciousness, glad to be out of it. His last sensation was that of his bladder emptying.

The Virginia Tech campus police desk sergeant went through the report with Janet Carter. It was 11:30 P.M. and some patrol cop was making a big deal on the radio-circuit speaker about a fender bender.

"Okay," the sergeant said. "So the complainant is one Barry Clark, third-year civil engineering student. Subject called nine one one at eighteen-fifty-five, semihysterical. Since he lived in the student housing area, we owned it. Responding officers said they found the subject naked on the floor, his clothes sliced up around him, a lump behind his ear and a puddle of piss on the carpet. Subject reported that a very large individual with no head assaulted him, cut his clothes off, threatened to kill him, and then coldcocked him. That's about it."

"Headless?" Carter asked, looking up from her notebook.

The sergeant shrugged, looking at his report. "That's what he said.

Subject showed evidence of being hit twice, and then the sleeping pill behind the ear. Can't move his arms. Point contusions. I got Montgomery County hospital to fax their ER report over. States direct blunt-force trauma to the—let's see—brachial nerve tie-in on both sides, causing complete but hopefully temporary paralysis to both arms. No sign of alcohol or drugs in his blood work. Hematoma behind the right ear but no skull fracture. Released after four hours of observation."

He put the report down on the counter. "We called you people because when the incident report went into our computer, there was a flag tying the subject's name to an interview list on the disappearance of those three Tech kids."

"Right. That was ours. This kid have red hair?"

The cop scanned the report. "Yep."

"I think I remember him. Snot mouth. Lots of attitude. Anything taken?"

"Apparently not. Right now, he's on some legal drugs and can't tell us anything—like why this might have happened, or what the headless horseman was after."

Janet shook her head. She had just gone to bed when the call came from the Roanoke duty officer to get over to Tech campus security. She had asked if it could wait until morning, but the duty officer said Special Agent Talbot, the first agent they'd called, seemed to think Carter would want to get on it right away. Thank you, Larry Talbot, she thought.

"Headless," she said again. "Okay, that's a new one."

The sergeant shrugged again. "College kids, what can I tell you. They've got seriously active imaginations. This isn't the weirdest one we've ever seen, believe me. You want a copy of this report?"

"Yes, please," she said. "Did the responding officers see any evidence of a burglary?"

"This all went down in the student ghetto. They checked the door lock, said it was easy pickings. It's not in the report, but the guys said the apartment was a double-glove situation. If there was evidence in there, none of them wanted to touch it or catch it."

She nodded again. "Got it. I think I'll go see Mr. Clark. How do I get there?"

Fifteen minutes later, she was knocking on the door of Clark's apartment. No one answered. She examined the door lock. The cops had been right: She could have taken it with a Q-Tip. She knocked again, then took off a shoe and used that to make enough racket to bring Barry Clark to the door finally. He was wearing an oversized Tech sweatshirt and flip-flops. His eyes were bleary, and she noticed that his arms were not in the arm-holes of the sweatshirt. She identified herself. She had heard a door open on the other side of the noisome stairwell, but it closed quickly when the name FBI rang out. He stared at her for a long moment, blinking slowly, and then nudged the door open with his foot, letting her in. She left the door cracked and wrinkled her nose at the mess in the apartment.

Clark sat down carefully on the only chair in the room and blinked up at her with dilated eyes. There was a single light on in the living room. His arms hung down uselessly inside the sweatshirt. She did remember him. He had been truculent, almost hostile, during the initial round of interviews on the Kreiss case, which was how she thought of it now, after the meeting with Edwin Kreiss earlier that day. She looked at her watch; yesterday, actually. She was pretty sure that either she or Talbot had rein-terviewed this one. She definitely remembered the orange-red hair and the pug-nosed, freckled-face smirk that begged every passing life-form for a slap. She remained standing and got out her notebook.

"So," she began. "I've read the campus police's incident report. What'd you leave out?"

"Leave out?" he asked blankly. "Nothing. I told them what happened. This huge bastard—"

"Look, Mr. Clark," she interrupted. "Let's cut to the chase. Why was he here? What did he want? You grope somebody's wife at Kroger's, or what?"

He stared at her, trying for a hard look, but then his eyes drifted out of focus. Hell, she thought, closing the book. He's zoning out. She wasn't going to get anything useful here. She looked around. There was a pile of cut-up clothes next to the far wall. There was a dark brown smear on the wall, and some paper towels stuffed under the rug beneath it. The room was such a mess of clothes, papers, athletic gear, bicycles, and tattered books that Sherlock Holmes would not have been able to tell if anything was missing. She could see a desktop PC through the bedroom door, but the bedroom looked even scarier than this room. Her toes curled at the thought of even going into the kitchen, which she could smell from where she stood. She looked back at Clark, who was staring dully at the floor.

"He scared the piss out of me, man," the kid said softly, shaking his head from side to side. Literally, she thought, wrinkling her nose again, trying not to breathe too hard.

"He had no head," Clark said, wincing at the memory. "And he had this huge fuckin' knife. He lifted me off the floor with one fuckin' hand. Like, I can move my fingers, but I can't lift my arms. One, two, wham, bam. I was fuckin' down on the floor like a rubber chicken. The EMT guys had to put this sweatshirt on for me. Now I can't go to class, can't take a shower, can't do shit. I may lose the whole fuckin' semester."

Fuckin' awesome, Janet thought. "So why'd this happen, Mr. Clark? What did this guy want?" she asked.

"Don't know," Clark said, shaking his head again, but now he was avoiding making eye contact. She gave up. The kid was hurting, but he was also lying. She put away her notebook and headed for the door. She stuffed her card between the door molding and the wall, dislodging a fat roach.

"Call me when you're ready to talk to me, Mr. Clark. Hopefully, *before* he comes back."

The kid's head came up as he registered that little comment. She smiled sweetly at him and went out to her car. She sat there for a minute before starting it up. This has to be Kreiss, she thought. That kid knows something about where those kids went, and Kreiss detected it back during the initial activity right after their disappearance. Tonight he came calling. Why now? Because today the Bureau announced it was backing out, of course.

The physical description didn't fit, of course, but it was a rainy night. He could have simply pulled his raincoat right up over his head, surprised the kid in a dark room, and disabled him with a couple of expert karate strikes. And with his head inside the coat, he would have appeared absolutely huge in the darkness. The question was, What did he get? She was tempted to call Kreiss right now, maybe go roust him at his mountain aerie. But of course, if it had been Kreiss, he'd have himself covered. Despite that, she felt a tingle of satisfaction. Talbot had been wrong.

She started up the car. Tomorrow, she would go talk to Kreiss. No—first she would find out some more *facts* about Edwin Kreiss, as opposed to rumors and legends. For some reason, the name Kreiss had been tickling a cord of her memory. But maybe it was just her. She felt him standing in front of her again, all that energy radiating out of him. It had been like standing next to a generator humming at full power. Then her professional side reasserted itself. Get real, Carter. The guy was out of line, hassling some college kid like that. Not that it had never occurred to her to smack the living shit out of Barry Clark. She smiled as she started the car. No more than once a minute, she thought.

Edwin Kreiss relaxed with a short whiskey in front of his fireplace. He felt better than he had in years, especially since now he had something to go on. He hadn't enjoyed beating up on a snot-nosed kid like that, but he had learned long ago that sometimes a direct, physical approach gets the quickest results. He wondered if the kid would go to the cops. Probably. No matter: He still knew how to go somewhere and leave no trace. He took a deep breath and let it out slowly. A cold wind from the ridge above his property was stirring the pine trees outside the cabin, causing the fire to flutter for a moment. It was almost springtime, but not up here yet, not at night, anyway.

He thought about what the kid had said. Site R. The only Site R he had ever heard about was the Alternate National Military Command Center up in the Catoctin Mountains, just north of Washington. That Site R was a self-contained mini-Pentagon. It had been built in a five-story steel box balanced on gigantic springs inside a man-made quartzite cavern. It was the hidey-hole for the president and whichever of his generals could make it out of Washington if nuclear missiles ever heaved over the ballistic horizon. No, this had to be something closer. And the kid had said they were going to *break into* Site R.

He closed his eyes and mentally reviewed the map of southwestern Virginia. Assuming they hadn't gone out of the area, as the cops were postulating, then what was around here that might be called Site R? It sounded military. He wondered if it could have anything to do with the Ramsey Army Arsenal, which was fifteen miles south of Blacksburg. He'd never heard that called Site R, although he had lived in this area only since Lynn had come to Tech. He didn't even know if the arsenal was still operational. But . . . *break into*? That implied a restricted area, so that could be it. *R* for Ramsey?

Lynn, Lynn, Lynn, he thought. What the hell did you get yourself into? The pit in his stomach asserted itself. He had only gotten to be her father, really be her father, for the past six years. Before that, there had been that eleven-year gap, when his ex-wife, Helen, had kept him firmly at arm's length, out of her life and Lynn's.

The whole sorry episode had been hurtful. Helen had cut him out of their lives with an iron curtain after the divorce—no visitation rights, no contact, no nothing. The judge had gone along with that when Helen refused child support and alimony. His wife and child could not have been more closed off to him if they had gone to another galaxy, even though they'd been right there in Washington the whole time. He had kept track of them, of course, keeping a distant watch on them between postings, until Helen remarried two years later to a coworker at the FBI laboratory. After that, he had pretty much given up and immersed himself in his work, which by that time was taking every bit of his time and energy, right up to the Millwood incident and the end of everything.

And then suddenly, just after Lynn turned sixteen, she had called him, right out of the blue. Left a message with the FCI Division central operator that she was Edwin Kreiss's daughter and wanted to talk to him. Just like that. Their first meeting, at a Metro café in Rosslyn, had been awkward; the second one better. For a year thereafter, they had met secretly, conducting a small conspiracy that was, for Lynn, a fulfillment of the normal teenage rebellion against her mother, as well as a filling of the hole in her heart that yearned for her father. For Kreiss, it had been the best of times, momentary islands of warmth and eager anticipation between sieges of increasingly acrimonious political developments in the Department of Energy Nuclear Laboratory case. Then came the plane crash, later that same year, which took Helen, her second husband, and eighty-eight other souls into the Chesapeake Bay at five hundred miles an hour. After that, it wasn't a secret conspiracy anymore, but Lynn on his doorstep, a pretty, tomboyish, bright-faced young lady with two suitcases, a tennis racket, and trembling lips that were trying hard to be brave and to hide the shock of it all. When she had been accepted at Virginia Tech, Kreiss, recently forced out of the Bureau, had moved down to the area to be near her.

Site R. Tomorrow, he would go investigate the Ramsey Army Arsenal. He recalled the redheaded FBI agent's warning about going solo. He snorted. I'm still Edwin Kreiss, he thought. I'll find her, and if someone's hurt her, I'll find him and his wife and his children and all his other living relatives and send a load of body parts FedEx into the lobby of the J. Edgar Hoover Building. Let Missing Persons sort that out.

4

On Friday morning, Janet Carter called Eve Holloway at FBI headquarters. Eve worked in the Fingerprint Division and had been Janet's racquetball partner before Janet's transfer to the Roanoke office. Janet explained that she wanted to find out about a retired senior agent named Edwin Kreiss.

"Is this official?" Eve asked.

"Yes, actually, although we're moving the case to MP. It's a disappearance case—three college kids, but, unfortunately, no evidence of a criminal act. Kreiss retired from the Bureau four, maybe five years ago. He's the father of one of the missing kids, and I have a feeling he knows something he's not telling us."

"Or working it off-line, maybe?" Eve asked. Eve's husband was a senior supervisory agent in the Professional Standards and Inspection Division. She knew a thing or two.

"Entirely possible. Supposedly, he worked in FCI, but he crashed and burned, and then he was sent home."

Eve was silent for a moment. "Kreiss," she said slowly. "I know that name. Hey, there was a Helen Kreiss who worked in the lab. That's right—she was an electron mis—misc—shit, I can't pronounce it. She ran the electron-microscope facility. Microscopist? Anyway, she and her second husband were killed in that plane crash in the Bay, remember?"

Janet remembered Talbot mentioning a crash to Kreiss. "She worked for us? In the Bureau?"

"Yeah. I worked a child murder case with her, when she was Helen Kreiss. I remember she was getting a divorce at the time. This was '88, '89 time frame. I think she later married an agent who worked Organized Crime. Nice lady. I remember the plane crash because we lost two people. It was late '94, thereabouts. But she wasn't called Kreiss anymore, of course. I'm thinking it was Morgan?"

"Right! Yes, I knew her. Helen Morgan. She worked some taskings for me when I was working in Materials and Devices. I'd been there—what?—just under two years, I think. So she was Kreiss's ex?"

"Yep. I think she had a medical degree."

"I would have liked to talk to her," Janet said. "You said she was getting the divorce when you worked that case together. She ever talk about it?"

"Not really. She seemed more sad than mad. There was one child involved. That must be your misser. But listen, I think she said she had talked to one of our in-house shrinks. Maybe there's a file?"

Janet thanked her and then called the Administrative Services Division at headquarters. An office supervisor listened to her question and promised that someone from Employee Counseling would get back to her. Then Janet went to the morning staff meeting.

At 2:30 that afternoon, the RA of the Roanoke office, Ted Farnsworth, called Janet into his office. The nearest full-scale FBI field office was in Richmond. The Roanoke office was subordinate to the larger Richmond office, and, as such, its boss was not called special agent in charge, but, rather, Resident Agent. Farnsworth was a senior supervisory agent who was nearing retirement age. He was generally a kind and not very excitable boss, but, at the moment, his New England accent was audible, which meant that he was perturbed.

"Got a call this afternoon from a Dr. Karsten Goldberg, number-two shrink in the headquarters Counseling Division. Says they received a call from this office concerning a Bureau employee, since deceased, named Helen Kreiss Morgan? I thought this missing kid case had been sent up to MP?"

"It has," Janet said. "Or it will be, as of Monday. I think Larry Talbot is still finishing up the paperwork." She then related the incident involving Barry Clark, and her suspicions that Edwin Kreiss might be going solo in the search for his daughter.

Farnsworth cupped his chin with his left hand and frowned. "And you're looking for some background on this former special agent, Edwin Kreiss."

"Yes, sir. His ex-wife worked in the lab in Washington. She was killed in that plane crash in the Bay in late 1994. A contact at headquarters told me she'd been to the counselors during her divorce proceedings. I was hoping—"

"Close that door," Farnsworth said, indicating his office door. Janet was surprised, but she did as he'd asked. In today's supercharged sexual harassment atmosphere, it was a rare male supervisor indeed who would conduct a conversation with a female employee behind a closed door. He had her attention. She sat back down.

"Now look," Farnsworth said. "What I'm going to tell you is not for general dissemination, despite what you might have heard from Larry. I hesitate even to go into this, because you're not supposed to be working this case anymore."

"Yes, sir," Janet said. "But as I understand it, we'll keep a string on it even when it goes to MP? And I haven't been assigned to anything else yet." Even as she said that, Janet realized her reply sounded a little lawyerish.

Farnsworth smiled patiently. "Janet, you're a smart young lady. A Ph.D. from Johns Hopkins in materials forensics, right? Almost nine years in the outfit, with two Washington tours and a field office tour in Chicago? And now you're down here with us mossbacks in the hills and hollows doing exactly what with all that specialized knowledge?"

Janet colored. During her first year back in Washington following the Chicago tour, she had twice managed to embarrass the assistant director over the laboratory by filing dissenting opinions in some high-visibility evidentiary reports. Subsequent reviews proved her right, but, given the rising legal storm over irregularities at the FBI lab, her mentor at headquarters, a female senior supervisory agent, had hustled Janet out of headquarters before she got into any more career-killing trouble. With Farnsworth's acquiescence, she had been transferred to the Roanoke office under the rubric of getting some out-of-specialty, street-level investigative experience. She nodded.

"Okay," Farnsworth said. "Now, there are two reasons why this case is going to MP. First, because I said so, and SAC, Richmond, agrees. There's no evidence or even any indication that there's been a crime, and we've got other fish to fry. Second, one of the kids was Edwin Kreiss's daughter." He paused to see if she would understand.

She didn't. "Yes, sir. And?"

He sighed. "Edwin Kreiss was not just a senior field agent who elected to retire down here in rustic southwest Virginia. He was Edwin Kreiss."

"Still is, I suppose, boss. I guess my question is, So what?"

Farnsworth got his pipe out, which told Janet she was not going anywhere soon. He didn't light it, in deference to the nonsmoking rules, but he did everything but light it. Then he leaned back in his chair.

"I don't know any of this directly, other than by being an RA and being plugged into that network. Okay? So, like I said, don't quote me on any of this. But Edwin Kreiss was a specialist in the Bureau's Counterintelligence Division. In the mid-eighties, he went on an exchange tour at the Agency. He got involved in that Chinese espionage case—you know, the one where they got into the atomic labs and allegedly stole our warhead secrets."

"Yes, sir. It supposedly went on for over ten years."

"Or more. Anyhow, you know that the Agency is restricted to operating *outside* the continental United States, while the Bureau is responsible for operating primarily *inside* our national borders."

"Except we do go overseas."

"Only when asked by foreign governments, or when we ask them. But the Agency may *not* operate here in the States, except when they feel they have a mole, an Agency insider who is spying. Then they sometimes team up with the Bureau FCI people to find him."

"And the Department of Energy case involved a mole? I hadn't heard that."

"Well, not exactly a mole. Our people began to wonder why the DOE's own investigation, as well as the Agency's, seemed to be taking so damn long. It turned out that the Chinese had some help."

"In our government?"

"Worse—in the Agency's Counterespionage Division. A guy named Ephraim Glower."

"Never heard of him, either."

"This wasn't exactly given front-page coverage, and, again, I've never seen evidence of all this. But here's the background on Kreiss. While he was on this exchange tour with their CE people, he supposedly uncovered Glower, who, at the time, was an assistant deputy director in the Agency's Counterespionage Division."

"Wow. Talk about top cover."

Farnsworth smiled. "Precisely. The Agency was furiously embarrassed. When Kreiss forced the issue, they got him recalled to the Bureau. J. Willard Marchand was the new ADIC over the Bureau's FCI Division, and he clamped the lid on Kreiss. They stashed him at headquarters for a while, but then the flap about the Chinese government making campaign contributions blew up, and Kreiss resurfaced his accusations. Marchand stepped on Kreiss's neck. Kreiss then apparently decided to go confront this guy Glower."

"You mean Glower still had his job?"

"Yes. Kreiss had no proof, or not enough to convince the Agency, so they got rid of Kreiss and left Glower in place."

"That's unbelievable."

"They do it all the time, Janet. Then if it blows up, they cover their asses by saying they were just letting the bad guy run so as to control what he did or gave to the other side. What's important is that the Glower episode ended in a very bloody mess out in a little village called Millwood, Virginia, up in the Shenandoah Valley. Glower ended up dead."

"Wow. Kreiss?"

"Well, after he got stepped on the second time, Kreiss went to Millwood and confronted Glower. Glower called for help from Agency security and they forced Kreiss out of the house. But then that night, Glower apparently killed his wife and two kids and then shot himself. The local law said the scene was right out of one of those chain saw–massacre movies. The Agency director called Marchand; for a while, they actually thought Kreiss had done it."

"So he was there?"

"Not when that happened, but of course they knew he had been there earlier. Fortunately for Kreiss, one of his subordinates at the Bureau could verify that Kreiss had been back at headquarters, writing up his report, at the time of the actual shootings. There were some questions about Kreiss's alibi, because it was one of his own people providing it. Needless to say, it was a helluva mess, and it became complicated by the fact that Kreiss wasn't done yet. He surfaced new allegations, that there wasn't just one scientist-spy at one lab; that there was a whole network. Based on what I've read since, he may have been right about that."

"Why did Glower kill himself?"

"That's unclear. According to Kreiss's theory, Glower was running top cover for the spy network. Being a deputy dog in Agency counterespionage, he could throw a lot of monkey wrenches into the various investigations, which is why it all went on for so long."

"Why would he do that?"

"There was the money."

"Money from?"

"Money from China, money that went into a certain prominent reelection campaign, which I'm sure you've also read about. Kreiss's theory was that Glower was only doing what he had been told to do—namely, to stymie the investigation at DOE and at the Agency, in return for keeping the Chinese happy, because the Chinese, of course, felt they had bought and paid for happiness."

"Could Kreiss back that up?"

Farnsworth sucked on his unlit pipe. "My guess is that if he could have, he would have. But it's kind of hard to tell when you start a fire at that level. Those kinds of fires usually get extinguished in a Mount Olympus–level deal of some kind. Although, from what I've heard, Kreiss was anything but a deal maker, as the Agency bosses found out much too late. Supposedly, this guy Glower came from a very rich family, so money should not have been a likely motive. But who knows. The upshot was that Marchand caught hell, and in turn, he forced Kreiss out administratively, using the bloodbath at Millwood as a pretext, via the Bureau's own professional standards board. That in itself should have defanged anything Kreiss had to say about what or who was driving Glower."

"A bitter end to an interesting career."

"Yes, a very interesting career. There are all sorts of stories about Kreiss. You've met him and I haven't, but he apparently went pretty far afield with some of the Agency's counterespionage specialists, some of whom redefine the notion of 'far afield.' I've been told that he actually trained with some of their people, the ones who are called sweepers."

"Yes, Larry Talbot mentioned that term. Said they were highly specialized operatives, guys who went after their own agents when they went wrong."

"And you think that's all a bunch of Agency bullshit. Ghost-polishing, right?"

Janet started to reply but then stopped. Those were her very words. Fucking Larry. The RA was still smiling.

"Let me tell you what I've heard, and let me again stress the word *heard*," Farnsworth said. "A sweeper is 'reportedly' someone our beloved brethren at Langley send when one of their own clandestine operations agents goes off the tracks in some fashion. We're not talking about their regular CE people, the ones who help us chase enemy agents around the streets of Washington. We're talking about a very special operative who hunts—and retrieves—that's the term they use—clandestine operatives who have gone nuts, gone over to the other side, or started running some kind of private agenda—like assassinating bad guys instead of playing by the rules. In other words, someone who is so completely out of control that he or she needs to be 'retrieved' from the field and brought back to a safe house in the Virginia countryside. Someplace where the problem can be attended to, quote unquote."

"'Attended to'?"

"Define that as your imagination might dictate," Farnsworth said. "The interesting thing is, if they develop a problem child out on their operational web, they *tell* the problem child that a sweeper is coming.

Supposedly, a sweeper notification is enough to bring said problem child to heel. Coming in is preferable to being brought in."

Janet didn't know what to say. "And Kreiss?"

"Kreiss was at the agency on an exchange deal, our FCI with their CE. Word was, he worked with the sweepers, trained with them. Did several years away from the Bureau. I talked to a guy, he's SAC now in Louisville, who knew Kreiss back in those days. Said he basically went native. Really got into the Agency hugger-mugger. His supervisors back in Bureau FCI didn't know what to do, because the one time they borrowed him back to deal with a rogue Bureau agent, the agent turned himself in, requesting protection. He was apparently so scared of Kreiss that he confessed to shit the Bureau didn't even know about. Then, of course, came Millwood. People who knew Kreiss tended to keep their distance."

"I can understand that," she said. "I got an impression of contained violence, I mean. And I found myself wondering about the degree of containment."

"That's the essence of it. Of course, no one knows what really happened at Millwood, or who else might have been involved by that point in the investigation. Once Glower was dead . . ."

"What do you mean? Oh, you mean—"

"Yeah. The Agency protested a lot, but our FCI people speculated that the Millwood bloodbath may have been the Agency itself taking care of business—you know, with one of these sweeper types. But once Kreiss started making accusations about the Chinese government, hundreds of thousands of dollars, and the highest levels of our own government, nobody either side of the river wanted it to go any further."

"Wow. And that's whose kid is missing."

"Right. And two others, don't forget."

"Could there be a connection?"

"I doubt it. But I've been given specific direction from Richmond to put a lid on this right now and shop it to MP."

"Just because it's Kreiss's kid who's involved?"

Farnsworth just looked at her with that patient expression on his face, which always made Janet feel like a schoolgirl. "Or are you saying the *Agency* is going to work it?" she asked.

Farnsworth put his pipe away in the desk. "Don't know, as we Vermonters like to say. Don't know, don't want to know. And neither do you. I am saying that *we*, the Roanoke office, are *not* going to work it, other than as a routine missing persons case. And *you* are going to move on to other things."

Janet thought about that for a moment. "But what if Kreiss works it?"

"What if he does? If someone was fool enough to abduct Edwin Kreiss's daughter, then, in my humble estimation, he'll get what's coming to him."

Janet sat back in her chair. Her instincts about Kreiss had been more correct than she had realized. Farnsworth was looking at his watch, which was his signal that the interview was over. "You, on the other hand," he said, "need to forget about making any more calls to Washington, okay? It'll be a lot better for you, all around. And for me, and for probably everyone in this office. Are we clear on that, Janet?"

She nodded. Clear as a fire bell, she thought. An image of Edwin Kreiss flitted through her mind: coiled silently in that rocking chair, those deep-set gray-green eyes like range finders when he looked at her. Crazy man or fanatic? She exhaled carefully. The few spooks she had met from that other world across the Potomac River, military and civilian, had mostly been pasty-faced bureaucrats. Kreiss was apparently from the sharp end of the spear. "Yes, sir," she said. "Got it."

"Knew you would," Farnsworth said with a fatherly smile. "You have a great day."

Janet went back to her cubicle, grabbing some coffee on the way. The coffee had a slightly stale, oily smell to it, which was typical of the afternoon batch, but she felt the need for a jolt of caffeine.

Billy was still snoring quietly in the next cubicle when Janet sat down at her desk. She was surprised to see a yellow telephone message indicating that a Dr. Kellermann, of the headquarters Counseling Division, wanted to talk to her. Whoops, she thought. Their deputy dog had called Farnsworth but probably had not canceled Janet's original query. She looked at her watch. It was 3:15. On a Friday.

She thought about it. Farnsworth had made things pretty clear: Back out. And yet, she could not get Edwin Kreiss out of her mind. She'd been in southwest Virginia for a year and a half, and had met absolutely zero truly interesting men in Roanoke. She'd been taking some postdoc seminars at Virginia Tech over in Blacksburg to fill the empty hours. And despite the fact that she had married and then divorced an academic before joining the Bureau back in 1991, she knew that she was at least subconsciously hoping she might meet some interesting faculty people.

As it turned out, so far at least, everyone old enough to interest her was either married or so completely engrossed in his or her work, S-corporation, or themselves as to bore her to tears. After her first few appearances in the local fitness center, a couple of the married agents in the office had made it clear they wouldn't mind a fling, but she had a firm rule about both married men and dating other agents. It wasn't that Kreiss stirred her romantically, but he sure as hell was interesting.

She decided to take Kellermann's call. Just to be polite, of course. The case was still theirs, technically, wasn't it? Maybe Kellermann had something that could keep it here in the field. She looked around the office. Talbot wasn't in. It was Friday afternoon; nobody would get back to Farnsworth with the fact that she had called this late in the day.

She dialed the number. A secretary put her through. "Dr. Kellermann," a woman's voice said. Janet identified herself.

"Ah, yes, Dr. Carter. Brianne Kellermann. I was Helen Kreiss's counselor. How can I help you?"

The voice was educated and kind, and Janet was momentarily flattered to be called doctor again. Here, she was just called Carter. She briefly described the case, then asked if Dr. Kellermann had any opinions, based on her sessions with Kreiss's ex-wife, that might bear on the case.

"Please, call me Brianne," Kellermann said. "And I'd need to think about that. I need to consider Mrs. Kreiss's privacy."

"I understand that, Brianne," Janet said. "Although she is, of course, deceased." She waited for a reply to that, but Kellermann didn't say anything. "And I should tell you that this case is being sent up to MP because we haven't uncovered any evidence that there has been a crime here—these kids might well have just boogied off in search of spotted owls, you know?"

"Let's hope so. But technically, they are missing? I mean, there's no evidence the other way, is that what you're saying?"

"Correct. There are three sets of parents involved, and they had no indication that the kids were just going to take off. Given that these kids were senior engineering students, I think it's highly unlikely that they did just take off. But—"

"And your boss is looking at his budget and wants you to move on."

Janet smiled. This doc knew the score. "Right. Which I can understand, of course. Even down here in the thriving metropolis of Roanoke, we've got plenty to do."

There was a pause on the end of the line, and Janet wondered if it was

Dr. Kellermann's turn to smile. She decided to fill in the silence. "I'm really calling because one of the parents is Edwin Kreiss. I'm actually more interested in him than in Helen Kreiss."

"Who is now deceased, of course," Kellermann said, as if reminding herself.

"Yes. I understand she remarried before the plane crash."

"Yes, she did. So your interest is really in what Mrs. Kreiss may have said prior to divorcing Edwin Kreiss. Do you suspect he has something to do with the three students' disappearance?"

Janet hesitated. If she said yes, she'd have some leverage she didn't have now. "Actually? No. But one of the things I'm learning here in the field is to pull every string, no matter how unlikely."

"I understand, Janet. May I call you Janet? And since this case goes back awhile—I think it was 1989 or even '88—let me review my files, think about it, and get back to you, okay?"

Janet hesitated. Get back to me when? she thought. As of Monday, the case officially went north. Well, in for a penny . . .

"That would be great, Brianne. Send me an E-mail when you're ready to talk, and I'll get in touch."

"I'll do that, Janet. Although I may not have much for you. There's the problem of confidentiality, and my focus is usually on the spouse I'm trying to help, not the other party. That way, we can move beyond blame, you see, and on to more constructive planes."

Janet rolled her eyes, spelled out her E-mail address, and hung up. She sat back in her chair. She'd given Kellermann her direct E-mail address to avoid any more phone message forms on her desk. Okay, she thought, but let's say Kellermann goes to her boss, who tells her that Roanoke has been told to put the Kreiss matter back in its box. How would she explain her call if Farnsworth asked? Kellermann contacted her *before* Farnsworth had called her off? She was only being polite in returning the call? Billy, that well-known Communist, did it?

The Communist woke up with a snort and some throat-clearing noise. He saw Janet.

"Hey, good-looking," he said. "How do you get a sweet little old lady to yell, 'Fuck'?"

"Billy—"

"You get another sweet little old lady to yell, 'Bingo!' "

She laughed. "Hey, Billy, why don't you get some of this wonderful coffee and let me run this missing college kids case by you."

Browne McGarand approached the smokeless powder-finishing building from the east side of the complex, staying in the shadows as he walked through the twilight. He had parked his truck well off the fire road that branched to the left off the main entrance road, then had hiked a mile southwest until he intercepted the railroad cut. From there, he had turned northwest, walking along the single track until he reached the security gates that bridged the rail line. When the installation had been shut down, the gates had been padlocked and further secured with metal bars welded top and bottom across, in case someone cut the chains and locks. Browne had left all the bars, chains, and locks on the exterior gate in place. Instead, he had used a portable cutting-torch rig to cut through the tack welds that married the chain-link fence to the round stock frame of the gates. By undoing one bolt, he was now able to lift a corner flap of the chain-link mesh and simply step through.

There was a second set of gates fifty feet inside, to match the double security fence that surrounded the entire 2,400 acres of the Ramsey Arsenal. These had been locked but not welded, and here he had cut down and replaced the rusty padlock with a rusty one of his own. The Ramsey Arsenal, which was really an explosives-manufacturing complex, had been in caretaker status for almost twenty years. A local industrial-security firm made periodic inspections. He had watched them often, but their people made all their security and access checks from *inside* the inner perimeter. More importantly, with the exception of the main gates, they never physically got out of their truck, choosing simply to drive around and look at everything from the comfort of their air conditioning.

He shifted the backpack with the girl's supplies down off his back and onto the ground. The water bottles made it heavy. He unlocked the inner gates, slid the right one back a few feet on its wheels, and stepped through with the pack. He closed the gate but did not lock it. Directly ahead lay the main industrial area, which covered almost one hundred acres. The complex consisted of metal and concrete buildings large and small, many connected by overhead steam and cooling water piping. There were mixing and filling sheds built down in blast-deflection pits, chemical-storage warehouses, metal liquid-storage tanks, the cracking towers of the acid plant, rail- and truck-loading warehouses, and the hulking mass of a dormant power plant with its one enormous stack. The complex was the size of a small town, behind which slightly more than two thousand acres of trees concealed the finished ammunition-storage bunkers. The rail line, a

spur of the Norfolk & Western main line that ran through Christiansburg, immediately branched out into sidings that pointed into the complex in six different directions.

He checked his watch. It was almost sundown. There was just enough
light to see where he was going. He did not want to use his flashlight until
he was well into the maze of buildings and side streets of the industrial
area. The only sounds came from his boots as he walked down the main
approach road. A slight breeze stirred dead leaves in the gutters. The
largest buildings flanked the main street, which ran from the admin building down to the power plant four blocks away. A series of pipe frames in
the shape of inverted U's gave the main street a tunnel-like appearance. At
fifty-foot intervals, there were large hinged metal plates in the street,
measuring twenty feet on a side. The plates gave access to what had been
called "the Ditch," which in reality was a concrete tunnel into which large
batches of toxic liquids could be dumped quickly in the event a reaction
went wrong. All the buildings were locked and shuttered, and, for the
most part, empty. Each building had a white sign with a name and building designation reference number for the use of the security company.
With the exception of the power plant, all of the machinery had long
since been taken away.

He reached the nitroglycerine-fixing building. He thought about the
girl as he walked toward the building, trying to figure out how she played
into his grand scheme. He had only mild regret about the two boys who
had been killed by the flash flood. In any event, many more strangers were
going to die. The girl and her friends were just a few more innocent
bystanders. In the six months that he had been producing the hydrogen,
no one had ever intruded into the Ramsey industrial complex. There were
long-standing rumors in the nearby towns that Ramsey had produced
chemical weapons during World War II. Even a hint that there might be
some nerve gas still locked away in the deep bunkers tended to keep people out of the facility, and such rumors had never been officially discour-
aged by the Army. It was all bunk, of course. The plant had been one of
several GOCO facilities: government-owned, contractor-operated by
various commercial companies to manufacture artillery propellant and
warhead fillers for the Army.

He could not imagine what the three kids had been doing here, but
Jared's traps had done their job. It would have been a lot simpler, of
course, if the flash flood had taken all three of them. But he could not
bring himself to execute her, even though she had seen their faces. In the

back of his mind, he thought she might actually become useful down the road, when he got closer to Judgment Day. That was how he liked to think of it: a day of reckoning, with him and his grandson delivering those agents of Satan into God's iron hands for summary judgment.

It was much darker now. He slowed and then moved sideways into the shadow of a loading dock and sat down to await full darkness. The concrete felt warm against his back. He always did this when he came in: sat down, listened and watched. Made very, very sure no one had followed him in. He closed his eyes and prayed for the strength to carry on, to go through with his mission of retribution. They had manufactured nearly three-quarters of the hydrogen, and the pressure in the truck was starting to register into the double digits for the first time. Not much longer. All they needed was the rest of the copper, and Jared said he had found a new source. There was plenty of acid, thank God. He opened his eyes and listened. There was nothing but the night wind and the ticking sounds of the metal roofs and the piping towers cooling in the darkness. Time to go.

There were two doors on the nitro building: one large segmented-steel hanging door big enough to admit a truck or railcar, the other a human-sized steel walk-through door. The building's sign was still legible in the gloom: NITRO FIXING. He struck the smaller door once with his fist.

"Put on the blindfold," he ordered.

He waited for a minute, then unlocked the padlock, removed it, and pushed the door open. The interior of the building was a single huge room, which now was in near-total darkness. With his eyes fully night-adapted, he could just make out the outline of the skylights far above. He could also just see the girl's face in the middle of the room, a pale blur of white hovering above the dark pile of blankets. He pushed the base of the door with his foot so that it swung all the way back against the concrete wall and then turned on the flashlight, fixing the girl's face in its blinding beam. She flinched but said nothing. The blindfold was in place, as he had ordered. The remains of the last food delivery were right by the door. He flipped the light around the open shop floor, illuminating each corner. Metal foundation plates that looked like the stumps in a cutover forest glinted back at him. The room smelled of old concrete, nitric acid, and a hint of sewage. He set the flashlight onto the floor, pointing at the girl.

He slid the backpack in and emptied it out on the floor. A roll of toilet paper, six plastic bottles of water, two deli-style sandwiches, two apples, and a Gideon's Bible. He picked up the flashlight and swept it around the building again, being careful to keep it low, away from the skylights. He put it back down on the floor so that the beam again pointed at the girl. Then he picked up the bag of trash by the floor and stuffed it into the backpack. She never moved, sitting cross-legged on the blankets as if she was meditating. He had never spoken to her, beyond the command to put on the blindfold, and she had never spoken to him.

He looked at her for a moment. She appeared to be well made, which was why he had stopped letting Jared bring the food. Jared was not entirely trustworthy when it came to women, a function, no doubt, of his youth. They had prayed together on Jared's womanizing problem several times, but he kept an eye on Jared just the same. He admired the girl's stoicism. She had to be strong, not to whimper and beg and carry on when he came. She must have a great deal of inner fortitude, he thought. The Bible would help sustain that. He should have brought her one a long time ago.

He picked up the light, swept the room one more time, and then backed out, turning the light off before he closed the steel door. His night vision was gone, of course, but he could put the lock back on and snap it shut without seeing it. He sat down on the steps leading to the door and closed his eyes, letting his other senses scan the surrounding area. Even after all these years, the air in the complex was tainted with the acrid scent of chemicals, as if decades' worth of nitric acid, sulfuric acid, ammonia, mercury, and a host of esters and alcohols had permanently stained the air. It had undoubtedly stained the ground, which was why the whole place was now sealed off. He wondered if all those people fishing that creek below the arsenal had any idea of what was sleeping in the sands of the creek bed, courtesy of some frantic flushes into the Ditch.

He opened his eyes and the shadows assumed shape as buildings again in the dark. The security company's truck would come tomorrow, even though it would be Saturday. Their contract required them to do at least two weekend checks a month, and it had been two weeks. Which is why he had doped the apples. She should be drowsy and sleep through most of the day. The security people were definitely lowest-bidder types: lazy and incompetent. They never even got out of their little truck. They just drove around the complex for an hour and looked out the windows and then went back out the main gates. He had toyed with the idea of doing something to them, perhaps just before Judgment Day. They deserved to be punished for not doing their jobs.

He got up, picked up the pack, and started back. The girl did not know anything, other than that they were here, presumably doing something illegal, or they wouldn't have taken her captive. He would have to decide what to do with her. In truth, if she could not contribute to the mission in some way, before or after, he could always just leave her. The walls of the nitro building were three feet thick, reinforced concrete. She would never be found.

5

Just before dawn on Saturday, Edwin Kreiss parked his pickup truck at the end of a fire road on the eastern edge of the Ramsey Army Arsenal. He shut it down, slid down the windows to listen, and waited. He had spent most of Friday looking for the arsenal, which, considering that it took up a couple of thousand acres, had not been as easy as he had anticipated. The state road map, which showed the installation fronting I-81 east of Christiansburg, was wrong. Unwilling to be remembered in Christiansburg for asking questions, he'd gone to the public library in the town of Ramsey and found a single book on the history of the arsenal. The reference librarian had told him the Ramsey Arsenal had been shut down for nearly twenty years.

He'd then found the main entrance south of town, but the intersection that led to what he assumed was a main gate was blocked off with concrete-filled barrels that had obviously been there for a long time. After that, he had followed every paved road, dirt road, and fire lane that seemed to point in toward the installation, trying to construct his own map. Every access that ran up against the arsenal ended the same way—in a firebreak and a tall double chain-link fence with barbed wire at the top, festooned with signs warning that this was a U.S. government restricted area and also a federal toxic-waste site. When he found what he assumed was a rail spur into the installation, he parked the truck out of sight and walked along the rusting rails for nearly two miles before seeing double gates. Assuming there would be surveillance, he had not approached the gates, but backtracked to his truck and continued with his mapmaking of the perimeter.

Now he was parked within two hundred yards of the spot he felt was the most discreet way into the reservation, the intersection of the security fences and a wide, quiet creek flowing out of the interior of the installation. The creek had been routed under the fences through a concrete conduit five feet in diameter that slanted down from the higher ground of the installation. There had been a heavy rebar grating out on the exterior side of the tunnel. It had looked intact, until he inspected it and found that the part below the surface of the water had long since rusted away. The creek widened considerably when it came out of the reservation, and the deep pool below the conduit showed evidence of being a local fishing hole, despite all the TOXIC-WASTE SITE signs decorating the fences.

According to the book, the arsenal encompassed about 2,400 acres, but the industrial heart of it appeared to be much smaller than that, if the pictures in the book were accurate. The bulk of the installation's acreage was occupied by the extensive bunker fields, where the Army's freshly minted ammunition had been stored. At least that's what the book implied; one never knew what other things the government might have secreted out here on a restricted area in the southwestern foothills of the Appalachian Mountains. The place was sufficiently remote and secure as to contain damn near anything. He didn't care about munitions; he wanted to know if the kids had ever come here. There had been no mention in the book of any Site R. He had considered walking the entire perimeter, to see if he could find any better prospects for easy access, but doing that covertly would entail at least several days. No, he had concluded, it was more important to get inside and do his looking there, where, if the kids had run into trouble, he might find signs of it. *If* this was the place, of course. Knowing his chances were slim to begin with, he sighed and got out. It was better than brooding in the cabin, and a lot more than the Bureau had done.

Birds were beginning to stir in the trees, but there was still little light. The mountains to the east would mask the direct sunrise for another hour and a half yet. The sky was clear and it was almost cold, in the low fifties. If there were Saturday fishermen coming, he should have at least an hour to get through the one very visible access point: the tunnel. He stripped off his shoes, jeans, and shirt and slipped into the wet suit: bottom, top, hood, mask, and boots. He put his street clothes back into the truck and took out a sealed waterproof duffel bag, which had a short lanyard ending in a snap attached to one end. He locked up the truck, put the keys in the exhaust pipe, and then headed for the pool.

The water was slightly colder than the air, but his only exposure was the skin of his face. He paddled out to the lip of the tunnel, towing the bag behind him. It was dark in the tunnel as he pushed the bag under the rusting teeth of the rebar grate, and then he ducked under and pulled himself up into the stream flowing over the lip of the tunnel. The concrete was slippery with old moss and he immediately found himself sliding backward, catching himself at the last moment against the top half of the grating. The structure swayed ominously, dropping bits of rusted metal all over him. He got one arm onto dry concrete on the side of the tunnel and worked his way back in, away from the grate. He then crawled on all fours through the stream, towing the bag behind him. The other end of the tunnel was about 150 feet away, visible as a pale circle of light against the blackness in the tunnel. He had to fight his way past a tree snag that was jammed across the tunnel about halfway in. Something dropped from the snag and went slithering past him in the dark water, but he pressed on. He knew that a snake's first instinct would be to get away from him. What he didn't know was whether or not the grate on the other end was intact.

There wasn't a grate at all. The tunnel opening gave onto a concrete-sided high-walled penstock shaped like a broad funnel in reverse. The creek came into the penstock via a waterfall at the far end. He spied a set of rusting steel rungs embedded in the concrete to one side, and he sloshed across the shallow water to get to the ladder. Once up on dry ground, he sat quietly for ten minutes, absorbing his surroundings. He was in a densely wooded area inside the security perimeter. The penstock appeared to be the only man-made structure other than the fences. He scanned the fences in the dawn light for cameras, but did not see any. He had checked the external fence during his reconnaissance yesterday for signs of electrification but had found no evidence of any wiring, not even alarm wires.

He pulled the duffel bag closer. He extracted a towel and a smaller, camouflaged bag. He stripped out of the diving gear, toweled off, and put all the diving gear into the smaller bag. Since he planned to make his daylight surveillance of the arsenal covertly, he had brought a crawl suit, into which he slipped quickly to avoid becoming chilled. The crawl suit was a one-piece camouflaged jumpsuit, which had padded knees, shoulders, and elbows, a wide elasticized waist, and elasticized arm and leg joints. The fabric at the back of his knees and under his arms was a breathable nylon mesh. The chest and upper back areas had segmented black plastic bands running vertically from just below his collarbone to a line level with his rib cage. The bands were made of Kevlar body armor and were separated by raised vertical strips of Velcro. There were tiny penlights sewn into the wrist cuffs on each arm.

Next, he pulled on a set of dark green high-topped boots, which were lined outside with Kevlar filament mesh to guard against snakebite. They had articulated steel ridges running vertically over a layer of rubber reaching all the way to the top of his calves. The soles were also rubber, with built-in steel shanks and heel cups. The boots were secured with four Velcro straps, and there was a built-in covered knife sheath on the left boot and a covered holster for wire cutters on the right. There were climbing studs embedded into heavy leather pads on the inside of each boot.

Next out of the bag came two flat mottled green packs, one for his chest and one for his back. Each pack was constructed of nylon netting with Velcro attachment pads. One contained two days' worth of food, the other his trekking equipment. He put on the backpack first, then the chest pack. The two packs were connected with Velcro straps under his armpits, preventing them from bobbling around.

He then pulled a lightweight camouflaged hunter's hood over his head, face, and neck. The hood was also mottled black and green, and heavily padded on top. It revealed only his eyes. His gloves were dark gray gauntlets that were made of cotton, lined outside with Kevlar mesh. He used a built-in bladder pump to inflate partially a two-inch cuff around both forearms, and then he attached a water bladder around his waist. He had not brought a gun; he rarely ever carried or used a gun. The last item out of the bag was a dull black telescoping titanium rod, which he extended to four feet in length before setting the locks. The rod had a broad hook topped by a black bulb on one end and a sharp spear point on the other.

He took the bags a hundred yards upstream of the penstock, then climbed up the bank to a knoll above the stream. The larger bag contained a low-profile camouflaged one-man tent, a lightweight sleeping bag, four military long-storage rations, a water-purification tube, and some cooking gear if he needed to stay longer. He sealed and then hid both bags in the middle branches of the largest pine tree on the knoll, then melted back into the woods and sat down to watch and listen for a few minutes. He could see the far edges of the fishing pool through the fences in the growing light, but he was confident that no one around the pool would be able to see him, even once the sun came up. He had seen no evidence around the inside penstock area that anyone else had come through the tunnel recently. Besides, Lynn hated confined spaces, so if the kids had come to the arsenal, it wasn't likely they had come through that tunnel. On the other hand, a creek this big probably did not originate within the restricted area, which meant there had to be another water cut through the fence, perhaps over on the higher, western side of the reservation. The creek appeared to run east-west.

His plan was to follow the south bank of the creek all the way across the arsenal and to look for signs of recent human intrusion along the way. If that effort turned up nothing, he would follow the north bank back and then cut over into the industrial area, which was north of the creek. He wasn't even puffing after the exertion of getting through the tunnel and getting set up in the crawl suit, which was a good sign. He was not in the shape he'd been when he was active, but he hadn't gone entirely soft, either. Except in the head, maybe, he thought. Those two agents had warned him against interfering, and he knew they were right. But since they weren't actually doing anything, he didn't feel too bad about it. He also knew that he might not like what he found. He took one last look around the pool area and then started west into the woods.

Browne McGarand sat in what had been the main control room of the power plant, watching the band of morning sunlight advance across the control room's wall from the skylights. He was keeping an eye on the pressure gauge of the operating hydrogen generator, which was a five-foot-high glass-lined stainless-steel retort into which he had put a sponge of copper metal. Suspended above the retort was a glass container of nitric acid, which was dripping down a glass tube at a controlled rate into the retort. The nitric acid combined with the copper to produce a slag of copper-nitrite and pure hydrogen gas. The reaction was exothermic, which required that the bottom of the retort be encased in a large tub of cold water to draw off heat. When the pressure in the retort rose to five pounds per square inch, a check valve lifted in its discharge line. The physical movement of the check valve activated a pressure switch, which, in turn, closed a contact connecting a small gas-transfer pump to its power supply. The pump drew the hydrogen gas out of the retort and pumped it through the wall into the tank of a propane truck that was parked in the maintenance bay next to the control room. When the pressure in the retort dropped back down to three pounds, the check valve reseated, shutting off the transfer pump, and then the whole process would wait for hydrogen pressure to rebuild in the retort.

Five pounds of copper took about two hours to produce as much hydrogen as it was going to make. Once the reaction began to decay, indicated by a steady drop in temperature, Browne would open valves to bring a second retort on line while he replenished the first one. He would don a respirator, divert the discharge line of the pump into the atmosphere of the control room, and operate the gas-transfer pump with a manual switch until a small vacuum was established on the retort. He would then close all the transfer valves by hand. He would wait, watching the gauge to make sure that it didn't creep back into the positive pressure range. Once certain that the reaction had stopped, he would open a vacuum-breaker valve on the retort, and then the main cover. He would remove the slag residue using tongs and rubber gloves, add five more pounds of metal, and close up the retort. He would run a short air purge on the retort, using the transfer pump again, until he had once more established a small vacuum in the retort vessel. Then he would start the nitric-acid drip going again.

It was slow, painfully slow. But it was a fairly safe way to make hydrogen, and, ultimately, an absolutely untraceable bomb. He had read with great interest all the news reporting on the Oklahoma City bombing investigation, and he knew all about the authorities' increasing scrutiny of all materials that had even the slightest explosive potential. This was why Browne had elected to make a hydrogen-gas bomb instead of using conventional explosives. And the container, well, that was going to be the really clever part. After nearly forty years of being a chemical engineer, assembling his little production lab had not required an elaborate scheme. The retorts he'd bought from a lab that had gone out of business. He'd obtained the small gas pump, as well as the larger one that would be required later to pressurize the truck fully, from a refrigeration and air-conditioning catalog. The small diesel generator, which putted away inside one of the two steam generators out in the boiler hall, was a Wal-Mart special. The rest of the hydrogen setup was conventional plumbing and catalog instrumentation, built into the existing piping of the power plant's boiler-water treatment and testing lab.

Jared had stolen the propane truck, with Browne's help. They'd hit a West Virginia propane company's lot one rainy night. While Browne kept watch, Jared hot-wired the truck and drove it away. They'd taken it to the arsenal and parked it out of sight down a fire lane close to the front gates. The next time the security truck came in, Jared had been waiting. The guards were in the habit of leaving the front gate unchained while they did their tour, which allowed Jared to drive the truck in once they were down in the industrial area. He'd hidden it in an empty warehouse until the security people had finished, and then he and Browne had maneuvered it into the power plant maintenance bay. They'd let the propane in the truck boil off to the outside air through its delivery hose for a week before sealing up the maintenance bay again and cleaning the truck tank and putting in new seals.

The pump came on, making a small racket in the room. Browne worried about the noise, and he knew the bigger pump would be even louder. He walked over to the interior control room door, which had a window in the upper half, and peered out into the cavernous steam-generation hall. The plant was about one-third the size of a commercial power station, but the two boilers were still forty feet high. He was pretty sure that the pump noise could not penetrate to the outside of the power station building, but he made frequent checks. His concern was that one day he would find a couple of deer hunters or college kids standing out there, poking around to see what that noise was. Just like the ones who had drowned in the creek.

Browne alone ran the hydrogen generator, working at night and on weekends. Jared, his older grandson, provided security. Jared had done his job well. Of his two grandsons, Jared was the one who looked most like his father, William. He was of medium height but strongly built. He worked as a telephone repairmen for the local telephone company, and he had been helping Browne with the bomb-building project right from the beginning. Browne knew that Jared held no great affection for his long-gone father, but, like his grandfather, Jared was sympathetic to the beliefs of the Christian Identity. He hated the government and all its works.

William's death during the Mount Carmel incident had just about shattered Browne. He had loved that boy in spite of everything that had happened—his disastrous teenage marriage, his slut of a wife running off like that, leaving William, and ultimately Browne, to raise the two kids. Jared had been a handful, no doubt about that, but Kenny, Jared's younger brother, had been born mildly retarded, and that had been really difficult. Although he had been angry at the time, he later came to sympathize with his son when he finally bailed out of Blacksburg. A high school education, two squalling kids, the cancer that rose up right about then and claimed Browne's wife, Holly—well, William never had a chance. Browne had had such high hopes. William had been bright enough to go on to college, maybe even Virginia Tech, right there in Blacksburg. With Browne's connections at the arsenal, William would have been a shoo-in for a high-paying job, except, of course, that the goddamned government had seen fit to close the arsenal, hadn't it? Damn near wiped out the town.

Jared had survived, which just about described it. He had been a dutiful, if resentful, child after both his mother and father left home. Raised in the orbit of his increasingly embittered grandfather, Jared had been a plodder. He had never talked to Browne about how he felt about being deserted by his parents, and Browne, with troubles of his own, had never raised the issue. He did often wonder how it might have all turned out if William had had a better shot at life. He had been such a great kid, full of life, friendly, easygoing, always trailing a clutch of giggling females, smart enough not to have to work very hard in school, and the apple of Browne's eye. Jared wasn't much like his father, except in one respect: He went through life seemingly obsessed with women. But Jared liked to live dangerously—he only fooled around with married women. Browne thought that this was probably Jared's way of guaranteeing that he would never repeat his own father's sorry family history.

Browne sighed as he thought about William and what might have been. All of Browne's hopes for the future seemed to have dissolved at the same time, right along with the arsenal. Jared was willing to help with Browne's revenge, not because he loved and missed his father, but because he heartily approved of the idea of the bomb, its target, and especially the timing of it, in the year 2000. Jared's other interest was what Browne called "the lunatic fringe," the militias and some of the more apocalyptic religious groups. One of Browne's continuing worries was that Jared would run his mouth to some of his dumb-ass militia friends over in West Virginia, but so far, security seemed to be intact. Jared was out there now, somewhere nearby, watching for the security people to begin their windshield tour.

The pump shut off to await the next pressure buildup of hydrogen. Browne crossed the control room and went into the maintenance bay via the connecting door. The power station was the one building on the installation where the government had not stripped out all the equipment. Two four-story-high steam boilers and all their auxiliary equipment still filled the open hall on the other side of the control room, and two locomotive-sized turboelectric generators crouched silently in the generating hall, beyond the boiler hall. Two twenty-four-inch cooling mains, now empty, used to bring water up from a reservoir back in the bunker farm to cool the main steam condensers. But it was all quiet now, quiet and secure, which made it the perfect place for what he was doing, especially since he knew the place like the back of his hand. Browne had been chief chemical engineer of the entire facility up until they shut it down two decades ago.

He opened the main pressure gauge sensing line and saw that the pressure in the truck tank was unchanged from yesterday's reading. He prayed there wasn't a leak somewhere, then reassured himself that any leak would have emptied the tank long before now. No, it was just going to take time to fill that huge volume. Browne nodded to himself. The mills of God were grinding away here, but they would indeed grind exceedingly fine when the time came. He went back into the control room. It was almost time for the security people to make their tour. When this cycle was done, he would shut off the electric generator until Jared came to tell him they had come and gone.

Edwin Kreiss moved through the woods like a shadow, gliding silently from tree to tree and cover to cover, using the warning cries of birds as his cue to stop and listen. He blended perfectly with all the vertical shadows among the trees. His rubber boots made no sound in the pine needles carpeting the ground. He was staying fifty feet inside the tree line on the south side of the creek, which was getting narrower as he followed it west back across the arsenal. He had crossed two fire lanes and two gravel roads so far, but he had seen no evidence that there had been any persons or vehicles on any of them in some time. He was warm in the jumpsuit, but not overly so, and he was handling with ease the gentle rise in elevation as he moved westward. It was nearly 11:00 A.M., and the sun was bright, creating pinwheels of light down through the pines.

So far, he had seen several deer, a raccoon, dozens of squirrels, and one rattlesnake sunning itself on a log. The creek was bordered on his side by a wide expanse of tall green grass, which was littered with branches and other debris, indicating that there had been at least one flash flood in the past month. The north bank, slightly higher and undercut about four feet, showed a tangle of roots and burrows against a face of red clay. Where the terrain allowed, he crept out of the forest and down to the creek bank to examine the watercourse for the signs of human life that seemed to litter every creek and river in America: plastic bottles, polystyrene hamburger wrappers, and aluminum cans. But this creek was pristine by comparison. The water was cold and clear, with waves of moss undulating on the stony bottom.

The only time he had to break cover was to cross a ravine that joined the creek from the south. It contained a tiny feeder brook, small enough to hop over. He crept down through the grass to the creek, stood up to jump it, and dropped back down into the grass. As he was scrambling up the other side, he thought he heard a vehicle off to his right. He dropped flat into the grass and made like a lizard, crawling carefully on all fours into the tree line at the top of the ravine, where he subsided into the pine needles to listen. He remembered doing this on the Agency training farm down near Warrenton: head down, face down, the smell of the dirt accentuating his other senses.

At first, he could hear nothing but the sound of a slight breeze soughing through the pines, but then he heard it again: the sound of a vehicle moving in low gear, far off to the right, beyond the pines lining the opposite bank. He lifted himself enough to see over his cover and was just able to catch a glimpse of a single chimney stack about a quarter of a mile or so to the northwest of his position. It looked like the concrete stack of a power plant, although only the very top was showing above the trees. I must be nearing the industrial area, he thought. He closed his eyes and concentrated, again detecting the far-off sound, a sound that came and went, as if the vehicle was changing direction constantly. Assuming it wasn't a trick of sound carrying across empty countryside, he figured there was definitely someone else on the reservation. The good news was that they were not getting any closer. The bad news was that he was not alone.

He shifted farther into the trees and the sound faded. He checked his wrist compass and then worked his way west through the woods for another fifteen minutes. He turned north to check on the creek and found that it was veering away from him toward a hard dogleg turn to the north. He moved back to his right in the woods until he came to the edge of the trees. He crouched behind a holly bush and examined his situation. Between him and the creek were fifty yards of waist-high bright green grass. He probed the ground with the rod—it was soft. The bright green meant that it was growing in totally saturated ground; he would have to be careful of quicksand and bogs.

At that moment, he felt the hair on the back of his neck lift. He flattened down onto the ground, the fabric of his face hood catching on the sharp spines of some holly leaves.

He was being watched. He was certain of it.

He kept perfectly still and reviewed his movements of the past fifteen minutes. The only open ground he had crossed was that ravine. Had he been spotted then? The woods noises remained normal; there was no sudden shrieking of jays or chatter of squirrels to announce that someone or some*thing* was behind him. Which meant that the watcher was probably on the other side of the creek. He waited for fifteen more minutes, listening carefully, and then began to crawl backward, flat on his belly, deeper into the woods. If there were someone watching from the other side, his movement back into the forest should be invisible.

He had seen something else when he tested the green grass area. Right at the elbow of the creek's turn, there was a massive twenty-foot-high pile of debris: whole tree trunks, shattered limbs, mud-balled roots, large rocks, and desiccated bushes, all caught up on the remains of a giant hardwood that had come down across the creek a long time ago. The huge logjam extended into the woods on his side for a hundred feet or so. On the north side, it had dammed the creek, which was now leaking through the tumbled mess in several small waterfalls.

He thought about that pile and wondered if he should cross to the north bank—there were bound to be snakes in that mess, and he needed to stay in visual contact with the creek. But there was no cover out there; he would have to crawl through that tall grass to the creek, and if someone was watching, they'd see the grass moving. He lay still for a few minutes, but the background noises did not change. He moved again, forward this time, but at a slight angle to the way he had come. He was aiming for the root ball of a downed pine tree that was fifty feet west of his original position, the place where he had sensed a possible watcher. He moved slowly, still making like a lizard, placing one hand and foot on the soft ground before moving the other one, inching back to the edge of the tree line. He had heard nothing and seen nothing specific that would indicate surveillance, but he had learned years ago to trust this particular instinct absolutely.

When he got to the root ball, he flattened himself down into the hole and then probed the roots with his rod. Sure enough, a copperhead lifted its diminutive triangular head three feet in front of him and tested the air with its tongue. He put the hooked end of the rod right in front of the snake's head and it froze. He tapped the snake's body with the rod and it coiled instantly, its delicate black tongue flickering in and out rapidly as it searched for a target. He angled the rod to line up with the snake's line of strike and waited. The snake also waited, its head making small angular displacements as it tried to form a heat image of whatever was in front of it. He moved the rod down to the ground and tapped it. The snake reset its coil and aimed in the direction of the rod. He raised the rod and jabbed at the snake, which struck at the rod straight on. He jammed the hooked end into the snake's maw and pushed hard, pinning the reptile against a thick root. It thrashed briefly and then stopped fighting, its jaws unlocked and wide open around the metal shaft that was stuck down its gullet. With his other hand, he pulled the knife from his right boot and cut down just behind the snake's head, killing it. He extended the rod and ejected the snake's body to his right.

He probed the root ball again to see if there were any more nasty surprises, but nothing moved. He checked to see that the snake was actually dead and then eased himself farther down into the hollow where the tree had grown. There was now a slight mound of dirt between him and the creek bed. If he lifted his head, the tops of that green grass were just visible over the rim of the mound. The feeling that someone was watching out there returned. He knew he had to be invisible from the other side, but he sensed that this was not the time to stand up and take a look. Using the hooked end of the rod, he began to cut a small groove into the rim of the dirt mound, working slowly and making sure the rod stayed perfectly horizontal. When he had cut a six-inch-deep groove, he widened the outside of it into an arrow slit. Then he produced a long, thin telescope from his front pack. He pushed it through the groove and out into the first strands of grass.

He raised his head and the telescope just high enough to see down into the area of the creek bed. Then he scanned the tree line on the opposite bank, inch by inch, degree by degree. The front lens was hooded to prevent reflections, and the sun was partially behind him anyway. He detected nothing in the woods opposite, but the sense of danger was strong now. He turned the scope westward, into the huge pile of the logjam. And then he saw it: a dull patch of color, a few feet inside the tangle of flood debris. He pulled the scope back and flattened himself into the root depression. Then he backed out of the hole and into the deeper cover of the woods, listening carefully and moving slowly enough not to scare up the birds. He angled back to the tree line, ten feet away from the root ball, and put the telescope back to the diamond-shaped eyehole in his head hood. He found the patch of color again and held his breath, hoping that he would not be looking into a set of binoculars. He focused the eyepiece. It was a ball cap, snagged on a branch. He felt the blood coming to his face and his breath catching in his throat. The ball cap was purple, with faded white lettering just barely showing. He thought he could make out one mud-splattered letter, the letter *L*.

Lynn owned a ball cap like that.

She wore it all the time, perched high up on her hair, the way the kids did now. That same color. With LHS embroidered on the front, for Langley High School.

He resisted the impulse to break cover, dash across the fifty yards of open grass, and tear into that tangled mess to retrieve the cap. He forced himself to sit perfectly still instead and deliberately slowed his breathing. It *had* to be hers. He pointed the telescope again, but now the cap was obscured. He closed his eyes and listened hard. Birds. Breeze. Crickets and other insects. Water splashing along the creek. No more vehicle noises. Now he had a decision to make.

He could go down there and get that cap, which is what he desperately wanted to do. But if there were people watching, he'd be at their mercy. Or he could wait for dusk. But then, if the watchers had a night-vision device, and they also were willing to wait, he would again be at their mercy. He visualized the area of the creek bed again. It was lower than the surrounding woods. He could wait until it was full dark, when the creek bed would subside into even deeper shadow. A night-vision device was a light amplifier: no light, no vision. Not like the infrared devices he'd used when he was active, which worked on contrast between warm objects and colder background. The hat was just inside the tangle of trees and roots, and just to the left of the leftmost waterfall. He memorized its location, took a deep breath, and began looking for a spot to hole up.

He decided to climb into the dense bottom branches of a big pine for the rest of the afternoon and wait for sundown. He still couldn't be positive someone was watching, but if they lost patience and came out of hiding, well, that would be all right, too. He couldn't think of a reason for someone to be skulking through the woods on this abandoned installation, unless there was something illegal going on, something that might account for the kids' disappearance. *If* that was Lynn's hat, he reminded himself. Another part of his brain tried not to think of all the possible ramifications of that last thought. Every hunt was a sequence of decisions: when to move, when to wait, where to watch, and when to sleep, which was as close to motionless as one could get. This was a time for sleep.

Janet Carter was finishing her lunch when the idea hit her. She had stopped for lunch after her Saturday-morning postdoc seminar at Tech.

The place was a vegetarian street café. Janet, a devoted carnivore, visited the nuts and twigs scene once in a while to salve her conscience. The seminars weren't terribly interesting, but at least they filled the beginning of the weekend. Over lunch, she had been thinking about Barry Clark. The kid was an insolent, slovenly pup, and Kreiss undoubtedly had applied exactly the right kind of pressure to make the little shit talk. On the other hand, he was probably still immobilized, and perhaps an unexpected act of kindness on her part might spring something loose. So why not take a pizza over there and see if she could get him to tell her what he had revealed to the headless horseman the other night.

She gathered up the paper plate and her Coke. It had to have been Kreiss, of course. Big bad bogeyman in the dark; in and out without a trace, and the kid scared shitless in the process, paralyzed physically and mentally by an encounter that probably had taken all of ninety seconds. *Professional* bogeyman. He must have learned some interesting things from those people at the Agency. She dumped her table trash and went across the street to the pizza place, resisting an urge to get some real food.

Twenty minutes later, she was banging on Clark's door. It took him a few minutes to answer the door, and his appearance hadn't changed much since the other night: dirty T-shirt, baggy shorts, flip-flops. His face was sallow and there were pouches under his eyes. The beginnings of a scraggly red beard covered his face. His arms still hung straight down at his sides, although he could move his hands now. He blinked at her for a moment, long enough for her to get a whiff of the apartment within.

"What?" he said, screwing up his face, as if the midday sunlight hurt his eyes.

"I'm Janet Carter," she said. "Still with the FBI. Brought you a pizza."

He blinked again. He must have been asleep, she thought. "Felt sorry for you," she said. "Want me to cut it up for you?"

"Damn," he muttered. "Yeah. Thanks. But, I mean, like, why?"

She took her last deep breath of fresh air, toed the door open, and stepped past him into the apartment. It hadn't improved. "Leave the door open," she called over her shoulder. "You need the fresh air. Where's a knife?"

He followed her across the room. She stopped at the kitchen threshold and let him pry a knife out of the sink. He could pick it up in his fingers but not lift his arm. "Why don't we just wash that," she suggested, taking it from his limp fingers and running it under some hot water. He just stood there. She cut the pizza into thin slices, scraped and washed a plate, and set him up in the single living room chair. She put the plate on a stool in front of him and watched him eat hungrily, bending over the stool and slurping it up like a dog. The light streaming in from the open front door showed more of the mess than she wanted to see.

"Actually," she said, "that's a bribe."

"Cops can do bribes?" he said around a mouthful. Now there was a hint of his previous insolence in his eyes. Must be the sudden carbo load, she thought. She no longer wanted any pizza.

"One-way rule," she said. "We can't *take* bribes; but we can *do* bribes, especially for information, see?"

He kept chewing while he watched her.

"I still want to know what you told the headless guy the other night," she said.

"Like I said—" he began.

"No, wait. See, last time I asked you what he wanted. That was the wrong question. This is a different question. What did *you* say to *him*? Exact words."

He sucked another piece of dripping pizza into his mouth. His eyes were definitely wary now, seeking some advantage. She pressed him. "Look, lemme lay it out for you. If you told him what he wanted to know, he's never coming back, so it won't matter if you tell me. If you *didn't* give him what he wanted, he will come back, and you'll need me to protect you. *Us* to protect you." She gave him a moment to absorb that "us." "So, what did you say to him? Exact words?"

He studied her face. "For a fuckin' pizza?" he said.

"You're out of your league, Barry. Way the hell out of your league. Think about how big he was. How much stronger he was than you, and that's when you had arms. Now think about other parts of your body, Barry. Soft parts."

He blinked at that, licked his lips, and then sighed.

"Site R," he said. "He wanted to know where Lynn and the guys went camping. All I knew was Site R. That's what I heard Rip say. They were going to 'break into' Site R. I don't know what that means. I told him that. And I still don't fuckin' know, okay?"

She looked at him. "Okay. And has it ever occurred to you that if you'd told someone this a lot sooner, maybe we'd have found them?"

He looked away. Janet got up and left.

Just before sundown, Browne McGarand watched the reaction on the last copper sponge fizzle out. The light coming through the four skylights of the control room was turning sunset red. He shut off the acid drip and was beginning the purge sequence when he heard two distinctive taps on the metal door, followed by two more taps. Jared was back. Browne turned out the single work light, got his flashlight, and went to the control room door. He tapped the door once.

"It's Jared," Jared replied from the other side. They had arranged a duress code when the project began. If Jared ever said, "It's me," Browne would know that Jared was not alone and that he should get out of there through the vehicle bays. Browne opened the door and Jared came through.

His grandson was a hefty-shouldered man with a large paunch and a heavy black beard. His job with the local telephone company had him spending days by himself checking the more remote lines in the county, where he tended to roadside tree falls, so-called backhoe interrupts, when customers or the other utilities unwittingly dug through a phone line, and feeder-box problems in the isolated cabins and trailers off the main county roads. His clothes always smelled faintly of pine needles and tobacco. Jared was perpetually suspicious, and he had a habit of squinting his eyes at people and things as if he expected them to lunge at him. Browne closed and locked the door and turned the work light back on.

"The security people stop anywhere?"

"Nope. Drove around like always. You could hear their damn radio goin' a block away—some damn rock and roll crap. Windows rolled up with the AC goin'." He sniffed. "Some security."

"Be thankful they're not real professionals," Browne said. "I've always wondered when they might start random building checks."

"Not that pair," Jared said, easing his heavy frame into one of the console chairs. "But we may have us another problem."

Browne finished the purge and began to set up the retort for cleaning. "What kind of problem?"

"You know how sometimes you see somethin' outta the corner of your eye? You wonder if you really seen it or you just imaginin' things?"

Browne eyed his grandson. "Things?"

"I was watchin' that there security truck from the rail sidin' control tower. I'd a sworn I saw a man crossin' that little ravine, joins the creek just below that big logjam? You know where I'm talkin' about? You can just see that stretch from the sidin' tower. But somethin' was off about it, what I saw, I mean." He shook his head. "Like he was wearin' a hood or somethin'. That's it—wasn't no face. I don't know. I think I saw it. But maybe not."

Browne rubbed his jaw. "A man, though? Not a deer or other animal?"

Jared nodded thoughtfully. "That tall grass out there along the creeks? Looked like he'd been down in that there grass, but had to stand up to jump that brook, comes through there. Then he was gone."

"What did you do?"

"When the security truck went out to the back bunker area, I went down there, to the north side of the creek. Hid out in the tree line. Waited for a coupla hours, see if he came out of the woods or showed himself somehow. But nothin'. And it didn't *feel* like there was someone there. Not like when you know there's deer movin' around in there, you know? Birds wasn't yellin'. No bushes were movin', no other noises." He rubbed the back of his leg. "Got into some damn chiggers, I think. Hell, I don't know. Prob'ly nothin'."

"A single individual," Browne said as he closed the retort back up. "Those traps still set?"

"Yep."

"Well, maybe we'll skip taking the girl her food tonight. Maybe we'll go out there and see what happens. If she ate those apples I fixed for her, she'll still be out of it anyway."

"You want me to go check on her?" Jared asked, a little too casually.

Browne wasn't fooled. "No, I don't think so, Jared," he said. "Besides, we shouldn't go near the nitro building, especially if there's someone here. He might be here because of those kids going missing. Wouldn't want to just lead him to her, would we, now?"

Jared nodded but said nothing. He continued to rub the back of his leg while Browne closed off all the valves to the truck in the next bay.

"We've got pressure showing on the truck tank," Browne announced, trying to distract Jared from thoughts of the captive girl. Jared didn't need to be messing with that girl. "From now on, we're building power. But I'm almost out of copper."

"Got me some back in the central office yard," Jared said. "Pallet of cracked switch plates. They're flat. We can grind 'em, or just put 'em in there and use more acid."

Browne nodded. Acid they had, in vast quantities. No government agency would be putting a pattern together on missing copper. He thought about the pressure. Maybe another thirty batches, if they could keep the process going. Pretty soon, they'd have to switch to the big pump. He finished up securing the hydrogen generator.

"All right. Let's go down there and look around," he said. "Maybe it was just a late-season turkey hunter sneaking around; those guys cammo up pretty good."

Edwin Kreiss made his move forty-five minutes after the sun went down behind the ridges to the west of the arsenal. He felt refreshed, having slept for a couple of hours in his hiding place. He had crept out to the tree line just before sundown and again memorized the features in the pile that were closest to the cap. Once darkness just about obscured the opposite tree line, he crept down on his belly through the tall grass, moving directly toward the creek. Mindful of that copperhead, he probed ahead with the rod, parting the grass carefully and probing the spongy earth on either side before slithering forward. The ground was not wet, but it was very soft, with occasional round rocks embedded here and there. It took him ten careful minutes to get down to within six feet of the creek bank, where he stopped to absorb the night sounds around him. His plan was to get into the creek itself and move upstream to the logjam, then get out and crawl sideways until he could retrieve the cap.

The sky above him was clear. A drone of night insects and frogs had begun and the creek burbled peacefully right ahead. What if it isn't Lynn's cap? Wrong question, his brain told him. What if it *is* her cap? Then what? He forced himself to concentrate on the ground directly ahead of him. He no longer had the sense that someone was watching up in those trees. Even if someone was watching, no one would be able to see him. Had all that been just a spook on his part? He thought maybe he should cross the creek, go up to the opposite tree line, and check it out for watchers. No. Focus. Get the cap.

He probed ahead with the rod while he inched toward the creek bank. The grass had a muddy smell. The cuff on his right sleeve hung up on something resistant in the grass. He pulled gently and heard a tiny chinking sound, like metal scraping on a rock. He froze. Metal? He backed up a few inches, turned his head very slowly to look into the darkness with his peripheral vision, but it was almost night now and he couldn't see anything at all. His sleeve was free, so he rolled very carefully to the left and began collapsing the rod down to a two-foot-long staff. Then he pointed it into the grass at his right and began parting the thick stems, moving the rod from side to side, advancing it an inch at a time, until he heard another clink. He put down the rod and snapped on one of his cuff lights, which threw a tiny red beam of light into the base stems of the grass. A sheen of steel reflected back at him. He parted more of the grass to expose the trap and gave a mental whistle. Had he been upright and walking through here, he might have stepped into that thing.

He considered his position. There were traps along the creek, big steel traps, capable of seizing, if not breaking, a man's leg. He directed the tiny bead of light at the trap again and found the step trigger and the tie-down chain. This trap was much too big for small game: These were *man*traps. So why in the hell were there mantraps out here? He carefully rolled the other way and began exploring the bank, going upstream until he found another trap. As long as he came at them low and from the side, they posed no threat. But for anyone walking along the creek, or down to the creek, to cross maybe . . . well . . . Then he wondered if there were any *in* the creek.

Browne and Jared walked quietly down the path toward the creek. The ghostly buildings of the industrial area were swallowed up behind them by the dense trees. Jared led, with Browne twenty feet behind him. They did not use lights, having used this path before. Browne trusted Jared's woodcraft instincts; his grandson had been hunting the foothills of the Appalachians since he was a young boy and he was a natural woodsman. Browne was also pretty sure that Jared's skills had more than a little bit to do with his penchant for comforting some of the lonelier women back up in those gray hills. Jared was a big boy now, and if he wanted to take chances like that, it was on his own head. If nothing else, fooling around with some of those mountain women had probably sharpened up Jared's defensive instincts. If Jared thought he'd seen something, then they needed to go take a look down along the creek area. That's where those kids had come in.

Jared slowed as the trees bordering the path thinned out. They were getting closer to the banks of the creek. Browne patted the Ruger .44-caliber revolver on his hip and began to pay close attention to his surroundings.

Kreiss finally reached the edge of the logjam pile and began to feel around for the bole of the big tree that had impounded all the flood debris in the first place. He was thirty feet away from the creek, moving back toward the trees on the south side of the water. The cap ought to be about six feet south of the root ball on the big tree, maybe five feet off the ground and a foot or so back in the tangle. He found the edge of the root ball and retraced his handholds on the trunk, using the rod to estimate the distance. He didn't want to turn on a cuff light until he thought he was very close. When he was finally in position, he paused to look straight up. It was a dark, moonless night, but there was plenty of starlight streaming down through the clear mountain air. He adapted his eyes to use the starlight by looking first up the stars and then down and sideways at the top objects in the logjam. When he could make out individual branches and snags, he looked down along the logjam until he could make out the tops of individual trees on the other side of the creek. If there was anyone out here tonight, they'd be over there in those trees, where they could see down into the broad ravine cut by the creek.

He began to scan the dark mass of tangled debris with his peripheral vision, searching for a lighter contrast among all the roots, limbs, packed leaves, and mangled grasses. When he finally thought he had it, he set a cuff light for the dimmest red setting and pointed it into the tangle. The hat was right there. Keeping the light on, he pushed the rod into the tangle, very slowly so as to make no noise, and snagged the hat. He turned off the light, retrieved the cap, and stuffed it quietly into the chest pack without looking at it. Then he subsided to the ground to listen to the night. The mass of the logjam rose up beside him. It felt like an avalanche, poised to drop on him. The hairs were up on the back of his neck again.

Browne stood to one side of the dim path. He was just able to make out Jared's silhouette as he stood ten feet behind him. Jared was sweeping binoculars down into the ravine. The wedge of night sky showing through a gap in the trees was clear; the air was cooling fast. He didn't really expect anything to happen tonight; if Jared had seen someone, they were at best long gone and at worst huddled around a campfire out in the deep storage area somewhere. For a moment, he had a prickly thought that whoever it was might have already gotten behind them and was even now creeping through the streets of the industrial area. The girl, he thought. Is this about the girl?

Jared was moving back in his direction. As always, Browne was amazed that such a heavy man as Jared could move so soundlessly through the woods. Not a twig snapped nor bush swished. He just seemed to get closer and closer, until Browne could smell the cigarette smell on him.

But then Jared reached for Browne's left hand. He took it gently, turned it palm up, and jabbed one finger down: He'd seen someone or something, and as best he could tell, there was only one of them out there.

Browne took Jared's hand. He drew the letter *W* on Jared's palm with his fingernail, followed by the letter *R*, meaning, Where exactly is he?

Jared took Browne's palm. He drew a wiggly line all the way across it. The creek. Then he bisected that line with the flat of his thumb, twice. The logjam, just below where those kids had drowned. Then he did it again, and where the two lines met, he drew his finger lightly up the logjam line and then jabbed his fingertip right *there*: south of the creek, on the other side, near the logjam, one individual.

Browne pulled the heavy pistol and pressed it into Jared's hand. Then he tapped Jared once on the chest and squeezed Jared's hand around the pistol grip, indicating he should take the gun. Then he took Jared's other hand, touched his own chest with it, and then his right ear, tapping Jared's fingertips on his ear two or three times, and then he pointed Jared's arm first to his own face and then off to the right, meaning, You take the gun. I'll go to the right and make noise. Jared nodded in the darkness, turned around, and melted back toward the creek.

Browne waited until he could no longer see the black shape of his grandson, and then he went off the path to the right, moving silently across the carpet of pine needles. When he judged he was about thirty feet away from the path, he felt around for a large stick, picked it up, took a deep breath, and then began yelling, *"There he is! Get him!"* at the top of his lungs while banging the stick against the trees around him and crashing noisily through the underbrush toward the creek.

Kreiss had crawled almost back to the edge of the creek when the hullabaloo broke out in the opposite tree line. He felt a stab of panic before his hunting discipline reasserted itself. Instead of springing into a dead run across the field of high grass, toward the safety of his own tree line, he lunged *toward* the noise and the creek, even as a heavy bullet smacked the bole of the big downed tree and a booming pistol report assaulted his ears from up on the opposite tree line. He rolled into the creek bed in the direction of the gunshot and made a split-second decision. If the watchers had been there for a long time, they'd expect him to run back the way he'd come, down the creek and then out through the tall grass, right into the mantraps. Instead, he scrambled as close to the undercut north bank as he could get and then slipped to his left under the big tree trunk and into the tangle of the logjam. He ended up lying on his belly in wet sand, with one of the small waterfalls pouring ice-cold water onto his back. Using the rod in his left hand and his fingers on his right hand, he moved sand aside like a giant sea turtle about to lay its eggs on a beach. As he wiggled deeper into the sand, he was able to move farther up under the logjam. With any luck, he could get all the way under it to the stream on the back side and get away, but, either way, they couldn't get a shot at him while he was under all this debris. He kept digging and inching his way forward.

When Browne heard the shot, he stopped making noise and stood still by the edge of the tree line, keeping one tree between himself and the creek and waiting for Jared. Obviously, Jared had been confident enough of seeing someone that he'd taken a shot. Then, to Browne's left, a bright white flashlight snapped on, its beam traversing the creek bed from right to left quickly, and then much more slowly. He pulled his own light and began doing the same thing, putting his beam where Jared's wasn't. They searched back and forth along the area of the creek bed, and along the downstream edge of the logjam pile. Browne saw the occasional glint of steel as his beam hit one of the traps. He moved left to join Jared.

"Well?" he said.

"Saw him at the edge of the creek and the logjam," Jared said, keeping his voice low. "Blind once the gun went off. Missed him, though; heard the bullet hit that big tree."

"Can you tell which way he went?"

"Into the creek. After that . . ."

Browne was silent for a long moment. He stopped his light when it illuminated Kreiss's original path through the tall grass leading down to the creek. "Well, nothing wrong with your instincts. There was someone out here. Question is, Why?"

"Way that grass is flattened down, he was crawlin'," Jared said. "Whoever it was, he wasn't huntin'. He was creepin' this place."

"This has to be about those kids, then," Browne said. "No way anyone could know about the other. Right, Jared?"

"Not from me anyways," Jared said as he flicked the powerful beam up to the opposite tree line, hoping to flash some eyes. Nothing shone back at him. "So that's bad, then."

"Yes, it is."

"You want to keep looking? Maybe go get the dogs?"

Browne thought about it. Jared had three mixed-breed hounds he used for hunting wild pigs, but it would be hours before they could get back here with the dogs. "No," he said. "I think we should get off the reservation for the night. Maybe leave it alone for a couple of days. In case this was just some guy wandering around. Tonight he's scared. Tomorrow he might bring cops."

"He'd have to admit he broke in here," Jared said, handing back the heavy Ruger. "If this wasn't purposeful, then he'll never come back."

"And if it was . . ."

"Then I need to start patrollin'. You stay on the generator; I need to start huntin'."

Browne detected the sound of anticipation in his grandson's voice. Above all else, Jared was a hunter. They made a few more sweeps of the ravine with their Maglites, and then Browne switched his off. He brought out a much smaller version of the big light and used it to guide them back up the path toward the industrial area.

Behind them, down in the ravine, Edwin Kreiss broke through the last of the tangle, pulled himself out onto a dry sandbar, sniffed the night air, and listened. Then he smiled.

6

On Monday morning, Janet Carter talked to Larry Talbot and Billy Smith about what she'd learned from Barry Clark. Billy Smith was manfully trying to stay awake, but there was a steady parade of yawns.

"Am I mistaken, or didn't the boss have a word with you Friday?" Talbot said.

"Yes, he did. Warned me off Edwin Kreiss and this whole case. But as I understand it, we get new info, we make sure it gets into the system. Billy, you finished the transmittal letter for the case file?"

"Nope, but I'll have it today," Billy said, giving another yawn. "I need to know which one of you is the official case officer."

If Billy wasn't such a nice man, all this yawning would have me yelling at him, she thought. Talbot, however, made a noise of exasperation.

"Look, Jan," he said. She frowned. She hated being called Jan. "I remember that kid Clark. Redhead, right? 'Fuck you' sneer on his face all the time? He's an asshole. He could be telling you anything, or the latest thing off the Dungeon Masters of Doom bulletin board. Leave the fucking thing alone. You want to put the campus cops' report and this Site R stuff into that file, fine. But if Farnsworth finds out you're still messing with this thing, he'll have you doing background investigation interviews on Honduran gardeners until the end of time. Okay? Enough already."

Janet acquiesced and slunk back to her cubicle. Billy rose up over the divider.

"What's the difference between a southern zoo and a northern zoo?" he asked.

She waited.

"A southern zoo has a description of the animal on the front of a cage, along with a recipe."

He winked at her over the divider and then did a down periscope. Sweet dreams, Billy, she thought. She started going through her E-mail and remembered that the shrink up in Washington had promised to get back to her, but it was only Monday morning. Then she saw an announcement on internal mail that Farnsworth was going to a conference of eastern region SACs and RAs for three days and wanted any pending action-items brought to him before close of business today. She looked around for Talbot, but he had stepped away from his desk. She cut over to the Web and hit her favorite search engine. She typed in Site R and received the usual avalanche of Web site garbage. So much for that, she thought, and went to refill her coffee cup. To her surprise, Billy was working, not sleeping. She offered to fill his cup, and he accepted. When she returned, she asked him about Site R.

"Only Site R I ever heard about was the alternate command center for the Pentagon; it's up near Camp David, in Maryland. Probably five, six hours from here, up I-Eighty-one, then east."

"Not a place you'd go camping, then?"

"Not unless you like sleeping with a lot of Secret Service agents. It's like that NORAD thing inside Cheyenne Mountain. You know, the command center for the ICBMs. For what it's worth, I took a look through that case file. I noticed something: They didn't take a lot of clothes, like for some long trip. Larry even made a note that Kreiss had questioned that. I don't know about this Site R business, but I'd be looking for something closer to home."

"Like what? Site R sounds military."

"Yeah, well, maybe go talk to some of the homesteaders here. Or local law maybe."

Janet nodded and went back to her desk. The homesteaders were FBI employees who had been in the Roanoke office for a long time, people who either had low-level technical jobs or were non-career-path special agents. Talbot returned to the office and looked over in her direction; Janet made a show of tackling her in box. She had half a mind to put a call into Edwin Kreiss, see what *he* knew about Site R. Yeah, right, she thought. Back to work, Carter.

Edwin Kreiss finished cleaning his trekking gear and then restowed his packs in the spare bedroom closet. He was waiting for a return call from Dagget Parsons up in northern Virginia. Kreiss had saved Parsons's life during an Agency retrieval in Oregon, when Dagget had been a pilot for the U.S. Marshals Service. Dagget had retired after the incident, but not before telling Kreiss that if there was ever anything he needed, just call. Kreiss was hoping that Dag was still flying for that environmental sciences company. The phone rang.

"Edwin Kreiss."

"Well, well, Edwin Kreiss himself. How the hell are you? *Where* the hell are you?"

"Nowhere special anymore, Dag; just another Bureau retiree. I'm down in Blacksburg, near Virginia Tech. What are you up to these days? You still flying for that Geo-Information Services?"

"Yeah. It's boring, but boring is what I'm after these days. How can I help you?"

Kreiss told him about Lynn. Then he got right down to it. "Dag, I need some aerial photography of a place called the Ramsey Army Arsenal. It's outside of a town called Ramsey, here in southwest Virginia. The place is a mothballed Army ammunition-production complex. Got any contacts who could maybe get me copies of some black-and-white overheads, say from about five thousand feet?" He phrased it that way in case Parsons didn't want to do it.

"Contacts? No. But I can do it. The company I fly for is over in Suitland, Maryland. Like you said, we do GIS stuff all up and down the East Coast. You know, field condition analyses for farmers, spectrum analysis for crop diseases, pond health, insect infestations, plant pathologies."

"I'm not active anymore, Dag. This is strictly personal. I can cover costs, of course."

"Understood. And you're working with local law, or in spite of local law?"

"They've declared it a missing persons case. The Bureau, I mean. The locals will follow the feds' lead on that."

"The locals know you're working it? They know who you are?"

"No. Not yet anyway. The local Bureau people do, of course, after my somewhat colorful departure, and I've been duly warned off. But I can't just sit here, Dag."

"Understood, Ed. I'll guarantee I'd be doing the same damn thing. Look, this stuff is all unclassified. We have a humongous database of aerial photography. We probably have coverage. Lemme work on it. How long's she been missing?"

Kreiss told him.

"Shit. That's rough." He paused, not wanting to state the obvious.

"I have to hope, Dag, but, like I said, the cops and the Bureau have given up looking. The feds say there's no evidence of a crime, so it's a straight missing persons beef now. But I got a tip about this installation, and I then found her hat there. It's not a place where she should have been, and I think there's something going on there."

"You tell your ex-employers all that?"

"I'd have to tell them how I found it. That wouldn't be helpful. For a variety of reasons."

Dagget was silent for a moment. "But maybe they'd start working it again," he said.

"I don't think so. There's still no crime, except mine. They're working stiffs with a budget and a boss, Dag. Basically, I'm going solo on this."

"Roger that," Parsons said. "I'm slated into southern Pennsylvania this afternoon, but we did some flights on some big apple orchards in the upper valley about six months ago. Let me look at the GPS maps for this Ramsey Arsenal, see if maybe we got coverage."

"I can pay for this, Dag."

"Not me you can't. The only thing that might take some cash is getting your data out of the center. But we're talking black-and-white photo recce here, so that ought not to be a big deal. This place restricted airspace?"

"Probably. There's a big double chain-link fence around the whole thing."

There was a moment of silence on the phone. Then he said, "I'll get it, Ed. Whatever it takes. I owe you big-time."

"No, you don't, but I appreciate it, Dag."

There was another pause. "Ed," Parsons said. "That incident at Millwood. I heard some bizarre stories about that. Next time we get together, I'd like to hear your side, you feel like it. The official version smelled like cover-up."

Kreiss didn't want to get into this. "The official story closed that book, Dag," he said. "Probably best for all concerned."

"A coupla guys made it sound like Custer's last stand, but with the Indians losing."

Kreiss stared out the window for a moment. "Ancient history, Dag."

"Yeah. All right. I've got your number. If we have coverage, I'll have something to you by Wednesday. And Ed, anything else—you just screech. You hear me? I've got my own plane, and I can still fly, even if I can't shoot."

"Appreciate it, Dag. More than you know." He got Parsons's beeper number, then hung up. He went out the front door to the porch. He looked into what seemed to be a golden green cloud of new leaves. The air was filled with the scent of pollen and fresh loam. The creek down below was just barely audible through the thickening vegetation.

He had made a mistake going into the arsenal without any idea of the layout. It hadn't occurred to him that there might be people in there, which showed just how much of an edge he'd lost over the past few years. It had taken him an hour to get out of the logjam tangle, and then another hour to traverse just the fifty yards from the creek back into the trees. That shooter had to have had a very good pair of optics or a night scope of some kind to get so close with the first shot. That meant they had been down there looking for an intruder. An intruder into what? What was going on in that place that there were men laying traps along that creek and coming after him with guns? A bunch of bikers running a meth lab, possibly? A hillbilly marijuana farm?

But then there was the hat. Lynn's hat. Carried down that creek until it got caught up in the logjam. Which meant—what, exactly? Had someone stolen that hat a year ago and gone into the arsenal with it? Or had the kids been camping outside of the complex, and the hat blew away and got carried downstream? There certainly were other plausible explanations. And yet, that kid had said "break into" Site R. While he was almost certain that hat was hers, he couldn't remember the last time he'd actually seen her wear it. He should call those FBI people and tell them he'd found the hat. But how would he explain the where part? And even if the Bureau people were sympathetic, would they *do* anything? Did they even have the case anymore? Did they care? Had they ever cared? He remembered the way that woman agent had looked at him, almost challenging him to interfere: "Do not go solo on this," she'd said. Pretty or not, she wasn't old enough to talk to him like that.

He sighed in frustration and went back into the house to make some coffee. He was being unfair. Agents were agents. There was an infinite supply of evil out there. Knock off a bad guy and two more rose up in his place. The working stiffs in the Bureau and the other federal law-enforcement agencies tended to work the ones they could, and the others, well, they did what they could until some boss said, Hey, this isn't going anywhere; let's move on, folks. As long as statistics drove the budget, the bosses would prioritize in the direction of closure. This was nothing new. The Agency had been different, but that was because they weren't really accountable to anybody except a committee or two in Congress, where accountability was an extremely flexible concept.

He stood at the sink, washing out the coffeepot, and considered the other problem, the larger problem—that Washington might find out he'd come out of his cave. The terms of his forced retirement after the Millwood incident had been excruciatingly clear, enunciated through clenched teeth by none other than J. Willard Marchand, the assistant director over Bureau Foreign Counterintelligence himself: Kreiss was never to act operationally again, not in any capacity. Not in private security work, not as a consultant, not even in self-defense. "Some asshole wants your car, you give it up. Someone breaks into your house at night, you sleep through it. You may not carry a firearm. You may not do any of those things you've been doing for all those years. You will forget everything you learned from those goddamned people across the river, and you will turn in any special equipment you may have acquired while you were there."

The deal had been straightforward: He could draw his pension, go down to Blacksburg, be with his daughter, and contemplate his many sins in the woods. But that was it. He remembered that Marchand had been so angry, he could speak only in short bursts. "We'll let you keep your retirement package. Despite Millwood, for which the professional standards board could have just fired you. You can live on that. You want to take a civilian job, it had better not be even remotely related to what you did here. And, most importantly, you keep your wild-ass accusations to yourself. In other words, Kreiss, find a hole, get in it, and pull it in after you. And speaking for the deputy attorney general of the United States, if we get even a hint that you're stirring the pot somewhere, any pot, anywhere, we'll ask the Agency to send one of your former playmates down there to retrieve *your* ass. And we *will* be watching."

All because of what had happened on a quiet Sunday afternoon in Millwood, Virginia, a tiny village up in the northern Shenandoah Valley. Millwood was home to a restored gristmill, a couple of antique shops, Carter Hall—once the huge estate of the Burwell family, which was now home to the Project Hope foundation—a post office, a private country day school, three dozen or so private homes, and a general store. It also contained the ancestral home of Ephraim Glower, erstwhile assistant deputy director for counterespionage operations for the Agency. Ephraim Glower of the Powhatan School, Choate, and Yale University. Whose ancestors had ridden with Mosby's Rangers during the Civil War, partnered with J. P. Morgan in the heyday of the robber barons, and served as an assistant secretary of the Treasury during the reign of Franklin Roosevelt. Ephraim Glower had risen to a position of real power within the Agency, while spending the last of the family's fortune on the family estate, a town house in Georgetown, foxhunting in Middleburg, Washington A-list entertaining, a high-maintenance socialite wife, and a string of young and beautiful "associates." His superior social standing had been matched by an equally superior attitude, and he had not been beloved by his subordinates within CE.

Kreiss's team, while working the Energy Department espionage case in collaboration with the Agency CE people and Energy's own security people, had begun to encounter an increasingly resistant bureaucratic field. Someone was subtly inhibiting the investigation. Kreiss eventually suspected Glower. When he checked out a rumor that Glower was almost broke, it turned out that he had been rescued by an infusion of mysterious cash. Kreiss, by then operating mostly on his own initiative, had followed the money trail. He had traced the money from its sources in Hong Kong, through the election campaign finance operations of the newly elected administration, directly to Glower. Who, for sums paid, was apparently obstructing the joint Bureau/Agency/Energy Department investigation by spinning a gentle web of bureaucratic and legal taffy over all the efforts to determine if there were Chinese spies at the nuclear-research laboratories. Glower didn't trade secrets for money, as most spies or traitors did. He provided an insidious form of top cover, and he did it so well that Kreiss eventually concluded that Glower must have been getting some help from over in the Justice Department.

All of this was happening as Kreiss was entering his eighth year of the exchange assignment with the Agency counterespionage directorate. As he and his small team developed the scope and depth of a possible top-level conspiracy, Kreiss, the team leader and prime mover, had been suddenly recalled to the Bureau. The word in the corridors was that Langley had complained about Kreiss, claiming he had begun to overstep his brief. Someone at the highest levels in the Agency had prevailed upon someone in Justice to make the Bureau recall him. He had been given an innocuous position within the Bureau's FCI organization, pending a new assignment. The pending went on for two years, while he watched the joint Energy Department/FBI investigation stall out completely.

This had convinced Kreiss that Ephraim Glower had a cohort over at Justice, and possibly within the Bureau itself. His timing turned out to be lousy, since there was already a great deal of bureaucratic acrimony between Justice and FBI headquarters. Since the FBI worked for the attorney general, no one in the Bureau wanted to hear Kreiss's conspiracy theories about any putative Chinese spy ring, and most emphatically, they did not want to hear about a high-level problem over at Justice. The Bureau was much too busy manning its own ramparts over Waco, Ruby Ridge, and, later, some unpleasant revelations about the FBI laboratory. When the story about the Chinese government's attempts to buy influence during and after the 1996 reelection campaign broke in Washington, Kreiss tried again. This time, he was shut down even more forcefully. The FBI director by then had his own problems with the Justice Department as he and the attorney general traded salvos and congressional testimony over independent prosecutors, a laundry list of presidential scandals, and growing talk of a presidential impeachment.

Kreiss, totally frustrated, went to Millwood to confront Ephraim Glower, which led to bloody results. He was preparing to challenge his expulsion from the Bureau, when something happened to change his mind: The Agency had threatened his daughter. The threat had been made indirectly, but it had been unmistakable. It had come during a seemingly casual telephone call from one of his ex-associates in the retrieval business. Langley was still furious about Glower, and the word in CE was that the big bosses didn't believe Kreiss's alibi for the time Glower had done all the killing. But they were willing to put the whole incident to bed as long as Kreiss shut up about what Glower had been doing. And if he didn't, Kreiss might get to experience his own family tragedy. Kreiss took the hint and subsided. He had done only one thing right that day in Millwood, and that one thing now constituted his only insurance policy.

So now he had a big decision to make: He could call Special Agent Larry Talbot, lay out what he'd done and what he'd found, take his licks from Talbot's peppery sidekick for intruding, and then get back out of the way. He could even plead with the Roanoke RA to keep his intrusion into the arsenal a secret from Washington. But that wouldn't work: The Bureau would never change. They'd yell at him and break his balls for going in there, while doing nothing about finding Lynn. So there really wasn't any decision to make, was there? What he had to do was to go back there, armed this time with some decent overheads, and find out what the hell was going on in the Ramsey Arsenal that might hopefully lead to Lynn, or at least to what had happened to Lynn.

He looked down at the muddy cap, which was lying on the kitchen table. Face it, he thought with a sigh, those kids may be dead. No, not those kids. *Lynn* might be dead. He couldn't bear to think about that. He himself would certainly have been dead if that big slug had hit him instead of the tree. Those people hadn't come out to talk. The shooter, taking his position up in the tree line, the other one acting as game beater, yelling and crashing forward through the woods to startle Kreiss into motion— that had not been extemporaneous. Those people were hunters and knew what they were doing. If the kids had blundered into people like that, they would have been easy pickings.

He felt the rage coming then, the familiar heat in his face, the sensation that his blood pressure was rising. He tried to contain it by deep breathing, but it came anyway, a wave of fury, the tingling sensation in his large hands, a scarlet rim to his peripheral vision. If he found out that those people had done something to Lynn, he would introduce them to the true meaning of terror, sweeper-style, and then he would slaughter them all, until there was blood to his elbows. He closed his eyes, savoring the rage. But even his fury could not entirely blank out the other possibility, the one he didn't ever want to think about. That it hadn't been locals who had taken Lynn.

To Janet's surprise, Brianne Kellermann called her back from headquarters right after lunch. After some more obligatory waffling about privacy issues, she told Janet that the fundamental issue leading to the breakup of the Kreiss marriage had been what Edwin Kreiss did for a living. According to Brianne's notes, the former Mrs. Kreiss implied that she had found out more than she wanted to know about what Kreiss was doing during his exchange tour with the Agency, and that it had not squared with what Kreiss had been telling her. There were also some indications of domestic turbulence, incidents of uncontrolled rage on his part that stopped just short of physical violence. The bottom line was that Kreiss's wife had become afraid of her husband. Four years after he went to the Agency, she sought the divorce.

"And that's it?" Janet asked.

"That's all I have in my file pertaining to him," Brianne said. "That was your focus, right?"

She had hoped for more, but she did not want Kellermann to detect that. "Yes, it was. Thank you very much. You've been very helpful."

There was a momentary pause on the line. "Have you met Edwin Kreiss?"

Her instincts told her to deflect any further interest in her call. "Yes," she said. "When we interviewed the parents. He seemed—I don't know—pretty normal? A lot of anxiety about his missing daughter, of course, and he wasn't thrilled when we told him the case was going to MP. But killer-diller secret agent? No."

"Secret agent?"

Janet swore under her breath. Damned shrink was quick. "Well, you know, that time he spent with the Agency."

"I see. Not a killer-diller, but not your run-of-the-mill, quietly retired civil servant, either?"

Janet had to think about that one. "No-o, not exactly," she said. "I got the impression that he was immensely self-controlled." She remembered all the things Farnsworth had told her, but she doubted Brianne Kellermann was in the loop on any of that. "I guess I wouldn't want the guy really mad at me, but closet psychopath? No. And he's not a suspect or anything. The kids just vanished. We've been clutching at straws the whole way. That's what pisses me off, I guess."

"Well, I wish I could have told you something significant," Brianne said. "But that's all I have."

Actually, you did, Doc, Janet thought. "Well, like I said, we have to pull all the strings. And thanks again for getting back to me. I can close our files now; let MP take it."

Janet flopped back in her chair after hanging up. Kreiss had a reputation for being a scary guy. Kreiss's wife had been sufficiently afraid of him to want out. Wait—correct that. Sufficiently afraid to want to go to a Bureau counselor. Having been divorced herself, she knew there was probably a lot more to the Kreiss divorce story than just that, but going to a Bureau counselor had to have been a big step for a senior FBI agent's wife to take.

With any luck, Kellermann would now just forget the call and move on. Janet had been entirely truthful when she had said she did not figure Kreiss for a part in the kids' disappearance. What concerned her now was the possibility that he might take up the hunt himself. Possibility, hell—probability, if the headless horseman trick was any indication. And, actually, *concerned* wasn't the right word, either. Face it, she told herself. It's Kreiss and his exotic career that's intriguing you. In fact, if Kreiss was on the move, she wouldn't mind helping him. She laughed out loud at that crazy notion and momentarily woke Billy.

7

A FedEx truck found its way to Kreiss's cabin late Wednesday afternoon. Kreiss signed for the package and took it into the cabin. Parsons had done well. There were two wide-area black-and-white overheads of the Ramsey Arsenal. Each had been taken from an oblique angle, because, of course, the aircraft had no business flying directly over the complex. One of them had been taken from a much greater height than the other, and it showed nearly the entire installation, including the creek that ran through it. The other was a shot that centered on the industrial area, and it gave a perspective to the buildings in the central area that allowed Kreiss to size them. There was one additional sheet in the package, which was a copy of the large overall shot with a global positioning system grid superimposed. The title box on the lower right of each sheet identified the site as the Jonesboro Cement Factory in Canton, Ohio.

Good man, Kreiss thought to himself. Parsons had disguised the identity of the prints from prying eyes at his company. There was a note in the package saying that Parsons had the photos in a computer file and that any of them could be blown up on one of their Sun workstations and reprinted to whatever level of detail he wanted. He had been unable to midnight-requisition the processing work, and he apologetically requested a check for fifteen hundred dollars be made out to the company. Kreiss got his checkbook and wrote the check immediately. Then he studied the photos for almost an hour, absorbing details of the industrial area. The individual buildings were blurry in the photograph, which told Kreiss that Parsons had already done some enlargement work.

The buildings of the industrial area took up no more than a small portion on the eastern side of the military reservation. The photo also showed the rail spur leading off the main line connecting Christiansburg to Ramsey and points north. Kreiss would have loved to get nighttime infrared photos of the entire complex, but that would have been pushing it. Besides, whatever those people were doing, they were probably doing it in the industrial area. The problem was that there appeared to be over one hundred identifiable buildings in the complex. He decided he would make one more reconnaissance intrusion, this time at night, and this time into the industrial area. It looked as if the railroad spur might be a better intrusion position, pointing directly into the industrial area and avoiding all the woods-crawling. It shouldn't be too hard to find his way back to that rail spur. If he could pinpoint where those people were operating, he would back out, come back to the cabin for some of his retrieval equipment, and then go after them. He was looking forward to talking to them, maybe sharing his thinking with them about their itchy trigger fingers.

Just after 6:00 P.M., Jared picked Browne up at his house in Blacksburg. Jared was driving his own pickup instead of his telephone repair van. There was a windowless cap on the back bed of the pickup, where Jared had packed their gear.

"Get the copper?" Browne asked.

"Yep. It's already stashed by the main gates. Coupla hundred pounds."

"We have to strip it?"

"No, it's four switch-gear plates. No insulation. Heavy, though."

On days they were going into the installation, Jared would drive the telephone company van to the concrete-filled barrels on the main entrance road of the arsenal. He would pretend to be doing something there. When there were no cars in sight, he would move two barrels slightly, just enough so that when they came later, he could pull off the main highway in the early darkness and drive straight between the barrels. From there, they would drive, lights off, to the actual main gate, about a quarter of a mile back into the trees from the highway. In front of the shuttered security checkpoint gates, they could turn left onto the fence-maintenance and fire-access road, which was a dirt path just big enough for the truck. They would take that around the fence until they intercepted the rail line almost a mile south of the main gate.

Tonight they would stop up by the gates, well out of sight of Route 11, to retrieve the bundle of copper plates. Browne planned to run the hydrogen generator for at least four hours. He also had some sandwiches and water for the girl.

"I think you better go on walking patrol while I do tonight's batch," Browne said. "We still don't know what we had out there the other night."

"We had us an intruder, that's what. Question is, Did he come back, or did that forty-four do the trick?"

Browne rubbed his jaw. They had seen the occasional hunter, who tended to stay away from the industrial area because of all the talk about toxic waste. But since the kids hit the traps, Browne was taking no chances. "No way of knowing that," he said, "without going down there for some tracking. We just need to be careful from here on out. I won't have some nosy sumbitch screwing this thing up, not now."

Jared didn't say anything for a few minutes, but then he asked Browne if he thought the intruder might be police.

"I don't think so," Browne said. "Cops come in crowds. Plus, they shoot back when shot at. We'd of known by now if that was a cop. Maybe next time, we ought not to go shooting like that."

"Paper said the FBI was lookin' for them kids," Jared said.

"That was almost a month ago; if the FBI thought those kids had come to the arsenal, we'da had a swarm of those sumbitches all over the place. Hasn't been anything like that. We just have to be extra careful for a while. We're getting pressure in the tanker truck now. Won't be much longer, I can do this thing."

Jared passed a clunker out on Route 11. "Killin' those kids, that could be some serious heat," he said.

Browne realized that the incident with the intruder must have spooked Jared a little more than he had anticipated. "We didn't kill anyone. That flash flood got 'em. There wasn't anything we could do about that. And we did save the girl."

"Them was our traps, got them kids," Jared said, slowing as he approached the darkened traffic signal marking the entrance intersection to the arsenal.

"They shouldn't have been in there," Browne said. "The Lord sent that flood. It was their time, that's all."

Jared was silent as he pulled into the turn lane. There was no one coming the other way, so he was able just to make the turn and douse his lights as he went between the barrels. Browne bit his lip, thinking about what Jared had said. The real question now was what was he going to do about the girl when Judgment Day came. She's insurance, he kept telling himself. But if the cops came, and they were holding the girl, she could tie them to what had happened to the other two.

Jared drove up toward the main gate through a corridor of tall pines, then slowed to make the turn onto the fire-access road. "The copper is over there," he said. "Behind that there transformer box."

He stopped the truck, and they both got out. The night was still and clear, but with no moon. The only sound came from the night insects and the ticking noise of the truck's engine cooling down. A big semi went whining down the highway below, but they were completely out of sight. They loaded the heavy copper plates into the bed of the truck, closed the tailgate, and then drove on down the access road until they came to the rail spur gates, where they stopped. Jared began to unload the plates while his grandfather went to move the wire and unlock the interior gates. They hauled the plates through the two sets of gates.

"We've been usin' these here gates for some time now," Jared said when all the plates were inside the perimeter. "Maybe we ought to lay down some things, like we got along the creek."

Browne thought for a moment. That might not be a bad idea. "Traps, you mean?"

"It's all gravel and concrete from here on in. I was thinkin' more along the lines of a counter. One a the guys in the Hats has one, Radio Shack 'lectric-eye deal. Tell us if it's just us chickens walkin' through here."

Jared belonged to a backwoods militia group, which called itself the Black Hats. They got together up on the West Virginia line to drink beer, tell racist jokes, and shoot up the woods, pretending they were guerrillas. Browne thought they were all a bunch of beer-bellied retards. William would never have stooped to that crowd. Jared, on the other hand, probably fit right in, but he kept that sentiment to himself. "I agree," he said. "Bring one next time."

Edwin Kreiss was making his way from building to building along the shadows of the main street of the upper industrial area, when he heard the truck. He had come up the rail spur from the switch point off the main Norfolk & Western line an hour ago. He had not discovered Browne's arrangements with the rail gates; he had simply climbed the fence a hundred feet from the gates, covering up the barbed wire on the top with the rubber floor mat from his truck. He had come in to make a one-night reconnaissance, so he'd brought only water and a chest pack with some implements of his former trade. His plan was to creep the main industrial area to see if he could find any signs of human activity, especially over toward the ravine on the south side that contained the creek. He stopped when he heard the truck.

The engine seemed to slow down. The sound was coming from the direction of the rail spur security gates. Kreiss looked around and found a steel ladder leading up the side of a three-story windowless concrete building that faced the main street. There was enough starlight in the clear mountain air to allow him to read the sign on the building, which said AMMONIA CONCENTRATION PLANT. One of the complex's internal rail subspurs ran directly behind the building, and the ladder went up the side of the building to its roof. He listened again. The engine was quiet, or perhaps idling. Then he heard it start back up, rev for thirty seconds or so, and then shut down. They were parking it. And coming in?

He tested the ladder. It seemed to be firmly mounted. He listened again, but there were only night sounds in the air. He made his decision and hoisted himself up onto the ladder and began to climb. At the top, the ladder rails curved up and over the edge of the roof. He stepped carefully out onto the roof, until he realized that it, too, appeared to be made of concrete. There were three large skylights embedded in the center of the roof, and he went over to one and looked down. The glass was clouded with grime and dust; below, there was only darkness. He thought about using a light, but not if there was the possibility that someone was coming. He felt a slight breeze touch his neck. He went back to the front edge of the roof, where there was a three-foot-high parapet. He knelt down behind the parapet and unzipped his chest pack. He pulled out a stethoscope, a flat cone-shaped object, and a small wire frame. He squeezed the cone open, creating a speaker-shaped object some twelve inches in diameter at the large end and one inch at the small end. He fit the cone into the wire frame and set it up on the parapet, pointing up the main street toward the rail gates, which were some three hundred yards distant. Then he screwed the acoustic diaphragm of the stethoscope into the back of the cone and put the sound plugs into his ears. There was a faint chuffing background noise sound of the night breeze, but otherwise nothing. He waited, keeping his head down behind the parapet in case someone down below was using a nightscope to scan the darkened buildings.

After five minutes or so, he detected the first footsteps, small, regular crunching sounds coming from the direction of the gates. He smiled in satisfaction as he listened. Two sets of steps, walking slowly, close to each other. They stopped, and there was the sound of some heavy objects hitting the ground. He wanted to take a look, but the cone was telling him what he needed to know. The footsteps resumed, coming up the main street, their boots making clopping noises on the concrete, alternating with a clanking cadence when they crossed the big metal plates in the street, until they passed beneath the cone. While he waited for them to pass, he pulled out his own nightscope. He attached its external power cord to a slim battery pack in his chest pack. He gave them another minute and then rose up behind the parapet and swept the street below. He almost missed them as they turned the corner a block away, went between two large buildings, and disappeared. Confirm two, and each of them was carrying something under both arms. One much taller than the other. He swept the street back in the direction of the rail gates, but there seemed to be nothing else stirring. Time to get back down on the ground.

He packed up the listening cone and his nightscope and climbed back down the ladder on the side of the building. Without making any noise, he moved as quickly as he could to the other side of the street and then down to the corner where they had turned. A quick look around the corner revealed a cross street with large- and medium-sized buildings on both sides. At the end of the street, about three blocks away, was what looked like a power plant. The street and the bottom of the buildings were all in shadow. He pulled out the nightscope and made a quick sweep, but no figures showed up. So they had gone into one of these buildings. He reversed course and crept back across the front of the building on the corner, then down the alley along its side wall. He found a steel ladder, but then he hesitated, because the building next to this one on the side street appeared to be taller than the corner building. He scanned the alley and then went farther down. The alley was almost in full darkness, but it was also empty: There were no trash cans or other debris, just the bare concrete and some weeds here and there. A noticeable chemical smell pervaded all the old concrete, and he was struck by the absence of any living thing.

He found the ladder at the back of the second building and climbed it. Where the skylights had been on the first building, there was a row of large metal ventilator caps, whose guy wires made it difficult to move around the roof. The parapet was much lower, so he set himself up at the corner of the roof nearest the power plant, from which he ought to be able to see both ways down the cross street. He rigged out the cone device and pointed it directly across the darkened street at the bare concrete wall of the opposite building. Since he didn't know which direction the men had gone, any sounds they made should reflect off the slab-sided building opposite if they reemerged. Just in case he had missed something, he put on the stethoscope and trained the cone to either side, first down the street and then back up toward the corner. He pointed it at each of the buildings, listening for any acoustic indication of humans inside. He did not expect sounds to penetrate all that windowless concrete, but there was always a chance of a machine making some noise. But there was nothing. He pointed the cone back across the street and waited.

Two men. Just like last time. Now that he knew what he was dealing with, and roughly where they were, this should be entirely manageable.

Browne got Jared to help him set up the retort for the first generating batch. The copper plates were awkward to move, but they would yield a much longer sustained reaction than the wire he had been using. He would have to cut them in half to get them into the retort.

"Once we get this going, I want you to take a look around the industrial area, make sure we don't have any close-in visitors. Got your nightscope?"

"Yep. And a three fifty-seven in my jacket, too."

"If you see something, try to come back here and get me before you use that. I'd rather catch 'em than shoot 'em. See who the hell they are. Two guns are better than one for that."

Browne set up the pump while Jared used a hacksaw to cut the plates. The soft copper cut quickly. Browne went into the boiler hall to start the generator. He came back and cleared all the lines coming from the retort, then went into the maintenance bay to line up the fill valve on the truck's tank. He came back and opened the acid feed line, and the reaction in the retort became audible. They waited for the pressure switch to activate the transfer pump, but it didn't happen. Browne tapped a gauge, then tapped it again. "Have to do something here; this thing isn't working."

"Can you jump it?" Jared asked, eyeing the pressure gauge. The frothing noise in the retort was getting louder. "That safety valve is fixin' to let go."

"I know that," Browne said irritably. Sometimes, he thought, Jared was a master of the obvious. William would have been suggesting solutions. He checked the lineup with the transfer pump once more and then hurried to hook a wire directly from the supply side of the pressure switch to the hot terminal on the pump motor. The pump kicked in and the pressure began to fall off in the retort as the hydrogen was sent to the truck next door.

"Looks like I'm going to have to run this thing manually," Browne said. "Go take the girl her food and water, and then have a look around the immediate area. Check back in an hour."

"All right."

"And Jared? No messing around with that girl. Tell her to put the blindfold on, open the door, check the room, make sure she's not hiding behind the door, leave the food, lock back out."

Jared acknowledged and grabbed up the paper sack. Then the transfer pump began to chatter and Browne swore. "Go on," he said. "Be back in an hour. This plate should be done by then and we can fix this switch."

Jared left the control room, an unfathomable expression on his face. He stood outside the power plant walk-through door for fifteen minutes to get his night vision back, and he thought about the girl. They had brought her here that first afternoon, blindfolded and restrained, and simply left her for several hours. Then they had come back, pausing outside the smaller door at the north end while Browne ordered her to put the blindfold back on. That had been the routine since then, each time they brought her food. She never spoke to them. She would just sit there, motionless, with her back to the door and the blindfold on her face, not even acknowledging their presence. And they, in turn, never spoke to her. Jared knew that she had seen both of them, but only that one time. The fact that she wouldn't speak to them kind of pissed him off. She was shining an attitude he wasn't used to.

He stepped off into the street and headed for the nitro building.

Kreiss was wondering if he should give up his listening position and go search for the two men, when the cone picked up something. He strained to listen, but the sounds were very small, almost beneath the threshold of the night sounds. There must have been some clouds coming through, because the ambient light had diminished, throwing the streets below into total darkness. He reached up and turned the cone to the left. Nothing. He turned it slowly to the right. Nothing, and then a sound. A footfall? No. He could not classify it. He wanted to use the nightscope, but that battery was limited, and he normally did not use it until he had a firm directional cue from the cone. If someone was moving around down at the end of the street, there was no way to tell precisely where in this maze of concrete buildings. Then the sounds stopped. He slewed the cone back and forth, trying to regain contact, but now there was only the small breeze. And then there was the unmistakable loud sound of a metal door closing, somewhere out there among all those buildings.

He took off the earpieces of the stethoscope and sat back on his haunches. That had been a door, which meant they were definitely doing something inside one of the big buildings. Probably a drug lab of some kind. He sniffed the night air, but the breeze was blowing toward that end of the street. He looked into the darkness; the only thing he could make out was the tall stack of the power plant, and that was beyond where he thought the noises had come from. Two men, who knew their way around this complex in the dark, were doing something in one of the buildings. Should he go down and probe that end of the street? And run into some more traps? He had to do something.

And then he had an idea. It had sounded as if they had parked that truck. He would back out and go see about that vehicle. It would have a tag, and a tag would lead to a name, and with a name, he could find an address. That would make things a lot simpler than prowling around this place, where they had had time to rig defenses.

Jared opened the door and shone the light inside. She was right where she was supposed to be. He flashed the light around the room, which was a hundred feet long, seventy wide, and four stories in overall height. There were several cableways and electrical boxes on the walls, and two large steel garage-type doors at either end. Prominent red NO SMOKING signs were painted every ten feet along the walls. A set of rusting rail tracks was embedded in the concrete floor, right down the middle. The lighting fixtures suspended overhead were devoid of bulbs, so the only light she would ever see was the daylight that came through the grimy skylights. There was a single steel walk-through door to one side of the larger sealed doors at each end of the building. Otherwise, it was empty, the machinery and the workers long gone, with only the smell of chemicals lingering in the old concrete to give any indication of its previous function.

He shoved the bag of food inside the door and then stepped inside. He put the Maglite down on the floor, pointing at the silent figure in the middle of the room. He pushed the door shut, then backed up against it.

"Stand up," he ordered. She didn't move.

"You want this water?" he asked, tapping the plastic bottle with his boot. "Or you want me to take it back outside? Stand up."

Slowly, reluctantly, she got on her hands and knees, and then stood up. The blindfold hid most of her face. The flashlight now pointed at her feet. She was taller than he had remembered, but the loose clothes could not disguise her fine figure. There was definite defiance in her posture, and Jared didn't like that. Jared liked his women compliant.

"Turn your back to the door," he ordered.

She complied, and he reached for the light and played it over her body.

"Take your shirt off," he said.

She just stood there. He waited for her to say something, but she remained silent.

"I said, take your goddamned shirt off."

She did not move. Jared reached down and picked up one of the three water bottles. He twisted the top off with an audible snapping sound, then poured the entire bottle out onto the concrete. It made an unmistakable sound, and he thought he saw her stiffen when he did it.

"Take your shirt off," he said again, discarding the now-empty bottle onto the concrete floor, where it clattered into a corner.

This time, she did it, pulling the shirt over her head and dropping it onto the floor.

"Now your halter," he said. "Do it."

She paused for a few seconds, then slipped out of her sports bra. He played the flashlight over her back and ordered her to turn around. She slumped a little and then complied. Her breasts were everything he expected, although her ribs were showing in the harsh white light. Must be the diet here, he thought with a mental guffaw.

"Now the rest of it."

She hesitated again, turning a little bit, as if to shield herself. He picked up another water bottle and shook it. "The rest of it. Do it! Now!"

She complied, bending forward to take off the rest of her clothes. Then she straightened up and took a deep breath. Her hands hung down at her sides.

"Turn sideways," Jared commanded, playing the flashlight over her white body. She did as he ordered, and then he told her to get down on her hands and knees. She bent her head to one side for a moment, as if trying to figure out what he was going to do. But then she got down on her hands and knees, her body in profile to him.

Jared walked over to the pile of blankets and then walked all the way around her, enjoying his rising excitement. Damn, she has a great body, he thought. She must work out.

"Put your head down," he said, still walking around her. She sighed, the first sound she'd made. Then she put her head down on the blankets.

Jared continued to walk around her, circling her like a predator, reveling in her utterly vulnerable position. He was just about to approach her when he thought he heard something out on the street. He immediately switched off the flashlight.

"Not bad, girlie," he said softly. "Not bad a-tall. Next time, we'll do something about all that."

He went to the door, listened carefully, and then stepped back through, pulling it shut softly but firmly. He replaced the padlock and closed the bail into the base of the lock as quietly as he could. He turned around and moved sideways to the corner of the building, waiting for his eyes to adjust to darkness again. As his ears strained to detect any noises out on the street, his mind's eye replayed the scene inside, the great-looking girl with her rump in the air, totally helpless, asking for it, he was sure. Not so defiant, was she, not once she was down there on the blankets. His throat thickened. He'd definitely come back, get him some of that. He listened some more, but there was nothing going on, no one here but him and that crazy old man in there, brewing up his bomb.

8

On Thursday morning, Janet Carter arrived a half an hour late because of a monster traffic jam. She was surprised to find Billy waiting for her at the security desk when she entered the federal building.

"Thought I ought to warn you," he announced as they badged in and bypassed the metal-detector station. "There are some people upstairs in Farnsworth's office, want to talk to you."

" 'Some people'?"

"Yeah. One guy's from the FCI Division at Bureau headquarters; the other one, a woman, is from Main Justice, I think. Looks like a pro wrestler in drag. Larry Talbot is acting like he's about to get fired. He thinks it's about that missing college students case."

Janet frowned. She'd dropped the Kreiss case after talking to the shrink. She's been busy for the past two days reviewing the evidentiary report on a complicated truck hijacking case that was going to be heavily dependent on physical evidence. It had been almost refreshing to work in her specialty again.

"Hasn't that whole deal gone up the line to MP?" she asked as they got on the elevator.

"Yep. Sent it up Tuesday to Richmond. I thought you were off that thing."

"I am. I haven't touched it since—"

"Since?" Billy asked quietly.

"Well, I'd already made one call, Friday, before the boss fanged me about it. Lady called back Monday, but it wasn't anything conclusive. Some history about one of the parents."

"Edwin Kreiss perhaps?"

"Well . . ." she said, making a face. She pushed the button for the fourth floor and then swiped her security card. She remembered that she'd briefed Billy on the case.

"Well, wait till you get a load of the political appointee gorgon from Justice," Billy said, suppressing a yawn. "Serious shit."

They went directly to their office, where they found Larry Talbot pacing around like a nervous cat. His eyes lit up when he caught sight of Janet. "We need to talk," he announced without preamble.

"What's going on?" she asked. "Billy said there're some people from Washington? To see *me*?"

"Yes, indeedy," Talbot said, taking her elbow and pulling her to one side of the office. He lowered his voice to a harsh whisper. "I think it's something about that Kreiss character. Is there something you need to back-brief me on?"

She explained about the call to the staff psychologist, keeping the exact timing of the calls a little vague. "But that was it, and Billy's already sent the case file to Washington via the Richmond field office. I've been on the Wentworth Trucking case since then. What's the big deal?"

Talbot looked around for Billy, but he had left the office. "Whatever it is, the boss had to leave his conference early and come back here to deal with it."

Janet blinked. "Not to be repetitious, Larry, but what's the problem? I tied off a loose end with a case that's been sent to MP. End of story."

Talbot shook his head. "Farnsworth is pissed. He's acting like you went up to D.C. and burgled the director's office." He looked at his watch. "Shit. You need to get downstairs."

"Jesus, Larry, can't I at least get some coffee?"

"I wouldn't advise it, Janet," he said. "This is no time to look routine."

Janet rolled her eyes and went back down to Farnsworth's office, which was on the third floor. His secretary, a professionally unpleasant woman who hailed from Arkansas, announced that the RA was in conference with some Washington people. Janet patiently asked her to tell Farnsworth that she was there. The secretary sighed dramatically and buzzed this news into Farnsworth. He appeared at the door to his office a moment later and asked Janet to come in.

The two Washington visitors were sitting at the conference table. One was a large woman, whose fat face reminded Janet of a recent Russian premier. She was looking at Janet with undisguised suspicion. The other visitor was a man in his fifties, also rather large, almost completely bald, with a reddish face and a permanently scowling expression. Farnsworth made introductions. The woman's name was Bellhouser; the red-faced man's name was Foster.

"Agent Carter, these folks have driven down from Washington. Ms. Bellhouser is the executive assistant to Mr. Bill Garrette, who, as I'm sure you know, is the deputy attorney general of the United States. Mr. Foster is the principal deputy to Assistant Director Marchand."

Janet noted Farnsworth's sudden formality. She knew that Marchand was the assistant director over Counterintelligence at FBI headquarters. She had heard of Garrette, but only in the context of his being acting deputy attorney general without benefit of Senate confirmation for the past four years. She nodded, waiting for Farnsworth to invite her to sit down. Surprisingly, he did not.

"Agent Carter," he said. "You apparently made recent inquiries about a certain Edwin Kreiss. Ms. Bellhouser and Mr. Foster are interested in why you're interested."

Janet took it upon herself to sit down in the only remaining chair. Farnsworth was acting as if he had never heard of Edwin Kreiss, so she decided to play along and speak directly to him, as if bringing him into the picture for the first time. She reviewed the circumstances of her involvement with Kreiss. She glossed over the call to the Counseling Division as tying off a loose end before sending up the case file.

"Let's dispense with the bullshit, Agent Carter," the woman said when Janet was done. Her voice was as harsh as her expression. "You persisted in asking questions about Kreiss after you were given specific instructions by the RA here to back off that case. We want to know why."

Janet looked at Farnsworth as if to say, I thought I just explained that. The RA kept his expression blank. She turned to Bellhouser. "I wasn't aware that I was indulging in bullshit," she said coolly. "I asked the original question before I was told to drop it. When Dr. Kellermann was courteous enough to call right back, I took her call. What she had to say didn't add anything substantial. It is entirely standard procedure to question parents in some detail when their kids go missing. It's also standard procedure to check them out. What's the problem here, if I may ask?"

"The problem is Edwin Kreiss," the woman answered. "Mr. Kreiss was responsible for an incident that deeply embarrassed both the Department of Justice and the Bureau. Inquiries about him or what he did are not authorized, and, in fact, are cause for alarm."

"Well excuse me all to hell," Janet said, trying not to lose her temper. "I was investigating the disappearance of his daughter. He is just another citizen as far as I'm concerned, a parent who's lost his kid. One more time: What's the problem?"

The woman sat back in her chair, her expression saying that she wasn't used to being spoken to like this. Foster intervened.

"Part of the problem is that we did not know Edwin Kreiss's daughter had gone missing," he said. "But—"

Bellhouser held up her hand in an imperious gesture, and Foster stopped. She gave Janet a speculative look. "Perhaps I should clarify a few things for you, Agent Carter. But I want your word that what I'm going to tell you will not be repeated to anyone." She had changed her tone of voice and was now being a lot more polite.

"Is this something I need to know, then?" Janet asked. "Because I'm willing to forget Mr. Kreiss, if that's the order of the day. My interest in him was entirely professional, not personal."

Bellhouser thought for a moment. Foster was strangely silent. "I think it is," she said. "Do I have your word?"

Janet looked again to the RA, but his face remained a study in neutrality. He'd told her all about Kreiss, but now he was acting as if he'd never heard of the guy. She wasn't quite sure what the game was here but if they wanted to play games, well, hell, she'd play. "Whatever," she said. "Yes. Fine."

"Very well. For many years prior to the current administration, there was tension between the Counterespionage Division at the Agency and the Foreign Counterintelligence Division in the Bureau. This administration determined that it would be constructive to break down some of those bureaucratic barriers. Edwin Kreiss was selected to be sent on an exchange tour of duty with the Agency, and one of their CE operatives was sent to Bureau FCI."

She paused to see if any of this meant anything to Janet, but Janet pretended this was all news.

"Kreiss's assignment to the Agency represented a dramatic step toward defusing those tensions. He trained under and worked with some of the best man-hunters in the business. It's fair to say that he participated in some operations that took place, shall we say, out on the less well-defined margins of national policy, with respect to who works where. Do you know what I'm talking about?"

"I assume you're talking about the rule that the Agency technically can't work inside the country."

"Yes, precisely, just like the armed forces can't chase criminals inside the borders of the United States. *Posse comitatus.* The problem is that sometimes the bad guys take advantage of this."

"And sometimes the good guys turn out to be the bad guys," Janet said, just to throw some shit in the game.

Bellhouser blinked, looked at Foster, and then they both looked over at Farnsworth.

"Um, yes, well, when I received orders to back out of the Kreiss matter, I told her about the Glower case," he said, looking uncharacteristically nervous. "Correction: I told her what I'd *heard* about the Glower case—I, of course, have no personal knowledge of what happened there."

Foster's eyebrows went up. "Really, Mr. Farnsworth. This is a surprise. Assistant Director Marchand was of the opinion that you knew *nothing* about the Glower incident."

Foster might be a principal deputy, but Farnsworth was still in charge of an operational office, and as such, he didn't have to take very much static from headquarters assistants, especially when they invoked their boss's power. He looked at Foster with an avuncular smile. "When something gets fucked up as badly as that situation got fucked up," he said, "*everybody* knows a little something about it, Mr. Foster. You need to remember that if you ever go back to the field." Janet felt a smidgen of relief that Farnsworth hadn't been entirely cowed by these two.

"Let's get back on point," Bellhouser said. "Which is: When Kreiss was forced out of the Bureau following the Millwood incident, he was given some very specific guidance in return for getting retirement instead of outright dismissal. And that was that he was never, *ever* to act operationally again, especially in those capacities with which he was formerly associated during his time at the Agency."

"So how was he supposed to make a living, then?" Janet asked.

"According to Larry Talbot's notes," Farnsworth said, scanning a piece of paper, "he's been teaching remedial math at the Montgomery County junior college. He quit that when his daughter went missing."

"The point is, Agent Carter," Bellhouser said, "that Kreiss was not permitted to engage in *any* activity related to law enforcement: federal, state, or local, or to have anything to do with the security field—commercial, personal, computer—anything along that line."

Janet nodded. "Okay, and—"

Foster leaned forward. "The question is, Agent Carter, Do you think Mr. Kreiss is going to actively search for his daughter now that Roanoke here is sending the case to MP?"

Janet remembered telling Farnsworth that she thought Kreiss was going solo. She had to assume he had passed this on. "Yes," she said. "In fact, I think he's already leaned on one of the potential witnesses, but I backed out before I could really follow up on that. And, of course, I can't prove any of that."

Bellhouser sighed. Foster frowned and began tapping a pen against the edge of the table.

"I mean," Janet said, "I guess I can understand it. From his perspective, the Bureau was backing out. He knows how MP works." No one said anything. "It's his daughter, after all," she concluded.

Bellhouser gave her a patient look and then got up out of her chair. She was even bigger standing up. The chair creaked in relief. "Thank you, Agent Carter," she said. "I think you've told us what we needed to find out. We will brief our respective superiors. We appreciate your cooperation."

Janet stood up, looking at Farnsworth. "Is that it, sir?"

Farnsworth glanced over at Bellhouser and Foster as if for confirmation and then said, "Yes."

"And if anything else pops up concerning Mr. Kreiss?"

"Inform Mr. Farnsworth here if that happens," Foster said. "We will attend to Mr. Kreiss if that becomes necessary. But we don't anticipate you will have any further interaction with him."

"Either at his initiative or yours, Agent Carter," Bellhouser said. All three of them looked at her expectantly to make sure she understood the warning.

"Okay," she said brightly, as if this all were totally insignificant. She left Farnsworth's office, shaking her head, and went back to her own cubicle. Talbot wanted to know what it was all about, but Janet told him only that it concerned Edwin Kreiss and that the matter had been taken care of. Talbot was clearly dissatisfied, so she said she'd been ordered not to talk about it and that maybe Farnsworth would fill him in. Talbot stomped out and Janet went looking for some coffee. She met with some other agents on the trucking case for half an hour, and when she returned, Billy had surfaced from his midmorning snooze. He asked her what all the fuss was about. Remembering her promise, she told him in only very general terms, concluding that she'd been clearly told to stay away from Edwin Kreiss and all his works. Billy got some coffee and they talked about the way headquarters horse-holders threw their weight around.

When Talbot reappeared, Janet went back to her cubicle. She pushed papers around her desk while she thought about the meeting with the two principal deputy assistant under executive pooh-bahs. What had that woman said—they would "attend to" Kreiss? For God's sake, the man's only child was missing. An image of Kreiss's face surfaced in her mind. She wondered if the two horse-holders were capable of "attending to" Edwin Kreiss. She thought idly about warning him.

Edwin Kreiss had obtained a county road map at the Christiansburg Chamber of Commerce that morning, and he was now nosing his pickup truck down a dirt road five miles west of the town. None of the land around these first geologic wrinkles of the Appalachian foothills was horizontal, and he had to keep it in second gear on the rough and winding lane. He had found their truck unlocked last night at the rail spur branch and retrieved the registration. The vehicle belonged to one Jared McGarand, whose rural postbox address he'd finally found on a rusting mailbox at the head of the dirt road. He came around a final bend in the trees and saw a double-wide trailer at the end of the lane. There were no other trailers or houses nearby, but there were some large dogs raising hell from what looked like a pen behind the trailer. He had anticipated the possibility of dogs and had the cure in a plastic bag on the seat. But first, he would see if the dogs' noise summoned anyone. It was the middle of the day, and the only other trailer he'd seen had been almost a mile back down the county road. It had looked deserted.

He turned around and then parked his truck in front of the trailer, pointed back out the lane. Then he waited. The dogs, still not visible, continued to bark and howl, but after five minutes, they lost interest. The trailer was mounted up on cinder blocks at one end to level it. The place looked reasonably well kept, with some side sheds, a separate metal car-port roof, an engine-hoisting stand, and what looked like a rig for butchering deer. The same pickup truck from which he'd obtained the registration was parked under a tree, but there were no junked cars or other hillbilly treasures stacked in the yard, and there was electric power and a phone line attached to the trailer. Whoever Jared McGarand was, he obviously had a job and was not just another member of the Appalachian recycling elite.

Satisfied that no one was coming, he opened the door, grabbed the plastic bag, and went up to the front door of the trailer and knocked on it. This set off another round of barking from out back. When no one answered, he went around to the back door and tried that, again without result. Then he walked over to the dog pen, which was fifty feet back from the trailer, under some trees. He took out some sugar-coated doughnut holes, into each of which he had put two nonprescription iron-supple-ment pills. The dogs were some kind of mixed breed, with pit bull pre-dominant, equal parts teeth, bark, and general fury. They were jumping and slavering at the sturdy chain-link fence. He pushed the doughnut holes into the chain link until he was sure each dog had eaten at least one. Then he went back to the truck and waited. The pills would not kill the dogs, but in about fifteen minutes, they would be feeling ill enough to lie down and whimper for the rest of the day. While he was waiting, his car phone rang. Ever since Lynn disappeared he had made a practice of hav-ing any calls that came into the cabin automatically forward to the truck if he was out of the house.

"Kreiss," he said, visually checking the trailer and its surroundings. The dogs had stopped their barking.

"Mr. Kreiss, this is Special Agent Janet Carter."

"You have something on Lynn?" Kreiss asked immediately.

"No. I wish we did, but no. This is something else." She described the visitation of Bellhouser and Foster.

He listened without comment, wishing he had been able to observe that little séance. Attend to me, would they? He took a deep breath to calm himself.

"Mr. Kreiss? Are you still there?"

"Yes," he said. "I'm on my car phone. I appreciate the heads up, Agent Carter. I really do."

"You didn't get it from me, Mr. Kreiss."

"Absolutely." He paused for a moment, not sure of what to say next. He was picturing her face, and, after their last meeting, wondering why she was doing this.

"Mr. Kreiss?" she said. "We asked you not to go solo on your daughter's disappearance, remember?"

"I remember."

"Well, let me reiterate that request. And of course, if new information does turn up, let me say again that you need to bring it to us."

How would two guys skulking around at night on a closed federal ammunition plant, setting mantraps and shooting at people, strike you? he wondered. "Of course, Agent Carter."

"Yes. Of course, Mr. Kreiss."

"Thanks again for the heads up. I owe you one, Agent Carter."

"Hold that thought, Mr. Kreiss."

He grunted, clicked the phone off, and got back out of the truck. He positioned a small motion detector on the hood of the pickup, pointed down the lane in the direction of the county road. It would start beeping if anything came down the dirt road toward the cabin. He took a canvas tool bag out of the passenger side and went behind the trailer. The dogs were circled on the concrete floor of their pen. One was drinking lots of water, while the other two were nipping at their flanks.

Fifteen minutes later, he was driving back out onto the county road. On the front seat beside him, he had some personal documents he'd lifted from a desk inside, enough to confirm that the occupant was Jared McGarand, a telephone company repairman. He also had taken a .357 Magnum he'd removed from the bedroom bureau's top drawer. He had found a .45 auto in Jared's night table but left that alone. The man liked big guns. He'd refilled the dogs' water buckets before he left; they were going to be very thirsty later on. He had mounted a cigarette carton–sized battery-operated box on the roof of the trailer, out of sight behind two vent pipes, and installed a listen-and-record device on the lone telephone. He turned onto the county road and headed back toward Blacksburg.

He had been tempted to tell Carter about the Ramsey Arsenal, except that he thought he could do a better job of finding Lynn than some posse of semihysterical feds, at least until he knew what the connection was between these two midnight gomers and Lynn's hat. He would have to find a way to pay Carter back for the favor of that warning; she absolutely did not have to do that, especially after having to take a meeting with Bambi Bellhouser and Chief Red in the Face. She'd probably called him because they pissed her off. He almost hoped they would be stupid enough to come out to his cabin, although he doubted a couple of horse-holders like that would ever venture too far away from an office. In the meantime, he had some preparations to make before returning to the arsenal tonight. He wanted to get into the industrial area just at twilight, because those two had shown up the last time about an hour after sun-down. This time, he wanted to be closer to that far end of the main street. Maybe he would be able to track them into a specific building.

That evening, Browne and Jared were delayed by a traffic accident on the Route 11 bridge over the New River. It was almost eight o'clock before they got to the entrance of the arsenal. Jared was in a bad mood, having found his three hunting dogs sick in their pen when he got home from work.

"Dog crap all over the place," he complained. "Had to hose it for half an hour. Dogs sick as babies."

"All three? Must have been bad feed."

"They got the same as always. They still ain't right." He drove through the concrete barrels and down the fire road with his lights off. There was a sliver of new moon up, which gave enough light to see the road and the high fence.

"You get that counter put up?"

"Yep. It's just inside the inner gates, waist-high." He pulled the truck into their regular parking place, between four bushy pines. "With them side fences, won't be no critters settin' it off. I got a line on some more copper, but it's gonna take some cash money."

"All right. We've got nearly thirty pounds of pressure in the truck tank now. I'll be shifting over to the big pump at fifty psi."

They got out and stood at the edge of the trees to night-adapt their eyes. There was a slight breeze blowing pine scent at them, and the rail-road tracks gleamed dully in the dim moonlight.

"I did one other thing 'sides that counter," Jared said. His grandfather looked at him. "I set me up a deadfall along the main street—wire trigger. Left the wire down for now. We get somethin' on that counter, I'll set the wire when we come out."

"We get a hit on that counter before we even go in, we're not going in," Browne said. "I may come back tomorrow during the day and do some hunting. Can you get some time off? Bring your dogs?"

"I can if there ain't a lot of tickets up on the western lines. Don't know about them dogs."

"All right," Browne said, picking up the bag of food and water for the girl. "Let's go check your toy."

They walked up the spur to the security gates, stopping a hundred feet out to watch and listen. Then they stepped through the flap of fencing and Jared walked over to the side fence and squatted down next to a high weed. He straightened back up and came back to where Browne was standing. "We've got us a visitor," he whispered. "Counter's showin' one."

"And that wasn't you leaving, after you set it?"

"Nope."

"Damn," Browne said, keeping his voice low. He had been hoping that the intruder the other night had been a onetime thing. "How far up is your wire?"

"Between the ammonia plant and the shell-casin' dip station. There's two hydrants, face each other across the main street. Got some pipe stock racked up on the overhead steam pipe crossovers between them two buildings. He hits that wire, it'll avalanche his ass."

Browne pulled out his gun. "You go up there, set your wire. I'll follow, fifty feet behind you. Then we'll back out, reset that counter to zero."

"What about the stuff for the girl?"

"Not tonight. Not if there's a chance there's someone in there. Let's see what your trap does first. We have to find out who this is, why he's here. We're too close for any mistakes now."

Kreiss was on the roof of the last building on the right side of the main street, listening to his cone. He was much closer to the power plant this time. The main street came over a low hill and turned slightly to its right as it approached the power plant, so he did not have a perfectly straight acoustic shot all the way to the rail gates at the other end. But if anyone came walking up over that hill, like they did the last time, he would be in position to hear their footfalls and then this time see into which building they went. There was enough moonlight tonight that he could use high-magnification binoculars rather than a night-vision device. He had put the stethoscope up to his ears when he first heard the truck approach the rail gates over the hill.

He'd been tempted to look around the complex of buildings when he first came in, right at sunset, but decided he would be better off getting set up in a good vantage point. Besides, there were nearly a hundred buildings, large and small, plus several wooden sheds that seemed to have been deliberately built down in circular earthen depressions. A methodical search would take hours, if not days. He was dressed out in a black one-piece overall, with the mesh head hood, gloves, and both packs. His plan was simple: watch to see where they went, creep that building to see how many entrances there were, close all but one, and then get the jump on them. The few buildings he had examined seemed to have only one human-sized door, but he had not had time to really look this place over. Besides, it didn't much matter: These guys had shot at him, which meant they were doing something in here that they should not be doing. If Lynn had worn that hat into the arsenal, these were the guys who would know something about what had happened to her. He settled back down behind the roof parapet to wait some more. They should be coming pretty soon, he thought.

Browne waited for Jared to pull the fence wire flap closed and to set the clips. "All right," he whispered when Jared joined him. "If there is someone up there, he heard the truck. We have to make the truck sound like it's leaving. You drive it out to the edge of the main gate plaza, then walk back in. I'm going to wait here and listen."

"This could take all goddamn night," Jared said. "Let's go back in there and find his ass."

"How? And where would you look? He could be anywhere. He could be wandering around, or he could be inside a building, waiting. No—we pretend to leave, he'll move."

"What if he goes into the power plant? Or knocks on that door at the nitro building?"

"Why would he knock on a locked door? All those buildings are shut tight, including the power plant. There's nothing to see, especially at night. He'll wait for a while, and then he'll walk out. We were going to be out here until almost eleven anyway. This way, we have a chance of nailing him. We can't let this go on, boy. Not now."

Jared grunted in the darkness. "Awright. I'll move the truck. Where'll you be?"

"That pine tree over there. That deadfall going to make some noise?"

"Oh yeah."

"You hear it, come running, 'cause I'm going back in if he trips it."

"We take him, what then?"

"He goes into the acid tank where those boys went. Get going."

Kreiss waited for two more hours before giving it up. He'd heard the truck leave and that had bothered him. The last time, they'd shut the truck down and then come right into the complex. Tonight, they'd come, spent about half an hour doing something, and then left. The worst possibility was that they had driven the truck away and then walked back and were waiting for him to move. That would mean they knew someone was here. The best possibility was that they had left and he now had the place to himself. But why the hell would they do that? They were doing something in one of these buildings. Why come and then just leave? Had he left some sign of his intrusion? It was almost eleven o'clock. He was tempted just to curl up and go to sleep up on the roof. Put the motion detector on the parapet to catch anything coming down the street and set it to buzz rather than beep. Then search the place at dawn. But suppose they waited, too? Or came in, set up, and waited? He'd walk right into them at first light. Going in circles here, he thought. He decided to get off the building and look around.

There were four large buildings at this lower end of the main street, which ended at the big power plant. He went down the ladder and set up the motion-detector box to point back up the street. He set the alarm to chirp like a cricket if it detected anything moving toward it. It wasn't much protection, but better than nothing. Then he spent half an hour circling each of the large buildings, creeping from shadow to shadow in the faint moonlight. The buildings were connected by what looked like steam and other utility lines that ran in bundled pipelines over the street. The musty smell of old chemicals was everywhere. The only identification on the buildings was a number, under which was a name printed onto a white block of paint near the entrance. The four buildings were called Ammonia Concentration, Nitro Fixing, Mercury Mix, and Case Heating. Each of them had large steel industrial cargo doors on the front, with a human-sized walk-through door to one side. None of them had any windows, and three of the four had a rail spur leading under the cargo door. He silently examined all the walk-through doors, but they were locked with massive padlocks. He didn't even bother rattling them.

Then he walked down to the power plant, keeping to the side, not wanting to make noise on those big metal plates out in the street. The power plant's doors were also locked. He was once again struck by the fact that there appeared to be nothing living in the industrial area: He had heard no rats, mice, birds, or insects, and seen little vegetation growing up through the cracks of the concrete. He concluded that not all of the nitro, ammonia, and mercury had remained in the buildings. There were parallel streets on either side of the main street, with more concrete buildings and pipe mazes running overhead. This was hopeless: Unless he could follow those people to a specific building, he could be here for weeks. He had located and identified one of the men, Jared McGarand; maybe he would be better off taking him down at his trailer and finding out what he knew.

He gathered up his motion detector and started back up the street toward the rail gates. It was now 12:30, and the moon was setting. When his foot hit the taut wire, his instincts propelled him forward and down, since whatever was coming was probably coming from the sides. To his surprise, there was a roar of metal from above him, and then he was pounded flat by an avalanche of steel pipes. One of them connected with the back of his head and he blacked out.

Jared dropped his grandfather off at his house in Blacksburg just after midnight and then headed home to his trailer. They'd waited until almost 11:30 before giving up, but nothing had happened up in the industrial area. He still thought his grandfather had been wrong about waiting outside. They should have gone in and rousted that sumbitch, whoever he was. Even if the guy tripped the wire, he could still get away if the pipe deadfall didn't put him down hard enough. But he had learned the hard way not to cross the old man, and especially not now.

He'd seen Browne McGarand focused before, but never like this. This whole bomb thing was all about William, of course. The old man was positively obsessed with William. That was how Jared thought about his father—William, not Father. Unlike the old man, Jared did not give two shits about William or what had happened to him. His mother, a swelling bride at seventeen, had decamped when Jared was only six, driven to desperation by the responsibilities of a motherhood aggravated by the fact that his younger brother, Kenny, has been born retarded. Not quite three years later, William pulled the plug as well, running off to California initially, and then eventually to beautiful downtown Waco, Texas, where he got himself mixed up with all those nutcases at Mount Carmel.

He slowed to make the turn into his trailer lot. If only William had just stayed home and done the right thing, none of this shit would be happening. But old Grandpaw Browne, he was a scorekeeper. He had raised both kids with a firm, often biblical hand, and to this day, Jared was still a little afraid of his grandfather, especially when he got some of that Methodist fire up his ass. His grandfather's eyes reminded him of pictures he had seen in history books of Stonewall Jackson or that abolitionist, John Brown. That old man, he wanted to make him a bomb, Brother Jared was not *even* going to get in the way. Even if it was about Saint William.

He sniffed as he turned down his own road. He thought he deserved at least some appreciation for helping the old man. He wasn't sure what old Browne would have done to those kids in the traps if that flash flood hadn't come along, but Jared knew he owned at least a piece of their deaths. Not that he cared too much—like the old man said, they shouldn't have come sneaking around like that. But he was now on the hook as at least an accessory, and had the old man even thanked him? He had not.

He pulled his truck into the yard and shut it down. There was other shit, too. He had stolen that propane truck for him. And hadn't he paid at least lip service to all that Christian Identity bullshit? Now there was another bunch of nut brains, always praying that the world would end when the year 2001 rolled around. Armageddon on demand, yahoo. He and the boys up in the Black Hats always had a great laugh when all those Doomsday Christians and their woolly-headed blood-and-fire predictions came up. Hell, he knew this wasn't about Armageddon or the second coming, or the so-called saints versus the sinners. What Browne was fixing up was pure mountain-style revenge, aggravated by his feelings about an oppressive government, out-of-control taxes, even more out-of-control federal lawmen, and the UN with its secret new world order. He'd told the boys his grandpaw was making a hydrogen bomb, and they'd laughed at that, too. Well, they'd see. The federal government had snuffed Saint William, and now Browne McGarand had gone and set his face against the whole damned government. The government was dead meat walking.

He got out and locked the truck. What he had to figure out was how to get back in there and get a piece of that pretty naked thing in the nitro building. He knew how to make her behave now, so maybe he'd sweet-talk her this time, talk some sense into her, then give her the ride to glory. He adjusted his considerable sexual equipment, smiled, and then went to check on the dogs. He refilled their water. They were lethargic, but there was no more kennel mess. He had a beer while he checked through the day's mail, and then he went to bed.

9

At just after 2:00 A.M., Jared snapped awake and sat up in bed. He tried to figure out what sound had awakened him. The windows were open, and the night was filled with the normal woods noise of insects and a chirping chorus of tree frogs. He rubbed his face and listened carefully. Maybe he'd been dreaming. Then it came again: the distinct sound of a dry branch breaking, and not far away, either. One of the dogs woofed softly, but they raised no general alarm. Was someone out there in the trees back of the trailer? He swung his feet over the edge of the bed and listened again. A few minutes later, it came again, the distinct crunching sound of someone stepping through the forest undergrowth, then the snap of another dry branch. He got up and went to the edge of the back window. His backyard was bathed in the orange glow from a security light mounted on his power pole. The light illuminated the yard, but it had the perverse effect of making the woods even darker. Keeping an eye out the window, he reached into the drawer of the night table and pulled out his government-model .45 auto. He stepped back from the window, racked in a round, and then crossed to its other side. He could see almost nothing out in the darkness.

He depended on the dogs to alert him to intruders, and they normally did a noisy job of it. But now there was silence in the woods. He went through the trailer, checking the other rooms and the locks and all the windows. There were no signs of intrusion. Then he went back to bed, leaving the .45 out on the bedside table. He was just about asleep, when he distinctly heard the muffled sound of a portable-radio transmission outside, followed by a distinct squelch of static. He sat back up and listened, wondering again if he had been dreaming. Then he got up and went through the whole trailer again, gun in hand, checking to see if he'd left the television or the radio on this time. It was just past 3:00 A.M., and this was pissing him off. Then he had a cold thought: A radio—were there cops creeping around out there?

He spent the next half hour going from window to window, looking for any signs of movement in the woods. He could not figure out why the dogs weren't raising hell. There was no wind, so maybe they heard the noises but caught no scent? Then he wondered if there was any connection between their being sick earlier and the possible intruders outside.

He kept watch for another half hour, and finally went back to bed, this time falling heavily asleep. He would have to tell the old man about this shit in the morning. Except there was always the chance he'd dreamed the whole thing.

Kreiss came to and tried to lift his head but could not. He was pinned facedown to the cold concrete, lying now beneath several objects. The moon was down and he couldn't see what had him. His right arm was caught, but his left could move. The back of his head hurt like hell, and there was a wet sensation on the back of his neck. He felt around and closed his fingers over a cold steel pipe, about an inch and a half in diameter. He felt around some more and realized he was under a pile of pipes. He tried to move his legs and found they were both free. After a minute or so of struggling, he was out from under the pile.

He rolled over on his back, fingered the trip wire at his feet, and looked up at the nest of steam lines looping over the main street between the buildings. Someone had gone to a lot of trouble, climbing up the steel rungs on the pipe crossover structure and piling a couple dozen lengths of steel pipe up there, rigged to the trip wire. The top padding in his head hood and the Kevlar shoulder pads along the top of the jumpsuit had saved him from serious injury. The Kevlar ribs that ran down the jumpsuit on his chest and back had also taken some of the shock, aided by the soft bulk of the chest pack and backpack. Otherwise, a couple of hundred pounds of steel pipe falling from twenty feet might have killed him. He stretched out on the concrete, took some deep breaths, and felt for bruises.

So they'd known he was in there. He'd walked down that street coming in and had not hit any wire. Plus, they'd gone to some trouble to rig that deadfall, which meant they'd *expected* him to come back. Not good. He looked at his watch; it was 3:30, Friday morning. The night was perfectly still, with not even the slightest breeze. He had some satisfaction in knowing that the little black box on top of brother Jared's trailer was going to make him lose some sleep tonight, too, unless he was dead drunk in that trailer.

So, how had they known? He had used the same ingress point twice, the answer must be there. He got up gingerly, brushed himself off, and explored the swelling cut on the back of his head. He got out a military battle dressing and taped it over the cut. Then he walked painfully down to the rail gates, where he quickly found the electric-eye counter. The counter went to 001 when he passed his hand through the beam. He hit the reset button to zero it, then recorded twenty-six hits. Let them think about that. He went over the gates, walked the three miles down the rail line to his truck, got in, and sat there for a minute in the pitch-black. He was no closer to finding Lynn, and he was still in the dark as to what these people were doing in the arsenal. If he went to the Roanoke feds, he would confirm the sharks from Washington's worst suspicions.

McGarand and his helper had been sure enough about an intruder to set up a deadfall. Hell with it, he thought, as he started up the truck. My objective is to find out what happened to Lynn. I can deal with the likes of Bellhouser and Foster if I have to. They're just admin pukes with fancy titles and privileged access. There was no more point to creeping the arsenal, where those two guys would always have the home-ground advantage. He decided to just go have a little talk with Mr. Jared McGarand. With a little luck, Jared would maybe give him the other one. Hell, Jared will absolutely give me the other one, he thought. And between the two of them, I'll get a line on Lynn. After that, well, with all the unknowns in the equation right now, there was no sense in making long-range plans.

He drove back toward his cabin west of Blacksburg, which would take almost forty-five minutes. He stopped in an all-night gas and convenience store out on Highway 460 to get some coffee. The clerk gave him a sideways look, and he realized he must look more battered than he knew. While he was refueling the truck, it occurred to him that perhaps the two Washington people had brought along some operational help. Who might be waiting at the cabin for him to return. He finished fueling, paid for his gas and coffee, and then pulled over to one side of the parking lot. He extracted a local county map from the glove compartment and examined the roads surrounding Pearl's Mountain. He knew that there was one paved county road that ran along the stream at the bottom front of his property, and another one that ran along the back slope of Pearl's Mountain. As he remembered, the two firebreaks that bracketed the big hill on either side ran all the way to that back paved road. The map confirmed this. If he could get his truck onto one of the firebreaks, and it wasn't too rough, he could drive partway up the slope and then hike up and over, ending up in a position above his cabin, where he had some toys stashed. He checked his watch. It was 5:15. It would take another half hour to get to the back of the mountain, and then at least forty five minutes to hike up and over. Sunrise was around 7:00 A.M. With luck, he could be in position just before dawn. If they had been waiting for him all night, they'd come out at daylight to Kreiss's version of the welcome wagon.

Jared called Browne at just after seven o'clock Friday morning. He told his grandfather what had happened the night before.

"And you hadn't been drinking? This wasn't some dream?"

"No, sir, I came home, had me one beer, checked on the dogs, and hit the sack. This shit started sometime around two this morning, a little after."

"And the dogs didn't alert on it?"

"No, sir. That's the weird part. You know them dogs—someone comes around here, they make like it's dinnertime."

Browne was silent for a moment. "I don't like the sound of this," he said finally. "We've got someone poking around the arsenal, and now this crap. Tell you what. Go outside when it gets full light and check for sign. Take a dog with you. See if he picks up on anything. Then I think we have to go back out to the site, see if your trap did any good."

"He hit that trap, his ass'll still be there," Jared declared. "That was a heap of pipe."

"We'll see. Maybe some bastard's just playing games. Call me back before you go to work."

Kreiss made it up to the south ridge of Pearl's Mountain just before sunrise. He had bought his front slope acreage from the old man who owned the entire mountain. He had permission to hunt all the slopes of the big hill, and he had gone out several times, often with Micah, to hunt deer, grouse, and turkey over its thousand-plus wooded acres. Given his previous career, he had also taken into consideration some defensive measures when siting his prefab cabin, which included arrangements for dealing with the problem of someone getting into the cabin to ambush him. But first, he had to determine if someone was there.

He crept along the south ridge until he reached the top edge of the tree

line on the eastern slope. Below was an open meadow littered with big boulders; it swept all the way down from the tree line to the back of the cabin. He was just able to see the cabin in the morning mist, some two hundred feet in elevation below his position and about three hundred yards distant. There were still large patches of shadow in the dawn light. A pair of early-morning bobwhites were calling across the grass in the meadow. Above them, a solitary hawk was testing for the first updrafts of the morning, but it was too early. It screeched once in frustration, dropped a wing, and slanted out of sight across the rock face of the upper mountain. There were no lights or other signs of life at the cabin, and he didn't see any vehicles. He checked again with his binoculars, and then he did see something: There was a Ford Bronco pulled behind some trees to the right of the cabin, well out of sight of the lower driveway.

Well, all right, he thought. So let's hold a little reveille. He moved along the tree line until the biggest boulder in the meadow shadowed him from view of the cabin, and then he trotted directly down the open meadow, remaining in the sight-line shadow of the boulder until he reached it. He got down on all fours and probed the base of the massive rock until he found the edge of a camouflaged tarp, which he lifted carefully, checking for snakes. Under the tarp was a well-greased five-foot-long steel box. He opened it and extracted a Barrett M82A1 .50-caliber rifle, complete with a Swarovsky ten-by-forty-two scope. The twenty-eight-pound rifle had a ten-round magazine loaded with RauFoss explosive, armor-piercing rounds. It also had a muzzle brake and a bipod. Beneath the rifle box was another, smaller box. From this, he extracted a black plastic device that looked like a television remote, and a battery pack, which he plugged into the device. He closed the boxes but left the tarp to one side. Then he lugged the huge rifle and the remote transmitter back up the slope to the trees, and once again he traversed the slope until he had a clear field of view of the back of the cabin and the clump of trees hiding the Bronco.

He checked the controller for electrical continuity with the battery pack, then put it down. He moved backward a few feet until he found level ground on which to set up the Barrett. He lay down beside the weapon, nestled the butt into his shoulder, and sighted down to the Bronco, aligning the crosshairs on the right side of the vehicle's engine compartment. Even though it was a .50-caliber rifle, the recoil wasn't too much more than that of a heavy shotgun, because the action was gas-operated and the weapon itself weighed so much. The heavy round would

drop substantially at three hundred yards, so he adjusted the scope accordingly and resighted. He fitted the magazine and then racked one round into the chamber. He didn't plan to use more than a few rounds. He checked his sight line again. Then he got the remote controller, pulled out a tiny whip antenna, and aimed it at the house. He selected amplifier, power on, volume 9, and hit the red button at the top of the controller. Then he selected program 1, and again hit the red button.

There were twelve Bose speakers placed strategically down in the cabin, all connected to an antique Fisher vacuum tube–driven 2,000-watt audio-amplifier, which was set up in the attic of the cabin. Connected to the amplifier was a CD player with a single compact disc and the radio transceiver, which accepted commands from the remote. The program he had selected was the recorded sound of roaring lions, which let go at close to 150 decibels. The noise was huge, even at Kreiss's position nearly one thousand feet away. Inside the cabin, it would be earsplitting. He could hear a chorus of dog howling start up from a mile down the country road, where Micah Wall kept a pen of coon hounds. The lion program ran for twenty seconds, and then it switched over to the second program, which erupted with the sound of a machine gun shooting out all the windows in a building. He shut it all down after another fifteen seconds and then sighted back through the scope on the Barrett as he settled himself into firing position.

Just before the machine-gun sounds ended, two men came tumbling out of the cabin's front door, holding their ears and running for the Bronco. He let them get within twenty feet of the vehicle before squeezing off the first round, which went through the right-front fender, the engine block, the left side, and then tore off a tree limb fifty feet down-slope from the vehicle. Well, maybe just a tiny bit more recoil than a shotgun, he thought as he fired again, this time moving the aiming point slightly to the left to hit the body, knocking a dent the size of a trash can's lid into the right-front door as the bullet went through the Bronco like butter and spanged off a rock down by the creek before decapitating a pine tree on the other side of the road. The third round he put through the rear axle, blasting both tires down and exploding the differential housing out the back of the vehicle. By then, the two men were flat on the ground, trying to reach China. He stopped firing and rubbed his sore shoulder. He checked the sight line again, but the heavy barrel hadn't moved.

He traversed the sight to where the men were. One of them sat up,

then got up and began brushing off his clothes. He then walked calmly out of the trees and up the hill toward Kreiss's firing position, acting as if nothing had happened. As Kreiss watched through the scope, the other man stayed down on the ground, his hands over his head, one eye visible as he watched the other man go up the hill. Kreiss sat up and took his finger off the trigger. Coming up the hill was a large black man, who grinned when he saw Kreiss.

"Fuck a duck, Ed, *lions*? And where the hell did you get a Barrett?"

"Hello, Charlie," Kreiss said. "Just something I picked up along the way. And kept. How you doing?"

Charlie Ransom had been in the Agency's retrieval Field Support Division for almost eight years and had worked for Kreiss from time to time. He was a deceptively agreeable-looking man who was lethally effective in bringing subjects back from urban environments. He stopped when he got ten feet from Kreiss, showed his hands, and then carefully extracted a cigarette out of his shirt pocket. Kreiss watched him light up.

"Bambi bring you guys along?" he asked finally, once Ransom had his cigarette going.

"Yeah," Ransom said, exhaling a cloud of pungent blue smoke.

"What's Foster's deal? He still Marchand's toad?"

"I think so. The request for our services came from Justice, so I'm not sure what the play is here."

Kreiss suddenly realized how badly he wanted a cigarette. He had quit smoking when he'd come down to Blacksburg. Now his neck hurt and he was aware that there must be visible bruises on his face. Ransom was looking him over.

"That was some sound show, man," Ransom said. "I think I pissed my pants when them lions did their thing."

"Who's the penitent down there?" Kreiss asked. He had not moved from his position behind the Barrett, which still had a round chambered.

"Nice young white boy," Ransom said. "Name's Gerald Cassidy. Career-minded. Married, too. I suppose that's why he's still grabbin' dirt. What do you think?"

"He's taking a reasonable approach to the situation," Kreiss said. "Sorry about the Bronco."

"DEA drug take. Ain't no big deal. But look, Ed. We were supposed to have us a little talk, not a firefight." He began to come closer.

Kreiss twitched the Barrett's barrel. "That wasn't a firefight. And I can hear you fine from right there."

Ransom stopped and flashed his palms at Kreiss in a gesture of peace. "All right, that's cool," he said, "but this isn't what you think."

The rifle wasn't pointed right at him, but it would not have taken much to fix that. Kreiss knew that from Ransom's perspective, the business end of a Barrett light .50 must look like the Holland Tunnel.

"Right," he said. "Then why were you two laying for me in my own house?"

"'Cause Bellhouser asked Agency CE for some off-line help. Apparently didn't want to use Bureau FCI people. Either that or AD Marchand didn't want the exposure."

"Help with what?" Kreiss asked patiently.

"Word is, Bellhouser's principal went postal when he heard that you've come out of retirement, so to speak. Apparently, one of the Roanoke agents told somebody you been operatin'. Word got back."

That would be Carter, Kreiss thought. "My daughter is missing," he said. He was tired and he was hurting. He could hear the edge in his own voice and saw that Ransom was struggling to hold his casual smile. "The local Bureau people fucked around with it for a little while, then sent it up to Missing Persons. That's not good enough. I know a thing or two about looking for someone. They're not going to look, so I am. You tell Bambi and company that this does not concern them, and to stay out of my way."

Ransom gave him a peculiar look, started to say something, but then put up his hands again. "All right, all right," he said. "That's cool. I'll tell 'em. Not saying that's going to go down so good, but I'll certainly tell 'em."

"You do that. You leave anything behind in my house?"

"Well, now, you know—"

"You go back down there. Take Tonto there with you. Get your insects out of my house, whatever you've done. Take your time; do a thorough job. I'll give you fifteen minutes. Then you come out and walk down the drive to the creek, and then walk south on that road. South is to the right. I'll call someone to come get you."

"Shit, man, we got the modern conveniences. We can take care of that."

Kreiss did not reply, but he indicated with his chin that Ransom should get going. Ransom gave him a little salute and then walked back down the hill, keeping his hands in sight. They might have cell phones, Kreiss thought, but they won't have a signal. They were in for a long walk. He also knew that their being rousted out of a stakeout was going to look bad enough without him, Kreiss, making the call to come get them.

He settled in alongside the Barrett and watched Ransom and his partner go back into the cabin. He would certainly have to do a sweep of his own. He swore out loud. This was definitely a development he did not need right now. The number-two guy at Justice had sent his own EA and another horse-holder from Kreiss's old department at the Bureau down here to step on his neck. He wondered where the heartburn was really coming from; the Agency shouldn't care. Upon reflection, he realized this probably wasn't about the Glower incident; this was probably about the Chinese spy case. If he had popped up on radar screens at Justice, the Agency, *and* the Bureau, then somebody very senior must be very nervous. Glower had been a major embarrassment, but his suicide should have long since tempered their pain. He wondered if this was about the money.

Janet Carter was summoned to the RA's conference room just after noon. The call came directly from Farnsworth's office, which once again set Larry Talbot off. To her surprise, the two Washington people were back, along with a large black man and a much younger white man. The two executive assistants were in business suits, but the other two men were wearing slacks, sport shirts, and windbreakers. Farnsworth asked her to join them at the table. He did not introduce the new players, and Janet saw that the RA was looking worried again.

"Agent Carter," Farnsworth announced formally, "This concerns the Edwin Kreiss matter. I've been requested to put you on special assignment. But first, Mr. Foster here has something to share with you. Mr. Foster?"

Foster looked down for a moment at some papers he had in a folder in front of him. "You said the other day that Kreiss went to see one of the people you interviewed about his missing daughter?"

"I said that I thought it was *probably* Kreiss." She replayed the story of the headless man for them.

"And the kid later told you that he told Kreiss they went to a 'Site R'?"

"That's right."

"Do you know what that is?"

"I never did find out. Nobody here seems to know about any Site R."

Foster shuffled his notes for a moment and then looked over at the woman, Bellhouser. Bambi, Janet thought. Perfect.

"We think Site R refers to the Ramsey Army Arsenal," Bellhouser said. "More properly known as the Ramsey Army Ammunition Plant. It's located south of the town of Ramsey, on the other side of the New River.

It's been shut down for almost twenty years and is technically in cadre status."

"Where'd that name come from, that Site R?" Janet asked.

"It's an EPA appellation. The industrial area of the site is highly contaminated, but since it's a military complex, the EPA doesn't name it as such on their lists of toxic supersites. They just called it Site R."

"And?" Janet asked. She was trying to figure out why the Justice Department cared about an abandoned military installation.

"There's some history here, Agent Carter. First, let me ask you something: Could you establish a working relationship with Kreiss if you had to?"

"Working relationship? With Edwin Kreiss?"

Farnsworth got into it. "Yes," he said. "Like if maybe you went to see him. Told him you were personally unhappy with the fact that the Bureau was just dropping his daughter's case like that. That you might be interested in helping him look for his daughter, off-line, so to speak."

She shook her head. "He was a special agent for a long time," she said, remembering her little confrontation with him in the cabin. "He would know that's bullshit. Agents don't work off-line and remain agents for very long."

"He's been retired for almost five years," Foster said. "You could play the line that the Bureau has changed a lot since then. And play up the fact that you are an inexperienced agent."

Janet cocked her head to one side and gave Foster a "Fuck you very much" look, but Farnsworth again intervened. "I've explained to Mr. Foster that your assignment to the Roanoke office was something of a lateral arabesque, Janet," he said. "Not for doing anything substantively wrong, of course, but for annoying a very senior assistant director at headquarters. You could tell Kreiss about that. Then imply that if you could solve the case, working with him, your career would be rehabilitated."

Janet felt her face redden. She sat back in her chair, embarrassed to have Farnsworth air her career problems in front of these people. "That all would be true, by the way," Farnsworth said to no one in particular. "Let Mr. Foster tell you what's going on before you say anything."

"This involves the BATF," he began, and Janet snorted contemptuously. Foster stopped.

"The *Texas toastmasters*?" she exclaimed. "You've got to be shitting me."

"Janet," Farnsworth began, but Foster waved her comment away.

"This involves a series of bombings that have been going on since the early nineties. Abortion clinics. The Atlanta Olympics bombing. And of course, some major incidents, such as the World Trade Center and the Oklahoma City bombing. Three letter bombs to federally funded universities that were *not* the work of the Unibomber. And three other potentially major federal office building bombings that did not succeed, or were derailed by security people."

"The theory of interest," Bellhouser said, "is that the anti-issue and antigovernment groups suspected to be behind these incidents are not technically qualified to design and construct some of the devices that have been used. Even more interesting is that the explosives used in several of the incidents were chemically similar. Some were identical."

"Basically," Foster said, "the BATF thinks that there is one expert or expert group that these anti-everything groups are using to get their big bombs from, because the kind of people who protest at abortion clinics are more likely to be soccer moms than explosives experts."

"So they use what, a consultant?" Janet asked.

Bellhouser nodded. "ATF and the Bureau have intercepted communications between some of the groups involved. We're talking one of the more violence-prone 'anti' groups, and some people who might be supporting that guy Rudolph, the one we're all chasing through the North Carolina woods."

"You're implying that there is a national conspiracy among the anti groups?"

The two Washington people nodded their heads. "Actually," Foster said, "there's been an interim national-level task force working that theory since 1994: Justice, the Marshals Service, the Bureau, and ATF. It's focused mainly on the anti-abortion bombings, but the feeling now is that it may be bigger than that. The task force is called the DCB, which stands for Domestic Counterintelligence Board."

Janet had never heard of any DCB, but she knew that Washington was full of interim task forces, a sure sign that the permanent organizations had become ineffective. "So what's this got to do with the Roanoke office?" she asked.

"The Board has only one lead on the so-called consultant," Foster said. "And that is, he's supposedly based in southwest Virginia."

Janet still didn't see the connection. Foster explained.

"You've told us Kreiss might be looking for something called Site R. Kreiss hunting anything is something that concerns us very much. We ran the national databases on Site R, and that surfaced the Ramsey AAP, an explosives-manufacturing complex down here in southwest Virginia. Our query brought the DCB staff up on the line, asking what we were looking for. We didn't really want to share our Kreiss problem with anyone, so we waffled. But ATF, which is a full member of the DCB, put an agenda item on the board's next meeting, asking what the Bureau was up to."

"And, of course, nobody at the Bureau wanted to give the ATF the time of day," Farnsworth said. Foster nodded. Janet understood, as did everyone in the Bureau, that after the Waco disaster, cooperation at the policy level in Washington between the Bureau and the Bureau of Alcohol, Tobacco and Firearms had become a very strained business. The BATF worked for the Treasury Department; the FBI worked for the Justice Department. The competition for federal law-enforcement budget dollars had always been fierce, but the Waco disaster had added an extra dimension of enmity between the two law-enforcement agencies. But there was something she did not understand.

"If you people or this board think there's something going on at this Ramsey Arsenal that's related to a national terrorist bombing campaign," Janet said, "why doesn't this DCB or whatever just send in the Marines, toss the place?"

"Because ATF already had," Foster said. "It did an inspection of all such sites two years ago, and it found nothing at Ramsey but a mothballed ammunition plant. For the Bureau to suggest otherwise now is to imply that ATF screwed up or missed something."

"What a concept," Janet muttered.

"More importantly," Bellhouser added, ignoring her gibe, "the proximate cause for such an allegation would be Edwin Kreiss's unauthorized activities. Speaking for the Justice Department, we do not want our Kreiss problem exposed, and certainly not to Treasury and the BATF."

"I guess I can see that," Janet said, although she sensed something was not quite making sense here. "So now what?"

"My principal, Mr. Garrette, has discussed this matter with Assistant Director Marchand. It has been decided that there might be a way to finesse this situation. We've told the ATF at the DCB level that an ex-operative of ours had maybe stumbled onto something related to the bomb-maker conspiracy theory, and that it might, emphasis on the word *might*, have something to do with the Ramsey Arsenal. We informed ATF that we proposed to let this guy run free for a while and see what, if anything, he turns up."

"But what makes you think there is something going on at this arsenal?"

"Because Kreiss recently contacted an old buddy who used to work for the U.S. Marshals Service," Foster said. "He did Kreiss a favor, but then his company security officer asked some questions, and in turn, the company reported the matter to the Bureau. They happen to have a contract with the Bureau, and they found out Kreiss used to work for the Bureau."

"What was the favor?"

"The friend is a pilot who does airborne geo-information systems surveys. Kreiss wanted an aerial map of the Ramsey Arsenal. He told his friend that something was going on there that shouldn't be, and that it had something to do with his daughter's disappearance."

Janet frowned. This was news. "Let me get this straight," she said. "You're saying that now you *want* Kreiss to go operational again, because you think he might lead you to some bomb-making cell operating out of this arsenal?"

"Correct," Bellhouser said. "Now, if we can put you alongside Kreiss, we can perhaps achieve two objectives: We can find out what he's doing, and maybe we can catch some serious bombers."

"Actually," Foster said, "nobody knows whether or not the antigovernment groups have organized nationally. It isn't out of the question that they have in a limited way—say in the matter of getting their bombs. But if this works, we might have a chance here to roll up not only the bomb makers but some of their customers."

Janet frowned, but then she thought she understood. Foster had an unspoken objective on the table: If the Bureau could unearth a bomber cell where ATF had failed to find them, the Bureau stood to count considerable coup. At the expense of ATF, she reminded herself.

"And you think that Kreiss acting independently has a better chance to find something than an overt joint ATF/Bureau operation?"

"The last one of those was something less than a signal success," Bellhouser pointed out.

"And Kreiss is that good?" Janet asked.

The large black man, who had been listening impassively up to now, snorted. Foster introduced him. "Janet, this is Mr. Ransom. He is a liaison officer to the DCB. The gentleman with him is Mr. Cassidy. Mr. Ransom here has had some, um, experience with Mr. Kreiss."

"Experience," Ransom said. "Yeah, you might call it that. Remind me to show you our Bronco."

"We're going to downplay this whole thing at the DCB meeting," Foster said. "The last thing we want right now is the ATF charging into the arsenal. Especially if there's nothing there, because that would necessarily bring the focus back to Kreiss."

Janet nodded slowly as she tried to work out all the lines in the water. Something was still muddled here. Then an awful idea occurred to her. "You people aren't holding back information on Kreiss's daughter, are you?" she asked, looking at Foster and Bellhouser.

"Oh, for God's sake," snapped Bellhouser angrily. There was an embarrassed silence at the table. Farnsworth was shaking his head. Foster took a deep breath before responding.

"I won't dignify that question with an answer, Agent Carter," he said. "Look, Edwin Kreiss is a tough nut. Even in retirement, as Mr. Ransom discovered earlier this morning. I'll let him brief you after this meeting. This Site R business may be entirely off the mark, in which case we'll break it off and find another way to deal with Kreiss. But the ATF people who went into the Ramsey complex said it would be an absolutely *perfect* place for someone to set up a covert explosives lab."

"But they found nothing?"

"A bunch of big concrete buildings, stripped down and locked up. The Army has some local rent-a-cops under contract. They make routine patrols of the physical plant, and they've never seen anything except signs of the occasional deer hunter back in the bunker area. It seems the central industrial area is known locally to be badly contaminated, which tends to keep intruders out. One of the security guards also said that there are rumors of chemical weapons, nerve gas, that sort of stuff, stored in the complex. We checked with the Army, which says that's total bullshit, but since it helps to keep out intruders, they've always been deliberately coy about denying it."

"Based on his reputation, if something *is* going on there, Kreiss will uncover it," Bellhouser said. "If and when he does, that's when the DCB would want to reassert control."

"And bring in some more assets, like maybe the ATF?"

"Or the appropriate Bureau people," Foster said. "And also because if someone hurt or killed his daughter, and those other two kids, you know—they broke into the arsenal on a lark, stumbled onto something, and somebody took them—Edwin Kreiss is likely to stake them out naked on the forest floor and build small fires on their bellies. For starters."

"Sounds about right to me," Janet said.

Ransom grinned in the background, but Foster and Bellhouser did not see any humor in it. "The objective," Bellhouser said, "over and above our Kreiss problem, is to see if we can smash the whole thing—the bomb consultant, his lab, and his conduits into the violent antigovernment groups."

"These are the people who bomb whole buildings full of innocent civilians," Foster said. "Remember OK City? The day-care center?"

Ransom stopped grinning. Janet nodded. That was certainly a worthwhile objective. "All right, I think I understand. And Kreiss is not to know anything about all this, correct? I offer to help him where I can, and then keep you people informed via our office here?"

"You said she was smart," Bellhouser murmured to Farnsworth.

Puh-leeze, Janet thought.

"This all assumes Kreiss will give me the time of day," she pointed out. "He doesn't exactly strike me as a team player."

"He may or may not accept *your* help," Foster said. "The first thing *we* want to know is whether or not he's been into the arsenal, and what, if anything, he's found there. How you get that information will be entirely up to you."

This guy's a master of the obvious, Janet thought. "It's been several days," she said. "Since the incident in that kid's apartment, I mean. We may be a little late here."

"For what it's worth, he was gone all night last night," Ransom said. "And when he came back, he also anticipated that somebody might be waiting there in his cabin."

"How? we wonder," Bellhouser asked rhetorically.

Janet kept her face a perfect blank. "Maybe he *is* just that good," she said. "Especially if he's working something after you guys told him never to go operational again."

"Perhaps," Bellhouser said, giving her a speculative look. "But for now, this is a Bureau/Justice Department play. With a little help from our Agency friends here."

Agency friends? Janet thought. Then she realized Bellhouser was talking about the two so-called liaison men. "And ATF doesn't suspect you've got something going?" she asked.

"We think not," Bellhouser said. "If Kreiss turns up solid evidence of a bomber cell, we'll take it to the DCB, and, of course, that will fold in ATF. But right now, Kreiss and what he's doing is our focus."

"What this 'we' shit, white woman?" Ransom murmured. "Maybe you should go deal with that crazy motherfucker. Him and his fifty-caliber rifle."

Bellhouser looked over at Ransom. "I will if I have to, since you failed to deliver the message."

"Didn't need to," Ransom said. "He doesn't think it's you."

"Huh?" Janet said. "What message? What are you two talking about?"

Bellhouser ignored her question. "We'll coordinate this through Mr. Farnsworth. You will report exclusively to him. Think of him as your field controller."

Field controller, Janet thought with another mental roll of her eyes. Just call me Bond, Janet Bond. "Okay," she said. "Boss, would you please back-brief Larry Talbot?" She looked at her watch. "It's Friday afternoon. I should get in touch with Mr. Kreiss ASAP, don't you think?"

"Absolutely," Foster said.

Janet hesitated, an image of Edwin Kreiss's watchful face in her mind. "You don't think Kreiss will tumble to all this?" she asked. "He seems pretty . . . perceptive."

"Not if it's done right," Foster said. "Think of it as the 'frog in the pot' analogy: You drop a frog into a pot of boiling water, out he comes. Put him in a pot of cold water and slowly turn up the heat? He boils to death without ever realizing he's in trouble."

Janet just looked at Foster. From her brief acquaintance with Edwin Kreiss, she saw a hundred things wrong with his little analogy.

"And Mr. Ransom here has some equipment to show you. Why don't you go with him, while we sort out communications and coordination with Mr. Farnsworth."

Janet glanced at Farnsworth, who nodded. She knew she would have to talk to him later, to make sure she understood the real bureaucratic ground rules here. As she got up to leave, the Bellhouser woman was giving her a studied look. It occurred to Janet that their scheme depended entirely on Mr. Kreiss going along with her offer of "help." The woman's expression somehow reminded Janet of a snake who'd just missed a rabbit.

She followed Ransom out of the conference room and closed the door behind her. The more she thought about this, the more she thought Kreiss would just blow her off. On the other hand, she had warned him about the Agency people showing up. Maybe he would be grateful. Edwin Kreiss grateful. Sure.

"So," she said, "what's this about a fifty-caliber rifle? And a Bronco?"

He shook his head. "It's in your impound lot. You know what a Barrett light fifty is?"

"I'm a materials forensics nerdette, so, no. What's a Barrett light fifty?"

They went down to the basement and then took back stairs out to the multistoried parking garage behind the federal building. A fenced area on the lower level held impounded vehicles. The Bronco was in one corner of the compound, hunkered down in a pool of its body fluids. Ransom walked them over to it.

"A Barrett light fifty is a big-ass rifle. Currently being used by Navy SEALs as a long-range personal communicator. The Army is using it to detonate land mines. He did this with three rounds."

"Wow. Was he after you guys?"

"Kreiss? No way. He normally doesn't use guns on people. He uses guns to scare the shit out of people. Like me and Gerald back there at his cabin. We were playing dive the submarine by the time that second round came down the hill. Somebody lets off a Barrett, you *know* you're in a world of shit."

Janet looked at the car and wondered what she'd gotten herself into. Ransom was watching her. "I guess I don't understand," she said. "Somebody pops a cap at Bureau agents, the immediate result is that a hundred more agents come kick his ass. Tell me some more about this Kreiss guy. And you work for the Agency? Did you work with Kreiss?"

"Nobody worked *with* Edwin Kreiss. *For* him, maybe, but never with him. That's part of his charm. And me, I'm just a glorified gofer."

Janet looked sideways at him. Ransom's flexible speech patterns were beginning to make her think that he was perhaps being modest. "Well, look, whatever you are, I'm a regular whizbang in a federal forensics investigation. You want courtroom-ready evidence to lock some wrong guys up, I'm your agent. I'm here in Roanoke to get some out-of-specialty field experience, which means I have next to no field experience. Get the picture?"

"Got the picture. Man upstairs said you pissed off some heavy dudes. What you do—tell the truth on 'em?"

"I was working in the Bureau laboratory. As you may have read, we've had some problems there. I told them what the evidence said. Not what they wanted to hear. You know, facts getting in the way of preconceived notions. Some of the bigger bosses hate that."

"See, we don't have that problem where I work."

"Oh really?"

"Yeah, see, at the Agency, ain't nobody ever asks for facts in the first place. That way, nothing interferes with their preconceived notions. Lot less friction."

She smiled. "I'll bet. Anyway, I do believe I'm out of my league getting mixed up with a guy like this," she said, pointing with her chin to the deflated Bronco.

"We all out of our league, Special Agent Carter. That's why he was so damned effective when he worked for us."

"I don't understand. If he's such a big problem, why don't you all just gang up and take him in, do some spooky number on him?"

Ransom stopped and looked around. "You really don't know, do you?" he said.

"No, I don't."

He looked around again. "Okay, there's two reasons. The first is because he's Edwin Kreiss. Listen, Gerald and me? We were sent to just have us a little talk with the man last night. Just talk, now, nothing heavy. He don't come home, and next thing I know, it's morning and I'm looking for coffee makings. I'm opening a cupboard door and a fuckin' zooful of goddamn monster-ass *lions* sound off in that big room."

"Lions."

"Fuckin' right, lions. I never heard a live lion in my fuckin' life outside of the movies, and I not only knew it was lions but that there was a hundred of them bastards *in* the house. We talkin' *loud* motherfuckers, awright? I mean, we talkin' a hundred fifty decibels' worth of roaring lions. Then it was a machine gun, blowing all the windows in the house out, along with our eardrums. I'm talkin' glass flyin', bullets blowin' through walls, dishes breakin'—and it's so loud, I can't hear myself screamin'."

"He shoot at his own house?"

"Naw, he didn't shoot nothin'—then. My man Kreiss does sounds. These were just sounds. I knew that—still scared the shit out of me. And Gerald? My man Gerald crapped himself."

"He does this with what—speakers? Tapes?"

"Tactical sound. It's a Kreiss trademark. See, if you can hear it but you can't see it, then your imagination automatically comes up with the worst-case monster, right? And if you get your target spooked enough, he's gonna move in straight lines. He put a rattlesnake tape in a guy's car one time—rattles, hiss, ground sounds, the whole nine yards. Dude drove it into a tree tryin' to find that snake. I gotta tell you, I knew all about this, but Gerald an' me? We both out the fuckin' door in about two nanoseconds, all that shit starts up, runnin' for the Bronco, and then, *then*, here come the crack of doom to split the engine block into four pieces."

"Okay, so he has a bad temper."

Ransom started laughing. "Temper? *Temper!* What are you, Special Agent, a comedienne? *Temper!* No, no, no, no. Kreiss? He wasn't mad. He cool as a fuckin' cucumber when I go up the hill to pay my respects, you know, say hello, see how *his* morning is goin'. No, no, see: This the kind of shit he does when he just workin'. Now, rumor has it he does have a teeny little problem with rage. That's when he does the really bad shit, the shit got him retired. And that leads me to the second reason. You sure you don't already know this?"

"I've heard a little bit about the Glower incident, if that's what you mean. I'm not sure I want to know any more."

"Well, you better, you be messin' aroun' with those executive back-stabbers in there. Edwin Kreiss, when he flamed out after the Glower thing, he supposedly said some things. Made some accusations. Like he'd been right about Glower, seein' as Glower offed himself and his whole family rather than answer to what was comin'. Some other people where I work thought the same thing, only they couldn't say so, because sayin' so wasn't such a healthy thing to do, careerwise."

"My boss said Kreiss thought there was someone else who had been obstructing the DOE laboratories investigation. Somebody in another agency."

"But that's the thing, Special Agent. That's the reason nobody willin' to order up a gang bang on Mr. Kreiss. Because, the way the jungle drums told it, brother Kreiss just might have some *evidence* to back up all those accusations he made. You know, *evidence?* Like what got you sent down here to East Bumfuck Egypt? Me, I'm just a workin' stiff, but my guess is there are some senior people in both your outfit and mine who just might be afraid of Edwin Kreiss."

She stared at the bleeding Bronco. "Fuck me," she said quietly.

"Now you talkin' like a veteran," Ransom said approvingly.

They headed back toward the building. Janet still felt that there was something wrong with the logic of what Bellhouser and Foster had asked her to do, but she couldn't put her finger on it. "So where does a retired FBI agent get his hands on a fifty-caliber rifle?" she asked.

"Probably got it when he was with Agency CE," Ransom said. "You gotta remember: Kreiss worked with the sweepers, and those are some serious spooks. Those guys can draw on any kind of equipment the CS—that's our Clandestine Services—have in the toy store, along with DOD's toy store. Word is, those dudes go out and get some of their own shit, 'cause the operatin' cash is, shall we say, loosely controlled? When it's time for them to retire, go raise plutonium somewhere, they turn in the issue stuff, but there's no tellin' what kinda shit they got stashed, or where. Ain't nobody asks 'em, either."

She stopped at the door, took a deep breath, and blew it out though pursed lips. "Maybe I need to go back and talk to Farnsworth. I'm definitely not qualified to do this by myself."

"Who says you be by yourself, Special Agent? You gonna have some top *line* backup while you on this little vacation."

She looked at him. He was smiling broadly. "You?" she said.

"One and only."

They went through the door and she stopped again. "And you just walked up the hill to talk to him?"

"Couldn't dance, Special Agent. Might as well go see what the man wants, makin' all that noise. Besides, I didn't like the sounds Gerald was makin'."

She shook her head. "He okay now?"

They started up the stairs. "I believe Gerald's had a small change of heart," Ransom said. "Brother Gerald has decided he's going into another line of work. He was in the computer-research end of the CS before he came to the retrieval shop. I believe the Barrett influenced his career thinkin' this morning. And maybe the lions, too. Hard to say which."

"Gerald sounds intelligent," she said. "So, what was significant about the message you were supposed to deliver to Kreiss?"

He looked down at her for a moment. "I can't tell you that," he said. "Because I don't know what it means. What I can say is that it involves somethin' way above your pay grade and mine. Now, let's go look at some of my surveillance toys."

Kreiss spent the rest of the day checking his property's perimeter, retrieving his truck, and then cleaning and restashing the Barrett. Micah Wall wandered up about midmorning to inquire if everything was all right at the Kreiss homestead. His eyes widened when he saw the Barrett.

"Been some years since I heard me a fifty-cal," he said, looking around for bodies. "Korea, I believe it was. They didn't look like that."

"Unmistakable, aren't they?" Kreiss said.

Micah eyed the bandage on Kreiss's neck but said nothing about it. "Fifty works real good on Chicoms, specially when they bunch up. We gonna have buzzards? You need a mass grave dug or anything?"

Kreiss laughed. "No, this was just a little domestic dispute. I think we got it all sorted out. For the moment anyway."

"Hate to hear you do a *big* domestic dispute, neighbor. Oh, and my dogs was inquirin' about them lions?"

"The wonders of modern science, Micah. Just a little something to make people move out of their prepared positions."

"Uh-huh," Micah said, nodding thoughtfully. "Well, like I've said before, you need me or any of my kinfolk to take a walk in the woods now and then, you just holler. Any word on Lynn?"

"I appreciate the offer, Micah. And no, nothing on Lynn from the authorities. I may have found out a couple of things, though." He told Micah about finding Lynn's hat inside the Ramsey Arsenal, and that he thought there was something going on in there.

"What kinda something, you reckon?"

"I'm not sure. My guess is a meth lab, maybe some other kind of heavy drug thing. Something that made those two guys willing to shoot first and talk about it later. I did find out who one of them is, however. We're going to have a talk."

"You think maybe them kids went in there and ran into the wrong kinda folks?"

Kreiss nodded, sighing. "It's possible, Micah. And that's not a happy thought."

"You want, I got some kinfolk who can go git this fella, bring him back to our place. We can put him in the caves for a while. Give him time to reflect. Then you can have that there talk in private, you want."

"I appreciate it, Micah, but I better do this one myself. There are some folks who are interested in the fact that I'm stepping out at night, and they're not people you want to meet."

"Like them two boys I seen goin' down the road this mornin'?"

Kreiss nodded his head. Micah thought about that for a moment.

"They revenuers?"

"Not exactly. They are federal. I used to work with one of them. There's some bad history here. I want to focus on finding Lynn, and I don't want them drawn into it."

Wall nailed a cricket with a shot of chaw. "Well, you know where we at," he said. "You git into a fix, you call, hear?"

Kreiss thanked him again and Micah trudged back into the forest, keeping a wary eye out for lions. Kreiss made a mental note that maybe he would take Micah up on his offer. Micah's clan had been walking these hills for decades. If Bambi and the Bureau had made some kind of deal with the Agency, there might be more watchers. The Wall clan might actually have some fun with them. Maybe he should lend them some lions, or maybe the tape of an adult male grizzly at full power, complete with noises of crashing through the brush and snapping limbs; that was a beauty for woods and cave work, especially if dogs were in pursuit. Their handlers might know it was a tape, but the dogs would inevitably leave the scene, sometimes with the handlers' arms attached to their leashes.

He had checked the house out for bugs and other electronic vermin, sanitized his phone line, and disconnected the house electrical power at the breaker box to scan the house wiring for devices that drew power by induction. His computer was strictly a communications device; as far as he was concerned, it was eternally unsecure. Everything that went out on the Net was an open book anyway, so he didn't bother to check it other than to do an occasional cookie scan. Once he was reasonably sure the place was clean, he checked his truck. There, his scanner found two bugs right away. They were so easy, he knew there had to be a third, which he finally found mounted on the inside of the right-rear wheel, where it drew inductive power from axle rotation via magnets fixed to the frame. If the wheel wasn't moving, there was no power signal to be detected by the scanner. Clever. He found it by getting on his back and looking.

Then he took a long, hot shower, dressed the cuts on his neck, ate a sandwich, and lay down for a long nap. He would redo the house sweep in twenty-four hours to pick up any delayed-action devices. He almost hoped they'd left one, because a bug you knew about was a wonderful way to feed back disinformation.

He was awakened at 3:30 by the phone. It was the FBI lady, Janet Carter.

"You have something new on Lynn?" he asked immediately.

"No, Mr. Kreiss, I don't. But I'd like to meet with you, if I could. Today if possible, before the weekend."

"Today is almost over and weekends don't mean anything to me, Agent Carter. Why do we need to meet?"

"To talk about something that shouldn't be heard on a phone, Mr. Kreiss."

He thought about that, trying to wipe the sleep from his eyes. His body was sore all over from his little pipe bath at the arsenal. He had planned to work on Jared McGarand tonight. If the FBI lady didn't have anything on Lynn, he wasn't sure he wanted to waste any time with her. She was pretty enough to look at, but until Lynn was recovered, he wasn't interested in women.

"Well, that's sufficiently mysterious to make me curious, but I'm busy tonight, Agent Carter. How about some other time?"

"Maybe I can help you find Site R; you know, the place Barry Clark told you about?"

That sat him up in his bed. She must have gone back to reinterview that little creep. And made him talk. He'd better hear this. "Okay." He sighed. "Where and when?"

"I live in Roanoke. You live well west of Blacksburg. You know where the Virginia Tech main library is? The university has a convention center hotel across the street. Called the Donaldson-Brown Center?"

"I know it." He'd had lunch with Lynn there a week before she disappeared. The memory of it pinched his heart.

"The bar at seven?"

"All right," he said, and hung up. What the hell is this all about? he wondered. First, she had warned him about the Washington people coming to town. Now she said she wanted to help him find Lynn, even though her bosses supposedly had closed the local case. He lay back in the bed. Were the Agency and the Bureau really working together? Not likely, he thought. Especially after the Glower incident. So what had brought Bambi and Chief Red in the Face to beautiful downtown Roanoke, Virginia, if not something to do with him? As further evidenced by the appearance of Charlie Ransom plus one at his cabin. Why? What had brought them now? Carter had just mentioned Barry Clark. She couldn't *know* that he'd been the headless visitor, but what if she'd reported the incident and named him as the most likely suspect? Would that generate Washington's interest?

He got up with a grunt and checked the time. It was going on four o'clock. Jared ought not to be home yet. He went to his desk and got out a file marked "Tax Return." He had transcribed all the pertinent numbers from the papers he'd taken from Jared's trailer into what looked like a personal tax record, and then he'd burned the McGarand papers. He got Jared's phone number and dialed it. When the phone had rung three times, he pressed the buttons marked 7 and 5 together for two seconds. This activated the recorder, which diverted the ring signal and initiated a ten-second wait period, in case the owner picked up his phone. Then it activated its playback feature. He listened to Jared's call to someone, pressed the star key, listened to it again, and then pressed 6 and 9. The digits of a phone number were read to him by a robotic voice. He copied down the number. He pressed the buttens 7 and 5 again. There was one incoming call, an older man's voice. It sounded like the same man in the previous call. The man told Jared that they would go out to the site tonight to get set up for tomorrow and to look for their "visitor." He listened to the voice again, memorizing the sound of it. There were no more calls. He pressed the zero button three times and hung up.

He looked up the number for the Donaldson-Brown Center and called for a room reservation, specifically requesting a room overlooking the parking lot. Then he went back to sleep, setting his clock in time to get cleaned up for his trip into that throbbing metropolis known as Blacksburg, Virginia.

Janet Carter arrived at Donaldson-Brown at 6:30. She was driving an unmarked tan Bureau Crown Vic, which she parked in the front parking lot. It was twilight, but the parking lot lights weren't on yet. She had had time to go to her townhouse in Roanoke before coming over to Blacksburg, and she was wearing a light wool pantsuit over a plain dark blouse. Earlier, she'd spent an hour with Ransom looking at various surveillance and communications gadgets, and then she had met with Farnsworth alone to nail down the ground rules for her new assignment.

Farnsworth had been pretty specific: All communications regarding what she was doing with Edwin Kreiss were to be via secure means directly to him—preferably via scrambled landline. No cell phones and no clear tactical radio unless it was an emergency. Ransom was to be her distant tactical backup—*distant* meaning that Kreiss was not to know that Ransom was operating with her if at all possible. She was not to go anywhere alone *with* Kreiss without clearance from the RA. If her situation got at all hinky, she was to back out and return immediately to the federal building, day or night, and notify him. They would not establish a response cell in the federal building unless something more than a surveillance operation developed. She was to be armed at all times, and she was to carry an encapsulated CFR—call for rescue—pod at all times. He gave her the phone codes that would forward any call she made to the FBI office in Roanoke directly to him wherever he was, twenty-four hours a day. Finally, Farnsworth told her that there was always the chance that the two horse-holders from Washington might have other assets besides Ransom in the area. If she detected that situation, she was to back out immediately.

"Unfortunately, all we know about this little deal is what those people have told us, no more, no less," he said. "I've got some calls into the Criminal Investigations operations center at our headquarters to verify this DCB thing—I've never heard of it, although that doesn't necessarily mean anything. And much as I hate the idea of working with ATF, I'm uneasy about cutting them out if this is turning into a bombing case. For all their Washington warts, their field people are pretty good at working bombs."

"I got the impression that those two weren't telling us everything," Janet said.

"You've got good instincts," Farnsworth said. "I've got to be careful here. Foster works for Marchand and the FCI people. As the Roanoke office, we *don't* work for Marchand. I have the authority to put you on this thing, but I want some top cover before it goes much further. I also want to know more about this purported bomb-making cell operating down here in southwest Virginia, which I damn well *should* have been told about."

"One final warning, Janet," he said. "I know you've had one previous field tour, but that was in your specialty, right?"

"Yes, sir, in Chicago. I didn't do much street work."

He nodded. "That's what I'm getting at, your lack of street experience, through no fault of yours, of course. But this guy Kreiss is the walking embodiment of street experience, and, apparently, then some. You're a smart young lady, but don't try to use those brains to outwit Edwin Kreiss. Use them to know when to back out and call me. Maintain situational awareness, and keep it simple, okay?"

Another "Yes, sir," and then she was out of there. And now she was here. The parking lot was almost full, and there were people unloading bags from cars lined up by the hotel's front entrance. She wondered if Edwin Kreiss was standing under a streetlight nearby, a newspaper in his face, watching her. Yeah, and a brown fedora, tan trench coat, and some shades to complete the ensemble. She smiled and automatically checked her makeup. She had deliberately put on plain clothes, not wanting to put any boy-girl elements into the meeting. He's just a retired Bureau agent, she reminded herself. Which isn't quite true, is it? she thought. Ransom's story of the acoustic attack and then the .50 caliber fire down the hill would have been almost funny except for one thing: Ransom and his partner had been frightened out of their wits. His partner was apparently quitting over what had happened up there. She closed her eyes for a moment and tried to imagine what lions roaring at 150 decibels would do to her own presence of mind. A flash-bang grenade was 175 decibels. And, yes, your forebrain would tell you there couldn't be lions in the house, she thought, but she was pretty sure her own instincts would have been to bolt out of that cabin while trying not to leave a trail. This Kreiss was a piece of work.

She got out of the car and walked directly to the front entrance. She was carrying a leather purse, which held her credentials. She had her Sig Sauer model 225 in a hip holster under her jacket. Farnsworth had asked her if she carried more than one gun, but, like most agents, she did not. She carried the CFR pod, which was the size of a change purse, in her pants pocket. If squeezed hard, it would begin emitting a coded signal on one of the satellite-monitored search and rescue frequencies, which in turn would key a reaction transponder at FBI headquarters. It couldn't pinpoint her precise location, but it would tell the system who was in trouble. Ransom had agreed to follow her to Blacksburg but to stay away from the hotel. She hoped he wouldn't get all independent on her and blow their cover, such as it was.

She found the lounge located to one side of the lobby and took a table at the back. There was a conventional bar running down one wall, booths along the opposite wall, and smaller tables out in the middle. A couple of men at the bar were looking her over. She went through the looking-at-her-watch pantomime to discourage any walk-ups. C'mon, Kreiss, she thought, and then realized she was the one who was early.

Three floors above, Edwin Kreiss kept watch on the parking lot from his darkened window. The building front faced northeast, so anyone looking up at the windows at sunset should not be able to see in. He had watched Janet drive into the lot in her rather obvious Bureau car, complete with the small whip antenna on the trunk. He had wondered what she'd been doing down there for ten minutes, but then she'd gone inside. He was waiting to see if any more unmarked cars showed up. He had, in fact, been watching the lot since five o'clock, looking for any vehicle that came into the area either to make repeated passes or to park, with no one getting out. His own vehicle was parked almost a mile away, on the other side of the Virginia Tech parade field, behind the main administration building. If Carter was working with a surveillance squad, her backup might try to plant something on his truck while she was inside with him. Assuming she had backup.

He was still suspicious about her call for a meet. It had to be more than something generated out of the goodness of her heart, and, regrettably, something to do with the firestorm he'd caused when he left the government. He swore quietly. If that's what this was all about, his life could get really complicated. Especially with Lynn missing.

And then he saw a minivan come into the parking lot, turn its headlights off, and start to cruise the lanes with just its parking lights on. That was okay, except that it went by two perfectly good parking spaces, and then a third and a fourth. He got out his binoculars, trying for a make on the plate, but the plate light was conveniently not working. The windows must have been tinted, because he could not see inside the van, either. The van cruised down one more lane and then came up past Carter's Crown Vic. There was a brief flare of brake lights, but then the van continued on. Bingo, he thought. The van went out of the parking lot and onto a small side street that led into the main campus. A passing car honked and flashed its lights at the van to get its main lights on. The van complied, then pulled into a handicapped space to one side of the hotel building. As Kreiss watched, a tall man got out and walked purposefully back to Carter's car, where he looked both ways and then bent down to put something under the left-rear wheel well. The man then walked back to the minivan and got in. A moment later, he drove away.

Kreiss pulled the drapes closed. It looked like Carter had backup all right, but not necessarily working for her. He slipped on his sport coat, having decided to dress up a little, in deference to the fact that Carter would probably still be in her office clothes. He went downstairs.

Janet saw him come into the bar and raised her hand. He was wearing khaki-colored slacks, a white shirt open at the throat, and a dark blue sport coat. With his gray-white hair and clipped beard, he looked almost professorial, except for the heft of his shoulders and a look in his eye that made other men in the crowded room ease out of his way as he came across to her table. He nodded to her as he sat down and ordered a glass of sparkling water from the waitress.

"Special Agent Carter," he said. "You called."

"Yes, I did," she said. The bar was really filling up now, and the noise level was growing. Up close, his face looked a little puffy on one side and there was a bandage peeking up over his collar.

"Hurt yourself?" she asked, looking at the bandage.

"Let's get to it," he said, ignoring her question. "I want to find my daughter. What do you want?"

"I reinterviewed Barry Clark. He said he told you they were going to Site R. I think I can help you identify what that is."

"I already know," he said. "It's the Ramsey Arsenal. What do you want?"

She was taken aback and suddenly didn't know what to say. She realized she should have had a plan B. He leaned forward, his eyes intense. "Listen to me, Special Agent Carter. I want to find my daughter. Three case folders gathering dust up in the MP shop don't cut it. I'm going to do what I'm going to do, regardless of the Bureau. If I determine that she's been abducted and injured or killed, I'll find out who did it and put their severed heads on pikes out on the interstate."

She blinked, desperately trying to think of something clever to say. This wasn't going anything like the way she had anticipated. She had forgotten how intense he was. Focus, she commanded herself. Focus. Then he surprised her.

"Who would want to plant a bug on your Bu car?" he asked.

"W-what? A bug?"

"I watched you arrive in the parking lot. Tan Crown Vic? You parked and stayed in the car for a few minutes. Then you walked in. Ten minutes after that, a nondescript minivan came into the lot, cruised all the lanes, paused at your car, left the lot, and then parked long enough for some tall white guy to walk back and put something under your left-rear wheel well. Who would want to bug a Bureau car?"

What the hell is this? she thought. "I looked for you," she said. "Where were you watching from?"

"My room, Special Agent."

His room. "Oh" was all she could manage.

He sat back in his chair and drank some of his water. "You're obviously not a street agent. What's your specialty?"

The look in his eyes was one of calm appraisal. She decided this was no time for bullshit. "I'm a materials forensics evidence specialist. Most of my assignments have been in support of Washington task forces, qualifying the evidence. I did one field tour in Chicago, but it was in-specialty."

"You do a lot of materials forensics over there in beautiful downtown Roanoke, Virginia?"

"Well," she said, "some senior people at the headquarters thought it was time for me to get some field experience."

"You mean you were playing straight-arrow in the lab, upset some prosecutor's preconceived notions about the evidence, and your mentor was concerned enough about your career to get you out of Dodge for a couple of years."

She colored and then nodded. To cover her embarrassment, she drank some Coke. It was watery.

"What brought Bambi and Marchand's lapdog down here?"

"I did, I guess."

"You guess?"

She winced mentally. Talking to him was like being back at the damned Academy. She kept forgetting he had been a senior agent with many years of experience.

"I made a routine inquiry. It's . . . it's perhaps not something you want to hear."

He just looked at her, so she described her conversation with Dr. Kellermann.

He nodded when she was finished. He had been coming at her like an interrogator. Now his expression softened. "And that inquiry got back to the Justice Department how, exactly?"

"That, I don't know," she said. The waitress buzzed by and asked if they needed anything else. Kreiss didn't look at her, just shook his head.

"I mean, I guess the Counseling Division notified somebody," she said. "Although I don't know why, exactly. My inquiry concerned your ex-wife, not you." She was trying to keep the conversation going, but there he was, looking at his watch. She had gotten nowhere. "Have you been to this Ramsey Arsenal place?" she asked.

He sat back in his chair and steepled his hands beneath his chin. "Who wants to know?"

"I do. Why did you ask that?"

"Because I don't believe the EA to the deputy AG and her counterpart from Marchand's office came down here to work a missing persons case. I think they came down here to find out what the hell I'm up to. Let me guess: They send you to get close to me?"

The question came so directly and so unexpectedly that Janet couldn't keep her expression from revealing the truth. Kreiss smiled wearily. "They're so damned transparent. They sit around in Washington for years and years, playing all these palace games. They think field people believe their bullshit."

"That's not quite it," she said. "They think there's some kind of bomb-making cell that might be working out of the arsenal. They—"

"*Bombs?*" he said with a snort. "The Bureau doesn't work bombs; ATF works bombs. If they thought that, they'd turn loose a herd of ATF agents in there and find out. This isn't about any goddamned bombs. If those two are here, they're here about me. Which is probably why two Agency CE worker bees were waiting at my cabin when I got back this morning."

She thought she saw an opening. "Got back from where, Mr. Kreiss?"

"That's my business, Agent Carter," he said, ignoring her gambit. "Now, I have a daughter to locate. I don't really think there's anything you can do for me. I appreciate your telling me about the Washington interest, but that's between me and them. If I find my daughter, I'll let you know. If I don't but I find the people responsible for her disappearance, you'll hear about that, too."

"Right," she said. "Heads out on I-Eighty-one."

He smiled, but his eyes remained grim. "It'd be a change from all those billboards," he said.

"Did you really operate alone?" she asked. She surprised herself, asking the question, but she couldn't imagine what that must be like.

He thought about it for a moment. "Not at first, but later, yes. The backup was available, but it was more technical than human. Once I went down a hole after somebody, it was an individual effort."

"But why? Why give away our biggest advantage, our ability to overwhelm a subject, with agents, with data, with surveillance, the whole boat?"

"We weren't sent after 'subjects,' Special Agent. We were only activated to retrieve professional clandestine operatives. That's not a game for groups. Besides, we applied a different theory of pursuit."

"Which was?"

"A single hunter. One-on-one. That made it personal, which gave us a chance to provoke an emotional reaction."

"Why?"

"Emotion distracts. The more emotion, the more distraction. Distraction leads to mistakes. Mistakes lead to capture. This is all news to you, isn't it?"

She shrugged. "I went through basic agent training. I've just never done it at the street level."

"And you probably never will. You're not tough enough."

She felt herself coloring. "That something you *know*, Mr. Kreiss?"

"Yes, it is. For instance, could you shoot someone?"

"Yes. Well, I think so. To save my life. Or another agent's life."

"Sure about that? Could you pull that trigger and blast another human's heart out his back?"

She started to get angry. "Well, the real answer to that is, I don't know. Probably won't know until the time comes to do it, will I?"

He smiled then. "Well, at least you're not stupid. I think we're done here."

He looked at his watch again, which was when she remembered something during the discussion in Farnsworth's office. "The Washington people were pretty specific about a bombing conspiracy. But one of them, the woman, said something I didn't understand. She jumped in Ransom's shit because he failed to deliver a message. I asked, 'What message?' but she wouldn't say, and neither would Ransom."

Kreiss looked away for a moment. "I don't know," he said, finally. "Like she said, Ransom didn't deliver any message."

He pushed his chair back. She couldn't just let him walk away, but she could not figure out a way of prolonging the conversation. She also wanted to be able to contact him again if something developed. "Wait," she said. She fished in her purse and brought out her Bureau-issue pager. "Would you take this?" she said, handing the device across the table. "In case I need to reach you quickly. You know, in case we get news of Lynn."

He cocked his head. "You want me to carry your pager?"

"It's not what you think," she said quickly, too quickly. "I mean, it's not a tracking device or anything. It's just a plain vanilla pager. Please?"

"Sure it is," he said, but then he took it and got up. "You have a good evening, Special Agent Carter. And remember to check out your passenger."

He left a five-dollar bill on the table and walked out. She noticed that all those intelligent-looking men at the bar again moved aside to let him by, moving quickly enough that he didn't have to slow down. Kind of like the Red Sea opening up for Moses, she thought. She took another sip of her Coke, grimaced, and left the bar. Great job, she thought. You co-opted him very nicely. Had him eating out of the palm of your hand, didn't you? You're supposed to be setting up on him, and he has to tell *you* somebody's put a bug on your car? And in compensation for seeing right through you, he's really going to walk around with your pager on his belt. *Jesus*, what had she been thinking?

She went out the front door and walked directly to her Bureau car. She thought about looking for the bug, then decided to take the vehicle directly back to the Roanoke office and let someone from the surveillance squad take a look. It had better not have been Ransom or one of his people planting that thing, she thought, because if it had, this little game was over before it began. She started the car and then just sat there for a moment. Kreiss had touched a nerve when he asked her if she could shoot someone. She was pretty damn sure she could never do that. Even in tactical range training, when the bad guy silhouette popped up right in front of her, she had hesitated. After the final qualifications, the chief instructor had given her a look that spoke volumes. It was probably still in her record. And here was Kreiss, reading her like an open book. She wondered if he was watching her now. She resisted the impulse to look up at the windows. Then she wondered how she was going to break the news to Farnsworth.

"Hold up a minute," Browne McGarand said. It was another cool, clear night, with moonrise not due until around midnight. The arsenal rail gates gleamed dully a hundred yards ahead of them. Jared stopped and looked back at his grandfather, who was scanning the gates and the dark woods around them through a pair of binoculars.

"You see somethin'?" Jared whispered.

"Nope. Just looking to see if anything's different."

"That counter'll tell the tale," Jared said, peering into the nearby trees.

"Unless he got by your little trap and laid down one of his own. He's been using the same gate as we have. Okay, let's go."

When Jared finally read the counter, he swore out loud. Browne looked at it and let out a long sigh.

"Zero it," he ordered.

"And then what? Twenty-six hits means thirteen people been in and out of here. That has to mean cops."

"Or one guy waving his hand twenty-six times across the beam," Browne pointed out. "If he tripped your deadfall, all this means is that he got by it."

"Why not a buncha cops?"

"Because there would have been a mess outside. Grass smashed down, vehicle tracks, cigarette butts. Cops come in a crowd; they leave sign. There was no sign out there. Let's go see your trap."

They found the pile of pipes where Kreiss had left it. Browne got down on all fours and searched the concrete of the street until he found the dried bloodstains where Kreiss had lain stunned after the initial fall. "Here," he said. "This mess got him, but he must have ducked most of it."

"That there's a coupla hunnert pounds a steel," Jared said, looking up at the steam pipe overpass. "I know. I carried it all up there."

Browne was standing back up again, looking up the street, and thinking. "One guy, not thirteen," he mused. "One guy who doesn't belong here, just like we don't belong here. And for some reason, he hasn't brought cops. Now who could that be? I wonder."

"Hell," Jared said. "After this here, he might be back."

"Yes, he might," Browne said. "Or he might be here now, watching us. Let's go exploring tonight. I want a look at these rooftops, see if he's been laying up, watching us."

"What about the girl?" Jared said, lifting the sack of food and water.

"Later. Leave it here in the middle of the street so we don't forget. She'll be out of water by now."

"Rats'll git it," Jared said.

"Chemicals got all the rats twenty years ago," Browne said. "And all the other critters, too. Hasn't been anything living in this area since the place closed down. Come on."

The first thing Kreiss did was to release the dogs. He climbed up on the side of the pen, ignoring the lunging, barking beasts below, and then blew hard on a soundless dog whistle. The dogs shut up immediately and began to run around the pen to get away from the painful noise. Then he tripped the pen's door latch and swung the door open, blowing the whistle hard as he did it. The dogs bolted into the woods and then came back to bark at him. He laid into the whistle again. This time, they yelped and took off into the darkness to do what they liked to do most—hunt. Within minutes, the sound of their baying was coming from over the next hill and diminishing as they went.

He climbed down off the pen, watching to make sure that one of the dogs hadn't doubled back, and then he went to the trailer. The telephone repair van was there, but Jared's truck was gone, which he hoped meant that he and his partner were up at the arsenal, doing whatever they did up there at night. And trying to figure out the number on that counter, and whether or not he or a posse of cops was waiting for them in the industrial area. He needed about an hour to get set up inside and outside the trailer, and then he would wait for Jared to return from his nocturnal operations. Then he would find out what Jared and his friend knew about Lynn and her friends. He dismissed the possibility that they might not know a damn thing.

Browne called it off at around 10:30. They'd looked over several of the buildings and found nothing, although Browne thought that some of the ladder rungs looked scuffed. Someone or thing had obviously tripped the deadfall. There were some stains on the concrete that could have been dried blood, although the darkness made it difficult to tell. The only other hard indication they had was the gate counter. Jared was still perplexed by the deadfall.

"That shoulda got him," he kept saying.

"He might have sensed it coming, or heard something above him and jumped back," Browne pointed out. "Or only part of it got him. If those stains are blood, it didn't do much damage."

Jared could only shake his head. Browne decided that they should stay away from the site during the day on Saturday. Let the whole area cool off. He told Jared to check the power plant while he took the food and water to the girl. Then they'd leave, and come back two hours after sunset on Saturday night. They'd do a quick night-vision sweep, and then Browne would run the hydrogen generator all night while Jared either patrolled the industrial area or hid out on one of the rooftops to spot any intruders. He told Jared to just leave the pipes out in the street, but Jared pointed out that if the security truck came on Saturday, they would see them and wonder what the hell had happened. Browne concurred, and they spent fifteen minutes moving the pipes into an alley. Then they split up, agreeing to meet up at the main gates in twenty minutes. Jared suggested setting one more trap, in case their intruder came back Saturday.

"This time, I got just the thing," he said.

Janet got back to the Roanoke federal building and drove her Bureau car into the security-lock parking area. She parked it near the vehicle-search rack and shut it down. It was Friday night, so the chances of finding one of the surveillance squad techs were slim to none. She was anxious to see if she could find the bug herself, but she knew she should let the pros have a clear field. If there was a bug under there, she'd have to call the RA. And he, of course, would want to know how the meeting had gone. Oh, just wonderful, sir. He told me that he didn't need any help from me and that I was much too inexperienced even to be out on the street by myself without a nanny. He saw through those two Washington wienies and didn't believe a word about the so-called bomb plot. Other than that, we bonded very well and formed an effective and maybe a productive partnership. And I did manage to get him to take my pager along with him.

She leaned back in the seat and tried to think it out. They talked, and then he left to do—what? He'd said earlier that he was busy tonight. Doing what? Going where? To Site R? What would he be doing down at the Ramsey Arsenal on a Friday night? Crashing the Anti-Abortion League's underground bomb makers' happy hour at the abandoned munitions factory? The place was a mothballed military installation, for Chrissakes. Why the hell didn't Farnsworth and his new playmates just send in the army and rake through the place with a few hundred guys and see what's what?

Because Foster and Bellhouser were blowing smoke. Kreiss was right: Their interest was in him, not some outlandish bomb plot and the mysterious message that didn't get delivered. He had ducked her question on that at the bar. There was a lot more going on here than just some simple bomb plot. That was why they didn't want ATF in on it. She exhaled forcefully, trying to clear her mind. For Edwin Kreiss, there was just one point of reality: He was determined to find out what had happened to his daughter. Those oily bastards from headquarters and the AG's office knew that and were trying to leverage his personal tragedy.

She banged the steering wheel in frustration. She literally did not know what to do. Then she remembered Farnsworth's instructions: "Any sign of somebody else in this little game, back out and call me." When in doubt, why not do what the boss says? What a concept, she thought, as she reached for her purse and her building key card.

Jared got back to his trailer just before midnight and parked his pickup next to the telephone company repair van. He went in the back door, as usual. He washed his hands, grabbed a beer out of the refrigerator, slugged it down, thought briefly of taking a quick shower and heading down to Boomers, a local gin mill, and then decided not to. The West Virginia motorcycle crowd usually arrived just about now, and unless some of his own Black Hat buddies were there, he'd probably end up in a one-sided brawl over nothing. He checked his answering machine, and there—thank you, Lord—was a message from Terry Kay. Her husband was out of town until Tuesday and she wanted to know if he would like to come over and make some Saturday-night noises at her place. He grinned, erased the message, and got another beer.

Terry Kay was a thirty-something housewife whom he had met on a service call out on Broward Road. He'd been out there once before, and she'd called in a second service call. Her husband was on the faculty at Virginia Tech and traveled a lot. Terry Kay was about five two, with black hair, teasing brown eyes, and a delectably round body. She had met him at the door wearing a short skirt, a straining cashmere sweater, and a pouty little smile. She was Terry Kay Olson, she said. With an *O*, rounding her lips to show him. The problem was in her husband's study; she thought it might be in the floor jack under the desk. When he had knelt down in front of the desk kneehole to examine the floor jack, Terry Kay had slid into the desk chair on the other side in such a fashion as to reveal what her real problem was all about. They had been together a few times after that, always on the spur of the moment, and always with an element of the danger of being discovered involved. Terry Kay liked it hot, hard, and fast, and Jared was just the guy for that. He had no time for the talkers. The prospect of an entire Saturday night with Terry Kay instead of another endless duty night with his grandfather at the power plant, well, hell, no contest. Besides, he was ready for a break. He finished the beer and decided to have just one more.

He called his grandfather, who always turned his phones off late at night, to leave him an excuse message. To his surprise, Browne answered the phone. Jared swore silently.

"What?" Browne said.

"Uh, I didn't tell you what I set up. In case he comes again and we're not there."

"Yes?"

"I did the Ditch. You know, those steel plates out on the main street? I set them one of them as a pit trap. Took out them center support bars. Anyone walks on that steel, he's goin' down twenty feet into the Ditch. That's all concrete down there. Break his legs, prob'ly. Then we'll have his ass."

"Yeah, that should do it. Which panel?"

"Second up from the power plant. That way, comin' in, he'll walk on several of them, and feel safe. Uh—"

"What, Jared? It's late."

"Tomorrow? I'm gonna be runnin' errands all day—laundry, grocery store, stuff like that? Then this lady friend called me. Wants to get together tomorrow night."

"Jared, we're almost finished with this thing. I need you there tomorrow night."

"I haven't had a night off in a long while," Jared whined. "I'm a young man. I've got my needs, for Chrissakes!" He winced, knowing what was coming next.

"Do not take the Lord's name in vain, young man. This is your father we are avenging, in case you've forgotten."

"He wasn't my father for very long, was he?" Jared said, and again winced, waiting for the explosion. But the old man didn't say anything. That was almost worse.

"Look," Jared said, rushing to fill that ominous silence. "It's just one night. Why don't we leave it all alone, let the place cool off. Let my trap do its job. Go in on Sunday instead, during the day. Change the pattern, screw this guy up, whoever he is."

"Because, for one thing, we're close to finishing. There should be enough copper. The sooner the truck is pressurized, the sooner I can get out of there. And for another, I've got to feed our prisoner."

Jared formed a quick image of Lynn's taut body. "Shit, she's in pretty good shape. She'll survive."

"And how would you know that, Jared?"

"I just mean, one night ain't gonna kill her," Jared said quickly. "Look, I promised this woman I'd go see her, all right? I'm a man, damn it. I've got needs."

There was an angry silence on the line. "You've got a short circuit between your brain and your dick is what you've got," Browne said. "Well, go on, you ungrateful pup. I'll do this thing without you. Go hump your slut. I hope her husband comes home with a shotgun and catches the both of you."

Browne slammed the phone in Jared's ear. Jared put the handset back on up on the wall, sighed, and finished his beer. Hell with him, he thought. He'll get over it. He'll want me back when we catch whoever the hell has been fucking around out there. Old man is half-crazy anyway. He felt a surge of resentment. The old man loved the memory of dead William a whole lot more than he loved Jared. He wondered why. Must have something to do with the way everything turned to shit for him after William left. The cancer. The closing of the arsenal. That shit with his pension. He shook his head. Screw it. It was almost over anyway.

He dropped down into the ratty old recliner and popped the television on. Three fat women in miniskirts were wrestling across a stage while a talk-show host watched with mock alarm and the audience screamed for blood. He smiled as he wondered what kinds of things might be down in that tunnel. The old man himself had probably sent thousands of gallons down there during all those years he'd been working there. Bet there's some regular mutant shit down there by now.

He settled back to watch the fun, when the lights cut out and the television went black.

"What the fuck?" he muttered into the sudden silence, getting up out of his chair. Then he realized he could see, because the orange security light on the power pole was still on. That meant that the power company had not dropped the load. He squinted out the kitchen windows, but there was nothing moving out there in his yard. Or in the dog pen, he realized. He squinted harder but could see no sign of his dogs. Was that pen door shut? They might all three be in their igloos, but usually one was stretched out on the concrete. He tried a light switch in the kitchen, but nothing happened.

He went to the junk drawer by the sink, resurrected a flashlight, and went outside. He checked the power box, where the overhead wires came down to his meter. There was no sign of trouble. Then he called to his dogs, to see if they were stirring. There was no reaction, so he walked over to the pen and found the door slightly ajar. This time, he swore out loud: "How the hell did this happen?" He listened for the sound of baying and rooing in the distance, but the only dog he heard was that little yapper belonging to that crazy old deaf woman who lived a mile down the county road. He was sure he had latched up this gate after feeding them. He was *sure* of it. Then he remembered the sounds he had heard the other night, and he hurried back into the trailer to get a gun. If somebody was out here fucking around, he wanted to be ready for the bastard.

He went back into the bedroom, got the .45 out of the bedside table, checked to make sure it was ready to go, and then went into the tiny utility closet to check the power panel. He cycled all the circuit breakers, but nothing happened; the trailer remained dark. Then he distinctly heard the sound of footsteps crunching outside. He backed carefully out of the utility closet, which was in the hallway leading from the living room–kitchen area back to the bedroom, and squatted down in the doorway of the trailer's second bathroom. The footsteps stopped. It sounded like the bastard was outside, right at the back of the trailer. Amazingly, the next sound he heard was that of a Zippo-type cigarette lighter cap being flipped back and the flame ignited. Bold as brass: The guy was lighting up a goddamned cigarette! Which meant at least one hand was occupied. Jared stood up and moved swiftly down the hallway to the edge of the kitchen, where he popped his head quickly around the corner for a look and then withdrew it. Nothing but the orange glow of the security light in the window; no silhouettes.

He waited. He was beginning to perspire, and his sweat smelled a lot like beer. Maybe he should call his grandfather. The phone was in the kitchen. He would have to go into the kitchen to reach it, but he knew the trailer's squeaky floors would give him away if he tried that. The next sound caught his breath right up in his throat: a shotgun being racked, again, somewhere out behind the trailer. He immediately got down on the floor, really sweating now. *What the fuck is this?* Then footsteps crunching again, but getting quieter, as if the guy was circling the trailer. After hearing the shotgun, Jared was afraid even to put his head up. Sumbitch had let his dogs loose so he'd be free to walk around out there. *Shit!*

Get to the fucking phone, a voice in his head told him. Call the old man. Hell, call 911! He crept around the corner of the entrance to the kitchen, trying to keep the floor from creaking, and reached carefully for the phone, listening very hard for sounds from outside. It was just out of reach. He grabbed a magazine off the table, rolled it up, and then used it to tip the phone off its wall jack, catching it just before it could clatter onto the floor. Then he hit the red button on the handset and heard the welcome sound of ringing. He felt a wave of relief.

"Nine one one. What is your emergency?" a male voice asked.

"Guy's outside my trailer," he whispered as loudly as he dared. "Bastard's got a gun, I need some help out here."

"Sir? I can't hear you, sir? Give me the address please and state the nature of your emergency." The voice sounded unnaturally loud, and he squeezed the earpiece to his head to keep the noise down.

"I need a deputy!" he said. "There's a guy with a fuckin' shotgun outside my trailer. One three eight County Line Road."

"Gee, that's too bad," the voice said, and then, to Jared's horror, there came the booming laugh of a fun-house scary monster. The huge sound reverberated in his ear as he swore and dropped the handset on the floor like a hot potato. The laughter went on, loud, very loud, as he backed away from the phone, waving the .45 around him, like cops did in the movies, until he was back in the hallway again, down on all fours, scrunching backward like a baby toward his bedroom.

Then a sound. Behind him. Some*thing* behind him.

He whirled around, and there was an enormous figure all in black looming over him. It was wearing a hideous mask, and there were bright round mirrors where the eyes should have been. Jared gasped but didn't hesitate. He brought the .45 up and fired, but all that came out was the pop of a primer. Then from the figure came the loudest sound he had ever heard, a roar, a lion's heart-grabbing, ear-pounding roar. The sound was so loud that Jared dropped the useless gun, clapped his hands to his ears, and scooted backward, flailing his way back into the living room, rounding the hallway corner on his hand and knees, scuttling toward the front door, which he never used, the bottom of his jeans warm and wet. There was a nightmarish scramble to get the door unlocked and open as a second roar came down the hallway, louder than the first. He screamed and then tumbled through the doorway, right into a tangle of wet, rubbery strands. It felt like a huge spiderweb. He fought furiously to get away from it, but the more he fought, the tighter it enveloped him, until he could do little more than twitch, and then the horrible mirror-eyed figure was filling the doorway and pointing something at him, something shiny and bright. He knew he shouldn't look at it, but he couldn't help it. There was an incredibly bright flash of purple light and he was just gone.

Kreiss pocketed the retinal disrupter and stripped off the hood and mirror-eyed horror mask. He looked down from the trailer's doorway at the stunned figure of Jared McGarand, balled up in the capture curtain at the side of the steps. Then he stepped past Jared and picked up a garden hose that was attached to the end of the trailer. He turned it on and sprayed water all over Jared and the curtain until all the sticky strands had dissolved, after which, he dragged Jared under the end of the trailer that was perched up on the cinder blocks. He positioned him so that his body was under the trailer, with his head just outside the metal edge of the trailer's frame. He went over to the engine-hoisting A-frame and brought back a large five-ton hydraulic jack stand, which he positioned under the edge of the trailer, about two feet away from Jared's head. He pumped the jack stand until it engaged the bottom edge of the trailer and then actually lifted it. Keeping an eye on Jared's inert form, he got a four-by-four from a stack of junk lumber and battered down the two cinder-block support columns until the trailer was supported entirely on the jack stand. Then he lowered the stand until the bottom of the trailer came to rest just barely on Jared's chest, pinning him firmly to the ground.

He went back inside the trailer. In the kitchen, he got the telephone recorder to play back Jared's calls. There was only one: to that second man. He listened to it twice, then disconnected the telephone dial intercept equipment, the recording device from the kitchen phone, the four inside speakers, and the breaker box diversion switch. He turned the lights back on in the trailer. The television boomed to life and he shut the obnoxious noise down. He gathered up all his equipment and Jared's .45, which he had previously disarmed by unloading it, leaving one shell case with no powder or bullet under the hammer. He spotted Jared's truck keys and wallet on the kitchen table, and he took those, too. Then he went out the back door, climbed up to the roof edge, and retrieved the sound box. He listened for the dogs, but the woods were still quiet.

He took all his equipment and Jared's weapon out to the truck and then took off the disposable blackout suit, under which he had been wearing khaki pants and a plain white shirt. He put on a dark ball cap with an extended brim, which he pulled down low over his face. He put on a pair of blocky black-framed glasses, which had a mildly reflective coating on the outside of the lenses. The glasses were magnifiers, which distorted the image of his own eyes while allowing him to see very well up close. He strapped a voice-distortion box onto his chest, put on a wire headset with a very thin boom mike in front of his lips. He pulled on rubber gloves and retrieved a box-shaped battery lantern from the truck. That's when he noticed the cover on the license plate.

He swore and bent down to examine it. It was not the plate cover that had been there originally, although it was very damn close. It was too new-looking, the metal too bright. He got out a Phillips screwdriver and took off the plate and its cover frame. He separated the plate from the frame and examined the back of the frame. He found the two stub antennas at once. Son of a bitch, he thought. This is a surveillance tag: Based on those antennas, it probably responds to a satellite interrogation signal. He looked down at the rear bumper. Gets its power from the plate light by induction. There were four rubber buttons glued onto the plate mounting to insulate the plate frame from the truck's frame.

He stood up. So he'd missed one. The question now was whether or not he'd been followed here. He didn't think so, but he'd better make sure. Jared wasn't going anywhere.

He slipped into the woods and made a big circle out to the road, where he looked for any signs of vehicles. The road was empty. He knew the plate tag wasn't a device used for following someone down the road. It could give a general location when the satellite transmitted a query signal, but it was not precise enough to do block-by-block surveillance. The question was, then, When would they query it? That would determine how much time he had out here. That tag changed the equation.

He walked back through the woods to where Jared was pinned under the trailer. He hauled over two cinder blocks and made himself a rough bench. He sat down and watched as Jared started to come around. He was whimpering and trying to move, and then he opened his eyes wide when he realized he could *not* move. Kreiss switched on the lantern and pointed it into Jared's face. He switched on the voice-distortion box.

"Can you hear me?" he asked. The box transmitted his words in the softly booming tones of a giant computer-generated voice, atonal and without any accent or inflection.

Jared blinked rapidly in the glare of the lantern's beam and tried to move again, pushing himself sideways as he tried to escape the weight of the trailer. Kreiss knew that Jared's vision would be a purple-rimmed haze for a few minutes. He waited motionless, while Jared figured out where he was. Then Kreiss reached over and lifted the handle of the jack stand one notch, which settled the trailer one-eighth of an inch downward. Jared made a terrified noise and stopped struggling. Both his hands were flat against the bottom of the trailer, as if he were going to hold it up. He had to look up and back over his shoulder even to see Kreiss.

"Can you hear me?" Kreiss asked again.

"Y-yeah!" Jared said, but his voice was little more than a hoarse whisper. "Get it offa me, man. Jesus Christ! Get it offa me. Can't breathe."

Kreiss leaned closer. "About a month ago, three college kids disappeared from Virginia Tech. I have evidence that one of them was at the Ramsey Arsenal. What do you know?"

Jared's expression changed from one of fear to one of suspicion. "Who the fuck are you, man? Why you doin' this?"

"I know you go there," Kreiss said. "You and one other. I've been watching you. I found your traps, the ones on the creek and the other one, remember? Do you want to die here?"

Jared's face hardened. "Don't know what the fuck you're talkin' about." He still had his hands in the push-up position. They were white and trembling. The trailer's frame was making ominous creaking sounds along its full length.

"Sure about that, Jared?" Kreiss said, reaching for the jack handle.

"Don't know—what—you're talking about," Jared gasped. The muscles in his upper arms were straining as he tried to push up against the trailer.

Kreiss lowered the trailer another eighth of an inch, and Jared would have screamed had he been able to muster the breath. He made a sound that was half wheeze, half whimper. His boots were pushing dirt around in an involuntary reflex. The trailer made some more creaking noises.

"Hope this jack has good O-rings, Jared," Kreiss said. "I want to know about the girl. What did you do with the girl?"

Kreiss thought he saw a flash of recognition in Jared's frightened, sweating eyes. He leaned forward, pushing the light right into Jared's red face. Jared was trying desperately to see around the light. Kreiss moved the lantern slightly, allowing Jared to see the outsized eyes staring back at him. His lips moved as he tried to say something. It looked like he was saying, Fuck you.

"What?" Kreiss said. He wiggled the jack handle.

"You're—one—of—*them*, ain't—you?" Jared wheezed. "You—killed—my—old—man. So fuck you!"

Kreiss didn't know what Jared was talking about. "Talk to me, dumbass," he said, "or I'm going to squash you flat, right now!"

"You—do," Jared gasped out, "she—starves!"

Kreiss experienced a flare of pure rage. He'd been right! Lynn must still be alive! He felt his heart racing and his face getting hot. It took every ounce of control he had not to release the jack and mash this creature into a bloody pulp under the trailer. He put the light completely to one side so Jared could see the fire in his own eyes through those enormous lenses. He adjusted the volume of the synthesizer output. "Where—are—you—holding—her?" he asked, enunciating each word very deliberately, letting the anger leak into his own voice.

Jared blinked his eyes to get the sweat out of them as he took a series of short, difficult breaths. Then he pushed up with all his might. He relaxed and then did it again, trying to get a rhythm in it, as if he were trying to rock the trailer off of his chest. All the while he kept mouthing the same thing, Fuck you. Fuck you. He actually got the trailer to move a tiny bit, and then, in a blast of adrenaline, he accentuated the rhythm. Kreiss slammed his gloved hand against the metal side of the trailer, trying to shock Jared into stopping it. But before he could say anything, Jared heaved again and the frame member slid just off the lift point of the jack. Instantly, the jack punched through the flimsy metal bottom pan of the trailer and all ten thousand pounds of the structure crunched down to obliterate Jared McGarand in one grotesque sound. Kreiss stared in fury for a second and then slammed his hand against the trailer again and swore out loud. Then he sat back on his haunches, closed his eyes, and took some deep breaths.

Control, control, *control*, he thought. The dumb son of a bitch had killed himself, and taken with him the one thing Kreiss had to know. But the important thing was that Lynn was *alive*! She was probably being held out there in one of those buildings at the arsenal. He knew there had been at least two men operating out there. Now they were going to be one short. He had to find the other man, and do so before the other man found out about this one.

He opened his eyes and looked down at the trailer. The only sign of what had just happened was the bent handle of the jack, which was sticking out from the dirt under the edge of the trailer like a broken bone. Then he caught the smell of Jared's corpse releasing itself. He thought about what to do. There probably wasn't another jack available, so he couldn't extract the body. And even if he did, he would be faced with a body-disposal problem. He had not intended for Jared to die, although he wasn't exactly sorry. "You do, she starves." Good news and bad news.

He stood up and retrieved the lantern. If he left the scene as it was, Jared would eventually be found. By the second man? Could he set up a trap right here? No. If he did that, he would have to wait until the second man showed up, if ever. Meanwhile, Lynn was locked up somewhere and the clock was ticking, assuming Jared's threat about her starving was real. No, he wasn't going to wait. He would *pursue* the second man. First, sanitize this scene, then go after the bastard. He looked back down at the trailer. He would make it look like Jared had gone under the trailer by himself for some reason, and then the thing had collapsed on him. It would stand a cursory investigation, as long as he set things right. If they got forensics into it, well, that would be another matter.

He looked at his watch. He had to assume that that tag had been tracked, so he didn't have the rest of the night to set the stage here. The taped conversation indicated the other man wouldn't be going back into the arsenal until Saturday night. He would sanitize this scene and then go out to the arsenal and spend Saturday looking for Lynn. But Jared here had already rigged one trap. He could probably spot another one of those, but what if there were others? Alternatively, he could call in that FBI lady: She had clearly offered collaboration. If the FBI believed him, they could flood the industrial area with people and search all the buildings. But what if Lynn wasn't in a building? What if she was hidden in one of those bunkers back out there in the two thousand acres? Or in a cave some-where? And what were the chances of the Bureau believing him? Espe-cially in view of the unholy alliance they apparently had going with Justice and the Agency. Charlie Ransom had been supposed to deliver a message, and now Kreiss thought he knew what that message was: We don't have her. He'd thought of that, of course, but he had kept his end of the bar-gain, and thus he had no reason to think they would not keep theirs. He could, of course, be all wrong about that.

All his instincts told him that he shouldn't trust anyone from Washing-ton, especially in view of the surveillance tag he'd found. That was sweeper gear. Maybe someone up there had decided to move against him *because* Lynn had gone missing. He had known all along that the deal might not survive if circumstances changed in Washington.

Focus, he told himself. Ambush the second man, find out where Lynn is hidden, and then retrieve her.

As he walked back to the truck to get his other gloves, he realized he still had no idea what those two men were doing out there at the arsenal. Then he realized he didn't give a damn. In a little over twenty-four hours, even if he had to pull some guy's limbs off one by one to find out where she was, he would have Lynn back. That was all that mattered. And she had better be unharmed.

She was *alive*!

Janet Carter was still disappointed with herself when she got up on Saturday morning. She had dutifully called Farnsworth the night before to tell him about the bug. There had been an embarrassed silence on the line for a long moment, and then Farnsworth somewhat sheepishly admitted that he had ordered the Roanoke surveillance squad to put a locator device on her car.

"Those Agency people made me nervous," he said. "I'm still not a hun-dred percent sure what the hell they're up to."

"Sir, I know I'm fairly new to street work," she said, "but somebody could have told me."

Farnsworth ducked that one. "I'm curious—how'd you spot it?" he had asked.

"I didn't. I'd proposed the Donaldson-Brown Center at Virginia Tech for the meet. Kreiss saw them put it on. He was watching from his hotel room. He told me."

"He took a room in the hotel where you did the meet?" Farnsworth said with a chuckle. "Told you, that guy is a pro. Just forget about the locator for the time being, Janet. What did you achieve with Kreiss?"

Janet had been unwilling to admit total failure. "He's thinking about it, but he made no commitments. He's focused on finding his daughter."

"Did you get any sense of where he's been looking?"

"Locally. He wouldn't admit to going into the arsenal, but he already knew that was Site R. I think he's been there."

"Based on what evidence?"

"Based on no evidence."

"And that was it?"

She hesitated. "I gave him my pager. Told him if we got anything on his daughter, we might need to get a hold of him."

"He took your pager? It's probably in the river by now."

"I'm not so sure. I'm telling you—he is totally focused on finding his daughter. Why not take the pager? If we get something, he'd want to hear it."

She realized later that Farnsworth hadn't reminded her of the obvious: No one in the Roanoke office was looking for Kreiss's daughter anymore. He did tell her to keep him informed and then hung up. She had gone back down to the parking lot to the Bureau car, where she searched for and found the tracking device. It was a lot bigger than she had expected. She'd pulled it off the frame, and then she went across the parking lot and mounted it on the RA's personal Bureau car. Then she had driven home.

Her Saturday seminar at Virginia Tech began at ten o'clock, after which she grabbed some lunch and then went back to her Bureau car. She found a gas station, where she changed into some outdoor clothes and refueled, then drove south out of Blacksburg through Christiansburg and Ramsey, until she came to the New River bridge on Route 11. From there, according to her map, it was five miles south to the arsenal entrance. She arrived at a little before 2:00 P.M., and discovered that she could not drive directly up to the main gates of the installation because of a concrete-barrel barrier. She got back on Route 11 and spent an hour trying to drive around the arsenal's perimeter, but she got nowhere. Then she went back to the main entrance road, got out, and wrestled one of the barrels out of the way. She drove through, replaced the barrel, and then drove up a short hill through a stand of trees to the main gates, where she came head-to-head with a small white pickup truck that was coming through the gates.

She pulled to one side, stopped, and parked. The pickup came all the way through the gates and stopped. She got out and identified herself to the two young men in the truck, which had a logo on the door proclaiming FEDERAL SECURITY SYSTEMS. One of them had a bad case of acne, while the other sported multiple earrings on both ears and a diseased-looking metal protrusion behind his lower lip. Judas Priest, she thought, this freak has pierced a *tooth*!

She told them she wanted to make a windshield tour of the arsenal. They examined her credentials and badge, then told her that she could not drive onto the reservation without prior authorization. She asked them to get it, and they pointed out it was a Saturday. They went back and forth like this for a few minutes, and then they compromised by letting her park outside the main gates and walk in. They would lock the front gates using the chain and combination lock, but they would give her the combination. They warned her gravely that they would change it the next time they came through. They gave her a map of the complex and told her that the industrial area was not a place she wanted to spend much time walking around in without a mask and gloves. She asked why.

"They made bombs and shit for the Army back there," Pimples said. "Like lots of seriously toxic chemicals, going back to World War One? As in, a long time before there was an EPA or any rules about disposal? We, like, stay in the truck. With the windows up, okay?"

"Don't go, like, kicking up any dust," the pierced beauty said.

"You've just made a tour of the entire facility?"

"Uh, no, not this time," Pierced said, glancing sideways at Pimples. "We did the bunkers. We did the industrial area last time."

"We want, like, to minimize the time in that area?" Pimples said. "That's why we did the bunker fields."

She solemnly thanked them for all their assistance and terrific advice. They waited while she got her FBI windbreaker, some gloves, a flashlight, and a bottle of water out of her car and locked it up. They stared at the sidearm holstered in her shoulder rig. Pierced made a big deal of writing down her name and badge number before they left, and she thanked them again. They waved as they left. She could hear their radio cranking back up as they drove down the access road to the main gate. She stared after the dynamic duo for a moment. Like, if that's security, the arsenal is, like, in trouble, man, she told herself.

Once they were out of sight, she went back and tried the combination. She unlocked the padlock, slid one side of the big chain-link gate back on its wheels, and then brought the car through. She closed the gate but left the heavy padlock unlocked, dangling on its chain. As far as she was concerned, this was a federal reservation and she was federal law. She wasn't about to answer to two postadolescent assholes from some podunk rent-a-cop organization. She put her stuff in the trunk, got back in the car, looked quickly at the map, and drove down the main road toward the industrial area.

Kreiss toyed with the idea of splicing together a voice message from Jared to the other man, in which Jared would agree to meet him at the site Saturday night after all. That way, the other man would get there and wait, which would make it easier for Kreiss to take him. But then he discarded the idea: It would take some specialized equipment and a lot of time to lift Jared's voice and words from the recorder and kludge together a workable message. He would just go out there three hours before sunset and set up in the area of the rail gate. And stay away from the steel plates in the main street of the industrial area, he reminded himself.

In the meantime, he'd learned that the second man was probably a relative. He had looked up the name McGarand in three local phone books and found, in addition to Jared, a B. McGarand located in Blacksburg, with the same phone number intercepted by the recorder. The man had sounded much older. A grandfather? Uncle? The listing gave him an address in Blacksburg, and he toyed with the idea of going over there and starting early. But there was too much he didn't know: Would there be family members? Children? A crowded neighborhood? He didn't want another Millwood, which ordinarily meant that he would have to do a lot of reconnaissance. No, it made more sense to wait for the man at the remote arsenal, in the darkness after sunset. There was always a chance that B. McGarand might call Jared back to convince him to make the rendezvous, but he doubted it: The older man had sounded genuinely angry. That left only one remaining complication: someone discovering Jared's body under the trailer. He thought that unlikely, at least in the next twenty-four hours. The mailbox was up at the head of the dirt road, and unless Mr. B. McGarand went out there himself, Jared would stay put until the buzzards gave him away.

He spent the early afternoon checking the perimeter of his property for any sign that the Agency people had come back. Then he reswept the cabin for delayed-action bugs. He even went over to Micah's to see if he'd seen or heard anyone creeping around, but Micah said he had people watching and that the woods were empty. If anything federal showed up on the roads or in the woods, Micah would give him warning. He checked out his truck again, but he found nothing other than Special Agent Carter's pager on his front seat. It was just a small black box with an LED readout window. He scanned it for a carrier signal, but it was a receive-only device. He started to turn it off, but then he thought about it: He was probably closer to finding Lynn than they were. But Carter might have another warning for him about the Washington contingent. If he'd successfully swept out all the tags, they might try to come find him. He was so close to recovering Lynn that he would do everything in his power to avoid them just now. So he left the pager on but threw it into the glove compartment. That way, if there was a transmitter in it, being in the glove compartment would attenuate the hell out of any signal that little thing could produce. Then he went back to the cabin to prepare for the night's ops.

Janet had driven around the entire Ramsey Arsenal for almost two hours, seeing mostly bunkers, more bunkers, and pine trees. Hundreds of bunkers and thousands of pine trees, to be exact. She had crossed and recrossed a creek that must have transected the entire installation, but that seemed to be the only moving thing on the entire reservation. The steel doors on all the bunkers were rusted and securely locked, with no signs or labels to indicate what had been stored there. By four o'clock, she was back at the industrial area, pausing on a street in front of what looked like the site's power plant. Around her, there were dozens of buildings, sheds, tanks, and towers scattered around a maze of streets, alleys, and rail-siding lines.

Okay, she thought, if this is Site R, it might have made an interesting afternoon exploration for three college kids on a camping expedition. But so what? She could well believe that the EPA had listed this site, based on the fact that nothing green was growing within a hundred yards of any of the buildings. Even with the air conditioning going, she could detect the chemical smell in the air. Could the kids have gone into one these big buildings and locked themselves in by accident? She hoped not—it had been four weeks now, and even with some camping supplies, they would be on their way to mummy status by now. None of the buildings appeared to have windows of any kind, and those doors looked like they had been made to restrain powerful forces. That Clark kid said they were going to break into Site R. Break into. So, it fit. Maybe the thing to do was to call out the Army or whoever owned this mausoleum and search every bloody building. She thought of Edwin Kreiss, pictured him sitting out here on the curb and watching a bunch of soldiers search the buildings. It was not a pretty image. Plus, there was all that bomb-cell theory the Washington people had been talking about.

Hell with it. This was pointless. Her assignment was to get close to Kreiss, see what he was doing. Find a leverage point. And then she thought once more about the mysterious bombers. She looked around again. Now that *would* make sense. The ATF was right: This would be an absolutely perfect place to set up a bomb lab. But they'd been through the place and found nothing. Assuming ATF knew what a bomb lab looked like, she was not likely to find something they had not. So go home, regroup. Get a line on Kreiss. Have a drink. Find a life.

She put the car in gear, went up the street in front of the power plant, turned left, and drove up the hill on what appeared to be the main drag. The car banged noisily over huge steel plates that were spaced every fifty feet or so. She slowed down so as not to hit them so hard, and she was reaching for her purse when the car suddenly banged on something and then tilted down at an impossible angle. She slammed on the brakes, but it was too late—the car was plunging down into a black hole. She started to scream, but the air bag smothered it as the car hit bottom with an enormous crash and all the side windows blew out in a shower of safety glass. The engine shut down at the jolt, and it sounded as if some major components had fallen off the underside of the vehicle.

She took a moment to recover her breath and to get her hands disentangled from the air bag. The skin on her face and wrists stung from the air bag, and the seat belt had damn near cut her into three pieces. She couldn't see much through a cloud of dust, and then she realized she was in darkness, or semidarkness—there was a cone of light coming from above. The windshield was intact but out of its frame. The concrete flanks of what appeared to be an immense tunnel rose up on either side of the car. Her ribs hurt and her shins were bruised, but she didn't think she'd sustained any major injuries. The car, on the other hand, felt very wrong. It was sitting too low upon whatever it had landed. And the angle was odd, with the back significantly lower than the front. She was in some kind of tunnel, and it felt like the tunnel sloped down behind her. She saw the rungs of a ladder embedded into the concrete wall to one side, so at least there was a way out of here.

As she reached to release the seat belt, the damn car moved! Backward. She reflexively stomped down on the brakes, but nothing happened except that the brake pedal went all the way to the fire wall. The car gathered velocity and the cone of light, now in front of her, became fainter as the car rolled down an increasingly steep incline. A horrible scraping and screeching sound came from underneath, as if the car was dragging its drive train or exhaust system over concrete. She tried to turn around in her seat, but the damned belt had tightened a lot and she had to fight hard even to get her neck turned, trying to see behind her, but of course it was pitch-black. She yelled almost involuntarily as the car slid faster, but the noise from underneath was incredible—a cacophony of scraping and grinding metal that drowned out even her thoughts. Then came the giddy sensation of launching off a cliff as the car went airborne for a second before crashing down again on something very hard and then slewing sideways and down into—water!

The vehicle stopped with a whooshing sound and then tilted ominously toward the driver's side, admitting a tidal wave of ice-cold water over the windowsills. Amazingly, the second impact had activated the cabin dome light over her head, and Janet tried to see where she was as she mashed the seat belt button and rose up in the front seat. The black water engulfed the interior in an incredibly few seconds. Outside was utter darkness, but Janet had no choice. She ejected herself through the driver's side window as the car filled completely and went down behind her, sucking at her legs as she scrambled to get away from it.

The water was frigid. It went up her slacks and gripped her bare legs and thighs like an ice pack. Her chest felt squeezed and she had trouble catching her breath as she treaded water in the darkness. Both her arms and her right leg stung from small cuts. She thought she saw the glow of the dome light beneath her, but then it was gone. She splashed around in the darkness for a minute before getting control of her panic and slowing everything down. She regulated her breathing and made her strokes more deliberate. Two huge invisible bubbles burst onto the surface nearby, the second one bringing up the stink of gasoline. She felt one of her shoes go and she kicked off the other one. The Sig in her shoulder rig felt like a brick, but she wasn't ready to get rid of that quite yet. Then she remembered her lifesaving courses and took off her slacks. Treading water with just her feet, she brought the waist of the pants up to her face, zipped the zipper, and closed the button. Then she tied an awkward knot in the bottom of each leg of the pants, took a deep breath, ducked her head, and exhaled into the billowing waist of the slacks. She did this five more times before the pants legs inflated enough to hold her up. She moved between the two puffed-up trouser legs and relaxed, bobbing gently in the utter darkness. She caught the smell of gasoline and oil again as the drowned car began to give up some more of its fluids. She yelped when something large moved under the water, but it was just another air bubble. Then there was only silence.

She tried to determine whether or not she was moving, but, without any visual references, it was impossible to tell. Probably not, she thought—that air bubble had come out of the car from almost directly beneath her. She called out, then listened as her voice reverberated from unseen walls. She knew there were flashlights in the car's trunk, but she had no way of knowing exactly where the car was beneath her, and she was definitely not going to let go of her life preserver in this darkness. From somewhere above her and far away, she heard what sounded like a large piece of sheet metal falling onto concrete. Then silence.

No, not quite silence. There was the sound of falling water somewhere nearby. Not a huge stream, but certainly a steady one. Dropping from a substantial height. She couldn't tell where the sound was coming from. She began dog-paddling in what she hoped was a straight line, and within a minute, she bumped into what felt like a concrete wall. She stopped and felt the surface. It was smooth and slippery, as if covered in moss. She felt her way along the wall for several feet but encountered no other features. The sound of falling water seemed to be louder in this direction, but still far off. Her limbs were beginning to tremble in the cold, and she knew she had to get out of the water before hypothermia set in. She stopped to think. If this is a tunnel, then the opposite side ought to be straight across from this side. She flattened her back against the wall and then shoved away across the surface, her eyes closed as she tried to visualize a tunnel. She paddled for what seemed like forever before her fingertips touched a hard, slippery surface.

She stopped. Had she gone in a circle? No, the falling water sound was coming from a different angle. Or at least she hoped so. She started her search again, this time bumping along the wall to her left, hand over hand, looking for a pipe or a ladder or steps—any protruding feature she could use to get her shivering body out of this water. She realized her chin was in the water, which meant it was time to refill her trouser legs. She bobbed under and exhaled five more times until she got her makeshift water wings back. Then she rested. Which way had she been going? The first tendril of despair wrapped around her gut and she wondered if she was just going to drown down here, alone, in this stygian blackness. She reached out for the wall, but it was gone. A lance of panic shot through her and she kicked out forcefully, only to bang her forehead on the wall. She reached out with both hands, bending forward into the Y of her inflated trousers, and rested again.

Think, she told herself. This is a man-made tunnel complex. The car had been climbing a hill when it had fallen through one of those metal-plate sections. The tunnel obviously conformed to the hill's slope, which meant it ran down to some bottom or collection point. The tunnel had been big enough to accommodate a Crown Vic, so there *had* to be some ladders down here somewhere, some means by which the tunnel could be inspected or cleaned out. All she had to do was find one, then climb up out of the water. If she could get back to the original tunnel, the one under the main drag, she could get back to the point where the car had fallen through. After that—well, first things first.

She continued her hand-over-hand search, stopping to listen and look for light. Finally, she realized she could no longer hear the sound of falling water. For some reason, that worried her, so she reversed course and went back the way she had come, going faster now, since this was wall she had already covered. Her legs were getting numb and her feet weren't there at all. She tried to ignore what this meant and kept going. At last, she heard the falling water again, and this time she headed for that sound. She was heartened when she smelled gasoline again, and she actually felt a slipperiness in the water. This meant she was back to the point where the car had come down from that big tunnel. She stopped and looked up, imagining that she could see light, but she knew it was an illusion. She could see nothing.

She kept going, past the oil slick from the car. The sound of falling water got steadily louder, and then she was in it, a small torrent of cold water dropping down from somewhere above. She stopped and put her head back, grateful to get the oil sheen off her face. Listening to the sound of the water, she realized there was a constant echo. Had she reached the end of this tunnel or pool or whatever it was? She kept going and immediately bumped up against a new wall. She followed it at what seemed like right angles to the direction she had been going for a distance of about twenty feet and then hit another wall, another right turn. So she had been right: This was the end of the cross tunnel. She felt the concrete and noticed that it was slippery underneath the water, although fairly dry above the waterline. She tried to think if this was different from what she had felt originally. It was getting hard to think. It was getting hard to do anything. Her chin was back in the water again, and this time she was less worried about that.

She snapped out of it and refilled the trouser legs again. She remembered the CFR device, but it was gone, probably slipped out when she'd taken her pants off. She sputtered and blew water out of her mouth forcefully just to make a noise and reached out for her wall. Her wall. That was a laugh. And then there was an ominous rumbling sound that originated somewhere way down to her right, a rumbling that seemed to be approaching. Dear God, what is that? she thought as she grabbed for the concrete, which was moving. Moving?

Moving!

No, it was not moving; *she* was moving, toward the rumbling sound. She grabbed again, but there was nothing to grab, just that slippery, mossy surface. She felt her fingernails breaking as she tried to stop herself, not wanting to go toward that awful sound. But go she did, faster as the noise got louder, her hand bouncing off the invisible wall, in a palpable current now, a rush of water as something huge happened in the tunnel. She tried to picture what was going on, but it made no difference if her eyes were open or shut—there was only blackness and that end-of-the-world noise. Then there were eddies and large air bubbles swirling around her bare legs, and a vicious sucking sound somewhere up ahead in the darkness. That's when she really panicked, screaming and kicking to get back up the current, her hands and legs flailing desperately as the water became even more violent. As the sucking sound approached, her hand hit on something metal, a vertical *thing*, which she grabbed for in one final, desperate lunge even as the current turned her whole body horizontal. She hung on with everything she had, grappling frantically to get a second hand on it. Her semi-inflated trousers were swept away in the maelstrom. She closed her eyes and held on with a virtual death grip until she realized the sound was subsiding. She was hanging from the thing she had grabbed. The water was going *away*, was beneath her, as if some giant had opened the drain on the whole system.

She probed with her left hand and found the other stanchion of what felt like a steel ladder. She felt for a rung to set her feet on and then let her head fall against another rung while she got control of her breathing. Below her, the water was subsiding into a rumble of air and noxious bubbles, and then it all went quiet, with the only sound being that of her own breathing. Her legs felt suddenly, terribly exposed in the clammy air. She could hear the falling water again, far to her left, but this time it sounded as if it was falling onto concrete instead of into water. She looked up, but there was only darkness. She began to climb, and after fifteen rungs, she came to what seemed like a ledge. The ladder arms arched up over the edge, so that she could continue climbing and pull herself onto the ledge. It wasn't wide, perhaps two, possibly three feet, but she sensed that it was above the water level. There was even a faint breeze, which felt warmer than the air down here.

She rested for several minutes before she realized she could smell gasoline again. The fumes were strong and seemed to be coming from right below her. The falling water, now to her right as she sat on the ledge, was definitely falling on bare concrete. The tunnel system must be some kind of giant siphon, she thought, remembering that the moss on the wall had been underwater just before the thing emptied itself. The water got to a certain level, and the pressure in the tunnel overcame the pressure in a drain system of some kind and the whole thing dumped. She nodded to herself in the darkness. It was urgently important that she understand how it all worked, because it had been terrifying when the water had started to move. Overcoming panic meant substituting known, man-made things for the huge unknown forces that had taken her down the tunnel.

Fumes, she thought. She wondered if perhaps the car had been washed down to this end of the tunnel, and whether or not it had gone out the drain. If the tunnel was empty, maybe she could get to the trunk and retrieve a flashlight. It meant climbing back down the ladder, and then letting go of the ladder as she groped around the bottom of the tunnel for the car. What if she got lost? Or couldn't find the ladder again? She shivered at that thought, because she knew that the falling water was probably going to refill this thing.

So go now. Do it. You must have light to find your way out of this nightmare.

With a reluctant sigh, she groped around for the ladder arch and got back on it. She climbed down slowly, the rusty rungs hurting her bare feet. Finally, she reached the bottom, discovered water already standing on the floor of the tunnel. She put her back to the ladder and tried to think of a way to lay down a trail of some kind. The smell of gasoline was even stronger, which meant that the carcass of the car was close. She bent down to feel the bottom, and she discovered a crack or seam in the concrete that led directly away from the bottom rung of the ladder. It felt like old asphalt, hard yet soft when she pushed a finger into it. If she kept her hand on that and never let go, she could follow it back to the ladder.

She tried it, going out six feet or so, then following it back to the ladder. It was all she had. She realized her eyes were closed, so she opened them. Better closed, she thought, because at least that way she could construct an image of what this place looked like. She stepped away from the ladder again, crouching down to keep her left hand firmly on the seam. She went all the way across the tunnel floor, through water that was getting deeper again, until she hit the opposite wall. No car. She went back, just to make damn sure she returned to the ladder again, and she did. She came back out to what she sensed was the middle of the tunnel, then said, "Hey!" She listened to the echo of her own voice, and did it again. This time, she thought she detected an object to her left. She called out again, listening like a bat to the reflected sound. She turned ninety degrees to the left, felt behind her for the seam, and then, taking a deep breath and a major leap of faith, stepped out and away from the seam. She had gone ten steps when she realized that in this direction lay the main drain. Was she walking straight toward it?

She called out again and sensed that there was something right in front of her. Was it the end of the tunnel, with some huge hole right in front of her? She began to take baby steps, her hands outstretched, trying not to think of how she would find the seam again, and then her hand ran into the smooth side of the car. She almost wept at the feel of it. She felt around until she could determine that the car was upright, with its nose to her right. She felt back along its side to her left until she came to the trunk. Which she was going to open how? She swore. The trunk latch release was a large button under the driver's side armrest. Would it still work? She worked her way back to the front door and tried to open it, but it was jammed shut. She felt the jagged edges of the glass in the window frame. She put her hand through and then her head and chest, until she could retrieve the passenger-side floor mat. She put that over the window coaming and climbed through, trying not to cut her bare legs. The Sig hung up on something, but then she was through and was able to feel her way across the front seat. She was within six inches of the button when she felt the car begin to move, a slow leaning motion toward its left side. She screamed and scrambled back out. She felt the car settle back down.

She crouched by the window, gasping, and tried to collect her thoughts. Damn thing must be balanced over what—the main drain? Was the drain big enough to suck down the whole car? Apparently not, or it would have already done so, right? Then why had it moved? God, she needed a light, any kind of light. She dared not climb over the hood; if it tilted, she might be thrown down into the drain. She realized the water was up to her midcalves. And rising, she thought.

Think, Janet, think. You need to reach that button. You have to go back in and try it again. She took a deep breath and climbed back into the front seat, being very careful about how quickly she moved. Then she drew the Sig out of its holster, hoping to use it to extend her reach. She knew right where that button was, even in the total darkness. She crept across the front seat, trying to keep her center of gravity over on the passenger side while stretching her arm out as far as it would go. The car didn't move. She stretched another few inches, tapping the Sig under the steering column, then extracting it when it got tangled in limp folds of the deflated air bag. She felt the car just barely sway, at which point she moved two feet back toward the passenger-side window. The car settled. She moved toward the driver's side, carefully, very carefully now, lunged with the Sig, and banged down on where the button ought to be, then scrambled back as the car began to tip again. To her relief, it settled back. She crawled out the window and went to the back of the car. The trunk was still closed.

Was the switch inoperative, or had she just missed it? She crept around the back of the car, keeping her hand on the trunk, until she got to the left-rear corner. She felt with her toes that the concrete dropped off, with the edge just inside the car's flattened rear tire. She erased the image that formed—of some dreadful drop-off into oblivion waiting to swallow up the car and her with it. Have to try again, she thought, and went back to the passenger-side window.

It took her four more tries before she heard the familiar chunking sound of the trunk hatch opening. She climbed out eagerly, reholstered her weapon, and went hand over hand back to the trunk, where she promptly hit her head on the raised hatch. Inside, everything was a total jumble, but at last her fingers found a rubberized flashlight. Crossing mental fingers, she switched it on. The bright white light hurt her eyes, but she didn't mind one bit. She could *see!* She swept the light around her and saw that she was in a large concrete chamber, with the tunnel she had explored over to her left. It appeared to be about twenty feet square. A pool of black water covered the bottom 10 percent of the tunnel. She swept the light over to the walls of the chamber and found the ladder, and saw the ledge above. She could see nothing above that. She turned the light downward, toward the far side of the car, and stopped breathing. The car was perched on the edge of a monstrous hole, which was already filled to the brim with shimmering black water as the tunnel system refilled. There was nothing holding the car back from tipping over into it; only the turbulence around the siphon drain had probably kept it from going over in the first place.

She exhaled nervously and went back into the trunk, where she retrieved a soaking-wet blanket, a second flashlight, the first-aid kit, and a plastic bag of green Chem-Lights. She gathered up her treasures in the blanket and followed the bright white beam of the light back to the ladder. She would climb up to the ledge, which would keep her out of the rising water. If that ledge ran all the way back to the intersection with the main tunnel, she could then follow that back to the point where her car had crashed through the street. Assuming the ledge was high enough for her to get back into the main tunnel.

But first she would have to rest. Her legs barely supported her, and her upper body was beginning to tremble. She knew she was close to exhaustion, as much because of her immersion in the cold water as from the fear, and she wasn't sure she could make the climb back up to the ledge. But even wet, that blanket would be warmer than nothing. She could use the Chem-Lights to provide ambient light and save the flashlight batteries for later. The main thing was that she could *see.* That made up for damn near everything. The water rising to her shaking knees reminded her that she need to get a move on. She walked over to the ladder rungs and began the long climb up.

Browne McGarand pulled his truck through the barrels just after sundown. He was still furious that Jared had gone chasing skirt when they were so close to finishing the hydrogen project. The intruder was an unwanted complication, but Browne wasn't willing to forgo another day. There was pressure in the truck tank now, which meant he was getting close. The target wasn't going anywhere, but if someone was snooping around, his setup here on the arsenal might be in jeopardy. He drove up the entrance road toward the main gates, slowed when he got there, turned off his headlights, and then turned onto the fire-access road as usual. And then he stopped. Something about the main gates was different.

He put the truck into reverse, backed up in the direction of the gates, stopped, set the hand brake, and got out. He left it in reverse so that the glow of the taillights illuminated the guard shed and the rolling chain-link gates. They were closed and locked as usual. No, not locked. That was it. The padlock and its chain were hanging on the center post of the gates. That's what had caught his eye.

Now what the hell? Were those security twerps in there? At night? He stared at the padlock. Then he went up and tested the gates, which, in fact, rolled back when he tugged on them. He walked over to his truck, shut it completely down, and listened for the sound of their truck, which he could usually hear when it was in the industrial area. There was nothing but the sounds of occasional traffic out on Route 11. Had they come in and then left, leaving the place unlocked? Not likely—he had never seen them do that.

The intruder? He got his flashlight and examined the padlock, but there were no signs of damage. Whoever had opened it had known the combination, and that had to mean the security people. Logically, then, they were in there. He looked down the main road inside the arsenal. It led through dense trees for about two miles before getting to the industrial area. The road curved as soon as it got into the trees, so there was no way to see headlights. For that matter, they might be on their way back to the front gate right now, having gotten a late start on their tour, or had trouble with their truck. He decided to go in this way and save himself a long walk up the rail line. He really wished Jared was here.

He went back to his truck, got the food for the girl and his night pack, and brought the stuff through the main gate, where he stashed it out of sight. Then he drove his pickup as quietly as he could back down the access road to the main gate, through the barrels, and out onto Route 11. He drove a mile south on Route 11 to a Waffle House, where he parked his pickup at the far end of the diner's parking lot. Waffle Houses were open twenty-four hours a day, so there were always vehicles in the lot. Then he walked back along Route 11 to the arsenal, waited for all traffic to disappear from sight, and turned back up the main access road. If anyone was in there, listening, and they'd heard his truck, they should now think he had come up to the gates and then gone away.

He walked to the gate and let himself through, rolling the gates shut again as quietly as he could. He hefted his pack and started walking down the side of the main road, stopping every few minutes to listen for any signs of the security truck. He still couldn't believe they were in here at night, but he would have to be careful, especially if they suspected intrusion and were waiting to see if anyone showed up. He thought about going back home, but that would mean admitting Jared had been right about waiting awhile to let the place cool off. He was damned if he was going to wait. He'd do a thorough look around the main street of the industrial area and then—he stopped dead.

Jared had left a trap.

Damnation, he thought. Those fools might have driven their little pickup truck over that steel plate and gone down into the Ditch. Great God, he thought, now that would be a real complication. They'd made their required weekend tour the previous weekend, so they should not have been here yesterday. But there was no getting around that padlock. And that would certainly account for their still being here, dead or injured in their little pickup truck at the deep end of the siphon chamber. He would have to check it out as soon as he went in, and then he might have to move the whole operation the hell out of here, like tonight. If the security patrol failed to report in, there would be a mob of cops and maybe even federal people out here pretty quick. Or would they? It was early Saturday night. He might have twenty-four, thirty-six hours. Appalled, he hurried down the dark road.

Kreiss listened to the vehicle noise on the access road and rechecked his position. There was a small concrete switch house just inside the interior rail-line gate, and he had set up shop behind it. The night was dark and clear, with decent ambient starlight. He planned to take the guy down right after he came through the interior rail gates, probably while he was occupied with looking at the electric-eye counter. When the vehicle noises subsided, he became still and listened hard. The sounds had stopped short of where those two had been parking their truck before. Now what the hell were they—no, not *they* anymore—what was *he* doing?

He waited for fifteen minutes. He was dressed out in the same crawl-suit rig he'd used on his first reconnaissance of this place. He'd thought about bringing Jared's .45, then decided against it. Guns were just extra weight, and he shouldn't need any firearms once he took this guy down, especially since he *knew* there would be only one of them this time. If Jared did show up, Kreiss thought with a grim smile, it would definitely be time to get the hell out of here. He closed his eyes to concentrate on what he was hearing. There were the usual night sounds coming from the forest outside the arsenal fence, but no more man-made sounds. Was this guy taking extra precautions because of the counter hits? Or had he discovered Jared? Kreiss wanted to go up the rail line into the industrial area. He decided instead to wait some more, and he concentrated on the rail line outside the gates, from which direction he expected the man to come. Assuming he hadn't changed his mind and driven away.

Janet crawled to the intersection of the main tunnel and the siphon chamber by the faint green light of a Chem-Light stick, only to discover that the ledge was at least ten feet below the lip of the main tunnel. There were no ladders visible, nor any other apparent way to climb up to the main tunnel. She sighed out loud and lay down on the ledge, wrapping the soggy blanket around her. Below, the water, invisible several feet down, was rising again. She hoped it stayed down there.

After what seemed to her like a few minutes, she looked at her watch and found it was almost 7:00 P.M. Her eyes opened wide—she must have slept for almost two hours. She shivered at the thought: What if she'd rolled off the ledge? The trusty Chem-Light was still going, so she held it out over the siphon chamber, and gasped. There was the water, right there, perhaps two inches below the ledge. The surface was smooth, but the great cold bulk of it felt as if it were compressing the air around her. She switched on the flashlight and pointed it to the left. The water level was almost up to the top of the siphon chamber, which should mean it would not rise all the way up to the ledge. *Should* mean.

She switched off the flashlight, shed the blanket, and got to her hands and knees. Holding the Chem-Light in one hand, she crawled along the ledge, past the intersection with the tunnel up above, looking for any way to get up there. Fifty feet beyond the tunnel intersection, she found a single vertical pipe anchored to the concrete wall. She held up the Chem-Light to try to see where it went, but it simply disappeared into the darkness above. She grabbed it. It was maybe two, three inches in diameter and seemed pretty solid. Could she shinny up this thing? To go where? It wasn't anywhere near the main tunnel.

Just then came the deep rumbling sound she'd heard before as the siphon pressures equalized and the chamber began to drain. She breathed deeply in relief, knowing that the water was going down now. The rumbling grew louder and louder, and the air pressure changed in the chamber, making her ears pop a little. She looked at the pipe again, and had an idea.

Browne stepped into a clump of trees when he got to the edge of the industrial area. The main road from the front entrance went straight down the hill into the main street of the building complex, but there was an open space of perhaps three hundred yards between the tree line and the buildings. He wanted to wait and watch before crossing that space. The buildings were slightly downslope from his position. Their normal way in, along the rail line, came from his left front as he looked down on the complex. The majority of the buildings fell away on a broad hillside that ended up in the tree line above the creek, almost half a mile away.

All those white concrete buildings looked like a ghost town in the starlight, and, of course, that's what it was now, ever since the government had shut it down with no warning. Were those security boys waiting down there, parked in a dark alley? Or had they driven into Jared's trap and were now dead or injured down in the Ditch? He kicked himself mentally for not anticipating that possibility; he should have told Jared to set up a different trap. He well remembered the Ditch. Each of the eight main chemical-processing buildings had a twenty-four-inch emergency drain main leading from the batch machinery to the Ditch, which in reality wasn't a ditch at all, but an enormous concrete dump channel built under the main chemical complex. He remembered the night he had ordered six thousand gallons of nitro-toluene dumped into the Ditch after the night-run manager lost temperature control of the TNT process. That was back before the days of all this environmental sensitivity, when the nation's armaments took clear priority over its air and water quality. The Ditch had been designed to flush any spills into a second tunnel, designed as a siphon chamber, which led to a natural cavern under the hillside. The cavern's depth was shown as being over five hundred feet on the plant's schematics, so where the spill ultimately went was anyone's guess. It went "away," as one of the company's managers had told him when he first started working there.

He concentrated on listening. He closed his eyes and let the night sounds sweep over him, searching for any noises that didn't belong. If those security people had gone into the Ditch, he had, at best, thirty-six hours. Was that enough time to finish pressurizing the truck? If he worked straight through Sunday night, it might be enough. Then he'd drive the truck out those front gates, take it to Jared's place. Then to the target. At least that part of the operation was already planned out.

And what about that girl? Leave her? Take her? He hadn't thought that one through well. She was insurance, but against what? A getaway hostage after he completed the attack? He had a vague plan of taking her to the target with him in the truck. If things went wrong, he would have something to bargain with. At least up to the point where the bomb went off. After that, all those very special agents would probably be in something less than a negotiating mood. The ones who were still alive, he thought, a savage grimace covering his face. He'd decide about the girl when the bomb was finished. And when he saw what, if anything, was down in the Ditch. He listened some more.

After half an hour, Kreiss decided to move up into the industrial area. Either the guy wasn't coming after all or he was coming in a different way. It had sounded as if that vehicle had stopped closer to the main gates. They had been operating on the arsenal for some time; it was conceivable they had cracked the front gates. He would move as quickly as he could up to the main complex of buildings, beyond the place where the pipe trap had been set, and climb a building. That would give him a vantage point from which to listen. This time he would stay off the main street and move through the alley behind the largest buildings. He checked his packs and then moved out, walking quietly but quickly up the rail line, past the first switch points, toward the cluster of the biggest buildings.

When he got into the alley behind the first building, he stopped to listen. There was some creaking and cracking going on as the buildings and the nests of pipes above the street contracted in the cool night air. The by-now-familiar chemical smell rose up from between his feet. He flattened himself against the still-warm concrete side of the building and crept around to the front corner to take a look-and-listen into the main street. He tried to remember where the main road from the front gates entered the complex, but then he realized he didn't know. He did remember a building that looked like it was more administrative than industrial. Probably the front road led to that building first. The main street appeared to be empty. It was much darker between the buildings, and he wished he had his cone set up. He could barely make out the big steel

plates interspersed at regular intervals along the dusty white concrete surface of the street. Except—were his eyes playing tricks on him? Down
toward the power plant, about a third of the way up the hill in his direction, it looked like there was a massive hole in the street. He remembered
Jared's description of the trap: second plate up from the power plant. Step
on it and fall twenty feet into some ditch. Break your legs. Sweet people.
Who are holding Lynn. Well, he was holding one of *them* now, wasn't he,
in a manner of speaking?

He slipped back away from the corner and found the ladder to the roof.
He stopped to listen again, then climbed swiftly to the top of the building.
This roof was flat and covered in graveled asphalt. There were steel ventilator cowlings spaced randomly around the top, with guy wires
anchored into the asphalt. He made his way through the maze of guy
wires to the front of the building, rigged the cone, and conducted a quick
acoustic sweep of the main street. There was a single, very faint sound
coming from the direction of the opened plate in the street, some hundred yards away. He concentrated but could not identify it. Whatever it
was, it was steady and not rhythmic. He repositioned the cone, but he still
could not identify the noise. He sat back, then trained the cone in the
opposite direction, hoping to catch the second man coming up from the
rail line. But there was nothing. He swung the cone back toward the hole
in the street. The noise was still there. What the hell was that? If it's not a
human walking up the street, he told himself, disregard it and focus on
finding bad guy number two. And Lynn. He dismantled the cone and put
the apparatus back into his pack.

Janet stood at the bottom of the siphon chamber, listening to the water
drip off the concrete walls, while she worked the section of pipe back and
forth in a slow, tedious arc. She had waited for the water to drain out
before going down the ladder and then coming all the way back to the
pipe, which terminated, as she had hoped, on the bottom of the chamber.
Some kind of instrument conduit, she assumed. She'd torn the bottom of
it loose from its rusted bracket and was now attempting to break off a section by causing metal fatigue. It appeared to be working. Each arc was
getting a little bigger. She was working by the light of her trusty Chem-
Light, which was plenty bright down here in the absolute darkness of the
tunnels. She actually felt as if she knew her way around the siphon chamber now, and the cold, clammy air swirling around her bare legs felt
almost normal. Better air than water, she realized. The Sig was still hang-

ing in her shoulder rig, and she giggled when she thought what she must look like, half-naked, with that big automatic under her arm. Despite its awkwardness, she was glad she still had it. Because if this worked, and *if* she got out of here, there was no telling what or who was up there in the ammunition plant complex.

She felt water around her ankles as the siphon chamber began to fill again, and she realized she did not have all night. She pushed harder on the pipe, putting her legs into it now, and felt it giving way somewhere up there in the darkness. Then suddenly, the weight of it was in her hands and she jumped back as she lost control of it. The pipe clattered to the floor of the chamber with a huge ringing noise of steel on concrete, barely missing her feet. She picked one end up and found she was able to move it. She put the end down and took a rough measurement. About twenty feet. Good. It had broken off about where she had intended it to. Now, she had to get it to the ladder, haul it up to the ledge, and then see if she could position it somehow on the ledge and shinny up the damn thing to the main tunnel. The trick was going to be locking the bottom end into something long enough for her to make the climb. She began dragging the pipe down the siphon chamber toward the ladder rungs.

Browne heard something. He opened his eyes, shocked to realize he'd been drifting off to sleep. What was that noise? He leaned forward and cupped his good ear, straining to hear it again. He swore silently to himself. His hearing was fair, for his age, but it was still the product of too many years working in an industrial environment without hearing protection. He looked at his watch; it was a little after 8:00 P.M. He was wasting time; he *had* to get going. He decided to wait another fifteen minutes, see if he heard the noise again, and, if not, go down to the main street and check out the plates. If nothing appeared to have happened, he would go to the power plant, start up the hydrogen generator, and get to work.

Kreiss got down off the roof as quietly as he could and began moving from building to building, staying in the deepest shadows and hugging the still-warm concrete sides of the structures. He stopped at each corner, listening carefully but hearing nothing but a slight breeze blowing down the empty street. When he was two buildings away from the power plant, he did hear something, a metallic scraping noise, like a pipe being dragged on concrete. He was about to go up on top of the nearest building to set up the cone, when he realized the noise was coming from the street—no, from that big hole in the street. He stopped where he was, and he heard it again. Definitely coming from that big hole, where the steel plate appeared to be missing. The guy must have come in the front entrance after all and was now doing something down below the street. Or had he fallen into his own trap?

Kreiss moved quickly to the edge of the hole. He listened. Definitely something going on, but at a distance—the sound was echoing up what had to be a tunnel, a really big tunnel, under the street. He pointed his finger light into the hole but could barely see the bottom. Something glinted back at him—glass? He heard another noise, coming up out of the tunnel from the direction of the power plant. His light illuminated the ladder rungs embedded into the concrete on one side. He decided to go down. He went over to the far edge of the hole, pointed the tiny light down, and saw where hinges had been ripped out of the concrete right above the ladder. He thought about that for a minute. A man walking out onto one of those big steel plates and falling through because the support was gone wouldn't have ripped the hinges off. He moved quickly around the perimeter of the hole until he found what he was looking for: scrape marks on the down-street edge of the hole, and a tire scuff on the concrete behind the edge. A vehicle had fallen through, not a human. He pointed his tiny finger light down the hole again. So where was it?

He listened again, but there were no more sounds. He went back to the ladder and climbed over the edge and started down. A cool draft eased by his face as he went down, one rung at a time, with pauses to listen. When he finally reached bottom he stepped away from the ladder and crunched on what turned out to be auto glass, a whole carpet of it, covering two large fluid stains. The steel plate was lying upward from the point of impact. The next thing he noticed was the slope: The tunnel angled down toward the power plant at a surprisingly steep angle. He turned on his finger light and examined the floor. Heavy metal scrape marks went down the tunnel. He stood up. The tunnel was big, its floor perhaps twenty feet down from street level and a bit over fifteen feet square. It smelled of chemicals and stagnant water, and the stream of air coming up from the bottom was heavy with moisture.

Okay. A vehicle had crashed through the plate, hit bottom here, and then slid down the tunnel into—what? Another metallic clank, this one much clearer than when he had been up on the street. From way down there, in the darkness. He stepped away from all the broken glass as carefully as he could and started down the tunnel, using the finger light in spot mode to sweep the tunnel floor directly in front of him. The farther he went, the steeper it seemed to get, until he had to walk alongside the tunnel wall with one hand on the sloping concrete sides to keep from sliding down out of control.

After going a couple of hundred feet, he thought he saw a faint green glow ahead. The smell of water was much stronger, and then he could hear falling water. He kept going, taking smaller steps now to maintain his balance. He must be near or even past that power plant building. The green glow was getting stronger, and then he realized he was listening to someone working, working hard, huffing and puffing a little, doing something with a metal object. Based on the shape of the glow, the tunnel he was in ended up fifty feet ahead, and whatever was going on was happening below the level of the tunnel. He decided to get down flat and crawl the rest of the way. As he got closer to the edge, he suddenly froze in place as a swaying snakelike object rose over the edge, backlit by the green glow from below. In silhouette, it looked like a large cobra.

Browne crept down the main street from the administration building, keeping to the sides of the buildings and walking as quietly as he could. He stopped frequently to listen for any more of the mysterious sounds, but there was only the normal nighttime silence. He'd probably imagined it. When he got to the hole in the street where the plate had been, he shook his head. He broke out his flashlight and played it around the edges of the hole, saw the scrapes and scuffs on the concrete, and then pointed the light straight down into the Ditch. He saw the steel plate, which had been torn off its hinges. The carpet of smashed automobile glass gleamed back at him, and he saw the drag marks leading down toward the power plant. He swore softly. They'd driven right into it. Right into it. He snapped the light off and sat back on his haunches. There was a ladder of steel rungs built into the concrete wall. Should he go down there? Confirm what had happened? What if they were still alive? He thought he heard distant noises from the tunnel, but then decided he was imagining things. He went to the up-slope side of the hole and shined the light as far down the tunnel as he could, but there was nothing visible. That cinched it: Their vehicle was probably down in the siphon chamber, so even if they'd survived the fall, they were gone. Really gone. Swallowed up by the endless caverns under the arsenal.

He stood up, wishing the plate had not come off its hinges. But it had and that was that. The clock was running. As of Monday morning, at the latest, someone would be in here looking for those two, and he would have to be gone. He and the truck would have to be gone. Time to get to the power plant. He had between twenty-four and thirty-six hours to finish pressurizing the truck. He grabbed the girl's supply bag and headed down the street.

The water was swelling in the siphon chamber below as Janet struggled with the heavy pipe, determined not to drop it. It had taken nearly all her strength to pull the damn thing up to the ledge, and now she was trying to stand it on end to reach the main tunnel up above. She had braced herself against the rusty steel ladder rails that arched onto the ledge and was trying to direct the swaying end of the pipe to the lip of the tunnel above. She had to get it perfectly vertical or it would simply roll off and she'd have to start again, and the Chem-Light gave off barely enough light. She was very conscious of how narrow the ledge was, and that her strength was waning. She had to get this right, then summon the strength to shinny up the pipe.

She landed the top of the pipe on the concrete above, made sure it would stay there, and then took a moment to rest. She kept one hand on the pipe as she closed her eyes and slumped against the ladder rails, breathing deeply. Her legs were getting cold again as the clammy air rose up to the ledge, driven by the rising water. She *had* to get out of here. Then she felt the pipe moving and she jumped to steady it. She stood up too quickly, lost her balance, and reflexively grabbed the pipe with both hands to steady herself and keep from falling over backward into the siphon chamber. But of course the pipe wasn't attached to anything, and she cried out as she realized she was going to fall. And then the pipe stopped moving. She swayed out over the edge for a terrifying instant, recovered her footing, and hugged the pipe. She looked up. There in the green glow from the Chem-Light, a frightening black-masked face was looking down at her. Blazing dark eyes framed in a horizontal oval of black fabric like a ninja.

Kreiss?

"Special Agent Carter," Kreiss said. "What in hell are you doing down there?"

She closed her eyes and started to laugh, although, even to herself, she sounded more than a little hysterical.

Browne had the hydrogen generator up and running in fifteen minutes. As pressure built in the retort, he went through the connecting door to

the truck. He found the battery charger on the front seat and pulled in an extension cord from the power strip so that he could begin to trickle-charge the truck's two batteries. The propane truck had been parked here for a long time now, and he wanted it ready to go when the time came to get out of here. The pressure gauge on the main propane tank had been shut off to prevent leakage. He cracked it open and saw it registered forty-two pounds. For weeks, it had registered nothing at all, but now that there was pressure, it ought to build faster. The copper supply should be sufficient; if not, he would tear down some of the circuit breakers in the turbogenerator hall. But he knew what his major constraint was now: time.

He went back into the control room and saw that the low-pressure pump had activated, sending pure warm hydrogen gas into the propane truck's tank. The retort was boiling happily away, with a chunk of copper still visible. He could hear the *putt-putt* sound of the little diesel generator next door. Nothing to do now but wait for this lump of copper to dissolve, switch over to the second one, flush this retort, and reload it. Once he began using the larger pump, the volume transfer would be smaller, but he might be able to get it up to three, maybe four hundred pounds before he had to get out of here. It all depended on when an alarm would be raised about the missing security truck. He was almost certain it would not be until Monday, or at least no one would come here until Monday. If he could generate straight through until early Monday morning, he might make his target pressure. He wondered if he could stay awake. Maybe Jared would come in Sunday morning. He checked to see that the row of five-gallon nitric-acid bottles were full, felt the side of the retort to make sure it wasn't getting too hot, and then picked up the food sack.

He switched off the single lightbulb and slipped out the door into the loading bay. The street was just outside. He stood there, letting his eyes adjust to the darkness and listening for any unusual sounds. When the street became visible as a pale avenue in the darkness, he walked out toward the nitro building. He still had not decided what to do with the girl. If it came to it, though, he could just leave her.

Kreiss steadied the pipe while the semihysterical woman down below on the ledge caught her breath. His question had not been rhetorical: What in hell was she doing down here? Or at the arsenal, for that matter? He looked over the side of the tunnel lip again. There was a Chem-Light sitting on the ledge next to her. She appeared to be in her underwear, except

for her blouse and her gun rig. He called her name. She looked up, her face a pale mask of fatigue.

"I have a rope. Have you looked for any other way up?"

"There isn't one." Her voice was dull. She was right on the edge of exhaustion.

"All right. I'm going to tie a harness into the rope and pass it down. Put it on, wrap your legs around the pipe, and I'll pull you up."

She nodded but said nothing. She still had a death grip on the pipe. He sensed there was water rising in the chamber beneath the ledge. He peeled the Velcro straps off the packs he wore on his chest and back and then shrugged out of the harness. He pulled the fifty-foot-long coil of six-hundred-pound test nylon line out of the backpack, then attached it to the harness using a bowline. He passed it down to her on the ledge. He had to instruct her on how to put on the harness, and her movements were unnaturally slow. Finally, she had it. He felt the lip of the main tunnel and found a segment of steel angle iron. Good. No concrete edges to fray the rope.

"Wrap your ankles and hands around the pipe," he ordered. "Pull yourself up like an inchworm, hands, then ankles. If the pipe starts to go, let it go, and hold on to the rope."

She didn't say anything. He said it all again and made her acknowledge. She did, but her voice was faint. The harness would hold her, but it would help a lot if she could assist. He wasn't sure if he was strong enough to pull up a deadweight, not with the way this tunnel sloped. He was very glad he'd worn the rubber-soled boots.

"Okay," he said. "Go."

He had wrapped the end of the rope around his hips and belayed it once over his right shoulder. Each time he felt the tension come out of the rope, he pulled gently by backing up the tunnel. He concentrated on the rope, feeling what she was doing: arm pull, hold, ankles, up, grip, arm pull, hold. He kept a steady tension on the rope, more to steady the pipe than to pull her up. He was alert for a slip, because that's what he expected. She'd get halfway up and then run out of steam. He was ten feet back from the edge now, keeping the tension on.

"Talk to me," he said. "Where are you?"

"A third," she gasped.

"Rest when you get halfway up," he said. "Grip with hands and feet. Relax the rest of your body. Deep breathing. The pipe and I have your weight."

She didn't say anything.

"Acknowledge," he barked.

"All right. Halfway. Rest. Got it."

He kept the tension steady, waiting until he felt her ankles grip and then pulling a little to help her. He had to save his own energy in case she slipped.

"Halfway," she said. "But I think I'm done."

"Grip with hands and feet. Deep breathing for two minutes."

"Okay."

He tried to picture her as he held tension in the line. The pipe at about an eighty-degree angle, almost straight up and down. She was halfway up the pipe, trying not to spin around on it. That would be a real disaster, because he couldn't get her over the lip if she was upside down. His own footing wasn't that solid as he backed uphill. He tried to think of another way to help her, but the pipe was about all they had. He looked around the tunnel for a projection to anchor the rope, but there wasn't anything visible in the green gloom.

"The pipe stable?"

"So far," she said.

"Can you climb any farther?"

"I don't think so," she said. "I'm afraid of rolling on the pipe."

"All right," he said. "You concentrate on staying upright. I'm going to pull you the rest of the way. Ready?"

"Very," she said. Good, he thought. A little wise crack meant she was still in charge of herself. He set his feet, took a second belaying turn around his shoulders, and then pulled back with his arms and his upper body, leaning backward at the same time. The rope moved. She must be 140, 150, he thought, and I'm losing some pull to friction at the lip. He stepped backward, leaning way back so as not to lose ground. Then he felt a slight slack in the line, which meant she was trying to help, probably using her legs on the pipe.

It took him fifteen minutes of excruciatingly slow effort to get her to the lip of the tunnel, and even then, it wasn't over. In fact, this was the dangerous bit, because he had to get her over the lip, and her whole body would add to the friction.

"Put your hands up on the top of the pipe," he called. He watched as she slid first one hand and then the other up to the top of the pipe, about four feet above the lip.

"Lock them there. When I tell you, try a chin-up."

"You've got . . . to be . . . shitting me," she said. It sounded as if talking was almost beyond her.

"No. Do it. The pipe's going to go when I pull again. Push off from it, let it go, and then let me do the rest. Now, deep breathing. One minute."

"Me or you?" she asked.

He almost grinned, except that his whole body was straining to hold her at the top of the pipe. But she had a point. He went into deep breathing, his body bent backward, his knees bent and flexing like springs, his hands hurting where he had the rope, the palms of his gloves actually hot with the pressure.

"Okay, stand by," he said. He needed her help to get some of her body weight over the lip. "One long pull on the top of the pipe, both hands, then let it go when it moves and stretch out with your arms, like you're diving. Then we're done."

She didn't answer and her head was hanging down. Her hands were visibly white at the top of the pipe. She was done. He had to go *now*.

"Pull!" he commanded. "Pull! Pull!"

He saw her try to pull up on the top of the pipe, and he laid into it, pulling back with all his might, jerking her right off the pipe, which disappeared behind her. Her head, chest, and arms came over the lip, but the heavy part, her lower body, stuck on the edge, just above her waist. Her head was down and he couldn't see her face. The pipe clanged softly once on something hard and then fell into some water down behind her. She was a deadweight now and he couldn't move her. He felt the line start to go backward, small tugs toward oblivion down the inclined floor of the tunnel.

Browne went through the procedure at the steel door into the nitro building, telling her to put the blindfold on, to turn around. He waited, unlocked the door, and shone the flashlight at her. She was right where she was supposed to be. He stepped in and put the food sack down. He didn't bother to pick up the remnants of the last food delivery. The big room smelled fusty and stale, and the stink of sewage was more pronounced.

"It's almost over," he said, not knowing exactly what he meant by that. She did not reply. He thought for a moment. "I have two options," he said. "I can either take you with me as a hostage or I can simply leave you here when I go."

"Take me where?" she asked.

It was the first time she'd spoken to him, and it surprised him. Her tone of voice was not what he had expected. There was a matter-of-fact-ness about it, almost a tone of defiance. His first reaction was not to tell her anything, but then, why not? She would either be with him in the truck, suitably subdued, or she'd be mewed up here in this concrete build-ing. No, wait: He couldn't leave her alive—if they searched the whole facility for the missing security people, they'd search all the buildings. So he either had to kill her outright or take her with him. He considered the prospect of simply pulling his gun and killing her right now. He shook his head. No, he'd kept her as a bargaining chip, and that's what he would use her for. He rehearsed his mantra: The two boys killed themselves when they stumbled into Jared's traps. They should not have been here. The flash flood had killed them.

"To Washington," he said.

She didn't answer at first, then coughed and asked him why.

"With a hydrogen bomb."

"Bullshit," she said immediately. "No individual can make a hydrogen bomb."

"Oh yes I can. In fact, I have."

"It takes a fission device to trigger a hydrogen bomb," she said. "You're going to tell me you made one of those, too?"

"I have made a hydrogen bomb," he said. "But it's not what you think."

"I'll bet," she said. "What do you want with me?"

"You are insurance. A hostage, in case things go wrong. I don't want to have to kill you."

"If you're taking a hydrogen bomb to Washington, you're going to kill lots of people; I'm supposed to believe you'll spare me?"

"That's different," he said, shining the light around the interior of the building, making sure she wasn't trying to distract him from something she'd set up. "This is personal, and as far as I'm concerned, this is an entirely legitimate target. You blundered into this by accident, which is the only reason you're still alive."

"Where's the other one?" she asked. "The one who likes to see me naked."

Browne felt a surge of anger. Goddamn Jared. "Don't worry about him anymore. His part in this is over, and he won't be going along. *I'm* taking the bomb to Washington."

"I'm hungry," she said. "Why don't you go away, so I can eat."

"I will. But we may be leaving soon. If you cooperate—no, if you sim-ply go quietly—I'll let you live. If I get cornered, I'm going to trade them you for me. If you won't go along, I'll put you out in one of the underground field magazines to starve. If you tell me one thing and then do another, I'll be forced to cut your throat and pitch you out onto the highway. Think about it."

He switched off the flashlight and closed the steel door. Outside, the night was still, only the faint buzz of insects from the nearby woods breaking the silence. He looked at his watch; he had a few minutes before the retort needed changing. He turned away from the power plant and walked up the main street for three blocks, turned right, and then walked down a side street and across an open area of hard-packed dirt to a low-lying concrete bunker that was fenced off from the rest of the industrial area. A dusty sign on the bunker read MERCURY-CONTAMINATED SOIL; KEEP OUT. He looked around and then opened a walk-through gate in the chain-link fence and went through. There were two doors to the bunker: one big enough to admit a front-loader tractor, and the man-sized door on the other end. He unlocked and stepped through the man-sized door, closing it behind him. He switched on his flashlight and checked through his getaway stash. Not even Jared knew about this. This was one of two supply caches he had prepositioned in the arsenal. This one was for his run to Washington. There was some cash, a gun, a fuel-delivery manifest from the company whose name was on the truck, and some spare clothes in a duffel bag. He gathered up what he needed and closed the bunker up again. Then he walked back down the dark side street to the power plant and went inside. He wished Jared was here to patrol against intruders, although there was no sign that anyone was out there.

Janet felt the rope slipping back and tried to do something, anything, but her muscles were turning to jelly and she couldn't force another ounce of strength into her hands. Her hips and bare legs were dangling out over the ledge and the lip of the tunnel was cutting into her middle. Her attempt to hoist herself on the end of the pipe had been a total failure. Despite the cold air in the tunnel complex, her eyes were stinging with sweat and she was having trouble breathing. The rope slipped back another quarter of an inch. He was losing it. She was going to fall, all the way back down into the black waters of the siphon chamber.

"Can you lift your legs?" Kreiss called through clenched teeth. His voice was filled with strain.

"W-what?" she asked stupidly. She'd heard him just fine, but she didn't understand.

"Your legs—can you lift a leg, get a knee over the edge?"

She tried, but the angle was wrong. Her knee just bumped into the hard concrete, and she crumpled back against the unforgiving wall. Her center of gravity was still below the lip. She knew she did not have the upper-body strength simply to pull herself over. But the effort gave her an idea, a last, desperate idea.

"Wait," she said, bending in the middle so as to get her feet flat against the wall.

"I can't wait. I can't hold you much longer."

"I'm going to straighten out my legs and then lock them," she said, hoping Kreiss would understand. She didn't have energy to waste talking. "As the rope comes back. Then I'll walk up the wall as far as I can. I think I can do it."

"Go ahead. Tell me when you're ready and I'll give you some slack."

"Just hold what you've got," she said. She didn't want him to let go, he was losing ground as it was. As the rope jerked back toward her in quarter-inch increments, she planted her feet firmly against the concrete and willed her legs to straighten. She would have a very brief window of opportunity to fly-walk up the wall, after which, she'd just have to let go and drop. She wondered how deep the water was down in the big chamber. She forced her eyes open but could not turn her head. Her left leg straightened out first, then her right. She locked her knees, but she was still bent like a hairpin. She would have to let him lose more ground.

She gripped the rope as hard as she could with her left hand and then quickly wrapped the loose end around her right wrist three times. She took up the strain on her right wrist and hand and did the same thing with her left, then equalized it. It gave her a much more solid grip, but then she realized she was losing circulation in both hands. Mistake. Big mistake, but there was nothing to be done. She had to go for it, and do it now, angle or no angle. She slid her right foot up two inches, and then her left foot. It was hard, very hard, and her arms felt like they were coming out of their sockets. She did it again.

"Hold it if you can," she grunted.

Kreiss didn't answer from up above, but the rope seemed to steady. She moved her feet again, getting the hang of it now, slide up, hold, slide the other one, hold. Breathe, she told herself; don't forget to breathe. She was hanging out like a wind surfer now, forcing herself to ignore the void below her and concentrating on the green swatch of concrete right in front of her. Her wrists were burning, but her hands were beyond sensation. She slid her feet again and realized she was close, only about two feet to go before they would reach the edge. Slide, plant it, bend the knee a little bit as her back flattened some more, slide the other one, plant it. Hold the fucking rope, Kreiss. Don't let go; don't let go. Thank God I'm barefoot. . . . And then she felt the toes of her right foot engage the smooth steel edge of the lip. She twisted slightly on the rope, trying to get a foot over. Wrong move. She had to get the other foot up to the edge first, then simply pull herself vertical hand over hand.

But she couldn't go hand over hand because her hands were completely wrapped in the coils of the rope, and paralyzed besides. She gave a small cry of total frustration and looked up the slope at Kreiss, who was barely visible except for the oval patch of white that was his face. She tried to speak, but her lungs were bursting with the effort of holding herself at the edge, her feet pinned against the cold steel, while the rest of her body hung out like some mountain climber enjoying the view. She was trapped, unable to go either up or back without falling. One of them had to do something, but she didn't know what.

Then Kreiss moved. He must have seen her predicament, because he locked his feet and leaned back hard, up the slope of the tunnel, so that the angle of the rope straightened. It produced a small tug, but it was enough to bring her body more vertical. He leaned some more, until his back was at nearly the same angle as hers, and suddenly she was able to simply step up into the tunnel. Kreiss sat down hard with a grunt as Janet sunk first to her knees and then down onto her shins and forearms. She resisted a temptation to kiss the concrete. Then Kreiss was there, unwrapping her hands and wrists.

"Nice outfit," he said softly. "Especially the Sig."

"They told us never to lose our weapon," she replied, unable to straighten up. Every muscle in her abdomen was cramping and her ribs hurt where the harness had cut into her. Then she began to shake as the adrenaline crashed. He turned her around gently so that she was sitting and wrapped his arms around her chest, below her breasts. She shook like a leaf, uncontrollably, and then realized she had urinated.

"It's okay," he whispered. "It's okay. Perfectly natural. Doesn't mean a thing. You're safe. Say it for me. I'm safe. *Say* it."

Her teeth were chattering and she was absolutely mortified, but he kept saying it until finally she got the words out.

"Now, deep breathing," he ordered, still holding her from behind, his legs alongside hers, both of them sitting on the cold concrete as if in a luge. He was warm and she was very cold, but there was nothing erotic or sexy about it. The hard ridges and buckles on his crawl suit felt odd, and she was keenly aware of her wet underpants. She suddenly just wanted to go to sleep until it all went away. Then he was lifting her up, strong, large hands under her armpits, dragging her gently to her feet.

"Come on," he said. "One more climb."

An hour and a half later, he pulled his truck alongside the curb in front of her town house. She had slept in the passenger seat of his truck the whole way into Roanoke, waking only when he asked her for directions. He had covered her up with one of his coats as soon as she got into the truck, and she'd gone down like a stone. Now she appeared to be disoriented, rubbing her eyes and looking out the windows.

"This it?" he asked.

"Yes," she replied, stifling a yawn. He had taken off his hood and gloves so as not to attract attention on the road. Her eyes were hollow with fatigue. "Thank you," she said. "For everything."

"I'll get the coat back later," he said. "That was a Bureau car that went down the hole, right? You've still got your own wheels?"

"Yes. My car's at the office. I suppose I have a significant paperwork exercise ahead of me."

He didn't reply. He was ready for her to get out of the car, but she wasn't moving. He was about to get out and go open her door, when she asked him why he had been crawling around the arsenal.

He'd been anticipating that question. "Because of what that kid said, that my daughter and her friends had gone to explore that place."

"But at night?"

"During the day, as much as half of a search area is in shadow. It's easy to miss something. I have a night-vision pack built into this crawl suit. At night, especially when there's ambient starlight or moonlight, almost everything's visible."

She hesitated, then asked, "You think she's there?"

He took a deep breath. He was not going to tell them anything, not until he'd had a chance to hunt down the second man and find out what he needed to know. Plus, now there was the little matter of the Jared pancake flattened under his trailer. "It's the best lead I've got," he said. "I've been there twice before. I'm going to look until I find something or satisfy myself that there's no trace of them."

"We could help with that, especially after—"

"No. I mean, I know I can't stop you, but you can't help without alerting those Washington people. Their focus is on me. That story about a bomb cell is probably bullshit. Besides, I can do this better alone. And it's not like I'm hunting someone you're hunting."

She missed the gibe. "My boss is suspicious about those people, too," she said. "But it's the weekend. He can't raise anybody in Washington in his chain of command to check them out."

He just looked at her, sitting bare-assed, exhausted, and bedraggled in the front seat of his pickup truck. She had the grace to be embarrassed. If it hadn't been semidark, he would have sworn she was blushing.

"I can still do it better than anyone you'd send." And, he thought, you'd bring a crowd, and then my one lead to Lynn might vanish.

"Okay, okay, so I'm not in your league," she said. "But surely we have people who are."

"I doubt that, Special Agent Carter," he said softly. "With the Bureau these days, it seems to be a question of quantity over quality. But in any event, I'm going back there tonight. I have nothing else to do. If I do find something concrete, I'll tell you. Would you like an escort to your door?"

"I can manage, I think." She glanced down at her bare legs. "Hopefully, my neighbors won't see me in this . . . outfit."

"They'd probably find mine even more interesting. I'd appreciate it if you'd find a way to leave me out of your report on how you got out of the tunnel. Maybe just say you climbed out."

She thought about that for a moment. "If you wish, yes, I can do that," she said finally. "But you did save my life. That should go into the record."

"Not my record, Carter. My record is closed. I'm just a father searching for his missing daughter now. Nothing more."

She kept looking at him in the dark. "What was the message that Ransom failed to deliver?" she asked.

He looked down at the white oval of her face. Even in the truck, he was taller than she was. He couldn't tell her, not without explaining the whole story. And if he was right about the message, he had little time to lose. He had to find Lynn before they decided to send someone.

"I can't tell you that," he said finally.

"Funny, that's what Ransom said when I asked him."

"Well, there you go," he said.

She hesitated, as if to see whether or not he would say anything else, but then she got out.

11

Janet was sitting in her kitchen, having a badly needed cup of strong coffee, when the phone rang. It was 7:30 on Sunday morning. To her surprise, it was Ransom on the line.

"So, Special Agent, where you been?"

"You miss me, Ransom?"

"Yeah, well, after a fashion, yes. Your surveillance folks found our little device on Mr. Farnsworth's car. Very funny, Special Agent. Not too bright, maybe, but very funny."

"I thought that was one of *our* bugs?"

"Let's just say that your boss was, um, agreeable to the notion of tracking your Bu car. Which is why I'm calling, actually: Where is said Bu car?"

"In China, somewhere, probably," she said. "Look, I'm just getting my first caffeine of the day. Can this discussion possibly wait?"

"You got more of that coffee around? Because I'm sittin' outside your town house right now, as a matter of fact, and we do need to talk. Sooner rather than later, as they say in the coolest circles of government."

"Oh, for God's sake, yeah, sure, all right."

She got another mug down from the cabinet and then went to let him in. He was wearing a short-sleeved black shirt, khaki trousers, wraparound black sunglasses, some expensive-looking boots, and a green windbreaker with a Boy Scouts of America logo. She realized she was naked under her bathrobe, so she tugged the strings around her waist.

He sat down in the kitchen, took off his sunglasses, and waited while she fixed him a cup of coffee.

"Nice touch," she said, pointing to the Boy Scout logo.

"Well, you know," he said. "We brave, loyal, thrifty, all that good shit."

"Right. So, what's the big deal about my Bu car on a Sunday morning?" she said.

"Where is said Bu car, again?" he asked, raising his eyebrows. "You say something about China?" She hesitated for a moment, then told him what had happened, including the fact that she had been rescued by Edwin Kreiss.

He whistled softly when he heard about Kreiss. "And this was basically at night? You sayin' Kreiss was creepin' the arsenal at night? *Last* night?"

She explained what Kreiss had said about night-vision equipment. He nodded, then asked her precisely when Kreiss had pulled her out of the tunnel.

"It was night. I guess I don't remember," she said. "Elevenish, I'd guess."

He said, "Uh-huh," and then looked around the kitchen as if seeing it for the first time. "You got plans for your Sunday, Special Agent?" he asked.

"Uh—"

"Now you do. Let me suggest you take that coffee upstairs, make yourself functional, if not too beautiful, and then I need to take you somewhere to show you somethin'."

She just looked at him.

"It shows better than it tells, Special Agent," he said. "And time, believe it or not, time is a-wastin'. Help if I say please?"

"Is this something I should call my boss about first?" she asked.

"No-o," he said. " 'Cause he's gonna ask you a million questions, and you won't have any answers whatsoever until I do my show-and-tell. Please?"

Half an hour later, they were leaving Roanoke and headed south on I-81 in his car. He was explaining how they had tagged Edwin Kreiss's truck.

"*Four* bugs? Whatever happened to the notion of the private citizen?"

"*Private citizen?*" Ransom said, slapping the wheel, as if she'd told a wonderful joke. "No such thing in America anymore. First of all, nobody's a citizen anymore."

Uh-oh, she thought. Brother Ransom has a hobbyhorse. She decided to go with it anyway. "Okay, I'll bite."

"Simple," he said. "We are what bureaucracies call us. Like law enforcement? We're 'subjects.' Pollsters? We're 'respondents.' Marketin' people? We're 'focus groups.' Politicians? We're 'voters.' Your Internet provider? You're a 'subscriber.' IRS? We're 'clients.' Clients—do you love it? Ain't no more 'citizens.' Last time there were citizens, in the way you mean it, Special Agent, was during the Roman Empire. And maybe the French Revolution, when they got into their guillotine phase."

She decided to shut up. She was in no shape for a philosophy discussion. The coffee was wearing off and she was still very tired. She settled back in the seat and let him drive. Forty minutes later, they were stopping next to Jared's lonely driveway. Ransom turned in and parked the car out of sight of the county road. They walked down the dirt lane to the trailer, which Janet could see was sitting at an odd angle.

"This here is the residence of one Jared McGarand," Ransom announced.

"What's that smell?" Janet asked, although she already had an idea.

"That is most likely related to brother Jared's final movement, if you get my meanin'. Under that end of the trailer, right there, where you see the jack handle stickin' out. And if you check that vehicle over there, you'll find one very expensive tag tracker on the back bumper."

"The one you put on Kreiss's truck?"

"That very one, Special Agent."

"Okay, I give up. I assume there's a dead guy under there. What the hell's going on?"

"I was kinda hopin' you could shed some light on that, seein' as you had a meet with subject Edwin Kreiss, apparently right before he came out here and wasted this McGarand individual. Least I think he did. I haven't gone and lifted that trailer up to make sure, but my nose is makin' an educated guess here, okay?"

"About a dead body, or Kreiss doing it?"

He grinned and shrugged.

"I got nowhere at that meeting," she said. "I've already told Farnsworth this. Sort of."

"Sort of?"

"Well, I didn't want to admit that Kreiss just totally blew me off, but that's what he did. He also saw through the proposition that we might work together, you know, to catch the mysterious bomb makers while I helped him find his daughter."

"Saw through it?"

"He said it was bullshit. That Washington being here was about him."

"Oh boy," Ransom said, blowing out a long sigh. "Here we go again."

"It was bullshit? Bellhouser and Foster's bit about the bomb makers?"

"Truth?" Ransom said. "I don't have any idea. My assignment was to cooperate with those two. And to keep my bosses at the Agency informed as to what was goin' down."

"So if those two were conspiring to trap Kreiss in something, you wouldn't necessarily know about it?"

Ransom hesitated before answering. "Lemme just say that if somebody managed to take Ed Kreiss off the boards, my bosses wouldn't exactly complain, okay?"

"Son of a bitch," Janet said softly. "Kreiss was right."

"What's his state of mind?"

She snorted. "I offered to help him find his daughter, you know, as cover for the other little project. He said he didn't need any help. He also said that if he found out someone had done something to his daughter, he'd catch them and put their severed heads out on pikes on the interstate."

"That's our Edwin," Ransom said admiringly. "Might be interestin' to see if this dude under there is headless. On the other hand," he said, squatting down on his haunches, "might not be much left to mount." He stood back up. "Now, you had this meetin' with Kreiss, he told you to buzz off, then you go home and he comes out here and does a number on this vic here, which we assume is subject Jared McGarand. You go to your weekend class the next mornin', then you go to the arsenal for your little field trip, and you encounter—Edwin Kreiss. Tell you anythin'?"

"That Kreiss might have found out something from this Jared whatever about his daughter. And that something points back to the arsenal. But—"

Ransom cocked his head. "Yeah, but what?"

"But Kreiss already suspected the kids had gone to the arsenal."

"At night? Why's he there at night? And didn't he tell you he was goin' back there last night? After he rescued you?"

"Yes." The smell was making her queasy. She backed away from the mess under the trailer. "Can we go now? And shouldn't we call in local law?"

"Yes, we can go now and, no, we will not call in local law. *We* don't have anythin' to do with local law and local homicides, seein' as we *never* operate domestically."

"Oh, right," she said sarcastically. "But we do."

"And you would tell the cops what, exactly?"

"That there's a dead body under this trailer."

"Which you found out about in the company of an Agency person, while investigatin' a missin' persons case that you've already shipped off to Washington. How you feel about explainin' why you did all that to the local sha-reef? Or to Farnsworth?"

She took a deep breath. Ransom was right.

"See, here's the thing, Special Agent. I buy Kreiss goin' out to that arsenal durin' the day, snoopin' around, lookin' for Injun signs. But if he's goin' at night, he's goin' co-vert. Wearin' some of those nifty black ninja threads, right? . . . Thought so. My guess is that he found *this* guy out there at the arsenal."

"If he did, and followed him back here, it was because he figured this guy might know what happened to his daughter. He'd want to talk to him, not snuff him."

"Unless he wouldn't talk. Not the first guy who wouldn't talk to Edwin Kreiss had him an accident of some kind."

"You think this was an accident?" she asked.

"Yeah. The kind that happens when folks resist a peace officer in the performance of his sworn duties, you know?"

"But how do you know it's Kreiss who did this?"

"Because our tracker tag is on that piece-a-shit pickup truck over there, maybe?"

"Who the hell knows? He could have discovered that while he was shopping at the local Piggly Wiggly and put it on the nearest vehicle. I mean, based on evidence, that's as reasonable an explanation as all this supposition you're coming up with. Those security people weren't alarmed about anything, and I sure as hell didn't see any signs of anything going on out there."

"From your tunnel perspective," he said. He closed his eyes and rubbed his face with both hands.

"Look," she said. "You think there's been a murder here. Okay, homicide is serious shit. I want to go back and update my boss, if only because I'm going to have to explain the loss of that car anyway. You come with me. I'll tell my sad tale: you tell yours. Let's see what Farnsworth thinks. Let *him* fold in your supervisors. If he wants to tell local law, I'm sure he'll give you guys a chance to cobble up a story to keep your precious Agency out of the picture. That's the right way to go here. You know that."

"Tell him today, Sunday."

"He's spoiled a couple of mine."

"And in the meantime, where the hell is Kreiss?"

"Who cares, as long as he's out looking for his daughter. Hell, he might find her. But I think all you guys are wrong about this arsenal bomb thing. That place is just a ghost town with a street-maintenance problem."

Kreiss awoke at dawn on Sunday to the sounds of a single mockingbird rousing the forest from atop a telephone pole. He had to think for a moment to remember where he was and why. His muscles were stiff and sore from his exertions down in that tunnel. He had come in from the direction of the rail spur rather than the main entrance because of what Carter had said about the security people. He'd climbed the rail gates and bedded down in one of the explosives filling sheds three blocks away from the main street.

He slipped out of his crawl suit and performed morning ablutions with a wet rag. Then he reversed the suit, exposing a tan-and-green camouflage color scheme to replace the all-black night-ops coloration. He reset the packs on his chest and back, put away the hood in favor of a camo watch cap, grabbed his staff, and headed for the back alleys behind the complex of larger buildings.

If he was correct about the vehicle noises last night, the second man had come and gone without entering the arsenal. Kreiss was now counting on him to show up this morning, because this was when the second man would expect Jared to show up. Since Jared would not be showing up anywhere ever again, the second man would have to make a decision: go to Jared's place to find out why, or come into the arsenal to do whatever they had been doing here. Kreiss planned to listen for sounds of a vehicle and ambush the second man. If no vehicle showed up, he would initiate a thorough door-to-door search. In the meantime, he needed to find a good spot to lay up.

He walked quietly down a side street between two large concrete buildings. The sun wasn't up yet, but there was plenty of light. As usual, there were no birds or other animals stirring in the main complex. He stopped when he got to the main street. To his right, going up the hill, were the two rows of large buildings. To his left were two more large buildings, an open space of road and rail lines, and then the big power plant building at the end of the street. The big hole out in the street where Carter had lost her bureau car was still there. He didn't relish her prospects for a happy and productive Monday morning. Whatever that tunnel complex was all about, he thought, it must dip down at a much steeper angle than the street. He checked his watch: It was still about forty-five minutes until actual sunrise. The air was still, and he could hear the occasional hum of a car way out on Route 11. He ought to be able to hear any vehicle that approached the arsenal perimeter. He decided to look around for a few minutes before setting up.

He walked down toward the power plant. It looked to be about five stories high, with one main stack attached to the back side. There were two huge combustion exhaust ducts slanting into the base of the stack, which indicated at least two boilers inside. The turbo generator hall, half the size of the main building, was on the right side, as evidenced by a fenced bank of transformers and high-tension cables that spread out into the complex. There appeared to be skylights at the very top of the boiler hall, but otherwise no windows. There was an admin building of some kind on the left side. Between the admin building and the boiler hall were four very large garage doors, one of which had a rail spur leading under it. There was a single man-sized door to the right of the garage doors, and he tried the handle, but it was locked. The metal garage doors had a row of one-foot-square wire-mesh-reinforced windows at head height, and Kreiss checked them, trying to see in. He could see nothing through most of them because of all the dust and grime, but he was surprised to see through the final one that there was a truck parked inside. It was a tanker truck of some kind. The cab was not as big as a semi, but bigger than a pickup truck, and a green-and-white tank was built onto the body of the truck. Other than that, he couldn't make out any more details. He wondered why a truck would still be here, since the other buildings had all been stripped down when the plant was closed. Probably wouldn't start when they closed the place and they'd just left it. Typical Army solution.

He walked all the way around the power plant, noting the four huge pipes rising out of the ground that brought water from somewhere to cool the condensers under the generating hall. There was probably an impoundment up on that creek somewhere. There were some steel doors at the back of the plant, but they were windowless and also locked. The stack was easily three hundred feet high, with a line of rusting steel rungs leading all the way to the top. He stopped to listen, and he thought he heard a mechanical noise of some kind, but it was very faint. It was probably far away. Behind the plant building was a tank farm. There were two large fuel-oil tanks, with a rail spur running between them and a pump-manifold house at one end. A third, medium-sized tank was labeled BOILER FEED WATER, a fourth POTABLE WATER. Built into a fenced enclosure were two somewhat smaller tanks, each encased in concrete and plastered with danger signs warning of acid. One tank was labeled H_2NO_3, the other H_2SO_4. Nitric acid and sulfuric acid, Kreiss realized. Why would these tanks be back here? he wondered. Because the pumps were in the power plant?

He continued around the building, sizing it up as a hiding place for a prisoner and then dismissing it: The rooms in the plant would be too big to provide an effective containment place. He came back around to the front of the plant and looked back up the street. Carter's crash hole was about three blocks up, just past the first two large buildings. The street appeared to disappear up the hill into a tunnel of overhead pipes and their support frames. He had a sudden feeling that his mission was hopeless: there were too many buildings, too many hiding places out here. No matter what that guy Jared had said, all this place offered was the silence of the tomb.

There was a sound behind him and he whirled around. A tall, black-bearded man was standing in the man-sized doorway of the power plant, holding a large revolver down at his side. The man had violent dark eyes and a face out of a Civil War photograph. They stared at each other for a fraction of a second, and then the man raised the pistol and fired from a distance of thirty feet.

Kreiss actually felt the bullet go past his head even as the stunning boom of the Ruger hit his ears, but he was already moving, sideways and then sprinting up the street, opening the distance with some broken-field running, knowing that the big .44 became almost useless as the range opened. He zigged close to the corner of the first building and felt, rather than heard, a blast of concrete above his head. He jinked left, using the stick to balance his running, aware that the big man behind him was not firing indiscriminately. He wanted to turn his face, if just for an instant, to see if the shooter was pursuing him, but he knew better than to slow down now, and then he was careening around the far corner of the first building into a side alley. He stopped just past the corner, spun around, and then ran full tilt back across the main street into the alley on the other side. This should surprise the shooter and also give him a chance to look left, but the man was gone, the power plant door closed.

Kreiss stopped short in the alley, close to the corner, catching his breath, and wishing now that he'd brought a gun. To do what? he asked himself. Stand there and shoot it out with that guy? The man appeared the next instant at the end of the alley in which Kreiss was standing. Kreiss jumped sideways as the .44 let go again, this time feeling a tug on his backpack. He bolted out into the main street, but with all those concrete walls, there was nowhere to hide, and the big man was pretty handy with that cannon. He ran left into the next side street, considered climbing a building, realized that would be a trap, and then saw the shooter's shadow coming down the back alley. He jumped back into the main street and went left, all those blank concrete walls, nowhere to hide, up the hill again, zigzagging as he ran, and then three more rounds came after him in quick succession, all low, but too close to have been anything but carefully aimed, building-steadied shots. He came to the big hole in the street and didn't hesitate. He scrambled, almost fell down the steel rungs into the darkness of the big tunnel, dropping the stick and retrieving it again when he got down. Knowing that the shooter would be there in a few seconds, he made no attempt to be quiet as he scrambled down the steep slope of the tunnel, using his stick for balance, until he was well down into the darkness. Then he got flat and waited.

After a minute, he could hear the sounds of falling water over the thudding of his heart. Getting too old for this shit, he thought. Five shots. One left if the guy kept coming and didn't stop to reload. And yet, so far, this guy hadn't done anything amateurish with that .44, so: safe to bet he'd be reloading. Why not? If he knew anything about the tunnel, he would know Kreiss wasn't going anywhere. Kreiss began to slide farther back down the tunnel, keeping his eyes on that cone of sunlight coming down through the hole in the street. When he thought he saw a change in the light, he stopped and grabbed the hooked end of his stick and twisted it sharply. It made a sound identical to a semiautomatic pistol's slide coming forward to the cocked and locked position.

Kreiss waited. Assuming that sound had carried back up the tunnel, the other guy now had a decision to make. The moment he started down into the tunnel, he'd be silhouetted in that cone of light and be fair game for the gun he's just heard Kreiss cock. Kreiss listened to his own breathing and then started sliding back down the tunnel some more, keeping very quiet this time. The tunnel grew increasingly steeper, until Kreiss was glad he was full length and not trying to stay upright like the last time. At last he felt the tips of his boots go over the ledge, at which point he stopped moving and then rolled off the centerline of the tunnel toward the side wall to his right.

He was now flattened on the concrete about three hundred feet from the cone of light. As he remembered from his little adventure with Carter, the ledge was below, and below that was a big water chamber. He pointed his finger over the edge and down, flicked it on, and thought he could see water. He had the rope in his pack; all he needed now was an attachment point up here, and then he could safely slip over the wall and down into the water below if he had to. He began exploring with his fingers, first to the right and then to the left, until he found a crumble of loose concrete underneath the steel coaming of the lip. He used the steel point of the stick to dig at that until he had enough room to slip the end of the rope under the coaming and knot it to the stick. He let the rest of the rope out and over the ledge behind him.

Still no sign of his pursuer, so his rack-the-slide noise must have done its job. As it had a couple of times before, he remembered. Having something that could make a noise like a gun was almost as useful as having the gun. But now the guy might still put his gun hand into the hole and empty it down the tunnel in his direction just for grins. He secured the stick, then clipped his chest harness onto the rope and went over the edge until just his head was up over the edge, with the rope belayed around his right hip, leg, and ankle for support. He did this just in time. A volley of random rounds banged down the tunnel at him, the big slugs ricocheting in every direction, with some coming back at him off the tunnel wall behind him and whacking into the concrete above the ledge. It was noisy and scary, but in the end, harmless gunfire, and Kreiss just hung on his rope, his head down now, waiting for it to end.

Now it would be stalemate, he thought. The guy knew he couldn't safely climb down into the tunnel without risking being shot. And he had probably just used up all his carry ammo. Kreiss's only regret was that he hadn't been able to get the jump on this bastard, because this was definitely the man he wanted to interrogate. On the other hand, if this was the other McGarand—and there was a definite resemblance to Jared there—Kreiss knew where he lived. It would have been better out here, but he'd go wherever he had to in order to find out what the hell they'd done with Lynn. He waited, his eyes just back up over the edge, watching the cone of light. Unseen water below him coiled in the siphon chamber, compressing the air around him.

Browne stood up in the street and jammed the empty gun into his waistband. The barrel was still warm from that last volley. He looked down at the line of steel rungs illuminated in the growing sunlight and knew he couldn't go down there. That guy was a cool customer, running like that and never once turning around. So it would be just like him to be sitting down there in the Ditch, drawing a bead on the ladder and waiting for Browne to screw up. Well, he wasn't going to do the intruder any favors. He looked both ways and then walked up the street to where they had piled the pipes from Jared's trap. He dragged three of them back to the hole in the street, where he placed them quietly over the hole nearest the ladder rungs. Then he got three more pipes and extended the grid, keeping the spacing at about eight inches. Then he rolled two of the heaviest pipes down and laid them crosswise on the grid, anchoring it. Now when the guy tried to crawl out of the tunnel, he'd find a barrier. He couldn't move those pipes without making noise, and Browne would hear him. Meanwhile, he had work to do.

He went back to the power plant and hooked up the electric motor on the leftmost garage door to the power strip and raised the door, revealing the truck. He had worked all night. He was sweaty and dirty and sand-eye-tired. He had brought the hydrogen pressure in the truck to just over four hundred psi. It wasn't the five hundred he wanted, but it would do, it would do. With those security guards going down the hole and now this lone ranger trapped down in the Ditch, the arsenal was blown as a base of operations. He had to get out of here and begin the final phase, Jared or no Jared. Goddamn kid, going through life with his brain hard-wired to his pecker. There'd be police and probably feds all over this place by morning, but by then he'd be on his way. Jared had painted the truck in the color scheme of a Washington fuel company a month ago from a picture Browne had given him, so now it was just a question of getting it out of here with no witnesses. He wasn't really worried about Washington; he knew those smug bastards would never see this one coming.

He had hauled the generator out of the boiler housing an hour before dawn and gathered all the other equipment into the control room with the retort. The generator fuel gauge showed it was one-quarter full. Good. Then he had gone around the boiler hall and sealed as many air-inlet points as he could find, including all the boiler fuel-burner registers and the ventilation-duct outlets. It had taken him nearly two hours, but he'd kept the retort chugging, letting the high-pressure gas pump squeeze the last bit of hydrogen into the propane truck. Then he closed all the interior doors in the power plant except the one leading from the control room into the boiler hall. He went to the truck, cranked it, and breathed a sigh of relief when it started up. Now all he had to worry about were the tires, but they seemed to be all right. He drove the truck out through the big door and stopped it out in the street, letting its diesel warm up. He checked the pipe grid on the hole in the street, but nothing had been disturbed. Good. Then he had an idea.

He went back into the control room, where he reloaded his .44 from a box of ammo he kept there. Then he ran a last flush on the retorts and added all the copper he had left in the room. He disconnected the pump piping from the tops of the retorts and recharged them with a double load of nitric acid. The reactions began immediately and he decided to add one more jug of water to their cooling tubs. Then he walked to the door, took one last look around, closed it, and duct-taped it. He went into the garage bay and taped the door leading back into the control room. He left the generator running and hit the switch to lower the heavy garage door. Then he ducked out under the descending door and went to the truck. The generator would run out of fuel in a little while, but there was now no more need for electrical power. Double-loaded like that, those retorts would generate hydrogen for hours, gradually filling the interior of the power plant with an increasingly explosive mixture of air and hydrogen. When the feds came knocking, there ought to be at least one smoker. That's all it would take.

He walked back up the street to the hole, knelt down, poked the .44 through the grid of pipes, and emptied it into the tunnel again. The noise down there must be terrific, he thought with satisfaction. And, hell, he might have gotten lucky. Then he went back to the truck and drove it up the hill to the tank farm behind the power plant. Leaving it running, he got out and went to the big valve-manifold station by the acid tanks. He searched around until he found a crow's-foot, a four-foot-long metal bar with three rakelike studs that just fit inside the rim of a big valve wheel and allowed a man to apply the full leverage of his body to turning the wheel. He closed the small valve that had supplied nitric acid to the reservoir bottles in the power plant's water-testing room. From this elevation, the acid would dump into the Ditch above the hole in the street. The other two valves, leading to the main explosive-manufacturing buildings, were already closed. He then opened the much larger dump valve marked EMERGENCY—DITCH. He heard a rumble in an eight-inch-pipe that disappeared into the ground ten feet from the tank. There was probably twenty thousand gallons of the acid left in the tank, which was now going to rain down into the Ditch, onto the intruder and the remains of the security guards. He considered waiting to see if the guy would pop up out of the street, but he imagined he could almost hear cops at the front gate. Every instinct was telling him to get the hell out of there. He got back in the truck and drove it out behind the power plant to the road that led back to the bunker farm and the arsenal's rear gate.

"Okay, so what the hell's been going on around here?" Farnsworth growled when he sat down at the head of the conference table. It was 11:20, and he was dressed in his church clothes. He was visibly angry.

Ransom and Janet sat on opposite sides of the table near Farnsworth, while two squad supervisors sat down at the other end. They, too, did not look pleased to have been brought in on a Sunday morning. A black triangular teleconferencing speaker sat in the middle of the table, nearest Farnsworth. After listening to Janet's preliminary report, Farnsworth had set up a conference call with Foster at his home in McLean, Virginia, and Foster was now on the line.

Janet began by recounting her meeting with Kreiss in Blacksburg, leaving out the part where Kreiss had expressed suspicion about what Bellhouser and Foster were really up to. Then she detailed her expedition to the Ramsey Arsenal. When she was finished, there was an embarrassed silence at the table. The two squad supervisors were looking studiously at their notebooks, undoubtedly very glad she did not work for them.

"All right," Foster said from the speaker. "Let me get this straight: Kreiss essentially told you he wasn't interested in any cooperative efforts, and that he already knew what Site R was?"

"That's right," Janet said. She had also left out his threat to put heads on pikes.

"Which means he *was* the headless horseman, then," Farnsworth said.

"I'd expect so," Janet said.

"How did he react to the theory that there was a bomb cell operating at the arsenal?" Foster asked.

"He thought it unlikely," Janet said, casting a quick glance at Ransom. She'd forgotten she'd told him what Kreiss had said. Ransom was looking straight ahead and saying nothing.

"And the next time you saw him, he was pulling you out of some tunnel?"

"That's correct," she said.

"And he said nothing about what he was doing there? Or how he happened to stumble on the fact that you were trapped down in the tunnel?"

She hesitated a half beat. "He said he was looking for his daughter. Which is what he said he would be doing. At our meeting in Blacksburg."

"How did he know you were in the tunnel?"

"He heard the noise I was making. I was trying to position a pipe to climb out. He was up on the street above, came to see what was making the noise."

"Did he think it was his daughter?"

Janet started to answer but then stopped. What had Kreiss been thinking when he heard the noises?

Random leaned forward to address the speaker. "This is Ransom," he said. "I think Kreiss *was* looking for his daughter, but there's another angle here." He went on to describe bugging Kreiss's truck, and his discovery of what he suspected was a dead body under a trailer, and the fact that his bug had ended up on the vehicle belonging to one Jared McGarand, whom he further suspected was the corpse under the trailer.

"So Kreiss had been there?" Foster asked. "That what you're saying?"

"That's correct." Janet noticed that Ransom's street speech was long gone. Enter the professional, she thought. Maybe gofer, maybe more.

"Local law into this trailer business yet?" Jim Willson asked. He ran the surveillance squad and was a senior special agent with nearly twenty years' experience in the Bureau. Willson had a reputation for being all business, all the time.

"We backed out without doing any notifying," Ransom said.

" 'We'?" Farnsworth said. Janet saw Willson whisper something to Paul Porter, the other supervisor.

"I took Special Agent Carter here out to the trailer this morning," Ransom said.

"Why?" Farnsworth asked in a tone of voice that Janet recognized as portending a bureaucratic turf fight. I knew this wouldn't work, she thought.

Ransom sat back in his chair. "Because it looked to me like a possible homicide. Domestic homicide isn't our area, is it? Putting electronic surveillance on Kreiss, on the other hand, was done at the Bureau's request. If Kreiss offed some guy, I figured it was time to get the Bureau into it, which is why we're having this meeting, I think."

Farnsworth looked like he was about to lose his temper. "With all due respect, boss," Willson said, "what the fuck is going on here?"

"Okay, everybody," Foster chimed in from the speakerphone. "Let's get back on track here. I'm hearing that Edwin Kreiss is operational. I'm hearing that there's evidence he's been at the scene of a possible homicide, and that he's made at least one illegal intrusion onto a federal reservation, which used to be an explosives-manufacturing plant. Correct so far?"

No one answered, so Janet spoke up. "Yes, that's correct."

"Then may I suggest that our theory might be correct after all? That this Jared Mc-whatever might in fact be connected to a bomb-making network we're all looking for."

"I disagree," Janet said immediately. "Kreiss is looking for his daughter. If there's a connection between Kreiss and the body under the trailer, it has to do with his missing daughter. Kreiss knows nothing about a bomb network. The only reason he went into the arsenal is that a single, somewhat questionable witness told him that's where his daughter *might*—and I emphasize the word *might*—be going. There's no evidence of a bomb-making cell at the arsenal."

"All right, all right," Farnsworth said. "We need to get local law out to that trailer, and then I think we need to get federal assets out to this goddamned arsenal. From where I stand, we have a missing persons case that might be a kidnapping-abduction case, and now, a possible homicide. One of my agents nearly lost her life, and a Bureau vehicle, in the process of what should have been a routine inspection of a federal facility. Mr. Foster?"

"Yes?"

"In deference to your bomb theories, I want to call in the local ATF. We'll look into this homicide situation in cooperation with the Montgomery County Sheriff's Department. Any information that develops with regard to Mr. Kreiss will be reported directly to you. How's that sound?"

"I'd prefer to keep the ATF out of it until we ascertain whether or not this Jared guy was doing something at the arsenal. For the reasons we discussed previously. I also need to confer with Ms. Bellhouser."

Janet saw Willson mouth the name Bellhouser and then shake his head.

"I can understand that," Farnsworth said. "And I know how much we might like to bust ATF's chops. But there's something wrong here. I've got agents getting hurt, and a possibly related homicide. No one has ever mentioned any southwestern Virginia bombing conspiracy to me before. Now you tell me something: Are you and Bellhouser serious about that, or was that just a ploy to get us to stir up Edwin Kreiss so Marchand and company could whack his ass?"

Wahoo, Janet thought. The boss is back. Willson and Porter were looking on in undisguised fascination. Ransom was hiding his face in his hands.

"We are absolutely serious about that," Foster said. "But—"

"Then we get ATF into it. Right fucking now. I'll make the call. Ken Whittaker is our local liaison guy."

There was a strained silence on the speakerphone. Then Foster said, "Well, may I at least request that the Kreiss angle be confined to Bureau channels?"

"We will try," Farnsworth said. "But if he becomes a suspect in a possible homicide—"

"He won't if you neglect to tell the local cops about the switched tracking device."

Farnsworth rolled his eyes and began shaking his head.

"I mean," Foster said, "if *they* come up with evidence linking Kreiss to the possible victim, then that's that. But in the meantime, I still think Kreiss may have tripped over something. If there's any chance that he has, that's more important to us, and I think to the DCB, than some hillbilly getting squashed under his trailer."

"The guy under the trailer might not agree with that," Farnsworth said. "And that's another thing: I need a phone number for a point of contact at that DCB."

"Uh, well, that may not be possible. I'll have to check with Assistant Director Marchand and the deputy AG's office. The DCB operates at a senior policy level. I'm not sure we can have field offices, ah, interfacing with that level within the interagency process."

Gotcha, Farnsworth mouthed silently to the people at the table. "Okay," he said. "I'll leave that to your discretion, since you're at the policy level. In the meantime, I'm going to send some people out there to that arsenal just as soon as I get some ATF assets folded in. You tell your people that, okay?"

"What if we encounter Kreiss?" Janet asked.

"We'll just ask the sumbitch what he's fucking doing out there," Farnsworth said. "If we have to, we'll pull his ass in, have an intimate conversation. In the meantime, let's take it one step at a time. It's Sunday. Let's see what we develop down here before everybody gets all spun up, okay? Mr. Foster, we'll get back to you."

"Very well," Foster said, and hung up. Farnsworth looked at the two squad supervisors. "Get ahold of Whittaker. Today. Now. Whip a joint team up and go into that arsenal. Notify the Army, and ask them to get their security people out there. Go have a look, see what the hell's going on out there, if anything. Paul, I want you to liaise with Sheriff Lamb's office, get them going on the trailer business."

"What do I tell them when they want to know how we know about this?" Porter asked. He was an intense, thin man and was a stickler for detail.

"Hell, I don't know—we had a CI call in? Keep it vague. You plus one go out there—I don't want a crowd. I do want info on the vic as soon as possible."

Porter nodded, got up, and left the conference room. Farnsworth turned to Janet and Willson. "You people be careful out there. If Kreiss killed someone looking for his daughter, then maybe this kidnapping business has driven him over the top. It wouldn't be the first time he has run out of control, and I don't want the Bureau embarrassed again if we can avoid it."

"What was that little phone game you just played with Foster?"

"That was an RA fucking with a headquarters horse-holder. That won't keep the heavies off our backs for more than twenty-four hours, if indeed this was all about Kreiss from the git-go, which I'm beginning to think it was. But we have to be sure."

"Why bring in the ATF?" Janet asked.

Farnsworth sighed. "Because, Janet," he said, "there's always the chance, remote as this may seem right now, that the people at headquarters know something we don't down here in the toolies of Virginia. And if there *is* some kind of bomb lab hidden at that arsenal, do you want to be the first through the door? Or shall we let our dear friends from the ATF have that honor? Hmm?"

Janet saw Willson and Porter grinning. It made her wonder if she was ever going to get ahead of the politics curve in this business. Like there had never been politics in the lab, she thought. Yeah, right.

"Mr. Ransom," Farnsworth said, "I'd like you to go along in case my team runs into Kreiss. And if you do, I'd like you to talk to him, see if we can keep Pandora's box shut until we see what the bigs in Washington are going to do next. Can you do that?"

Ransom looked down at the table for a moment. "I can try," he said, not very convincingly. Janet thought he actually looked a little scared.

Kreiss heard the noise of something happening up in the tunnel about the same time as the siphon chamber began another dump cycle. The roar of the water escaping the dark chamber beneath him overpowered all other sounds and filled the air with a fine wet mist. He decided to pull himself back up to the floor of the tunnel and was doing so when a sharp, noxious smell enveloped him. It was not only hard to breathe; it hurt to breathe. He swallowed involuntarily, causing his eyes to water. He could still hear nothing but the rumble of the chamber emptying into the earth below, but when he got his hands and shoulders up onto the concrete lip of the tunnel, he realized that there was a small, viscous, fuming river headed right for him. He pulled hard right as the stream hit the center of the lip and shot over. The corrosive fumes were so strong now that he dared not breathe, and then he saw a flat branch of the fluid sweep sideways along the lip. His rope disintegrated right in front of his eyes, and the metal on the end of the stick foamed ominously. He knew that smell.

Acid. Nitric acid!

He buried his nose and mouth in the vee of his crawl suit and took one deep breath, and then he got up and sprinted up the tunnel, trying to ignore the swelling stream of acid, until he reached the cone of sunlight and the ladder rungs. He stopped just outside of the light and took another deep breath, straining air through the tough fabric of the crawl suit. Was the shooter up there, waiting for him to stick his head out? His lungs were bursting, and his eyes were tearing so badly, he could barely see. No more choices here, he thought, and scrambled up the rungs, straining for the bright sunlight of the main street above. The makeshift grid of pipes slowed him down, but not much, and he rolled off the edge of the hole and kept rolling until he was all the way across the street and into a side alley. Finally, he could breathe, and, so far, no one was shooting at him. He lay back on the warm concrete and concentrated on clearing his lungs and eyes.

Acid—a flood of it. Where the hell had that come from? Obviously, the bearded man had initiated that catastrophe. This place wasn't the ghost town it appeared to be. He rolled over onto his side and looked around. There was nothing stirring in the morning sunlight. He could hear a faint slurring sound coming up from the tunnel, but nothing else. He took one final deep breath and got up. He'd lost his stick down in the tunnel, but he was lucky to have escaped. He didn't want to think about what would have happened if the rope had been eaten before he'd made it back up to the tunnel.

He climbed the nearest building and spent the next fifteen minutes scanning the entire industrial area from the roof, but there was nothing different about it—same collection of concrete buildings, empty streets, and dilapidated sheds on the bare, dusty hillsides. The man who had pursued him from the power plant was nowhere in evidence. The power plant. He studied the front of the building, with its four garage doors and windowless exterior. The man had come out of the power plant, so whatever they were doing here, that's where they were doing it.

He climbed back down from the building's roof and went down a back alley to the side of the power plant. The tank farm up on its side hill was visible behind its concrete mass, and he wondered for a moment if the acid had been dumped down out of one of those tanks up there. Then he saw what looked like fresh tire tracks coming out of the tank farm's dirt road. Big dual tracks, the kind a truck would leave. He remembered the truck in the garage bay of the power plant. He wanted to take another look into that garage bay, but he did not want to cross the open space between the explosives finishing building and the power plant, in case the man was in there, waiting for him. He'd taken enough chances already. He looked at the tire tracks again, then knelt down and fingered the ridges in the dirt. Fresh indeed.

He checked his watch. It was almost eleven o'clock. He decided to go back to his own truck and then go to Blacksburg and look up Mr. Browne McGarand. That green-and-white tanker truck should be pretty easy to spot. Find that truck, find his shooter. And, he hoped, find Lynn. This time, maybe he would take a gun. He still had Jared's .45 in his truck. He'd have to find some ammo.

At 3:30, Janet, Ransom, and Ken Whittaker were waiting out in the bright sunlight on the main street of the arsenal's industrial area. The two young rent-a-cops were finishing unlocking the padlocks on the final two buildings adjacent to the power plant. The Bureau team had arrived at the front gates at just after two o'clock, where they had been met by Ken Whittaker, the local ATF supervisor, and the same two kids in their little rent-a-cop pickup truck. The group had done a quick windshield tour of the bunker area and then descended on the industrial complex. Whittaker, a tall, thin man, wearing oversize horn-rimmed glasses, was in nominal charge. Sunday or not, he was dressed in khaki trousers and shirt, and he had his ATF windbreaker and ballcap on. When Willson had briefed him, he had been all business, and he surprised Janet by asking none of the bureaucratic ground-rule questions that had been swirling around this case from its inception. He agreed that it would be a joint scene, but he insisted on being in charge of any inspection for possible bomb-making facilities. Willson and Porter agreed to this immediately. Willson noticed Janet's bewilderment, and while Whittaker was giving orders, he quietly pointed out that, at the working-stiff level, federal agents were federal agents and tended to focus on the business at hand. It was Washington where winning the turf battles seemed to be as important as the case, he said, which was the reason he was permanently homesteading in Roanoke.

Janet showed them the hole in the street where the car had gone down. There was an eye-stinging smell coming up from the hole, which Janet recognized as being the fumes of nitric acid. The rent-a-cops said they could smell it, too, but they insisted there hadn't been any industrial activity in the arsenal for years. Janet didn't remember all those pipes being near the hole, but then she didn't remember much about getting out of there, period, after Kreiss had shown up. They had then driven up and down the streets and side alleys in a four-vehicle procession, seeing nothing but bare concrete walls. Ransom suggested that they ought to climb down into the hole in the street, but the fumes were too strong.

"There was nothing like that when we came out of that hole," Janet said, staring down into the darkness. "That's new."

"What's the purpose of this tunnel?" Whittaker asked. One of the rent-a-cops said the site maps showed it only as the Ditch. Willson guessed that it was an emergency dump channel for the big buildings lining the street, someplace that an entire batch of chemicals could be dumped if something went wrong while they were making explosives.

"Wow," Whittaker said. "And I wonder into whose drinking water that would go."

Neither of the two kids ventured an answer to that one. Whittaker had asked them if they had keys to all these buildings, and they said, yes, they had the series master-lock keys for every building in the complex. Whittaker had just looked at them until they understood what he wanted. With lots of dramatic sighs, they started at the high end of the street and began taking down padlocks. Whittaker split the joint FBI-ATF team up into groups of two. He briefed them on potential booby traps and told them to go through all the buildings, with orders to stop and back out immediately if something seemed wrong. He kept Janet and Ransom with him.

"And we're looking for?" one of the agents had asked.

"These buildings are supposed to be empty," Whittaker said. "If you come on one that isn't, back out and sing out. And be careful how you open doors: Bomb makers are into booby traps."

The FBI agents looked at one another, and then Willson said, "Gee, with all that ATF bomb experience, maybe Whittaker ought to be the guy opening doors." Whittaker laughed and even agreed, but then Willson said, "No, we'll do it." Whittaker, Ransom, and Janet had remained down near the big hole in the street. One of the rent-a-cops came back to where they were standing.

"That's all the main process buildings," he said. "How about the power plant?" He was perspiring, but that hadn't kept him from lighting up a cigarette. Cigarettes and pimples, Janet thought. Don't they just go together.

Whittaker checked back with Willson's team up the street by radio. They were still working their way down, building to building. So far, they had reported seriously empty buildings.

"Yeah, open it up," he said in a tired tone of voice. "The weekend's shot anyway."

The kid gave a two-finger salute and trudged across the empty space between the last of the big buildings and the looming facade of the power plant. Whittaker followed him halfway down, then stood in the street, talking on his radio to the two team leaders. Janet walked with Ransom over to a building marked NITRO FIXING.

"Now there's a great name for a building," Ransom said. "How'd you like to work in a place that did—"

Janet felt rather than saw a great wave of intense heat and pressure on her right side. The blast compressed her body with such strength that her chest, lungs, and extremities felt like they were being stepped on by some fiery giant. She wanted to turn to see what it was, but then she was literally flying through the air and right through a wooden loading-dock fence before rolling like a rag doll out onto the concrete of a side street, until she slammed up against the wall of the next building. She tried to focus, but there was an enormous noise ringing in her ears, and then she felt herself screaming as an avalanche of things began to fall all around her, *big* things that hit the ground with enough force to make her helpless body bounce right off the ground. The sun had gone out and she could not get her breath. Her right side felt as if she had been kicked by a horse, and she found herself spitting out bits of concrete and lots of dirt and dust. Then a huge mass of reinforced concrete wall, big as a house, crunched into the street right alongside her and she screamed so hard, she fainted.

When she came to, her whole body was buzzing with pain. She wasn't able to get a good breath because of her side, and she was dimly aware that there were sounds around her she couldn't quite hear. Her eyes were stuck shut by a coating of concrete dust. When she was able to get them open and focus, she could see that the whole industrial area had been wrecked, with great mounds of concrete rubble piled everywhere—in the street, between the shattered buildings, even on top of the buildings that were still standing. The last two buildings in the row had been partially knocked down, and where the power plant had been, there was only the stump of the main smokestack presiding over two piles of twisted metal that must have been the boilers. She saw Ransom come staggering out into the street from somewhere, his clothes torn to ribbons, bleeding from the head, eyes, ears, and mouth. He tripped over a mound of rubble and went down like a sack of flour, lying motionless in the street. She was horrified to see a rod of metal sticking out of his head like a featherless arrow. A great cloud of dust hung over the entire area, thick enough to turn the daylight yellowish brown.

She looked around for Whittaker, but he was nowhere in sight. Her knees felt like they were on fire, and she looked down and saw that she had skinned the knees of her pants down to two bloody patches of road rash. She tried to get up, but there was a large piece of concrete with its rebar still embedded lying on her right leg, and her right hand didn't seem to be working. She tried calling out for help, but all she managed was a whimper, and that turned into a coughing fit, which hurt her lungs.

Then someone was there, levering the big chunk of concrete off her leg. It was one of the surveillance squad agents—Harris, she thought his name was, pretty sure that's what it was—and he was saying something to her. She absolutely couldn't hear him. She pointed to her ears and shook her head, which turned out to be a big mistake. She experienced a major lance of pain, followed by a cool rose haze that enveloped her consciousness, and then, blessedly, it all went away.

When she regained consciousness the next time, she found herself inside an ambulance, but the vehicle was not moving. Her whole body felt awash in some soothing balm, and she was hooked up to IVs in both arms. A young paramedic was talking urgently on a telephone down near her feet, and she could see out the back doors of the ambulance that it was parked on the main street of the industrial area, looking down toward what had been the power plant. She was shocked by what she saw: The power plant was essentially gone, with nothing remaining but the wrecked boilers on the wide concrete expanse of what had been the floor. The two large buildings at the far end of the street nearest the power plant had been mostly destroyed, with only their uphill side walls still intact. The streets were littered with pieces of concrete, big and small, and there were two body sheets lying out on the street between her and the open space in front of what had been the power plant. The medic turned around and saw that she was conscious. He said something into the phone, which she could not hear, and then hung up. Then he was talking to her, but she could barely hear him. She shook her head, much more carefully, but couldn't move her arms. She was able to read his lips.

"Can you hear me?" he was asking.

She winced and mouthed the word *no*. Her lips felt twice their normal size.

"Can you breathe all right?"

She tried out her lungs. It hurt to inhale, and her ribs were throbbing under the warmth of the painkiller, but she nodded.

"How many fingers am I holding up?" he asked. *Three* she mouthed, and then she said it out loud: "Three."

"Okay, good." She realized she could hear him now, although his voice was still distant. He saw that she could understand him. "Your vitals are okay," he said. "Your pupils are a little bit dilated, and I think you've cracked a couple of ribs and maybe your right wrist. I'm guessing a mild concussion, but otherwise, I don't see anything major, okay? The IVs are for pain and shock, and we've got you on a monitor. Just relax. We're gonna transport in just a few minutes."

"What happened?" she croaked.

"Looks like an A-bomb to me, lady. There're a million cops out there right now."

"What about . . . them?" she asked, pointing with her eyes to the body sheets down the street.

"Don't know, ma'am. I mean who they are. The cops in suits are pretty pissed off, though."

At that moment, Farnsworth's head appeared over the medic's shoulder. His face was a mask of shock and concern. He saw Janet looking at him and tried for a smile. It was ghastly, Janet thought. "Hey, boss," she said weakly.

"Thank God," he said. "Can she talk to me?" he asked the medic.

"Yeah, but she can't hear so good," the man said, and then crawled out of the way so that Farnsworth could climb partially into the ambulance.

"Janet, can you tell me what happened?" he asked, and then swore. "Listen to me: Are you okay? Are you hurt badly?"

"I took a flying lesson," she said, trying for a little wisecrack to get that mortal look off his face. "We were standing next to some building, down there, called Nitro Fixing. Then the world ended. I don't know what happened."

"The surviving team members said the power plant blew up," he said. "One of them was in the doorway of a building when it went up. Said the whole fucking thing literally disintegrated in a fireball. No warning."

"Who—" she began, looking past him into the street.

"Ken Whittaker is dead, and definitely one of the rent-a-cops, if not both of them. They were out in the street, we think."

Janet felt her stomach go cold. But Farnsworth wasn't finished. "Ransom is . . . well, it's gonna be touch-and-go, I'm afraid. He had a bastard of a head injury. They've heloed him out already. Our guys who were up the street inside buildings are pretty much okay. But, listen, we have a development."

"What?" Despite the pain medication, her side was beginning to really hurt, and it was getting harder to breathe. She tried not to panic. Development?

"The state police pulled Lynn Kreiss out of that last building down there. She's injured but alive, Janet. She was able to tell us that two guys have been holding her here since those kids disappeared, but then she became incoherent. Started babbling about Washington and a hydrogen bomb. Then she passed out. This is all secondhand—I wasn't here yet. But now we have to find out what the hell happened here."

"Is ATF taking over?"

"Oh, hell yes, they've taken over. In force. They're delaminating about Whittaker. Their lead guy is foaming at the mouth about why Washington never told them they suspected this place of being a bomb factory."

"Brilliant," Janet muttered. "This whole place was a bomb factory."

"Sir?" the medic said, looking at his monitors. "I think you're all done here, okay? We gotta transport now."

Farnsworth nodded and withdrew. "Get well quick, Janet," he called as the attendant began shutting the doors. "Fucking Kreiss—he was right!" he added.

And Kreiss had known a lot more than he had been letting on, she thought as the attendant slid forward and rapped on the window to the driver. She wondered if Kreiss was out there among all the rubble, or still in pursuit of these people who had been building—what out here, a *hydrogen bomb*? She was no explosives expert, but she knew that wasn't possible. No way. But assuming Kreiss was alive, somebody did need to tell him that they'd found his daughter. That he could stop chasing the phantoms of the arsenal and come in and talk to them. The ambulance was rolling and the attendant was doing something with one of her IVs. She suddenly felt very sleepy. Have to remember that, she thought as she slipped off again.

Browne waited until dark to go back to the Waffle House on Route 11 to retrieve his pickup truck. Earlier, he'd driven the propane truck out to the interstate and five miles north to the big TA truck stop, where he'd parked it among a hundred other big trucks that were idling out at the back of the cinder lot. He'd cooled his heels for an hour at the truck stop before hitching a ride back down I-81 into Dublin, south of Ramsey. From Dublin to the Waffle House on Route 11 had been a four-mile walk. He'd seen all the emergency vehicles running up and down Route 11, so somebody must have finally opened the door to the power plant. His suspicions were confirmed when he went into the Waffle House for a cold drink and everyone was talking about the big bang out at the arsenal.

As he drove his pickup back to Blacksburg, he was satisfied that any evidence of what they had been doing out there for all those months, including the retort, the pumps, the generator, and even the acid tank were now somewhere in low earth orbit. He'd also put enough acid down that tunnel to obliterate any trace of the security truck and any number of intruders. Leaving the girl . . . well, he'd done what he had to do. Regrettable, but necessary. That nitro building's big vertical expanse of concrete wall facing the power plant should have taken care of the girl once the explosion occurred. Keeping her had been a dumb idea all along, he thought now. It was just that he had never been quite able just to shoot her. He was ashamed about Jared fooling around in there. He should have known that would happen. He would go out to Jared's this afternoon, find out why that oversexed young pup hadn't shown up. William had been headstrong, but he would never have taken advantage of the girl that way.

The thought of his dead son stole some of the satisfaction out of what had happened out at the arsenal. The radio was talking about ATF agents. These were the same federal cops who'd killed William. But two weren't enough. The goddamned government, with all its alphabet soup of cops, was out of hand. Killing women and children in the name of the law, sending snipers to gun down women with babies in their arms, then lying through their collective teeth about it, then being exonerated in court. He'd followed the Waco standoff on the television, but had missed the exact moment when they drove their tanks into the building and burned those deluded bastards out. He was convinced that there was the mother of all cover-ups in place over Waco. William, William, William, he thought sadly. Why did you have to go down there? Why did you join up with such a bunch of misguided fools? I lived for the day I could get you back. And now you're nothing but a pile of greasy ashes out in some dusty field near Waco.

He took a deep breath to calm himself. Remember what you're going to do, he told himself. You're going to show those bastards that they'd killed the wrong man's son. The arsenal was just the beginning.

His plan now was to wait twenty-four hours to let the hubbub surrounding the arsenal explosion subside, and then he'd head north with the propane truck for the final stage. There was only one thing that could link him to what happened out there, and for that, they'd have to go through every one of the nine hundred ammo bunkers out on the back reservation. Bunker number 887 looked like every other bunker—partially buried, 150 feet long, 40 feet wide, and 20 feet from floor to the top of its curved ceiling. It contained his post-attack getaway stash: cash, clothes, passport, food and water for two weeks, and even a car. Assuming he got clear of what he was going to do in Washington, he would come back here, hide out in the bunker for a while, and then disappear. There were people in splinter groups of the Christian Identity network who would help him hide.

What he had to do right now was to make Jared understand he needed to keep his head down and his mouth shut from here on out, no matter what happened up in Washington. He'd deliberately not told Jared specifically what he was going to do with the hydrogen. What the boy didn't know, he couldn't tell. The propane truck was safe for the moment—just one more truck parked at a truck stop, right out in plain sight, which effectively made it invisible. The only other person who knew anything was dead. Just like his William. Fair was fair.

He crossed the New River bridge and headed north toward Blacksburg. He decided he would go directly to Jared's trailer before going home. See if the dummy had disentangled himself from his current whore long enough even to know about what had happened out at the arsenal.

Kreiss ended up going back to his cabin. He had driven down Canton Street where Browne McGarand lived and had seen the house. It was a medium-sized two-story brick house on a half-acre lot in a well-kept, heavily treed neighborhood. He had spotted a detached garage at the back of the house, and the yard looked well attended and free of trash. An elderly man had been raking his lawn next door when Kreiss drove by. He had glanced at Kreiss's truck, but he had not really looked up. One more pickup truck going down the street was apparently not remarkable. There were other people about, and he heard some dogs barking when he stopped at the corner, as if checking a set of directions. There had been no sign of the tanker truck. He turned at the next corner and discovered an alley that ran behind the houses on Canton Street and the houses on the next street over. The property lines were marked by clusters of metal trash cans standing guard along the alley.

He had decided not to go past twice, not with that geezer out there. Old people noticed things, and, unless Kreiss was willing to stop and go knock on the door, he didn't want to be remembered. It looked like a quiet middle-class neighborhood, which told him absolutely nothing about the occupant of number 242 Canton Street. He would come back tonight and try for that alley. He might need to create a diversion of some kind. If the neighbors were mostly elderly, there would be people about, not to mention dogs. A NEIGHBORHOOD WATCH sign emphasized the point. He saw what looked like a mom-and-pop corner gas station one block down from Canton Street where he might be able to park when he came back at night.

After cruising Browne McGarand's house and neighborhood, he decided to drive out to the area of Jared McGarand's trailer. On the way out there, he thought he heard thunder, but the sky seemed to be clear. When he approached the intersection of Jared's road with the state road, a Highway Patrol car was blocking the entrance. He kept right on going, catching a quick glimpse of more flashing blue lights back in the trees. Okay, he thought, Jared's demise is no longer a secret. He drove on down the state road and turned onto Highway 460, which would take him back toward his own cabin. He decided to go home, catch a quick nap, and then he had some preparations to make for his call on the other McGarand. Maybe this guy would be more forthcoming, and would live long enough to give him what he needed to know. Given the man's cold, quick decision to begin shooting out there at the arsenal, he might be a tougher nut to crack than the beer-guzzling Jared.

Focus, he reminded himself. The objective is not revenge, the objective is to find Lynn, and this bastard probably knows where she is. As he drove home, he turned on the truck's radio to get a weather report, and he found out that it had not been thunder he'd heard earlier.

Janet was fully awake in a semiprivate room at the Montgomery County Hospital when Farnsworth showed up with a small crowd that included the red-faced Mr. Foster. Her ribs had been taped, and there were bandages on some of her bandages. The most painful points on her body were actually where the IVs had been. Sounds still echoed in her ears, and she felt as if she had been pummeled all over. The other bed was empty, and the RA sat down on the edge of it. His expression was somber, and then she remembered that Ken Whittaker had been killed, along with those two kids, the rent-a-cops. Farnsworth was accompanied by Ben Keenan, who was his number two in the Roanoke FBI office. Keenan, who had been away on annual vacation, had come back in after the explosion. There were three other men, whom she did not recognize, but they looked like feds. They filed in behind the RA and gathered around the end of the bed. She saw a state trooper standing on guard outside her door before Farnsworth shut it. She was almost glad to see them, until Farnsworth introduced the three other men as being from the ATF. Two of them appeared to be in their early thirties, and the third was much older. She nodded carefully as each was introduced, then promptly forgot their names.

"How's Ransom?" she asked, remembering his crumpled form.

"Not terrific," Keenan said. "Took a piece of rebar through the head. He's in a coma. We're all praying that he'll come out of it. But actually . . ." He shrugged.

"Janet, can you go through it again?" Farnsworth said. "What happened out there at the arsenal?"

Janet described their tour of the bunker fields—nothing out there but empty concrete mounds surrounded by tall weeds. Then she described their search in the industrial area, and where she had been standing when the world ended. "I remember that one of those kids—one of the rent-a-cops—had gone down to unlock the power plant, but I wasn't paying a whole lot of attention."

One of the younger ATF agents leaned forward. "We're trying to figure out what kind of a bomb it was," he said. "The girl they recovered? She made a fragmentary statement at the scene, said something about a hydrogen bomb and Washington? You have any take on that?"

She shook her head again, carefully. There was a monster headache lurking back in there. The ATF guy must be talking about Lynn Kreiss, she thought. The second ATF agent, the other young one, asked her if she could describe the explosion.

"Felt it, never saw it," she said. "Pressure, heat, no noise—I think the sound was there, of course, but it was overwhelming. You all are echoing when you talk."

"We have a tech team from the Washington NEST at the site right now," the ATF agent said. "You know, that nuclear emergency response team? They're making a radiation survey, just in case, although we think the nuke angle is unlikely. We've backed all the local response people out until we know something, one way or the other."

Janet didn't know what to make of all that. She'd caught only a glimpse of the area through the doors of the ambulance. She supposed it could have been a nuclear bomb, given the extent of the destruction, but shouldn't she have been flash-burned? On the other hand, that power plant had been absolutely flattened. She could still visualize the molten and smashed boilers where the building had been, and the crumpled tank farm behind it.

"Janet," Farnsworth said. "Did you personally see any signs of human activity within the arsenal? Anything in any of the buildings that looked recent? Trash in the street? Shiny metal surfaces?"

"No, sir," she said. "I'd been there earlier, of course, and the hole was still in the street where my car went through that plate." She paused for a moment. Something about pipes. Then she remembered. "There were some pipes piled next to the hole in the street that I don't remember being there when Kreiss got me out. But I may not have seen them—I was pretty exhausted by then."

"Who is this 'Kreiss'?" one of the ATF agents asked.

Foster and Farnsworth exchanged a quick guarded look that the ATF agents could not see. "A security guard at the arsenal," Farnsworth said. "They were making a patrol and found the plate gone. Back to these pipes—you're saying they could have been put there *after* you got out of the tunnel?"

"Sir, I don't know. I just remember seeing them and not remembering their being there the last time."

Farnsworth nodded. "Okay," he said. "Once the NEST people are backed out and the place is verified radiation free, we're going to do a really comprehensive search of the wreckage area and the rest of the installation. If people have been using this installation, especially if it's been going on for a while, we should find evidence of it: intrusion routes, trash, chemicals, bomb-making equipment, residues, stuff like that."

"ATF will be honchoing that effort," the older agent said, as if to remind Farnsworth whose jurisdiction bomb makers came under.

"Absolutely," Farnsworth said, looking at Janet with a slightly annoyed expression. "But we can't go forward until the nuke people say the place isn't a hot zone."

Janet tried to think of something else to tell them, but she couldn't. Her body hurt enough to distract her. Farnsworth got up.

"Well, okay, folks," he said. "Let's leave Agent Carter here some room to recuperate. Of course she'll be available for further questions in due course. I'll have an interviewer come up and take a dictation for the record tomorrow morning, and we'll make that available for all concerned."

The men made sympathetic noises and backed out of the room, leaving only Farnsworth behind. He again nudged the door closed behind them.

"What's the deal with Kreiss?" she asked softly.

He shook his head. "Beats the shit out of me. Foster came down here with his hair on fire when word of the explosion got back to D.C. But now ATF has everyone spun up with what the girl said about a hydrogen bomb. Washington thinks she's hallucinating, but she's still out cold, so no one wants to take any chances."

"Foster want to pin this one on Kreiss, too?"

"I'm no longer in that loop. But there's something going on, and it involves the damned Agency."

"I'd like to tell Kreiss we've rescued his daughter," she said.

"Well," Farnsworth said, glancing over at the closed door, "that guy Foster has a slightly different slant on that proposition. But the focus right now is on the Kreiss girl talking about a hydrogen bomb and the capital. People in D.C. are seriously spun up."

"An H-bomb? That's kind of ridiculous, isn't it? I mean, don't you have to have an A-bomb even to initiate an H-bomb?"

"I'm no physicist, Janet. All I know is that when the girl said that, the BATF people did not laugh. In fact, they went semi-apeshit, got that nuclear response team heloed down here on an hour's notice. They were scaring the locals with all those Geiger counters and guys in moon suits until we cleared everybody out of there. Thank God the press didn't get onto that."

"But, boss—an H-bomb? C'mon."

"Did you see that building, Janet? The Army people had some pretty good pictures of the industrial area before the explosion, and that power plant was a big fucking building. It's now a concrete deck. The debris field is a half mile in every direction, and every vertical wall facing the plant has been damaged or knocked down. They found some pieces of the boiler tubing out on Route Eleven, for Chrissakes. You tell me what kind of bomb that was."

Her head was hurting and it was hard to concentrate. "But what has this to do with Kreiss? He was just looking for his daughter."

"The homicide of Jared McGarand is the key to that, we think. Look, we're keeping ATF in the dark about Kreiss and the rest of it, because you know that crowd: They'll go off half-cocked. That's doubly true if they think there's Agency shit involved here. They do bombs, and we have the mother of all bombs for them to focus on right now."

"What's their theory, if not a nuclear device?"

"The older guy, the one who didn't talk much? While everybody else was running around yapping on their radios and pretending they hadn't pissed their pants, he was making a drawing of the bomb site. When I asked him what kind of bomb was in that building, he said something interesting. He said it looked to him like the building was the bomb."

"And what the hell does that mean?" she asked. She was having trouble keeping her eyes open. She hated being in the hospital, but right now, there was a sleep monster in this bed and it was whispering her name.

"Don't know, Janet, but Foster is insisting we keep ATF in the mushroom mode for a little while longer, while certain people way above our pay grade, quote unquote, work the Kreiss angle. You get some rest now, okay? Hey, and you did fine out there."

Janet closed her eyes after Farnsworth left. He was upset—hell, they were all upset—after losing Ken Whittaker. And apparently Ransom's prognosis wasn't wonderful. ATF headquarters would of course be asking why a Bureau resident agency had called for one of their people without clearing it through Washington, and why they had even been out there at the arsenal. Farnsworth, anxious at this point to keep the bullshit swirling, had probably told them that it was part of the missing kids case.

She turned in the bed to ease the pressure on her aching ribs. She vaguely remembered going through a wooden railing. That wood must have been very dry. The docs said she had no broken bones, and that she could check out in the morning, as soon as they made sure she hadn't suffered a cardiac tamponade, whatever the hell that was. Her right wrist was swollen but usable.

The fly in all this ointment, of course, was Edwin Kreiss. She tried to remember if the DCB had been told about the Kreiss angle or not. Because if they had, then Farnsworth's game with the ATF wasn't going to hold up for very long. And poor Kreiss: tearing up the visible world, looking for his daughter, and now the feds had her and weren't going to tell him? She cursed all bureaucratic rivalries and fell asleep.

Browne didn't see the cop car until it was too late; he was already signaling his turn into Jared's entrance road. He slowed as the cop got out and waved him over. With a sigh, Browne shut down the truck and prepared himself. There was no way someone could have made a connection between the arsenal explosion and him, he reassured himself again. Or Jared, for that matter, so this had to be something else. Had to be.

"Evening, sir. May I see some ID, please?"

"Certainly, Officer," Browne said, reaching for his wallet. "What's going on here?"

The cop didn't reply as he looked at Browne driver's license. He asked him to please wait in the truck, then went back to his cruiser to make a radio call. When he came back over, he said, "There's a sergeant coming out to speak to you, Mr. McGarand. It'll just be a minute, sir."

Browne saw that the cop was uncomfortable, rather than angry or suspicious. Had something happened to Jared? Was this why he hadn't shown up? Then he had an alarming thought. Had that woman's husband caught them? Jared had said someone had been creeping around his trailer. He felt a pang of conscience—he remembered hoping that the woman's husband would catch them. He knew the old rule: Be careful of what you wish for.

A dark four-door sedan nosed alongside the cruiser. Two men in civilian suits accompanied by a bulky state trooper with sergeant's stripes got out and approached his truck. The trooper took his hat off and informed him that a man, whom they believed to be Jared McGarand, had been found fatally injured. Was he related to Jared McGarand? Browne said yes, he was Jared's grandfather and his only local next of kin. Would he be able, and willing, to make a next-of-kin identification at the scene? Browne, a cold feeling in his stomach, nodded a soundless yes. The trooper cleared his throat and began to explain that the victim had been crushed by the trailer, and that identification might be difficult. Browne blinked. Crushed by the trailer? That didn't sound like some irate husband. He took a deep breath and said that, yes, he'd do it.

He got out of the truck and waited for the trooper to introduce the two men in suits, but the sergeant did not do so. He almost didn't have to; Browne was almost positive they were government agents, probably FBI. The city suits, the faintly supercilious expressions on their faces, and the body language of the local cops told the tale. Browne forced his expression to remain as neutral as he could get it. This was the enemy: The FBI, along with its incompetent cousin, the BATF, had taken William from him. It was one thing to talk about a formless, faceless, and powerful enemy, and quite another thing altogether to be standing three feet away from two of its agents. On the other hand, he realized, they would expect him to lose his composure if his grandson had been killed. But why were they here?

They walked, rather than rode, back down Jared's entrance road to the trailer, Browne with the local cops, and the G-men bringing up the rear. They rounded the corner and Browne saw the yellow Mylar tapes, a Crime Scene Unit van, two police cars, two unmarked police cars, and a coroner's black-windowed ambulance. Jared's pickup was parked next to his phone company repair van. Technicians in white overalls were wandering around Jared's yard, while two men who were probably detectives stood talking and smoking cigarettes near the back of the trailer. The trailer's doors were open and there were obviously people inside. Browne tried to think if Jared would have anything in the trailer that might tie him to what they'd been doing at the arsenal, but he didn't think so. Unless he had a stash of copper, and even that could be explained, since he was a telephone repairman. Or had been one.

The trailer was no longer level. The space underneath the downed end of the trailer was curtained off with a temporary railing, on which some kind of fabric had been stretched. There was a portable light stand set up on one side, which a tech turned on as they approached. Browne hadn't even noticed that it was getting dark. The cops put out their cigarettes as the sergeant escorted Browne to the curtain, offering at least a public show of deference to impending grief. Browne wasn't worried too much about grief. He'd spent all he had when William had been killed. By some of these people, he reminded himself, glancing sideways at the two feds. He still couldn't figure out why they were here. Had something turned up in the trailer to draw in federal agents? And were they FBI or ATF?

The sergeant explained that Jared had been found underneath the trailer, next to a hydraulic jack, and that the jack had broken through the floor of the trailer, causing the trailer to drop directly onto Jared. Browne was conscious of a bad smell coming from behind the curtain. One of the Crime Scene Unit techs walked over and offered a small bottle of Vicks VapoRub. Browne understood at once, and he rubbed a dab into each of his nostrils, then stepped forward. It was not a pretty sight. The end of the trailer had been jacked back up. Jared's entire body was flattened and his head was swollen, the familiar face almost unrecognizable. There was an industrial-sized hydraulic jack positioned to hold up the near end of the trailer on a steel plate next to the body.

He saw as much as he wanted to see and then stepped back. He put the back of his hand to his mouth, closed his eyes for a moment, and then nodded. The cops were watching him, probably to see if he was going to throw up, but the wave of nausea passed, replaced by a pang of long-lost familial hurt, the kind of hurt he had not experienced since watching the news tapes of those federal bastards cremating his son at Waco. Hate them, he told himself silently, suddenly very conscious of those two federal agents behind him. Hate them and feed on that hate. Maintain control of yourself. Jared's beyond help or hurt, but you are the bringer of retribution. But you must not attract further attention.

He caused his shoulders to slump and his face to wilt. "That's my grandson, Jared McGarand. I guess I don't understand what happened here."

"Well, sir, we're all looking into that. Do you know of any reason he'd go underneath that trailer like that? Or knock down those cinder blocks?"

Browne looked down at the twisted jack stand. He shook his head.

"Them cinder blocks were either knocked over or they fell over, one or the other," one of the detectives said, pointing with a flashlight. "Any idea why or what did that?"

Browne shook his head again. "It doesn't make sense, those blocks just falling over. Why would they do that? He hit it with his truck or something?"

The two federals, who had kept back while remaining within earshot, exchanged glances but didn't say anything. Why are they here? Browne wondered again, fighting off the urge to look at them.

The sergeant was nodding. "Yes, sir, that's kinda what we thought. But there's no sign of that. And it would take something pretty big, what with the weight of the trailer and all. We figured he may have been jacking the trailer so's to reset the blocks or something."

"What have you done with the dogs?" Browne asked, looking over their shoulders at the empty pen.

The cops all looked around and then at one another. "How many dogs we talking about, Mr. McGarand?" the sergeant asked. "We saw the pen, but there weren't any dogs here when we got here."

The sergeant had a bit of a mountain accent, so Browne decided to countrify his own language a bit. "He had him some pig dogs—three of 'em. He never let 'em run free less'n we were hunting."

One of the detectives introduced himself then, flashing a leather credentials wallet with its golden shield at Browne. He, too, spoke with a southwestern Virginia country accent. "Your grandson, Mr. McGarand?

He have him any enemies? Anyone who would have wanted to do something like this?"

All Browne could think about was that intruder at the arsenal, the big man in the weird coveralls, or whatever they were, looking right at him with those intense eyes, almost like he knew him. The cool way he had just run off when Browne opened up with the .44, not bothering to shoot back or try anything fancy. That had taken calm professionalism, and Browne was beginning to think that there was something going on here, something much bigger than the disappearance of those college kids. Instinctively, he decided to throw them a red herring. He looked down at his shoes for a moment and shuffled his feet, creating the picture of a man making up his mind to tell the cops something embarrassing about his grandson.

"My grandson?" he said with a parental sigh. "He liked the ladies." The Vicks was making his eyes water, which was perfect, actually. "And they liked him, if you know what I mean. Some of those ladies had husbands. I was supposed to see him Saturday night, but he called, said he had him a hot date. By the way he was talking, I think she was maybe one of the married ones. I warned him, right there and then, but with Jared, well . . ."

The cops were writing in their notebooks and nodding. This was something they understood right away. It was also something to go on.

"Any idea of who she was?" one of them asked.

"No, sir," Browne said. "Jared, he wasn't one for naming names; knew I disapproved. But my guess is it was someone who'd had a telephone problem, called it in, got Jared as the repairman. Something like that, I imagine. He usually operates alone, working the backcounty trouble tickets."

One cop closed his notebook and headed for his car to make some calls. Browne kept his eyes downcast. Why were *they* here?

"Sir, how's about we go inside, see if you can tell us if anything's missing?"

They went into the trailer, past a tech who was scraping some gooey-looking substance off the edge of the front steps. They walked around inside the sloping trailer, but everything seemed to be in place. Browne went through the bureau and night table drawers but didn't say anything about the missing guns. He wasn't entirely sure that Jared had obtained the guns through lawful channels, since Jared frequented the gun shows in Roanoke and up in Winchester. Plus, there was a lot of gun swapping that went on among those Black Hats idiots. While back in the bedroom, he asked, as casually as he could, who the other people were outside.

"Those guys? They're Roanoke FBI agents. They're doing some investigation at the phone company, some kind of interstate wire fraud case. Your grandson worked for the phone company, so a couple of them came out when we made the tentative ID. Me, I think they're just curious to see how us local yokels do a homicide investigation."

That settled that, Browne thought with relief. Nothing to do with the arsenal explosion. They walked back through the trailer, although Browne felt weird walking over the area atop of Jared's body like that. They asked him for some background information on himself, where he lived, and whether he would be seeing to the funeral arrangements. They informed him that, due to the suspicious circumstances, there would have to be an autopsy, after which the body would be released to him. They let him go after that, and he walked back out to his vehicle by himself. He was pretty sure that the two FBI agents watched him go.

He drove away and headed back to Blacksburg, watching his rearview mirror. Now that the propane truck was parked out at the truck stop, the clock was running. He had planned to leave late that night, but now he would have to make sure there was no one operating in his backfield, like maybe those feds, before he set out. After what had happened at the arsenal, he should be in the clear. If the Bureau would be occupied by anything in southwestern Virginia, it'd be with that explosion. He looked forward to watching it on the television news; he wanted to see what the hydrogen had done to a reinforced-concrete building like the power plant. It would give him a feel for what it was going to do to a certain mostly glass and steel office building in downtown Washington, D.C. He smiled in the darkness. He had few doubts on that score: It would absolutely, positively obliterate an office building.

At 10:30, Kreiss drove Jared's phone repair van down Canton Street and turned at the block just before he would have reached Browne McGarand's house. He had gone back out to Jared's trailer at 9:30, hoping to find the cops gone, which they were. He knew he couldn't operate in Browne's neighborhood in a crawl suit, but he had kept Jared's keys. He'd decided that if he could get his hands on that phone company repair van, he'd have some pretty effective cover in town. The cops had apparently towed Jared's pickup truck away, but the repair van was still sitting there. The dogs were still not back, and the only signs of what had happened there was all that yellow tape fluttering in the semidarkness. He had watched the trailer for fifteen minutes to make sure no one was still there, and then he'd gone in, after parking his own truck behind an abandoned house a half mile beyond Jared's road. He had put his surveillance equipment, car phone, Jared's .45, and Janet Carter's pager into a bag and taken it with him in the van.

Kreiss was dressed in plain dark blue overalls, and he had Jared's white plastic phone company helmet sitting on the seat next to him. He also had Jared's Southern Bell ID pinned to the overalls, although the picture wasn't even close. He might fool a civilian, but not a cop, so he would have to take some care as to where he parked the van. The vehicle smelled of cigarette smoke and the front seat was a trashy mess of fast-food wrappers, technical bulletins, repair-order manifests, and empty soft-drink cans. The back was a slightly more orderly mess of wire bins, parts shelves, opened boxes, coils of telephone wire, a pair of red traffic cones, and a variety of tools and tech manuals. He had Jared's .45 auto in a pouch behind the seat, but still no shells. Sometimes an empty .45 was as good as a loaded one, though: People tended to make assumptions when it came to looking a .45 auto in the eye. He found the entrance to the alley that ran behind his target's house, pulled in, came to the first telephone pole, and doused the main headlights.

Browne McGarand was almost ready to go. His pickup was in the garage, with the cap mounted on the bed to protect his tools and equipment. He had called the weekend number for a local funeral home and made arrangements for them to pick up Jared's remains for cremation once the autopsy was completed. Then he'd called the detective who'd given him his card and left a voice-mail message that he would be out of town for a couple of days, that he was going down to Greensboro, North Carolina, to inform Jared's younger brother face-to-face about what had happened. He explained that the boy was mildly retarded and that the news would take some special handling. He expected to be back on Wednesday. Not asking them, just keeping them informed, everything perfectly routine and normal. That should keep them at bay if they decided they wanted to question him further.

He went out the back door to the garage and put the last bags into the passenger seat. He had everything he needed for the operation in Washington. He hadn't planned to leave on a weekend, but it wouldn't matter at the target's end, because any weekday morning would do for what he had planned. He went back into the house, turned out all the lights, and locked up. He had no dogs or other pets to worry about, and his mailbox was big enough to let his bills pile up. He had actually considered burning the house, but in the end, he'd decided against it. If he succeeded at the target, they'd never be able to trace him to the propane truck, which might not even survive the explosion. If the bombing at Oklahoma City was any indication, they would eventually be able to trace the truck back to the town in West Virginia where Jared had heisted it a year ago, but there the trail would end. There was no physical evidence of his clandestine activities in the house, because he had never done anything illegal there.

He looked around the darkened house from the inner kitchen door. He had lived there for over thirty years, twenty-four of them with Holly, until the cancer took her. William's room down the main hall, untouched since the disaster in Texas. Jared and Kenny's room across the hall. While raising William, Browne had risen from ordinary chemical engineer to chief engineer of the Ramsey Arsenal. His life had gone as he'd planned it: Hard work, a persevering attitude toward marriage, regular churchgoing, and a good wife had taken him to the number-two management position at the arsenal. And then it had begun to come apart: William getting that girl pregnant, their aborted marriage, Holly's cancer, and then a major blow, when the government unexpectedly closed down the arsenal. Holly had worked for seven years at the arsenal in one of the mercury-recovery plants, and Browne was pretty sure that's where her cancer had come from. There had been three other women who had died of cancer from that unit, but the government scientists all proclaimed that there was no possible connection. Once the plant shut down, the government didn't want to discuss the problem anymore. They'd even cheated him out of part of his pension, and then, adding insult to injury, made him oversee putting the plant into mothballs in case the Army ever required it again.

He missed Holly as much as he missed William. His wife had been a strong, taciturn woman who never complained, even when the cancer rose in her. When he found out that Holly was going to be taken from him, he had consoled himself with the knowledge that he would still have his son and his grandsons, but then William had gone off to Waco. And always, behind most of his troubles, was the government. Unfeeling, devoid of conscience, overweening in its power over the lives of the individuals it smashed flat without a second glance. He might have saved William if it hadn't been for everything else that happened, courtesy of the government. He had once been appalled at what those sick boys had done in Oklahoma City, but now—now he could well understand the impetus to strike back. There was retribution due, by God.

He sighed and stepped out the back door, shutting it and locking it, knowing he'd probably never see the house again. It had all begun so well, and ended in pieces. Holly was dead, Jared was dead, the arsenal was dead, and Kenny . . . well, Kenny had truly never lived and never would. He was a virtual ward of the state, working a menial job at the state mental hospital in Greensboro and living there as well in one of the supervised homes. Browne almost wished he *could* go down there and tell Kenny that his brother was gone, but Kenny would only smile sadly, accepting this bit of news with the same equanimity as he would the fact that it had begun to rain outside.

He went to the garage. The pickup truck was pointed nose out, so he simply got in, started it up, and drove out into the street, turning right to get to Highway 460 and then make his way out to the interstate. His own life was over. Now he would see how well he could finish it, and the bastards who'd cremated his son.

Kreiss sprinted for the telephone repair van when he heard the truck's engine start up in the garage. He had been twenty feet away from the back of the garage when McGarand had come out of the house and started up his truck. Once in the van, he blasted straight down the alley, knocking over two trash cans as he turned right and then right again and gunned it back the way he had come in on Canton Street. He ran a stop sign three blocks up. There was no sign of McGarand's truck ahead, and he almost thought he'd lost him, when he saw the lights of a major traffic intersection a half a mile or so ahead. By the time he got to it, the light was still red and he saw McGarand's F-250 stopped in the left-turn lane. The truck was sporting a cap over the bed, so this was probably not a trip to the grocery store. He slowed down dramatically to allow a few cars to get ahead of him into the left-turn lane, then closed it up in time to make the turn behind McGarand. He followed the pickup truck for eight miles, until it turned onto the hamburger-alley strip that signaled the approach of the I-81 interchange. Traffic was heavy, but he was having no trouble following the pickup.

This was a complication he hadn't planned on, and when the F-250 turned onto I-81, he had a decision to make. Follow him? Or break it off and go back out to the arsenal to search some more for Lynn? But of course, that wouldn't work, not after that big explosion there this afternoon. The place would be crawling with feds. He didn't want to think about the possibility that Lynn might have been caught up in all that. He'd seen a television news report when he got home, a film clip taken from an airplane or a helicopter in the late-afternoon sun, showing the bare concrete floors of what had been the power plant. Big bomb, that, he thought. Really big bomb. The surrounding buildings had all been damaged in some fashion, with the two process buildings nearest the power plant semiflattened. He'd checked those buildings, all those buildings, and had found everything locked tight and no signs of recent entry.

Should I go back to the guy's house? he wondered. The pickup was three cars ahead of him, its big taillights distinctive enough that he didn't have to stay too close. The traffic out on I-81 was heavy, as usual, with wall-to-wall semis jockeying for that vital extra hundred feet of progress down the congested roadway. Where the hell was McGarand going? And then turn signals—the pickup was getting off.

Kreiss slowed down, slipped between two semis, and then turned off, going as slowly as he could so as not to come right up on the pickup at the end of the ramp. He almost did that anyway, but McGarand's vehicle turned right and then right again into the front parking lot of the big TA truck stop. Kreiss waited for as long as he could at the ramp, but then headlights flared behind him and he had to move. He went right, then into the truck-stop plaza, which was brightly lighted. He caught sight of McGarand's truck going behind the main building, through the big rig fueling lanes, and disappearing out into the back parking lot, which was filled with dozens of semis idling in the smoky darkness. He pulled the repair van up to the auto-fuel lanes and turned out the lights. The lanes weren't filled to the point that there were cars waiting, so he got out, locked it, and hurried around the corner of the restaurant and store building, dodging incoming vehicles and weary-looking drivers filing in and out of the building. The whole area was brightly illuminated by sodium-vapor lights coming from several towers, and the air was filled with the smell of diesel exhaust from the trucks parked out behind the building. He paused when he got to the back: There was no sign of the pickup truck.

Had McGarand spotted him and ditched him? He didn't think so. So what was he doing back here among all the semis? He watched the occasional truck driver walking back out of the restaurant building, cradling a thermos of coffee or some carryout gut bomb from the choke and puke inside. There were three women hanging around a set of phone booths over on the other side of the plaza, kids, really, standing out in their cutoff shorts and halter tops, eyeing the rigs as they rumbled back out through the plaza. AIDS victims in the making, he thought. But where had the pickup gone? He wasn't thrilled with the thought of walking out into that dense pack of trucks out there, where the only lights were the running lights of the tractor-trailers. There was a high chain-link fence around the whole area, so that truck had to be out there somewhere. Doing what? And then he squatted down behind a Dumpster by the back of the building as McGarand's truck reappeared from between two semis in the farthest parking lane, lights out now, going slow and headed back into the main plaza area. The truck went right by the Dumpster, and Kreiss got a good look. Yes, the same guy who'd opened up on him at the power plant. Which wasn't there anymore. Courtesy of this guy? Had they been running a bomb factory in that power plant? An illegal bomb factory at an ammunition plant—what a concept. He'd told Carter that Foster and Bellhouser had been blowing smoke; maybe not.

He moved to the corner of the building as the pickup truck cruised out into the open area, did a careful 180, and pulled into a parking place right in front of the restaurant. He watched from around the corner as McGarand went into the restaurant, carrying a thermos, just like any other trucker. Just as soon as the bearded man had gone in, Kreiss hurried back to the telephone company van and checked the fuel gauge. Half-full. He put Jared's telephone-company credit card in, cranked up the fuel pump, and filled the tank, keeping an eye on the front door while trying to keep the van between him and the building. Would McGarand see the telephone repair van? Recognize it maybe? He finished fueling and restowed the hose. There were cars waiting now, so he couldn't stay there. He got in, started up, and drove out toward the front area of the plaza, looking for a place to park where he wouldn't stand out quite so obviously. Then he saw an Appalachian Power truck parked all by itself in one corner of the plaza, and he drove over there, turned around, backed in, and shut down. He could see the main entrance door and McGarand's pickup, while the larger truck masked his van. Then he waited.

Janet woke up at 11:00 P.M. and had a confused moment trying to remember where she was and why. The hospital was quiet, and her room was in semidarkness. Lights from the parking lot below illuminated the windows of the hospital building. She sat up carefully. She could hear nurses talking quietly at the charge desk out in the hall. She hurt in a general sort of way, but her mind was alert. Her wrist was not as swollen, and she was able to breathe without nearly as much pain. She wondered what was going on with the arsenal case. She rolled over very carefully, found the phone, got an outside line, and put a call through to the Roanoke office. The secretaries weren't there, of course, but one of the agents in the fraud squad answered and told her everyone was still in the office trying to sort out the disaster over at the arsenal. There were a million questions coming down from both FBI and ATF headquarters in Washington, and everyone was pretty upset about the loss of Ken Whittaker. She told the agent that she was ready to escape from the boneyard and asked him if someone could come get her at the hospital in Blacksburg.

An hour and a half later, she carded into the federal building and went directly to Farnsworth's office. His door was closed, but there was a group of agents, including Ben Keenan, Farnsworth's number two, in the RA's conference room. The conference table was piled with papers, site diagrams, photos, teletype messages, and a dozen very used polystyrene coffee cups. They all stopped talking when they saw Janet, which is when she realized that she probably looked a mess.

"Janet, what are you doing here?" Keenan asked, his tone of voice belying his brusque question. Keenan was known for his people skills and was extremely well liked within the Roanoke office.

"Got tired of staring at the ceiling," she said, coming in and clearing away some papers so she could sit down. "And it not being my honeymoon and all." This provoked some smiles as she sat down. "Since I was there when it happened, I thought maybe I could help."

Farnsworth's door opened and the RA came out, accompanied by Marchand's red-faced executive assistant. They stopped short when they saw Janet. Farnsworth looked like he hadn't slept for a long time and his suit was a rumpled mess. Foster's expression was flat. He didn't make eye contact with anyone.

"Ransom didn't make it," the RA announced. "Died an hour ago. Never woke up." He turned to Foster. "That makes two agencies who are going to be mad at us now, ATF and the spooks."

Foster nodded as he looked down at the floor. Then he said he needed to make some calls, stepped over into Keenan's office, and shut the door. There was a grim silence in the conference room, and then Farnsworth greeted Janet, asked how she felt, and asked her to come into his office. He closed the door behind her and asked if she wanted some coffee. Her brain did, but her stomach vetoed the idea. She was now beginning to think that leaving the hospital had not been her brightest idea. She sat down gingerly in one of the chairs while the RA poured what looked like used motor oil from a pitcher on his desk into a mug. The smell of the stale coffee confirmed her stomach's opinion. He poured in a paper packet of sugar, which literally floated on top of the noxious-looking brew. He sat down heavily.

"Five years here as RA, never lost an agent," he said quietly. "Until today. Even if he wasn't technically one of ours, this really sucks. Ken Whittaker was a good man. You know his wife, Katie?"

She shook her head.

"She's devastated, of course. Kept saying, 'So close, he was so close.' Meaning close to retirement. This *really* sucks. And now Ransom. I liked him, too. Shit."

"Plus the two security kids," she said. "I feel responsible. If I hadn't gone out—"

"No, no, that's all wrong, Janet. You had every right to go out there, although I fault you for going alone. But there obviously *was* something going on at that place."

"I guess so. But still . . . How's Kreiss's daughter?"

"She's alive but in and out of a borderline coma. Took a head shot from flying debris. Damn wall nearly crushed her. She was saved by the fact that she was up by the front door. Hasn't said anything beyond those few words when they pulled her out of that nitro building: Washington and hydrogen bomb. Intriguing combination, huh?"

She nodded distractedly. "So, where do we stand?" she asked. "What's ATF found out?"

Farnsworth shook his head, then ran his fingers through his graying hair. "Their people on the scene called out one of their own national response teams, after the nuke guys backed out. Even though the casualty count wasn't that big, it was one hell of an explosion. The NRT is still there."

"I'm not familiar with that," she said. Her stomach growled and she realized she hadn't eaten for a long time.

"It's an ATF special team. An NRT has chemists, forensic experts like you, arson and bomb dogs, postblast and fire-origin experts, intel people, special vehicles and mobile labs, all that good shit."

"The NEST people find anything radioactive?"

"Nope, just radon. I still can't figure out what that was all about. But nothing to indicate it was nuclear, although the bang sure seemed big enough."

"And?" she prompted. She realized she probably sounded impertinent, but Farnsworth was too tired to notice.

"And they haven't called it yet. Blast origin point in the power plant. Eureka. But type of explosive? They can't find it. Some nonstructural physical evidence scattered around the site, but almost every piece of it can be traced back to equipment that was probably installed inside the power plant. Boiler tubes, plant machinery, turbine parts. Otherwise, stone-cold mystery right now. They haven't found even a *trace* of the security kid who went down there to unlock the place."

Janet shifted in her chair and exhaled, causing Farnsworth to look more closely at her. "You all right? How about a glass of water?"

She nodded and said she thought she needed something in her stomach. He went out and came back with a cup of water from the jug cooler and a stale-looking doughnut.

"We sent some people in chem-suits down into that tunnel system and found a couple of things, the most interesting of which was evidence of somebody shooting a large-caliber weapon down there. That ring any bells?"

She shook her head, but not too hard. The doughnut helped, and she sipped the cold water.

"The fumes in the tunnels tested to residue of nitric acid. One of the tanks out behind the power plant appeared to be the source of that, although it was, like all the others, flattened."

"No cars?"

"No cars," he said with a fleeting smile. "But the divers reported that the whole thing appears to dump to an even larger underground cavern system. They pulled a guy in there from the Army who used to be what they called a 'plant rep' when the civilian company operated the place. He confirmed that the tunnel was called the Ditch. It was used when something went wrong with a chemical batch and they had to dump it quick to prevent an explosion. Said where it went after going into the Ditch was something no one ever knew, or at least he didn't know."

"Wonderful," she murmured. "And what about Kreiss?"

"Well," Farnsworth said, trying to get the sugar to dissolve in his coffee, "that's getting interesting. Foster and Bellhouser may have something there. First of all, no one can locate Kreiss—at least we can't and the local law can't. I don't know if Foster and company have asked for more help from the Agency. That may be hard after losing Ransom."

"Might he have been there—when that place blew up?"

"Willson's troops talked to some of Kreiss's neighbors, of sorts. Bunch of hillbillies living down the road from Kreiss's cabin. They weren't exactly forthcoming, but indications are they'd seen Kreiss alive and well late this past afternoon, which was after the blast. But that's all they would say."

"And Kreiss is a suspect in the Jared McGarand homicide?"

"Yes and no. You'll remember what Ransom told you about putting bugs on Kreiss's vehicle? How he got all but one off, and then Ransom finds that one at that McGarand guy's trailer, where McGarand got dead?"

She nodded. The doughnut felt like it might be changing sides. She drank some more water and tried to ignore the queasy feeling in her stomach. It was hurting to breathe again.

"Local law hasn't been told anything about that, or Kreiss. I sent a couple of our people to the scene after seeing Ransom's report. Told the cops that it might, emphasis on *might*, relate to a case we're working on telephone company fraud. Our guys weren't fully briefed on the Kreiss angle, either. I simply told them to go see what the local cops came up with on this possible homicide and report back."

"And—?"

"And the locals are definitely calling it homicide, but the physical evidence points all over the map. Jared McGarand's wallet and keys seem to be missing, and there was evidence that someone had been into his phones, although he himself was a phone repairman, so that might not mean anything. There's some unknown substance they recovered from the front steps that they were really interested in, because there was some more of it on the body, which for some unknown reason seemed to have been hosed down. But that's not as important as what we think *we've* found out."

"Foster still trying to tie this bomb-cell conspiracy theory to Kreiss?"

Farnsworth nodded and leaned forward. "This is close-hold, for now anyway. I'm telling you because you and Kreiss know each other, at least superficially. We've tied Kreiss to the arsenal and to Jared McGarand. Believe it or not, Foster apparently has a line of some sort into the ATF's national response team. The NRT people found evidence of vehicles being parked near the rail line entrance to the arsenal, and that the gates at the rail line were not in fact locked, which they should have been. They also found an electric-eye counter mounted on the interior rail gate. So Foster directed us to ask the local cops to see if there was any evidence that Jared McGarand's truck had been to the arsenal, and damned if they didn't get a match in samples of mud off Jared's pickup truck. From that parking area outside the rail gates."

"That quick?"

"The NRT has a mobile lab."

She was confused. "Are you saying Jared was a bomb maker? And what's that got to do with Kreiss?"

"No, all I'm saying is that Jared has been going into the arsenal. Why, we don't know. But Foster thinks, based on what you've told us, that Kreiss may have stumbled into Jared or his truck at the arsenal, then followed Jared home to question him about his missing daughter. This happens, as best we can tell, on Friday night. Jared ends up dead, and Kreiss ends up back at the arsenal, bailing you out of the tunnel. Why did he go back? Did Jared reveal something? And then, when *we* go into the arsenal to see what the hell's going on, a very big bomb is waiting for us. For you, maybe."

"Or for Kreiss."

"Yeah, okay, maybe for Kreiss. And then, who should we recover but Kreiss's daughter, who's babbling about H-bombs and Washington."

"But—"

"Wait. Jared's grandfather shows up at the homicide scene today. His name is Browne McGarand. He ID's the body, agrees with the cops that something is fishy in Denmark, tells them Jared liked to live dangerously with married women, then leaves. Then later, he calls the cops, says he's leaving town, purportedly to break the bad news to Jared's brother, his other grandson, who's down in Greensboro, North Carolina. Cops try to get back to him, go by the house, but he's already gone. They've asked the state cops to see if they can spot him out on the interstate and confirm he's headed for Greensboro. In the meantime, it turns out the chief of d's on the sheriff's force knows this guy Browne. That's Browne spelled with an *e*, by the way. And based on what he says, Foster now thinks his theory was right and that *this* guy might be the second half of the bomb team."

"Jared's *grand*father?"

"Because it turns out that the grandfather is a retired chemical engineer, whose entire career just happened to be spent with the company that ran Ramsey Arsenal for the Army. He was the chief chemical engineer there when it closed."

"Holy shit."

"It gets better. You know Mike Hanson, our own arson and bomb guy? He was one of the people I sent out to Jared's trailer. He comes back, runs the name McGarand through the NCIC just for the hell of it. There are several McGarands, but only one hit that ties to this area: There was a William McGarand, formerly of Blacksburg, Virginia, who had a local rap sheet of minor offenses and was listed as having ties to an antigovernment, quasi-militia group called the Black Hats. They're based up in the mountains west of here in Bluefield; combination Aryan Nation, moonshine runners, and marijuana farmers who like to take pot shots at revenuers—that's ATF these days. Jared McGarand is also listed as being involved with them. But that wasn't the kicker."

"Let me guess: William's related to Browne McGarand."

"Yes, he is—or was—Browne's only son. But more importantly, he was one of the people killed at Mount Carmel."

"Mount what?"

"Mount Carmel, otherwise referred to in these hallowed halls and in the media as the Waco disaster. William was Browne's son; Jared was William's son. William's wife ran off with some guy, and then William took off, leaving their two kids, Jared and the brother, to be raised by their grandfather."

"Browne," Janet said. Her stomach was forgotten. "God, if there's a Waco connection, then maybe the theory of a bomb cell in southwest Virginia wasn't just some wash job to cover up for losing control of Kreiss."

"Hell, Janet, I don't know. My guess? It was a smoke screen that just happened to be true. But now we've had a bomb, a big fucking bomb, and we have an ATF agent dead, and an Agency operative dead, not to mention two civilians, and now this Jared McGarand."

"So what happens now?"

"The director is into this one, according to the SAC in Richmond. And because the Justice Department, deputy AG Bill Garrette, and Edwin Kreiss are involved, the director is ordering shields up."

"He remembers the Kreiss affair?"

"Vividly. Plus, there's been no love lost between Justice and the Bureau for the past four years. Now Kreiss is missing. Foster says there's a fair chance that he's hunting down Browne McGarand, not because of any bomb plot, but because he's still searching for his daughter."

"Oh God, that's right: Kreiss doesn't know we recovered his daughter."

"Didn't you tell me you gave Kreiss your pager?"

Janet blinked. "Yes, I did."

"I want to activate that pager, and keep calling it until Kreiss answers. We'd really like to know where the hell he is and what he's doing, but more importantly, I want you to tell him something."

From the expression on his face, she thought she knew what was coming next.

"This is coming from the deputy AG at Main Justice, okay? And I don't much like it. But you are instructed to tell Kreiss that his daughter *was* there in the arsenal—but that she was killed in the bomb blast. Second, you tell him that this guy Browne McGarand was responsible for abducting her and getting her killed. We'll even give him McGarand's vehicle description."

"Sweet Jesus, boss," she whispered. "You don't mean it!"

"Look, Janet, if there's even an outside chance that some maniac is loose with a hydrogen bomb and headed for Washington? You bet your ass I mean it. According to Foster and his pals at Justice, Kreiss will react by hunting this McGarand bastard down and boiling him in oil."

"But what the hell is the Bureau doing turning loose a—what is Kreiss anyway? A retired bounty hunter? I thought we wanted to tie these bomb people to the antigovernment groups. You know, make a case in court and all that good stuff? With evidence, even?"

"The deputy AG has apparently spoken to the Secretary of the Treasury. ATF headquarters has worked up an official spin on the explosion. They're reporting that it was an accident—a buildup of gases over the years in the industrial complex. Big bang, but end of story. Public and media interest goes south. Privately, of course, they're still looking."

"Because of the word *hydrogen*?"

"Right. That fact has spun official Washington up pretty good, especially when ATF admits it can't identify what kind of explosive did the deed. The Justice Department's internal response was pretty simple: Find this guy and stop him. Forget building a case. Essentially, the Bureau and the ATF are gearing up to defend the capital, but we're the only ones besides the Agency who know about Kreiss."

"Who is a professional loose cannon!"

"But he's no longer *our* loose cannon, Janet. He's now the Justice Department's loose cannon. Which is why the director, while officially ignorant about Kreiss, is going along with this. He's saying, Let him run.

Assuming McGarand is loose with a bomb, if Kreiss tracks down McGarand and does something off the wall, Washington's immediate problem is solved. If it later turns to shit, the director will state that Kreiss was not our asset."

"Kreiss will be Bill Garrette's asset," Janet said wonderingly. She blinked again. This sounded like bureaucratic hubris on a grand scale. "I've got to tell you," she said, "when Kreiss finds out you lied about his daughter, you personally may move to the top of his hunting list."

"That's where the Agency will come in, Janet," the RA said. "Bellhouser told Foster that Deputy AG Garrette has made some arrangements with the Agency, which probably knows Kreiss even better than we do. While we're all hunting the bombers, they're going to be hunting Kreiss."

He paused to let her absorb the import of what he was saying. Jesus, she thought, this was more than she wanted to know. Kreiss had grabbed a real tar baby here, and Garrette and company were now going to use this bombing hairball to do what they had always wanted to do.

Farnsworth got up and paced around his office for a minute. "What we're going to tell Kreiss may not be that far off the mark, by the way," he said. "The docs aren't overly optimistic about the girl's probability of survival anyway."

"Then it's doubly cruel to tell Kreiss she's already dead," she said.

"Maybe so. But the urgent mission right now is to prevent a replay of what happened at the arsenal. That building was a power plant: reinforced concrete with no windows. It was just about vaporized, and the ATF guys who've seen it are genuinely worried, which is scaring Washington. Now think federal office building in downtown D.C. You were there, Janet. Ken Whittaker was there, too."

Janet had a "But, sir—" all ready to go until Farnsworth mentioned Whittaker. If her bosses were putting the picture together correctly, the clan McGarand had blood on their hands and more in their eye. Browne McGarand had lost a son at Waco. The son and the grandson had ties to a known quasi-militia group in West Virginia. Browne and Jared had apparently kidnapped Kreiss's daughter and done God knew what to the other kids. Now Kreiss's daughter said there was a threat to Washington. But when? And from whom, exactly?

"I'll tell you what: Give *me* that pager number," Farnsworth said. "And then you go home. I'll have someone activate the pager once I know you're home. If he calls in, we'll call-forward it to you at home."

She stared down at the floor. This was wrong. It smelled of the old "operational necessity" ploy. Farnsworth came over and put his hand on her shoulder. "I know you disapprove of this, Janet, but your voice is the one he knows."

She nodded, trying to think of a way to get out of this, but her brain wasn't working all that well. The best hope she had was that Kreiss had pitched the pager into the New River. Her fatigue must have shown, because Farnsworth called in one of the agents outside and asked him to drive her home.

After thirty minutes, Kreiss saw McGarand come out of the restaurant, still carrying his thermos. He got in his truck, backed out, but then he drove diagonally across the plaza, toward a Best Western motel that was right next door. Their parking lot was contiguous to the plaza, and about the time Kreiss was starting up the van, McGarand parked right on the edge of the motel's lot and got out. He looked around for a moment, then walked back toward the restaurant. Halfway there, he cut diagonally behind the main building and strode purposefully toward the truck park in the back. Kreiss shut down the van and got out to follow. As he did, the doors on the power company truck next to the van opened and two very large men got out. They were wearing green trousers, over which hung expansive T-shirts. Each had on a ball cap that had the TA logo on the front. Both of them carried large black Maglites. One of them had the steroid-enhanced build of a professional weight lifter; the other one was a whale who sported an enormous beer gut, but he had the upper body, shoulders, and arms to match.

"Excuse me, sir," the weight lifter said. "We're TA security, and we'd like you to come with us into the office." His voice was surprisingly high and no match for his body, but he made sure Kreiss saw him reach behind his back and pat the lump under his T-shirt where the gun was. The second one was already moving behind Kreiss in case he decided to run. From their expressions, it looked like they almost wished he would.

"What's the problem?" he asked, trying to see if McGarand was still visible.

"The problem is you've been hanging around here, acting in a suspicious manner, that's the problem, sir. Now let's go."

They walked with Kreiss in between them, close, but not too close. He thought fast. If they got him inside, he'd miss McGarand leaving. He stopped, but the one on his right quietly folded a massive paw around his upper right arm and he was walking again, conscious of the stares from two truckers coming out of the main door. They had to wait in the middle of the plaza while a big semi roared by them in second gear, followed closely by a propane truck. They escorted him down a hall between the restaurant and the shop, past the men's room and the showers, and into a small office at the back of the building. There, the whale patted him down and then indicated he should sit in a straight-backed chair directly in front of the desk. Kreiss chose to remain standing just to the left of the chair. The weight lifter sat down behind the desk, while the fat man kicked the door shut and then stood close behind Kreiss.

"So: what the fuck you up to here, bud?" the weight lifter asked. "You pull in, park at the gas pump, walk out back, come back, gas your van, then park it over next to our truck—not your smartest move, now, was it?—and you sit there and wait."

Kreiss said nothing. Then the weight lifter picked up a Polaroid camera from the desk and shot it off in Kreiss's face. While waiting for the photo to develop, he explained to Kreiss that unless he could explain what he was doing here, they'd call the state cops and have him arrested for trespassing.

"Actually," said the whale from behind him, "we'll tell 'em that we caught you wearing panties and waggling your wienie through that little hole in the partition between the stalls in the men's room." Kreiss felt the man's foot rubbing suggestively up the inside of his leg. "They'll take you over to the Roanoke city jail, and, hell, you know cops, they'll tell everybody they see."

"See, we've got this hijacking problem out here in the truck stops," the weight lifter said. "And you were acting a whole lot like a lookout, okay?"

"I still think he was just cruisin'," the whale said, patting him on the ass now and sniggering.

"I *was* looking for something," Kreiss said. He reached into the upper pocket of his coveralls and withdrew a retinal-disrupter cube. He felt the whale behind him shift when he reached up into his pocket but then relax when all he produced was something that looked like a fat flashbulb cube.

"One of these," Kreiss said, offering it to the weight lifter and closing his eyes tightly. As the man reached for it, Kreiss fired it into his face. The big man grunted and then just sat there, stunned, as Kreiss turned, went down on one knee, grabbed the chair by its legs, whirled around, and hit the fat man behind him across both lower legs. The whale grunted and bent forward, giving Kreiss, still crouching low, the opening he needed to drive his fist into the man's fleshy throat. The man's eyes bulged and he started to gag, then sank down to his knees, both hands at his throat, his face already turning red. Kreiss checked on the man behind the desk, but he was still just sitting there, his pupils the size of BBs. The phone rang at that moment, but Kreiss ignored it and went out the door. There was a fire exit to his right, which he took. The door let him out into the back parking lot, which was still wall-to-wall semis. There was no sign of McGarand. He swore and walked rapidly to the van. The cube flash would keep the big man immobilized for another few minutes, and the whale—well, the whale might wish he had a blowhole about now.

He got to the van, jumped in, and took off across the plaza. When he got to the exit, he paused. He looked back and saw McGarand's truck still parked right where he'd left it. He didn't know what to do, other than to get the hell out of there. But not too far, he thought—somehow he had to get back on McGarand's tail. There'd be state cops there pretty quick, and the security people had seen him in a phone company van. Then a cold wave washed over him—he'd forgotten the Polaroid: They had his fucking picture! He turned and drove the van into the motel's parking lot and took it all the way behind the second building of the complex. What he needed now was another vehicle. He could steal one possibly, but it wasn't likely that people pulling into a motel were going to leave their keys in their cars. Then he remembered McGarand's truck. A pickup truck. Every pickup driver he'd ever met always stashed a spare key somewhere outside the truck.

He walked as casually as he could back through the motel complex, staying away from the check-in lobby and keeping an eye on the big truck plaza next door for cop cars. He got to McGarand's truck, knelt down on the side that faced the plaza, and began feeling along the frame for a magnetic key box. He had reached the tail end of the truck when the first emergency vehicle came down the ramp from the interstate, lights and siren going, and wheeled into the plaza. It wasn't a cop car, but an ambulance. Good, he thought—a little more time to look. He searched all along the bumper and frame on the back of the truck, then up the left side. May be out of luck here, he thought. The ambulance had pulled up in front of the building and the attendants were hurrying in. He fingered the exhaust pipe, which was where he often put his key. Nothing. Cops here any minute now, he thought, and went back to the rear bumper. There was a Reese hitch welded to the back frame, and the receiver had a ball tang inserted and locked with a pin. He pulled the pin, extracted the tang, and felt inside the receiver. Nothing but some grease on his hand. He was putting the tang back into the square hole when he saw the wad of duct tape on the very end of the tang. Bingo.

He peeled the key out of the tape and reinserted the tang just as more blue strobe lights lit up the plaza. He looked over his shoulder and saw a state police cruiser bristling with Lo-Jack antennas pull into the truck stop. Kreiss let himself into the truck, started it up, and quickly drove it over to the motel and behind the front buildings to where the phone company van was parked. He grabbed his bag and the gun out of the van and threw them into McGarand's truck, locked the van with the keys inside, and then got into the truck.

Now what? he thought. No—now *where?* Where the hell was McGarand? He wanted to go cruise that back parking lot next door, but that was out of the question now, and besides, there was something sticking in his mind. Very conscious of the commotion next door, he closed his eyes and tried to reconstruct what he had seen McGarand do. Come out of the building, carrying a coffee thermos, move his truck to no-man's-land between the motel and the truck stop, and then walk back out to the parking lot out back, where the big rigs were. Then what? The security cops had grabbed him up, and they had walked across the parking lot to the office. No, wait—they had stopped for a truck. No, two trucks. A big semi and a propane truck. A *propane* truck! Son of a bitch, it had been that green-and-white tanker truck he'd seen in the power plant maintenance bay!

He started up the pickup and drove out of the motel lot and back up toward the interchange. There was a second cop car in the plaza now. Which way? McGarand had been going south, so south it was. He pulled onto I-81 and merged quickly. The pulsing blue lights were visible in his mirror for almost a mile beyond the interchange. He put it up to just under eighty; McGarand had a pretty good head start. Then he heard Janet Carter's beeper start to chirp in his equipment bag.

Janet awoke to the sound of her phone ringing. She sat up and groaned out loud. Every muscle in her body protested the sudden move. She opened her eyes and tried to focus on the clock. It looked like two something, but her eyes weren't working. Neither was her brain. The phone kept ringing, so she sat up straighter, cleared her throat, and answered.

"Janet, this is Ted Farnsworth. I'm sorry to be rousting you out like this."

"That's okay, boss," she said, clearing her throat again. "What's happened?"

"We think we got an answer to the pager, but it's a mobile and the signal died away. We've set up a conference call-forward tie between your line and the number I sent to the pager. Assuming he calls back, it will come in direct to you, but we'll be listening. The question of the hour is, Where is he and what's he doing? And then—"

"And then you still want me to tell him his daughter died in that explosion?"

Farnsworth hesitated, then said, "That's affirmative. And that this Browne McGarand guy was responsible for that explosion. McGarand's driving a '98 Ford F-Two fifty south on I-Eighty-one toward Greensboro; in fact, we've just had a sighting report on the vehicle from the state cops."

She said nothing for a moment. "Janet," Farnsworth began, but then she cut him off. "If McGarand's driving *south* on I-Eighty-one, then he certainly isn't going to Washington with a bomb," she said. "So why are we doing this to Kreiss? Why not have the state cops pick up McGarand and bring him in for questioning?"

"Because we have no grounds for a warrant, and the state cops won't arrest him unless we produce a federal warrant. I already thought of that."

"But still, if he's going south—"

"He may very well be going south because he knows we're onto him. He goes south in plain view while members of his cell take a big bomb to D.C."

Janet didn't know what to say.

"Janet," Farnsworth said. "You're the only voice in our office Kreiss will listen to. He can find out what the rest of us can't—whether or not there is a real threat to Washington."

"You're assuming Kreiss will give a shit about a bomb threat to Washington. Hell, if this guy hadn't kidnapped his daughter, he'd probably help the guy drive. I think he'll just hunt down McGarand and do whatever he does to him. And then we won't know anything."

It was Farnsworth's turn to stop talking.

"Look, boss," she said. "Telling Kreiss his daughter is dead is bullshit. Why not tell the truth here? Tell Kreiss we've recovered his daughter, that she's alive but comatose over there in Blacksburg. Let him go there, see her, satisfy himself that she's at least safe, and *then* tell him about the McGarands."

Farnsworth didn't say anything.

"I still say, if that guy is headed south, there's no immediate threat. Put surveillance on him, track him, maybe even let him see the tail. Personally, I think Kreiss might play ball, as long as we tell him the truth. The converse is not true: You do not want Edwin Kreiss coming to your house one night after you've lied to him about a thing like this. And it would be a really cruel lie, wouldn't it, especially if she does die and he never gets a chance to see her?"

Farnsworth still didn't say anything.

"Let me tell him what the hell is going on. I'll even go meet him at the hospital. These bureaucratic games with the Agency, ATF, those executive lizards from Justice—who knows what that's all about? The kid in the hospital is real. And she's somebody's daughter."

"Shit," Farnsworth said. "I've been up too long. This whole thing. Ken Whittaker was a good friend—"

"Sir, you don't have to tell Foster and company *anything*. Let me tell Kreiss the truth, let him see his daughter, and then let's work this bomb problem. By the book this time. Our book, not these other assholes' book."

"Okay, Janet," Farnsworth said with a sigh. "You're probably right. I guess if this McGarand's headed into North Carolina, it gives us some time to straighten this thing out. Okay. We'll patch the call in as soon as Kreiss tries again."

Janet felt a surge of victory. "I'll be waiting," she said.

12

Kreiss stood by his daughter's hospital bed and tried to control himself. She looks so thin, he thought. Lynn was an athlete and normally radiated good health and fitness. Now her face was gaunt and slightly jaundiced. He held her hand under the blanket and just watched her breathe. She wasn't on a ventilator, but there was an IV drip going into her left wrist. Her face was bruised, and her normally vibrant hair lay limp on her head like a skullcap. A bank of machines kept score on her vital signs above the bed. Coma, the docs said. As opposed to profound vegetative state. The "good" kind of coma—if there was such a thing—where a badly abused body checks out for awhile to work on healing itself without having to deal with the outside world. The room lighting was subdued and there was a quiet music stream coming from somewhere.

"She was conscious at the explosion site?" he asked.

"I didn't see her," Janet said. "I was being scraped off the concrete myself." Kreiss eyed her, probably noticing for the first time her own puffy face and stiff posture. "Apparently, she spoke to whoever found her. They got 'hydrogen bomb' and 'Washington' out of her, but that was all."

"Hydrogen bomb and Washington. Sounds good to me. We're at just about the right distance, down here in Blacksburg, and the prevailing winds are on our side."

"Washington is taking a somewhat different view," she said. "But this whole bomb theory is pretty screwed up. One moment, we're all running around at top end because we think some bad guys are on the way, as we speak, to bring an H-bomb to Fun City. The next, we're standing down in the regroup mode. The Bureau is fucking around with the ATF, and the Justice Department is fucking around with the Bureau, and ABC is fucking around with DEF. You know."

Kreiss nodded. "Palace games," he muttered. He let go of Lynn's hand and smoothed the hair on her forehead. "Our divorce was unnecessary," he said finally. "Helen got scared of what I was doing while I was with the Agency. She knew more than she should have, and she just wanted out. I could understand that. Accept it, even. But I never wanted to lose Lynn."

"Did your wife poison the well? Set Lynn against you?"

"Not deliberately, no," he said. "This wasn't a spiteful separation, adultery, or anything like that. Which made it almost worse, because Helen was so reasonable. She just wanted away from me and what I was doing. Like most men, I thought the career, what I was doing, the things I was learning, were terribly important. I let her go with *my* pride intact."

"Mine was different," she said, surprising herself. "My husband turned out to be a no-load. He was sort of a career ectopic pregnancy—he was never going to produce anything, but he was determined to stay in the general area of the academic womb. I think that's one of the reasons I joined the Bureau about then; I wanted to be around real men."

"'Real men,'" Kreiss said. "Inspector Erskine, where are you?"

They both smiled. "Lynn had to believe that everything her mother was afraid of was true," he said, smoothing her hair again. "Kids can sense bullshit, and Helen was genuinely afraid."

"And you and Lynn were reconciled after the plane crash?"

"Just before, actually." He told her about Lynn's unexpected visitation. "And then this mess." He sighed. "You said that the McGarands were probably responsible for the bomb. And that they had been holding Lynn the whole time? At the arsenal?"

Janet suggested they go outside. He seemed reluctant to leave his daughter, but there was obviously nothing he could do for her that wasn't already being done. He followed Janet down the hall, past the ICU nurses' station. Janet smiled at the nurses and the lone orderly, but they were all staring at Kreiss, whose gaunt face and hulking shape stood out among all the white-coated hospital personnel. He looked as out of place among all the gleaming cleanliness and order of the ICU as a bear fresh out of the woods. It had taken a lot of FBI badge waving and friendly persuasion to get them to let Kreiss in to see his daughter. Kreiss had called back fifteen minutes after she had persuaded Farnsworth to stop and regroup, and she had told him immediately that they had found Lynn, that she was alive and in the Montgomery County Hospital. She had asked him where he was, but he wouldn't tell her. Then she had suggested that she meet him at the hospital, and he had said, "one hour," and hung up.

Farnsworth had been listening. He called her back immediately to say he would send along some backup, just until they knew what they were really dealing with. She had asked that they stay well out of sight, because she was going to be on thin ice when Kreiss showed up. The RA agreed and they set up a surveillance support zone outside the hospital. She would park her car somewhere where it was clearly visible in the lot. The backup agents would set up around that car in two unmarked vehicles. There was no time to equip her with a portable radio, so Farnsworth said that if Kreiss put her under duress in the car, she was to do something with lights. When she went into the hospital with him, there would be two agents inside in hospital orderly clothes who would keep her in sight at all times. Her signal that everything was all right would be to open her purse and touch up her makeup.

They reached the main elevator bank and waited for a down car. An orderly carrying a bag of what looked like bed linens joined them at the door. They got in and punched the ground-floor button. The orderly punched the basement button. She had told Kreiss the bare outlines of the McGarands' suspected involvement in the explosion at the arsenal, but he had offered no response to that. He had wanted to see his daughter; any discussion of the rest of it could wait.

No one spoke until they got to the lobby and the door opened. Janet stepped out and Kreiss followed, turning at the last minute to tell the orderly that his shoulder rig was showing. As the elevator doors began closing in front of the surprised agent, Janet made an "I'm sorry about that" face, but Kreiss was already headed for the front door and the parking lot. She caught up with him when he stopped under the marquee at the entrance and looked around at the nearly empty parking lot.

"I have things to do," he said as he scanned the lot. "You have backup out there?"

"Of course," she said.

"I don't want them following me," he said.

"They're out there to protect me," she said. "Not to follow you."

"That something you know, Special Agent?" he asked, looking directly at her for the first time that evening. Actually, it's this morning, she realized. His eyes were rimmed with fatigue, but there was a fierce determination back there, unfinished business.

"No," she said. "My boss sent them. They may have other orders."

"I don't want that," he said, looking around again. "What did you say about standing down? Earlier, up there in Lynn's room."

"Mr. Kreiss, I need to fill you in on a lot of things. Why don't we go back inside and let me tell you—"

"I'll make a deal with you," he said impatiently. "I don't want a war with the Bureau. I do want to leave here without having to take evasive measures. You know what a claymore mine is?"

She had been shown a claymore during the training for new agents at Quantico. "Yes, of course," she said. "But—"

"My idea of evasive measures is to strap a couple of claymores to the tailgate of my pickup truck and then get someone to chase me in a car. Get the picture?"

She didn't know what to say.

"I'll make a deal with you," he said again. "I'll tell you something vitally important about your bomb plot, and you make sure no one follows me. Deal?"

She looked around at the parking lot. There were islands of trees between the lanes for parking, and about thirty vehicles scattered around the lot, which sloped gently down toward the main hospital building. Tall light standards illuminated the entire lot. Her car was visible, but she had no idea where the other agents were. Kreiss was waiting, staring at her.

"All right, but there's a lot you don't know. As in, they've tied you to one Jared McGarand, for instance?"

He stared at her for a moment but then dismissed with a shrug what she had just said. "Give them the all-clear signal, and then I'm going back into the hospital. Tell them I've gone back upstairs. I'll take it from there."

She still hesitated.

"Look," he said, "I'm not armed. And like I said, I don't want trouble with the Bureau, or with you. I'm willing to bet that your superiors weren't going to tell me that Lynn was here, alive. I suspect that you convinced them otherwise. So I owe you. Again. Give them the signal." His eyes were boring into hers with a commanding force. She found herself complying, opening her purse, taking out a compact, opening it so that the round mirror caught the marquee light and reflected it out into the parking lot. She pretended to touch up her nonexistent makeup.

Kreiss nodded and relaxed fractionally. "Okay," he said. "Here's my half. You said your people were all spun up about the possibility of a bomb going to Washington but that now they're standing down, right?"

She nodded, trying to think of a way to keep him here, to get control of the situation. But this was just like their other meeting, the one at Donaldson-Brown.

"Well, here's the thing," he said. "It was *me* driving McGarand's truck south on I-Eighty-one, not McGarand. I believe McGarand's gone north." Then, before she had a chance to ask any questions, he spun on his heel and went back into the hospital. She watched him go straight back down the main hallway, until he disappeared through some double doors. She turned and hurried out to her car, where her cell phone was. What was Kreiss trying to tell them? Farnsworth had said the state police tracked McGarand going to North Carolina.

She stopped, seeing it now. Not McGarand—McGarand's vehicle. Which, for some unknown reason, Kreiss had been driving. She waved her arms at the parked cars, calling in the backup agents to converge on her car. Lights came on in the parking lot as she got to the car and two Bureau vehicles slid into place on either side with a soft screech of tires. Ben Keenan got out of one of them, pulling out his portable radio.

"Where's Kreiss?" he asked.

"He said he was going back in to be with his daughter," she said. "But we need—"

Keenan ignored her, and he ordered the agents standing around them to go into the hospital and apprehend Kreiss. Then he got on his portable radio and contacted the agents disguised as orderlies inside the building. They reported that they had not seen Kreiss return to the ICU.

"Shit!" Keenan exclaimed. He ordered a search of the hospital building, and then he turned to Janet. "Do you know what he's driving? The state cops want him now, for a felony assault out at a local truck stop."

"That's what I was trying to tell you," she said. "*Kreiss* was driving McGarand's truck."

"Wonderful. So what is it? A Ford? A Chevy? What?" And then, with a horrified look, he understood. "The earlier sighting? That wasn't McGarand?"

"No, sir, it was *Kreiss*, driving McGarand's vehicle."

Keenan shook his head. "What the fuck's with that?" he said.

"He didn't really elaborate," she replied. "But it means McGarand could be halfway to anywhere by now. With a bomb."

Kreiss drove down the street that went along the back side of the hospital parking lot. He had earlier parked McGarand's pickup truck in front of a private residence and walked over to the hospital. Now he was going to go back out to Jared's trailer and switch trucks yet again, leaving McGarand's truck and retrieving his own. Then he was going to go *north* on I-81 this time and hunt down that propane truck. Acting on the assumption that the Bureau had requested traffic surveillance out there, he had been careful about what he had and had not told Carter. As for what McGarand was really up to, Kreiss didn't care. His daughter was safe. Jared was dead, and his grandfather on the move. He was going to find this bastard and crush him for what he'd done to his daughter, period. The Bureau wanted McGarand for the explosion at the arsenal; fine. He didn't want the Bureau getting to McGarand before he did. The good news was that the Bureau wouldn't know anything about the propane truck. It took almost five hours to get from Blacksburg to downtown Washington, D.C., and McGarand had a good head start on him. If at all possible, he wanted to be in Washington before they stopped looking for McGarand's pickup truck and started looking for his.

Browne McGarand turned off the northbound lanes of I-81 at 2:30 A.M. and eased into a truck stop. He'd been driving for almost three hours and needed a rest break and some more coffee. It had been a long time since he had made a really long drive, especially at night. The propane tanker, thankfully, was holding up just fine. With this refueling, he could make it all the way to the final setup point in Crystal City, on the Virginia side of Washington. He wanted to be there by dawn, and before the major Monday-morning traffic snarl coiled around the Washington Beltway. He would lay up the truck for the day and make a final reconnaissance run to the target. If the situation hadn't changed since the last time he and Jared had scoped it out, he'd make the attack tonight, before all those feds down in Roanoke put two and two together.

He parked the truck out in the back lot after fueling it and walked into the restaurant-store area. The place was not as dead as he had expected, with several zombie-eyed truckers wandering rubber-legged around the brightly lighted store and half the tables in the café occupied. He went to use the bathroom and then sat down in a booth and ordered coffee and a bowl of hot cereal. Two Highway Patrol troopers came into the café and sat down at a table near his booth. Browne felt a tingle of apprehension, but then he relaxed—there should be no reason for anyone to be hunting him. They were sitting close enough that he could hear their shoulder mikes muttering coded calls, although the weary-faced cops weren't paying any attention to anything but their coffee.

He knew the federal authorities must be elbow-deep in the wreckage of the arsenal by now. They would think they'd broken up a major bomb-making cell of antigovernment terrorists. They would probably never solve the mystery of Jared being under his trailer. Browne felt there were three possibilities: Jared got drunk and went under the trailer for some reason and the jack collapsed; an irate and cuckolded husband who was playing by mountain rules; or the hard-looking man who had been snooping around in the arsenal. He was betting on the second theory. His own conscience was clear on that score: He had warned Jared often enough about his philandering and his boozing. They had both been careful not to have anything at home that could tie them to the arsenal.

That concrete power plant would have acted like an auto engine's cylinder when the hydrogen ignited: a momentary compression, and then a massive power stroke and vaporization of the building. The only device that could indicate what he had been doing in there was the retort, and it had been made mostly of glass. He had put all the spent cinders of copper-nitrite into the boiler fireboxes, where they would look like ordinary slag. The two pumps would have been smashed to pieces, so they should look like just another piece of wrecked machinery in the power plant. The ATF would be all over the place, but he was betting they were stumped. A hydrogen explosion left no trace other than water vapor, which would dissipate almost immediately. A nice *clean* explosive.

One of the cops at the next table was talking into his radio, repeating a license plate number. As Browne listened, the number suddenly registered. The cop was writing down *his* pickup's plate number.

He turned away from the cops slightly, not wanting to be seen eavesdropping. The cop had written down the number and was now back to talking to his partner. But it had been his pickup number; he was sure of it. Why? Who wanted him stopped out on the interstate? The Blacksburg cops should not have been all that interested that he was going to Greensboro. He tried to think it through, but he was just too tired. He had parked his pickup truck between the TA truck stop and that motel, out in no-man's-land. The state cops should be looking for it out on the road, somewhere between Blacksburg and the North Carolina line. But he was now 150 miles north of that, thirty miles from the interchange with I-66, which would take him down into Washington. But you're not in your pickup truck, he told himself. So—so what? He sighed. He was more tired than he'd thought. He rubbed his eyes and signaled the waitress that he needed his thermos filled.

The cops got up and went to the cashier's stand. He watched them go, as did the other truckers in the room. He might not be thinking all that clearly, but one thing was certain: The only person who had ever seen him at the arsenal was that fire-eyed big guy. Suppose he had been a fed of some kind? They had had signs of an intruder for a couple of days. Suppose it had been the same guy all along, and this guy had been a fed and had somehow survived the nitric-acid dump into the Ditch. If the feds tied the bomb at the arsenal to him and Jared, then his target in Washington might have been alerted. If so, that was going to make his plan very, very difficult to carry out. But maybe not: If he could count on one thing, it was the enduring hubris of federal law-enforcement agencies. He could just as easily see them concluding that some bad guys had been screwing around with explosives and there had been an accident. The key was that there was nothing to tie him to Washington. Jared had known he was going to take a bomb to Washington. Jared may have been a skirt-chaser and a boozer, but the boy could usually keep a secret.

He got up and went to the cashier's counter to pay up. The cops had gone back out into the night and their interstate patrol. He stepped outside into the cool air and told himself to relax. There was simply no way they would see this coming.

At 7:30 on Monday morning, Farnsworth called an urgent all-hands meeting in the Roanoke office. Janet had come back to the office by herself after meeting Kreiss at the hospital. Keenan and his agents had gone haring after Kreiss in the night. She had told Keenan about the claymores. Keenan shrugged that off, but the other agents were giving one another uneasy looks. She had given them two chances of finding Kreiss: slim and none. Farnsworth had gone home by the time she got back to the office, so she slept on the couch in the upstairs conference room. She was awakened by agents coming down the hall, talking about the hurry-up meeting, and just had time to wash her face, comb her hair, and find some coffee before going down to the next floor to the big conference room.

When she got there, the room was pretty much full. It was easy to tell which of the agents had been out all night and which ones were coming in fresh. The older man who had been with the ATF squad out at the arsenal was sitting next to Farnsworth. This time, there was no sign of Foster. Being a worker bee, Janet stood by the back wall while the supervisory agents took chairs around the table. Her ribs still hurt, but the headache was gone and she could hear much better than yesterday. Farnsworth looked like he'd aged considerably.

"Okay, people," he said, "Let's get going." The room quieted right down. He introduced the ATF senior special agent as Walker Travers, who stood up and walked to the briefer's podium.

"I don't have a formal slide show or anything," Travers said. "But I've got the preliminary results of our NRT's work out at the Ramsey Arsenal."

"What was it?" Keenan asked. He hadn't shaved and was obviously frustrated by his search for Kreiss, which had turned up empty.

"It was what's known in the trade as a BFB," Travers said with a perfectly straight face. Janet got it about one second before he explained it: a big fucking bomb. There were some chuckles around the room. Janet noticed that neither Keenan nor Farnsworth joined in. The loss of Ken Whittaker was still weighing heavily.

"We don't know what it was," Travers went on. "We've had our EGIS people on it; they're from our National Laboratory Center. EGIS uses high-speed gas chromatography and chemiluminescent detection systems to identify explosives residue. The weird thing we're finding with this one is that there isn't any. Residue, I mean. And it's complicated by the fact that this was an explosives-manufacturing facility, so once we spread out the search beyond the actual power plant, of course we got the world's supply of residue."

"But nothing in the explosion focus?" Keenan asked. He had done a tour with ATF five years ago and knew something of their technical procedures.

"No, sir," Travers said. "The remains of machinery—you know, pumps, pipes, wiring, control instrumentation. Emphasis on the word *remains*. The plans say there was a boiler-water–testing laboratory next to the control room, and we've raised chemical residues in that area, but nothing that points to anything. It was a very hot and powerful blast."

"With no readily identifiable residue," Farnsworth said, shaking his head.

"Which tells a tale, actually," Travers said. "From looking at the wreckage, we see a reinforced-concrete building that was leveled in four directions damn near instantaneously, and it released a wave front that flattened everything nearby. Only one substance does that."

"Which is?"

"A gas," Travers said. "An explosive gas. Ever seen a building where somebody left a gas stove on with the pilot light turned off? Or a hot-water heater? Then someone comes home and lights a cigarette?" There were nods of recognition around the room.

"A hydrocarbon-based gas, such as propane, so-called producer gas, or natural gas builds up in a structure until the mixture of gas and air becomes an explosive vapor, just waiting for ignition. It doesn't take as much as you might think, depending on the hydrocarbon involved. When it does let go, it creates an instantaneous overpressure on every square inch of the structure's interior. Unlike, say, a truck bomb, which punches a wave front *at* a building, an internal vapor explosion exerts a huge force on every element of the building from inside. Remember your math: Force equals pressure times the area affected. You take a wall, twenty feet long by eight feet high, that's a hundred and sixty square feet, or a little over twenty thousand square inches. Times a pressure of a hundred pounds per square inch, and you get an impulse force of a little over two million pounds. That is somewhat outside the normal load-bearing specs for buildings."

"So you're saying this explosion might really have been accidental?" Janet asked from the back of the room, remembering what Farnsworth had told her. Agents turned to look at her. "Like a natural buildup of methane or some other bad shit left over from when the plant was open, and when that guy went down there to open the building with a cigarette in his mouth, boom?"

"That's exactly what I'm saying," Travers replied. "As you may or may not know, that's our official conclusion. Originally issued to choke off media speculation. But that's in fact what it's coming down to—a gas explosion. We found piping connections between the turbine hall and a large underground chamber where cooling water for the turbogenerator condensers was discharged. There are chemical residues of all kinds, including nitric acid, of all things, in that chamber."

"I have some personal knowledge of that chamber," Janet said. There were some covert grins around the room. "I don't remember smelling nitric acid down there."

"Would you recognize it if you did smell it, Agent Carter?"

"Yes, I would."

"Well. That's a mystery, then. The explosive vapors may not have originated in the underground area. There are several gases that can become explosive air-gas mixtures, and they have no scent whatsoever. For that matter, the gas in your house comes odorless—the gas company puts the sulfur smell in to alert people to leaks." He stopped for a moment to look at his notes.

"That place has been shut down for a long time. The security company's records don't indicate that they *ever* went into that power plant. There were rumors of toxic wastes and even chemical weapons going around about the Ramsey Arsenal. A small accretion of methane, which occurs in nature, could build up in that building over the years, creating a huge bomb. Which is what we got, folks."

"And that's how you're calling it?" Farnsworth asked. "An act of God?"

"Basically, yes, sir, that's what we're calling it. There is no evidence of any chemical or commercial explosive residues, and the way that heavily reinforced-concrete building blew up—it all points to a gas explosion."

"Could it have been hydrogen?" Farnsworth asked, shooting Janet a cautionary look.

Travers frowned. He had obviously heard about what Lynn Kreiss had said. "No, sir, I don't think so. I mean, hydrogen would certainly have done the job, but it doesn't occur in nature in concentrations like that. It tends to dissipate, rather than concentrate, due to its molecular structure. No, my guess is methane, and though we can usually smell methane, this explosion so completely leveled the building that there was nowhere for any residual gas to pocket. I think it was methane, coming up from that underground cavern, where, I'm told, they used to dump chemically unstable batches of feedstocks when a reaction went out of limits. God only knows what kinds of things are lurking down in that cavern, or in what amounts."

There was a surprised silence in the room. Everyone had been thinking a conventional, chemically based bomb. Farnsworth stood up.

"Okay, folks, there we have it. These people are the foremost experts in reconstructing explosions in the country. How many bombing incidents has the ATF investigated in the past five years, Mr. Travers?"

"Sixty-two thousand and counting," Travers said. This produced expressions of surprise and some low whistles.

"Good enough for us country folks," Farnsworth said. "All right, everybody, it's Monday and there's paperwork to be done. I'll have word about the funeral service this afternoon."

The meeting broke up and Janet started back to her office. She had to wait for the crowd that was bunched up at the elevator. Ben Keenan escorted Travers to the front door of the security area. She was toying with the idea of going home to get fresh clothes and a shower, when Farnsworth gave her the high sign that she was to join him in his office. She had to wait for a few more minutes while some supervisors cornered the RA. When they were finished, she went into his office. Ben Keenan was already there, along with someone she had not expected to see: Foster. Her heart sank when she saw Foster.

The RA, his deputy, and the Washington executive assistant. This isn't over, she thought. Foster had another man with him, someone she did not recognize. Everyone sat down. Farnsworth looked at Keenan.

"No word on finding Kreiss?"

"No, sir, he plain vanished. We have local law looking for his vehicle, another pickup truck, like McGarand's, but no hits so far."

"And he didn't return home last night?" Foster asked.

"No, we had some of our people in position."

"Now that ATF has taken a formal position on this explosion," Farnsworth said, "we've got to find Kreiss."

"Why?" Janet asked.

"We've got too many pieces to this puzzle: The McGarands are linked to Waco, Kreiss is linked to Jared McGarand's homicide. Jared's truck has been physically linked to the Ramsey Arsenal via samples from his truck's tires. Kreiss has revealed that he was the one the state cops sighted driving the other McGarand's truck south on the interstate, not McGarand. We have a very large explosion that ATF is classifying as an act of God. But now Browne McGarand, ex–chief explosives engineer at the Ramsey Arsenal, is missing, Kreiss is missing, Jared McGarand's dead, and Kreiss's daughter was heard ranting and raving about a hydrogen bomb and Washington, D.C. Mr. Foster thinks we still have a problem here."

"Do we think Kreiss killed Jared McGarand?" Janet asked.

"Maybe," Farnsworth said. "The local cops say that it could have been an accident. They're all hung up about some goo they found on the trailer and also on the body."

"Goo?" the man with Foster said. "What color was it?" He was what Janet would have called "an M-squared, B-squared" if she had to describe him: medium-medium, brown-brown, and totally forgettable.

"I have no goddamn idea," Farnsworth replied, obviously exasperated and also still very tired.

"Purple," Keenan said, consulting his notes. "It was purple and very sticky. And who are you, sir?"

"This gentleman is from the Agency," Farnsworth said.

The man nodded as if introductions had been made. "That 'goo,'" he said, "is a substance used in something we call 'a capture web.' It comes in a spray can. It's like a spiderweb, only much thicker. Very sticky. The more you fight, the more you get entangled, until you are immobilized. When you're ready to release your subject, you hose him down—it's totally water-soluble."

Jared's body had been wet when they found it, Janet remembered. "Okay, so maybe it was Kreiss who got Jared," Janet said. "But I'm willing to bet that was about his daughter, not any bomb plot. And, Kreiss was right: They did have his daughter. So if they had his daughter captive at the arsenal, the McGarands weren't using that place for a fishing hole. They were doing some bad shit out there. If this is about Waco, we need to warn Washington."

"That's going to present a problem," Keenan said, and Farnsworth nodded, obviously already knowing what Keenan was going to say.

"What?"

"The ATF is going on record, as we speak, that this was an explosion resulting from natural causes. Without direct evidence of a bomb, what you suggest is purely supposition. ATF will view any alternative theories we bring up as a challenge to their authority in the area of explosives determination."

"Oh, for crying—"

"Think about the state of relations at the Washington level among our respective agencies just now," Farnsworth said. "Which haven't been helped by Ken Whittaker's death, during what was essentially a Bureau deal."

Janet took a deep breath and then let it out. "So if we could find Kreiss," she said, "maybe we could firm this up a little?"

"If you find Kreiss, he goes in a box somewhere where nobody can get to him, and that includes ATF," Foster said. "Assistant Director Marchand has those instructions from the deputy AG's office. Edwin Kreiss isn't going to testify to anything. We can't allow it."

"Hell, I suspect he wouldn't allow it," Janet said.

That last remark produced an uncomfortable silence, which Keenan finally broke.

"Look, boss," he said, addressing Farnsworth. "It's time to elevate this hairball to headquarters. Tell 'em what we know, tell 'em what we think, and then hunker back down in the weeds, where we belong."

"I represent headquarters," Foster told him.

"Not my part of it," Farnsworth said. There was a strained silence in the room. Finally, Farnsworth instructed Keenan to keep looking for Edwin Kreiss. He told Janet to notify Keenan if she had any further contact from Kreiss, and to get with the surveillance people to put a locating tap on the hospital lines into the ICU, where his daughter was. The RA and Foster then went into the secure-communications cube to get on the horn to Richmond, which, as the supervisory field office, was directly over the Roanoke RA.

Keenan stopped Janet outside Farnsworth's office. As Farnsworth's deputy, he dealt primarily with the four squad supervisors, so he had not had very much direct contact with Janet. "You've met this guy Kreiss," he said. "Whose side is he on if this does turn out to be a bomb plot against the seat of government?"

Janet had to think about that. "I've met him, but I wouldn't say I know him. All these bomb conspiracies notwithstanding, the only thing Kreiss has ever been focused on was finding his daughter. She is now at least safe, if not fully recovered. I don't know whose side he'd be on."

"You're the last person who spoke directly to him," Keenan said gently. "Take a guess."

Janet sighed. "Well, sir, if Kreiss thinks the older McGarand had a part in kidnapping his daughter and getting her hurt, he'll pursue him and punish him, maybe even kill him. Everything else would be incidental to that objective. I don't think Edwin Kreiss takes sides anymore, and I don't think he takes prisoners, either, or at least not for very long."

Keenan nodded thoughtfully. "Do you understand what Foster and his buddy over at Main Justice are up to?" he asked.

"No, sir, I haven't a clue. But if Foster's really acting for Assistant Director Marchand, I think it has something to do with what happened when Kreiss was forcibly retired."

Keenan looked away, nodded his head slowly. "Lord, I hope not," he said, and then went back into his office.

Kreiss had left the interstate near Harrisonburg and made his way east over to the Skyline Drive, the mountain road. It would be much slower than running the interstate, but it accomplished two things: It got him out of the state police's primary surveillance zone, and the narrow, winding mountain road made it easy to spot a tail. He left the Skyline Drive south of Front Royal and worked the back roads along the Blue Ridge and the Shenandoah River into Clarke County until he cut U.S. Route 50, at which point he turned east and joined the morning rush-hour traffic. An astonishing number of cars were headed into Washington at that hour of the morning, but the heavy traffic would be a good place to hide his vehicle in case the northern Virginia cops had been alerted. By the time he'd made it down through Upperville, Middleburg, and Aldie, it was nearing 7:00 A.M. He was now in familiar territory, having lived in northern Virginia for many years, so when he hit Route 58, the Dulles Airport connector, he got off the main highway and stopped at a diner next to a large shopping mall for some coffee and breakfast.

As he watched the sluggish stream of commuter traffic drag by on the four-lane highway outside, he thought about his next steps. Ideally, he needed another vehicle. Second, he needed a place to stay while he hunted McGarand. Third, he wouldn't mind a nice GPS position on McGarand and the propane truck. He smiled grimly. Actually, finding McGarand shouldn't be all that hard, as long as he stayed with that distinctive green-and-white truck. The Washington area was served by a large metropolitan gas company, which meant that there were not a lot of propane customers in or near the city. Driving something like that downtown, especially in Washington, was strictly regulated, which left the Maryland and northern Virginia suburbs. If he intended to park it, he would most likely use a truck stop along the Beltway. The biggest trucking terminals in the Washington area were in Alexandria, on the Virginia side of the Potomac River, and near the rail yards on the Maryland side. Browne McGarand had come up from southwest Virginia, so Kreiss would begin his search in Alexandria along I-95 and I-495.

The easiest way for him to get a new vehicle would be to rent one. For that, he needed to get to a couple of ATMs. He had brought some cash with him, and there was a motel right behind the diner. He would prepay a room, park his truck in the back somewhere, get cleaned up, and walk over to the mall, where there were bound to be ATMs. Then he would taxi over to Dulles, rent a van, find a trucker's atlas or an exit guide, and get to work. Then it would be a matter of slogging through the Washington-area trucking centers, looking for that propane truck. He remembered that there had been a logo on the truck, but he couldn't recollect what it said. Something about that logo had not been quite right, but he simply could not remember it. So, first a motel room and a shower. Then some scut work.

Browne McGarand got off the Beltway and made his way up U.S. Route 1 into the rail yards on the Reagan National Airport side of Crystal City. He parked at an all-night diner and got some breakfast. He and Jared had scouted out this phase of the plan some months ago. He would drive into Crystal City proper after rush hour, staying on the old Jefferson Davis Highway until he reached the Pentagon interchange, just before Route 1 ascended onto the Fourteenth Street Bridge over the Potomac. Then he would get back off the elevated highway, loop underneath it, and drive down a small two-lane road that led into the Pentagon parking areas. Just before the turn that would take him into Pentagon South Parking, he would turn into the driveway that led to the Pentagon power plant.

The power plant had originally been a coal-fired facility, then an oil-fired one, designed to provide emergency power to the huge military headquarters. Now it housed a dozen large gas turbine generators in a fenced yard next to what had been its coal yard. Because the gas turbine emergency generators could be started remotely from the Pentagon, the facility was no longer manned. Its entrances had been chained and locked. All except the parking lot, which was really an extension of the old coal yard. The parking lot had a long chain across it, but no lock, probably to let fire trucks get in. The coal yard, now empty, was surrounded on three sides by high concrete walls, originally used to contain a small mountain of coal. He would back the truck out of sight of the entranceway and shut it down. It had been Jared who had found this spot when he'd gotten lost in the maze of roads around the approaches to the Fourteenth Street Bridge. He'd blown a tire right in front of the power plant, pulled into the driveway to change it, and discovered the perfect hiding place. Someone would have to come into the driveway and then all the way back into the old coal yard ever to see the truck.

From the power plant, it was a five-minute walk to the Pentagon Metro station. Browne was dressed in what he hoped were suitably touristy clothes: khaki slacks, short-sleeved shirt, a windbreaker, and a floppy sun hat and some sunglasses. He wished he had a camera to complete the outfit, but, as long as nothing had changed, this would do. The Pentagon Metro station was on the east side of the Pentagon building. He would take a Yellow Line train into the District, then get off at the Mount Vernon Place station. His target would then be within easy walking distance. He ordered another cup of coffee, and, as the caffeine kicked in, wondered if he should bother getting a motel room.

Janet got back into the office at 11:30. She picked up a sandwich at the first-floor deli and took it upstairs to her office. She had just popped open her Coke when the intercom buzzed and Farnsworth's secretary called her down to a meeting in the RA's conference room. She sighed, poured her Coke into her coffee mug, put the sandwich in the office fridge, and went downstairs. Farnsworth was there, along with Keenan, Special Agent Bobby Land from the Roanoke surveillance squad, and two uniformed police lieutenants, one from the Virginia State Police and the other from the Montgomery County Sheriff's Department.

The person who got her attention, however, was a woman who was sitting by herself at the other end of the conference table from where the men were standing. Janet struggled not to stare at her. She had a striking, witchlike face: intense black eyes under thin eyebrows, a slightly hooked nose, wide cheekbones, and dark red lips. She appeared to be in good physical shape, tall, with wide shoulders and a fit tautness to her skin. She looked to be in her late forties, and the way she was sitting at the table, still as a grave, staring quietly into the middle distance, projected an attitude of total composure that made her utterly unapproachable. As the only other woman in the room, Janet would normally have gone over to introduce herself, but something in this woman's demeanor gave her pause.

"Okay, gents, this is Special Agent Janet Carter," Farnsworth said. "Let's get going." Everyone took a chair, leaving the other woman in semisplendid isolation at the far end of the conference table. Janet forced herself to face Farnsworth, who shuffled some papers before beginning.

"We've had some developments in the McGarand business," he announced. "Not to be confused with progress, however. Janet, for your benefit, this is Lieutenant Whitney from the Virginia State Police, and Lieutenant Harter from the Montgomery County Sheriff's Department."

Farnsworth glanced down at his papers for a second while Janet waited for him to introduce the woman, but he did not. "There've been some musical chairs with vehicles in the arsenal case," he said. "Browne McGarand's pickup truck has been located at his grandson's house, where it was *not* present during yesterday's sweep, except for the brief time that Browne McGarand visited there. Jared McGarand's telephone company repair van, which had been parked at Jared's trailer, was found by another phone company crew at the TA truck stop above the Christiansburg interchange. This is the same truck stop where two security guards allege that an unknown subject, later identified as Edwin Kreiss from a Polaroid photograph the security guards took, attacked them without provocation in their office. They'd detained him in the parking lot, where they had been watching him 'case the place,' to use their words."

"Unprovoked attack'?" Janet asked.

Farnsworth shrugged. "Both of them were steroid junkies. One of them nearly died from a partially strangulated larynx, and the other reported being disabled with a . . . weapon, I guess, that another branch of government said was something subject Edwin Kreiss might have been carrying. They called it 'a retinal disrupter.' "

"A retinal what?" Keenan asked.

"They described it as a very powerful flashcube, tuned to the optical frequency of a purple substance in the human eye that can be overloaded by a strong pulse of light. Firing a retinal disrupter into a subject's eyes renders him stunned and immobilized for up to sixty seconds, if not longer, which has its obvious tactical advantages."

"Where can I get me one of those?" Lieutenant Whitney asked. He was a large-shouldered man in his fifties, with buzz-cut gray hair and a huge pair of mirrored sunglasses hanging down from his perfectly creased shirt pocket.

"You can't," Farnsworth said. "If it's any comfort, neither can we." He gave the lieutenant a second for that to sink in, then continued. "Kreiss's personal vehicle is also a pickup truck. It is not at his house, nor is Kreiss. Browne McGarand is not at his house, and we have information that he did not go to Greensboro, North Carolina, as he told the local police he was going to do. His other grandson, whom we located in Greensboro, confirmed he had not heard from his grandfather, and he also did not know about Jared McGarand's demise."

"Sir, what's the status on Kreiss's daughter?" Janet asked.

"She's stable, comatose, but breathing on her own. The docs now think she'll come out of it, but they can't say when."

"You guys designated a prime suspect for the Jared McGarand homicide?" Keenan asked.

"We like this guy Kreiss, based on what you folks have told us," Lieutenant Harter said. He was a dark-haired, well-built young man, whose short-sleeved tan uniform shirt fit him like a glove. He had been giving Janet the eye while Farnsworth spoke.

Janet was surprised to hear this: Now what had Farnsworth done? The last thing she'd been told was that they were going to stay quiet about Kreiss. And she was still wondering who the woman was. She was wearing a visitor's badge, but it was not one requiring an escort. She had not moved a muscle, reminding Janet of an exquisitely made Japanese robot she had seen at Disney World several years ago. She did not even appear to be listening to the discussion. Her hands rested motionless on the table. Janet noticed that the outside edge of the woman's right palm was ridged with calluses, which fairly shouted karate training. She jerked her attention back to what the lieutenant was saying.

"Is there a federal warrant out?" Harter asked.

"No," Farnsworth said, looking down at the papers in front of him. "And we've asked the state and local authorities to hold up on obtaining a warrant for right now."

"Because of what happened out at the Ramsey Arsenal," Janet said, concentrating again on the discussion.

"Exactly," Farnsworth said. "The purpose of this meeting is to confirm that we will continue to press our search for Edwin Kreiss and Browne McGarand, but we will do so in conjunction with a larger federal investigation being conducted in cooperation with the ATF." Farnsworth shot Janet a quick glance to make sure she wasn't going to blow his cover, but she had caught on—Farnsworth wanted local law to think the Bureau was working hand in glove with the ATF.

"This is all about that big explosion, out at the arsenal?" Lieutenant Harter asked. His expression indicated that he wasn't exactly following what was being said.

"Yes, and we have reason to believe that subject Browne McGarand may be engaged in a bombing conspiracy, which might involve the capital city," Farnsworth continued.

"Do y'all think the explosion at the arsenal was their lab going up?" Whitney asked.

"*We* think it was, but the ATF national response team is leaning toward natural causes. A methane buildup. Given the size of that explosion, we're treating the whole matter very seriously. If there was a bomb-making cell operating out of the arsenal, and they blew themselves up, then end of story. ATF tells us that happens sometimes. But if that explosion was a package left behind to entertain federal authorities who might come snooping, then they're capable of making one hell of a bomb, and we have to assume a clear and present danger."

"We'll play it any way you want to, Mr. Farnsworth," Harter said. "But when it's all over, we're still going to want to have a talk with this Kreiss fella."

"And you'll get it. I guess what I'm saying is that we just want to make sure that there isn't a bigger deal going down here. You know, like an Oklahoma City–scale conspiracy."

"What's this Kreiss guy's role in that theory?" Harter asked.

"Kreiss's daughter was one of those college kids that went missing, remember? As we told you, he's been looking for his missing daughter, who turned up at that arsenal."

"And right now, y'all think he's chasing down this Browne McGarand?"

"Yes."

Harter and Whitney looked at each other and then back at Farnsworth, who knew what their question was. "Kreiss used to be pretty good at hunting people. We wouldn't necessarily be upset if he finds McGarand, especially if it prevents another bombing."

Janet watched as Whitney nodded his head slowly. Farnsworth was obviously confusing the shit out of the locals "Oka-a-y," Whitney said. "But how do we get him for this homicide deal?"

"His daughter is now hospitalized in Blacksburg. I'm requesting that she be placed under police guard. Eventually, we're pretty sure Kreiss will come back here to see her. Can you help?"

"Yes, sir, he comes back, we can take it from there, I think," Harter said. "And we'll get some assets into that hospital."

Farnsworth stood up, and so did the two uniformed cops. They shook hands and Farnsworth asked Agent Bobby Land to escort them out. When they were gone, he sat back down and ran his hands through his hair.

"Okay, so much for local legends. Janet, we'd been meeting for a while before you got back to the office. That little charade was for purposes of keeping local law occupied while we sort out what we're really going to do. The U.S. attorney for the Southwestern District of Virginia is running top cover for us, but I thought I'd better add my personal reassurances to those guys."

"Sir?" Janet said. "I thought we were going to keep the Kreiss angle away from local law?"

Farnsworth cleared his throat, glancing nervously at the woman at the other end of the table.

"Yes. Well. We've had some new guidance from Washington on that score."

Janet couldn't stand it anymore. "May I know who *she* is?" she asked, pointing with her chin to the woman at the end of the table. The woman did not even look at her.

"When I'm finished, yes. Now, as usual, there's a turf fight shaping up. ATF headquarters is circling the wagons around their 'natural causes' theory of the arsenal explosion, apparently because their director found out that they had cleared the arsenal during a previous inspection of the place."

"And the Bureau?"

"Bureau headquarters is officially deferring to ATF, but somehow, ATF has found out that we're hunting two subjects, McGarand and Kreiss."

"ATF is saying there's no threat to Washington?"

"ATF is saying there's no threat unless, of course, *we* have evidence to the contrary. I think they're looking for a fig leaf, in case it turns out somebody has actual *evidence* that some bad guys were in fact making bombs down there."

"But we do, sort of—Kreiss. And what his daughter said."

"No, we do not, Janet," he said. "As of this morning, based on guidance I've received through our regular chain of command, we no longer know anything about any Edwin Kreiss, except as the parent of a girl who is no longer missing."

Janet sat back in her chair. "But don't you think he's chasing McGarand? Shouldn't we tell Kreiss that we think McGarand is going to bomb something in Washington? That's there's a tie between McGarand and Waco?"

"Officially, I no longer have any opinions on the matter of Edwin Kreiss," Farnsworth said, setting his face into a blank bureaucratic mask. Janet, baffled, just looked at him, and then at Keenan, who was now intently studying his hands.

"But I do," the woman at the end of the table said. Her voice was low, but filled with quiet authority.

"And you are . . ." Janet said, turning in her chair.

"I am the person assigned by an appropriate authority to attend to the problem of Edwin Kreiss," the woman said. "I understand he is or was carrying a pager you gave him?"

Attend to—Janet remembered those words. She didn't know what to say, but she found herself nodding.

"Very well," the woman said. "I want you to page him at eighteen hundred tonight, exactly. Then key in a number I'm going to give you. It's a northern Virginia number, but it will bounce back here to this office. Assuming he calls in, I have a message I want you to give him."

"Not until I know who you are, or *what* you are," Janet said. She was beginning to suspect that the "what" would be more important than the "who." "The last guy who wanted me to page Kreiss wanted me to tell him his daughter was dead. And guess what: That didn't happen."

Farnsworth looked up at the ceiling. The woman stood up, and Janet was surprised by how tall she was. She was wearing an expensive loose-fitting pantsuit, and she was clearly over six feet tall even in her flat shoes. She picked up a handbag that could have doubled as a briefcase. She asked the two men in the room if they would mind excusing themselves. To Janet's further surprise, both of them stood and left the room without a word, closing the door behind them. Looking at the expression on the woman's face, Janet suddenly found herself wishing she was carrying her sidearm. The woman walked around the conference table and came up next to Janet. She perched one hip on the table and looked down at her, forcing Janet to crane her neck to make eye contact. The woman's expression was disturbing; she was looking at Janet with a flat, slightly unfocused, zero-parallax stare.

"When we're all done making the page call and delivering the message, I will return to Washington to attend to the matter of Edwin Kreiss," the woman said. Her diction was precise and clear. "Your director has assured my director that you *will* make the call, and that you *will* deliver the message. Which goes like this: three words—*tenebrae factae sunt.* I'll write it down for you, if you'd like. It's church Latin for 'night has fallen.' It will tell Kreiss that I'm coming for him."

Janet didn't like the sound of that, so she tried for a little defiance. "And he'll give a shit? That *you're* coming?"

The woman's unfocused look went away, and she looked right into Janet's eyes with a wolfish smile that made her own black eyes glow. "Oh yes, Special Agent Carter. He'll absolutely give a shit. Anyone who knows me would." She stood back up, smoothed her clothes, and retrieved her handbag. "I'll see you in Mr. Farnsworth's office at eighteen hundred. That's six P.M. by the way."

The woman walked calmly out of the conference room, leaving Janet alone at the table, her face burning just a little, and wondering what in the hell this was all about. She was tempted to page Kreiss right now and warn him that some female cyborg in an Armani pantsuit was after him, but the woman had mentioned her director and Janet's director. This implied that the woman was an Agency operative of some kind. Another "sweeper" perhaps? What kind of outfit needed to have people like that in their stable? The woman's mention of directors had been deliberate, though. And if the heads of the Bureau and the Agency were involved, it was definitely not time for junior special agents to be taking any sudden initiatives. Then she remembered what Farnsworth had speculated earlier: They were going to let Kreiss hunt McGarand, but the Agency was going to join the hunt for Kreiss.

Tenebrae factae sunt. Darkness has fallen. She felt a tingle run up her backbone. Yeah, that would do it for me, she thought. My director and your director. She closed her eyes to think. Something didn't quite add up here: The people originally interested in Kreiss had been Foster, of the Bureau, and Bellhouser, of the Justice Department. FBI counterintelligence and the deputy AG, to be specific. And now the Agency. Why would the FBI director be supporting that ugly little axis?

She wanted to go talk to Farnsworth again, but he was acting as if he had been stepped on from above and was now in the "yes, sir, no, sir, whatever you say, sir" mode most beloved of the Bureau when it was circling its own bureaucratic wagons. What had Farnsworth told her earlier? They'd let Kreiss run free. They didn't *know* there was a bomb threat, but if Kreiss solved that problem, fine. And if he created bigger problems while he was doing it, there'd be no stink on them. He wasn't their asset. He was the Justice Department's asset. So what did that make Janet? Farnsworth's secretary stepped into the conference room.

"Agent Carter?" she said. "The Blacksburg hospital is calling? About a Lynn Kreiss? Can you take it? I can't find the boss, and I know you were involved with that case."

Janet said sure and went into Farnsworth's outer office to take the call. The nurse calling reported that they thought Lynn Kreiss might be coming around. Their log said that the FBI people wanted to be notified when she surfaced. At this very moment, Janet wasn't sure what her current assignment was, but she said she'd be right over. She went back upstairs to collect her sidearm and purse, grab her sandwich, and then go down to the garage.

There was a street-level sandwich shop diagonally across the street from the office building at 650 Massachusetts Avenue. Browne bought a cup of coffee and a newspaper and sat down at one of the café tables out on the street itself. It was a warmish day, although nothing like what was to come in the horrific Washington summertime. There was a steady flow of government workers walking by, some stopping in for coffee or to get a ready-made sandwich to take to the office for lunch.

He studied the ATF headquarters building surreptitiously while pretending to read his newspaper. There did not appear to be any new security cameras on the building or its neighbors, although he could not see what might have been added to the building right above him. He reminded himself to check that when he got up. The attack depended on two factors. The first was that there was a parking garage right next door to his target, separated from the ATF building by a narrow alley. The garage had an outside ramp that led directly up to its roof-level deck. More importantly, that ramp, which was on the side of the garage away from the ATF building, did not appear to be in the field of view of any of the cameras guarding the ATF's headquarters. It was also just wide enough to accommodate the propane truck.

The second factor had to do with the ATF building's heating, ventilation, and air-conditioning system. Like those of most office buildings, it was a recirculating system. A small amount of outside air was taken in and passed over the cooling coils of the chiller plant housed in a small HVAC building at the back of the alley between the garage and the ATF building. It was then circulated throughout the building via the duct system, but instead of being exhausted from the building, it was recooled and redistributed again and again, so as to maximize the efficiency of the air-conditioning plant. His plan was simple: Very early tomorrow morning, he would drive the propane truck up the ramp to the top deck of that garage and park it next to the outer wall on the alley side of the building. The ATF headquarters was ten stories high, with a wall of windows overlooking the top deck of the garage. But no cameras looked at the garage; he and Jared had both checked. Instead, a single security camera, mounted on the front corner of that air-conditioning building, looked into the alley, toward the street.

The propane truck came equipped with a four-inch diameter wire-reinforced 150-foot-long hose, whose fittings he had modified to handle the hydrogen gas. He would park the truck, wait until nearly dawn, and then unreel the heavy hose down into the alley behind the air-conditioning building, a distance of perhaps forty, forty-five feet. A big truck like that in the alley would draw instant attention from the security monitoring office, assuming they were awake at the switch at that hour of the morning. But the hose would come down in the predawn darkness *behind* the security camera, and so would he.

Once on the ground, he would spread a large plastic tarp over one of the HVAC building's two air intakes to block it off. He would then drape a second tarp, with a receiver fitting sewn into it, over the remaining air-intake screen. The screens were eight feet high and six feet wide. At that hour, the building's environmental-management system would be running the intake fans at very low speed. They wouldn't speed up the fans until the heat of the day called for more cooling. He had taken rough volumetric measurements of the building by pacing off its length and width on the sidewalk and then multiplying that number by one hundred. Then he had computed the heating/ventilation/air-conditioning volume using the *Civil Engineer's Handbook*. The propane truck was designed to hold eight thousand gallons of liquid propane. Now, filled with pure hydrogen gas under nearly four hundred pounds of pressure per square inch, it held more than enough hydrogen to fill the ATF building, using the building's own recycling ventilation system, in about an hour. What made the building most vulnerable to this kind of attack was the fact that none of its windows could be opened. In fact, he had almost twice the hydrogen he needed to achieve an explosive vapor mixture, but he knew there would be small leaks here and there. No man-made gas system was perfect.

He was going to treat the ATF the same way they and their allies at the FBI had treated the people at Mount Carmel. He would start the odorless, invisible hydrogen injection at around 6:00 A.M. Sometime in the next 60 to 90 minutes, the building would achieve an explosive mixture of air and hydrogen, courtesy of its own closed-cycle ventilation system. Because it was the start of the day, the intake fans would be running slowly, and the recycling air-handler system would keep almost all the air inside the building to achieve maximum cooling. Sometime after that, as the building filled with ATF agents and their bosses, someone, somewhere, would slip into the men's room to sneak a cigarette. Or fumble with an aging light switch. Or turn on an entire floor's worth of fluorescent light fixtures all at once. Or summon the elevator and mash the button several times, making those copper contacts up in the elevator shaft open and close, open and close. He had been a chemist and an explosives engineer for decades. The industrial-safety manuals were filled with stories of how the most mundane objects were capable of producing a static spark: a doorknob in winter, the switch on a desk fan, panty hose on a dry winter day, the keyboard of an electric typewriter, the ringer in a telephone.

In that silent, invisibly deadly atmosphere, one spark would reproduce what had happened down at Ramsey. Only this time, the building wasn't made of reinforced concrete: It was wall-to-wall windows.

"Some more coffee, sir?" a pleasant young woman asked, pausing at his table with a Silex coffee pitcher.

"Thanks, I'm all done," he said, smiling up at her through his dark glasses. His heart was actually thumping with excitement. Today, after months of labor at the arsenal, he was finally here. This afternoon, he would find a motel near the airport to crash and get some sleep. Early in the morning, he would take a taxi to the Pentagon, then go retrieve the truck. There was security-camera surveillance of the Pentagon building itself, but he had seen not one single camera on the old power station building. Then he would drive the truck into the city; he even had an official-looking dispatch ticket, lifted when Jared had appropriated the truck. And sometime early tomorrow morning, all those criminal bastards in that building were going to get a taste of what it must have been like at Waco when they burned William along with those Branch Davidians to death, while their agents stood around the perimeter, drinking coffee and making crispy-critter jokes.

He hoped there *were* cameras on that building. They were going to get the shot of a lifetime.

Forty-five minutes later, Janet was sitting in Lynn Kreiss's hospital room. A uniformed sheriff's deputy sat outside the door, watching the television in the empty room across the hall. Lynn was still hooked up to an IV, but she actually looked better than the last time Janet had seen her. It's amazing what some sleep can do for you, Janet thought. The girl was tossing and turning a bit in the bed, and making small noises in the back of her throat, as if she were having a bad dream. Her face had some color in it, and the monitors on the shelf above her head were busier than they had been the last time. Janet had talked to the attending physician, who told her that Lynn had started talking—*babbling* might be a better word for it—at 3:30 that morning. The collective opinion was that she would be coming around soon. Janet asked how soon was soon. The collective opinion was that it was anybody's guess. The marvels of modern medicine, Janet thought.

As she watched the girl wrestle with the web of unconsciousness, Janet was struggling with her own dilemma. In her mind, she was coming down on the side of a real human-made explosion out there at the arsenal, if only because of the timing. That thing had gone off when a bunch of people had come in there and started unlocking doors. If there had been a pool of explosive vapors down there in that tunnel complex, her own little adventure should have set it off, especially when that car went scraping along the concrete. Then there were the two civilians, the McGarands, one a possible homicide victim, whose truck tires had traces of arsenal mud on them, and the other a retired chemical explosives engineer. And not just any engineer, but the senior engineer at the Ramsey Arsenal. Both of them were blood relations to a guy who had been incinerated at the Waco holocaust. And now the surviving McGarand has just flat-assed disappeared, with Kreiss apparently hot on his tail. And all three federal agencies involved, two of which had been responsible for what happened at Waco, were busy going head down, tail up in the bureaucratic ostrich position. Oh, and now some shark-eyed dolly with a half-inch-thick karate callus on her hands wanted Janet to relay a love note to Edwin Kreiss.

She looked up. Lynn Kreiss was staring at her, trying to speak. Janet got up and went over to the bed. The girl's lips seemed to be dry, so Janet poured her a glass of water.

"I'm Special Agent Janet Carter," she said softly. "I'm with the FBI. Are you thirsty?"

The girl nodded and Janet helped her sip some water. Lynn cleared her throat and then asked Janet what time it was.

Janet told her what day it was, what had happened out at the arsenal, and how long she'd been out of touch here in the hospital. The girl drank some more water and then Janet said she was going to summon the nurses but that she needed to talk to Lynn after that, if she was able.

"Where's my father?" Lynn asked.

"We don't know," Janet said after a second's hesitation. "He wasn't involved in the explosion. Personally, I think he's up in Washington chasing down the guy who kidnapped you."

"Guys," Lynn said. Her voice was gaining strength, and she sat up a little in the bed. "There were two of them, a young guy and an older guy, although I only got a quick look at them, when my friends hit the leg traps."

"Leg traps?"

The girl explained what had happened to her two friends. She reiterated that she had seen only the two men, one much older than the other. Both guys had black beards and looked like mountain men.

"Yes, that's what we have," Janet said. "The younger guy's name was Jared McGarand; he's dead. The older guy is his grandfather, Browne McGarand, and he's missing." She told Lynn what had happened to Jared, then asked her what had happened to the boys' remains. Lynn didn't know, other than that the water had covered them up. She closed her eyes for a moment, and Janet gave her a minute to rest.

"The younger one—you said he's dead?"

"Yes," Janet said. "An apparent homicide." She didn't feel it was the time to discuss her father's possible involvement.

"Good riddance," Lynn said. "That guy was a serious creep."

"Lynn, when the medics picked you up, you were sort of babbling something about a hydrogen bomb and Washington."

"I was?"

"Yes. It didn't make much sense, but it got everybody's attention."

Lynn frowned for a moment, and then her face cleared. "Oh, yes, I do remember. The other one, the older one, told me he was taking a hydrogen bomb to Washington. I said, Yeah, right, like he could just make a hydrogen bomb with some plans off the Web. He said it wasn't what I thought."

Oh shit, Janet thought. "Any indication of what he was going to do with this bomb?"

Lynn frowned again, trying to remember. "No," she said. "Wait—yes. He said he was going after what he called 'a legitimate target.'"

Janet studied the girl. There was a toughness there, despite her current physical frailty. Definitely her father's daughter. "Did he sound like a nutcase?"

"Yes and no. He wasn't raving. He was calm, sort of matter-of-fact. But fanatical, maybe—remember, I could only hear him. He said he'd made a hydrogen bomb, that he was taking it to Washington. Like it was a routine deal, something he did every day. That made it kinda scary, you know?"

Janet nodded, writing it all down in her notebook. "I wonder why he would tell you," she said.

"He implied I was supposed to be insurance, a hostage or something, if things went wrong. He told me to get ready to go, but then he never came back. The next thing that happened was that the building fell in on me. But that was much later."

Something was playing in the back of Janet's mind. What had that older ATF guy said—that this had been a *gas* explosion? "When he said hydrogen bomb, and you challenged that, and he said it wasn't what you thought—I wonder if he meant a hydrogen *gas* bomb?"

Lynn shrugged and then winced. Janet knew that feeling. She stepped out into the hallway and summoned the nurse. Then there was a crowd and Janet backed out into the hall to let the docs do their thing. She went down the hall to the waiting room, which was empty. She fished out her cell phone but then hesitated. She needed to call her immediate supervisor, Larry Talbot, to tell him what had happened to the two boys. There were parents to be notified, and, of course, remains to be found. But there was a bigger question here: That Agency woman wanted her to page some kind of a warning threat to Kreiss. But here was the daughter confirming that Browne McGarand was up to something that did involve a bomb and Washington, D.C. She should report that immediately, but would anybody listen? Her bosses seemed to be so caught up in protecting their rice bowls right now that there might be nobody listening.

She called Talbot, got his voice mail, and told him what Lynn had said about the missing kids. Then she put a call into Farnsworth's office. The secretary said he was not available. She asked for Keenan, but he was with Farnsworth. Where was the RA? Out, the secretary said helpfully. Feeling like a child, Janet almost hung up, but then she gave the secretary the news about Lynn Kreiss being awake, and that she, Janet, needed to talk to the RA urgently, as in, Now would be nice. The secretary was unimpressed, but she said she would pass it along. Janet gave her the number for her cell phone.

She went back down to ICU to talk to Lynn some more, but the doctors were busy and the nurses forbidding. It was now almost three o'clock. She stood there in the busy corridor, thinking, while a stream of hospital traffic parted indifferently around her, as if she were an island. In three hours, she was supposed to page Kreiss for his wake-up call. If he still had the pager, and if he had it turned on. She could just hear him saying, Now what, Special Agent? In that weary voice of his. Now what, indeed. I've got good news and bad news. Your daughter is conscious and apparently doing okay. She says one of the guys who kidnapped her is taking a hydrogen bomb to Washington. If you're interested, that is. Oh, and an old friend of yours stopped by with a message—want to hear it? And Kreiss would go, Nope, busy right now. Bye. Her cell phone rang. It was Farnsworth's secretary: "Get back here now."

Kreiss nosed his rented Ford 150 van into the truck stop off the Van Dorn Street Beltway exit in Alexandria. It wasn't much of a truck stop, not compared with the interstate facilities, but he had to check it out. His exit guide listed only two such facilities on or near the Beltway, not counting trucking terminals. This was the third trucking terminal he'd stopped into on his circuit of Washington's infamous I-495. It was midafternoon, and he knew that in about a half hour or so he would have to quit until after rush hour, because nothing moved during rush hour around Washington.

There were a dozen trucks parked at this stop, and three more filling up in the fuel lanes. No propane truck was in evidence. It was possible, of course, that McGarand had put the thing in a garage somewhere, and he had made a mental note to look up fuel companies in the area and make the rounds of those if the truck stops came up empty. But there was something so nicely anonymous about a truck stop that he was pretty sure that's where the propane tanker would be. Kreiss believed in the theory that if you want to hide something really well, you hide it in plain sight. He drove the van around the parking lot and behind the store and rest facilities building. No propane tanker. He got back out onto the Beltway and headed east, toward the Wilson Bridge and the crossing into Maryland. He had a terrible feeling he was wasting time.

A stone-faced Farnsworth was waiting in his office when Janet got back to the Roanoke office. Keenan was with him when Janet took a seat in front of the RA's desk. He asked her to debrief him on what Lynn Kreiss had told her. When she was finished, he turned in his swivel chair and looked out the window for a long minute. Janet looked over at Keenan, but his expression was noncommittal. He seemed to be uncomfortable with what was going on, but willing to go along. Farnsworth swiveled his chair back around.

"Okay," he said. "I'm glad the girl's going to recover. I'm sorry the other two kids didn't make it. Larry Talbot is going to make family notification, and we're sending in some search teams to see if we can find remains."

"The county people are getting up a search team and a canine unit," Keenan said. "Larry's coordinating it."

"Good," Farnsworth said. As best Janet could tell, the RA was only minimally interested in the resolution of the case of the missing college kids. "Now, this other business: You have a page to make at six P.M., right?"

"Yes, that's what Mata Hari wanted me to do. I wanted to ask you about—"

Farnsworth was shaking his head. "No," he said. "Make the page. If he calls back, give him whatever message she wants. Then I hope we're done with the Edwin Kreiss affair. His daughter's been recovered, and the other two missing persons have been . . . accounted for."

"But what about the girl's statement? That Browne McGarand's going to Washington with a bomb?"

"You said she said she was blindfolded," Farnsworth said. "We have no *evidence* that Browne McGarand has ever even *been* to the arsenal or that he was the man who abducted Lynn Kreiss."

"Then show her his picture," she said. "She saw them both in the storm. It just about has to be him. She described him as a big man with a huge beard. Looked like a mountain man."

Farnsworth and Keenan exchanged looks. "What we *know* is that Jared McGarand's truck had been parked *outside* the arsenal fence. We have no evidence that he himself penetrated that arsenal perimeter, either."

Janet frowned. What the hell was this? Farnsworth was sounding like a barracks lawyer. "There were two people involved in Lynn's abduction," she said. "One young, one much older. She was abducted inside the arsenal. She saw them both and can identify them. We found her inside the arsenal, so they *must* have been inside the arsenal, too. Doing what? She said that the older man told her he was holding her as a possible hostage, in case things went wrong with his little H-bomb project in Washington. She was found in a building right near that power plant. *What more do we need?*"

Her voice had risen with that last question, and she became acutely aware of the way her two supervisors were looking at her. Impertinence was not an attribute much admired within the Bureau. Farnsworth leaned forward.

"We *need* to adhere to the very explicit guidance we have been given from headquarters. Now, I would very much appreciate it if you would comply with my orders. Make the page. Give Kreiss the message if and when he calls in, nothing more, nothing less."

What the hell is going on here? she wondered. "Can I tell him his daughter is back among us?"

Keenan made a noise of exasperation. "What part of 'nothing more, nothing less' don't you understand, Carter? How about doing what you're told for a change?"

Janet had never heard Keenan speak this way, but she had about had it. "How about telling me what's going on around here?" she countered. "Why is this office so hell-bent on mind-fucking Edwin Kreiss?"

"You've got it wrong, Janet," Farnsworth said. "That page will conclude your involvement in the Edwin Kreiss matter. Then you can help Larry Talbot close out the missing persons case."

"But what about the bomb? Are we just going to sit on that?"

"You're talking about wholly uncorroborated information, obtained from a young woman who has just awakened from a coma, as if it were evidence. There is no evidence of a bomb, and if there were, bombs are the business of the ATF, and even they are saying there was no bomb."

Christ, Janet thought. This was like being back in the lab: We know the answer we want; how about a little cooperation here? "But they don't know what we do," she protested. "Of course they're saying there's no bomb!"

Farnsworth closed his eyes and took a deep breath. "I am ordering you to drop this matter." He opened his eyes. "And if you can't accept that order, you have an alternative."

That shocked her. She sat back in her chair, unable to think of what she should say next. Both Farnsworth and Keenan were watching her, almost expectantly. Then, surprising herself, she fished out her credentials and leaned forward to put them on Farnsworth's desk. Then she hooked her Sig out of its holster, ejected the clip, and then racked and locked back the slide. A single round popped out onto the floor. Keenan automatically bent to retrieve it. She put the gun on the RA's desk, as well.

"You guys page Kreiss," she said, getting up. "This is all fucked up, and I quit."

She walked out of the RA's office and went straight upstairs to her cubicle. Larry Talbot and Billy were in the office. Talbot took one look at her face and asked her what was wrong. She told him she'd just quit. He sat there at his desk with his mouth open.

"You did *what*? Why? What's happened now?"

"There's something way wrong with this Kreiss business," she began, but then she stopped. Talbot probably wouldn't know what she was talking about. His expression confirmed that. The intercom phone on his desk buzzed. He picked it up, listened, said, "Yes, sir," and then hung up. "Mr. Keenan wants to see you."

"He can fuck off and die, too," she said. "He's not my boss anymore. I quit and I meant it. I'll come back later for my desk stuff. They have my piece and credentials. I'm outta here."

"But, Jan, what the hell—" Larry said, getting up. "Obviously there's been some misunderstanding. Look—"

"No, Larry. The more I think about what I've just done, the better I like it. You got what you need on the missing kids?"

"Um, only the basic story of what happened to them; I was on my way to talk to the Kreiss girl before I did the actual notifications. Hey, look, Jan, why don't you just take the rest of the day off. You've been through a lot. Go home and think about this. Quitting the Bureau—that's a big deal."

"It's the Bureau's loss, as far as I'm concerned. Think of it as a logical consequence of my being sent down here to this . . . this backwater. I'm a Ph.D.-level forensic scientist, for Chrissakes. I'm here because I wouldn't come up with the quote-unquote right answer in an evidentiary hearing. Now here we go again. I should have quit the last time. And for the last goddamned time, don't call me Jan!"

Talbot put up his hands in mock surrender and left the office. Billy got up and came over to her cube.

"Hey," he said gently. "What the hell was it they wanted you to do?"

"They won't go after this guy who's on his way to D.C. with a big-ass bomb. And they won't let me tell Kreiss that his daughter is in safe hands. It's outrageous!"

"What *did* they want you to do? Quitting is a pretty big step, Janet."

"The Agency sent some gorgon down here to give Kreiss a message.

I'm supposed to be the messenger. I'm just tired of all the lies, Billy. First in the lab, now here. This isn't what I signed up for. Nice knowing you."

Billy seemed lost for words, so she grabbed her jacket and her purse and left the office. She was home in thirty minutes, and she went directly into the bathroom to take a long shower. As she stood in the streaming water, she reflected on her decision and concluded that it had been the right move. She realized she needed to put it in writing, and that she also needed to get something in that letter referring to the arsenal case. She smiled then: Bureau habits died hard—she was still thinking about covering her ass, even in the process of resignation.

She turned off the shower, got out, and dried off. She put on fresh underwear and was combing her hair when she heard a noise from the bedroom door. She whirled around and found the Agency woman standing in the doorway. She was wearing slacks and some kind of safari shirt with lots of pockets. Her eyes were invisible behind wraparound black sunglasses.

"Brought you something," the woman said, proffering a shiny object in her outstretched hand. Janet blinked, focused on it, and then there was a shattering pulse of purple light. The next thing she knew, she was on her back in her bed, completely enveloped in a sticky web of some kind. The individual strands were the consistency of raw yarn and smelled of some strong chemical. Her arms were pinned down at her sides, her hands turned palm-in against her hips. Her legs were bent to one side. She made an instinctive move to escape, but the effort only caused the web to contract everywhere it touched her body. She felt as if she were in an elasticized-rubber onion sack. Only her head was free. Everything she looked at had a purple penumbra, and the center focus of her vision was a haze of small black dots. The woman was sitting calmly at Janet's dressing table, watching her, her sunglasses gone now. Janet tried to think of something clever to say, but there was no escaping the fact that she was lying on her bed, in nothing but her underwear, trussed like a deboned turkey. She tried to blink away the haze of purple-black spots. The woman's expression was totally blank.

"So that's a retinal disrupter?" Janet asked.

"Yes. The spots will go away in about an hour. Usually, there's no permanent damage done."

"Usually? That's comforting. And you did this—why?"

"To ensure you'd make the page, Agent Carter."

"I'm not Agent anybody anymore," Janet said.

"Especially because of that." The woman looked at her watch. "We have a little over an hour. I've arranged for the return call to bounce here, and then you'll give him the message I asked you to give him. Still remember it?"

"What if I don't?" Janet asked. "What if I simply tell him to run like hell?"

"Same difference," the woman said. "That's what my message is designed to do anyway. It's just more effective if he knows it's me. But I think you'll want to do it my way."

"Why?"

"Because if you don't, I'll go get another capture curtain and wrap it around your throat. Then you could practice some very careful breathing until someone finds you. Think of it as Lamaze with a twist. Whenever that might be, now that you're . . . unattached, shall we say? Why don't you relax now. Attend to your breathing. That stuff's like a boa constrictor: It tightens on the exhale, as I suspect you've discovered."

Janet had indeed discovered that. "Why the hell are you doing this? Taking down another federal agent?"

"But you're not a federal agent anymore, are you, Carter?" the woman said sweetly. "Not that you ever were. An agent, I mean."

"Huh?" Janet said.

"You were a glorified lab rat, Carter. As a street agent, you're a joke. You've got the situational awareness of a tree. I was standing in that doorway the whole time you were taking a shower."

"Enjoy the view?" Janet asked.

The woman cocked her head to one side and gave Janet the once-over, staring at her body just long enough for Janet to blush. "You're nicely made, for a breast-Fed," she said. "Was that why they sent you to get close to Kreiss?"

"That probably wasn't their brightest idea," Janet said, trying to feel how much give there was in the yarn. Not very damn much.

The Agency woman laughed once. "Edwin Kreiss has zero time for amateurs," she said. "Of any stripe. What'd they do—tell you to show a little leg, bat your eyes at him?"

"Why are you doing this?" Janet asked again, trying to strain against the sticky web without showing it.

"Because now you're just another annoying civilian who's getting in my way. Stop testing the curtain. You can permanently damage your circulation. Lie still. Rest your eyes. Take a nap. I'll wake you when it's time."

The woman left the room, and Janet immediately tried to move her hands. The sticky rubbery substance clung to her skin like shrink-wrap, but it did give when she pushed out with the back of her right hand. But when she relaxed, it tightened, and she realized that it was now noticeably tighter than it had been. She thought about several coils of the chemical yarn around her throat and involuntarily swallowed. Then she remembered the discussion in Farnsworth's office about the capture curtain, and the fact that it was water-soluble. If she could roll off the bed and get to the bathroom without Medusa out there hearing her, she could get it off. She looked around, trying to figure out how to move quietly with her legs bent sideways like that, and saw the three strands that went around the right-hand bedpost. Shit. So much for that idea.

She closed her eyes. Okay, she thought, so make the call. Do what this bitch says. Hell, Kreiss might not even answer the page. She opened her eyes, suddenly afraid. He'd better answer the page, she thought. She wondered where he was.

Kreiss was sitting in the parking lot of a fast-food joint three blocks from the Beltway interchange with U.S. Route 1. He was munching on a lukewarm, well-oiled three-dollar heart attack when he heard the pager chirping in the duffel bag behind his seat. He put the greaseburger down and turned around to get at the pager. He'd forgotten he had it. The number in the window made him sit right up, though: It had been his own unlisted office number when he was at the Agency. Now who the hell was sending this little summons? He didn't have to write the number down, so he simply cleared the pager, which beeped at him gratefully. There was a phone booth at the edge of the parking lot, but there were two very fat teenaged girls hanging on it, so he went back to his gourmet extravaganza. He had been through all the truck stops and terminals on the northern Virginia side and was now working up the nerve to cross the Wilson Bridge, Washington's monument to uncivil engineering. He had planned to wait another half hour for rush hour to subside somewhat and to make sure no big semis had fallen through the bridge deck today.

The girls finally left the phone booth in gales of laughter, multiple chins jiggling in unison. He started to get out but then hesitated. It was just after 6:00 on a Monday evening. The pager had belonged to Janet Carter, which meant it was Bureau equipment. Now someone had called it and left a northern Virginia phone number on it that no one in the Bureau should have had access to. Ergo, this wasn't a Bureau summons.

He turned on the cabin light and examined the pager for signs of a second antenna, something that might transmit his location when he had acknowledged the message. Then it occurred to him that this might be about Lynn. Hell with it, he thought.

He got out and went over to the phone booth, which reeked of chewing gum and cheap perfume when he cracked open the door. He dialed the number. It rang four times before being picked up, and, to his surprise, it was Janet Carter.

"Is this about Lynn?" he asked.

"I have a message for you," Janet said in a wooden voice.

"From whom?"

"The message is as follows: *Tenebrae factae sunt.*"

"What—" he said, but the connection had been broken. And then the message penetrated. Almost in slow motion, he put the handset back on the hook and backed out of the booth. He walked back to the van, got in, and started it up. Hamburger forgotten, he drove out of the parking lot, turned left when he came to Route 1, and headed south, away from the Beltway.

Well, well, well, he thought. *Tenebrae factae sunt.* Darkness has fallen. Misty's coming. That was the nickname she'd been given, in memory of the psychotic woman character who kept calling Clint Eastwood to play "Misty" for her in that movie. The message was her trademark. It was supposed to spook him, and in a way, it did. Misty was in her fifties, looked forty the last time he had seen her, and had been the preeminent stalker in the stable, bar none. Kreiss had concluded a long time ago that Misty had a Terminator personality. She was either sitting up there on her shelf, like some neighborhood black hole, absorbing light, motion, sound, everything that was going on around her, with those disturbing black eyes staring into infinity with perfect indifference, or she was on the move, morphing through keyholes or running down cars, a human Velociraptor, leading with her teeth. She tracked like a damned adult mamba, moving fast through the bush on a molecular prey trail, its head and upper body occasionally coming up and off the ground, testing the air with its tongue, looking, eager to deliver a fatal strike, hunting because it liked to.

He had trained under her supervision for two years before getting his first operational assignment, so there was nothing that he knew that she didn't also know. Well, maybe a couple of things, he thought hopefully. But realistically, he was now, officially and irrevocably—put it on the evening news, folks—in deep shit. He would have to abandon immediately his pursuit of Browne McGarand and look to his own defenses. Maybe head out to Dulles and get on the evening flight to Zanzibar, or, better yet, lower Patagonia. That would be about the right distance. Except he'd probably just be finishing the evening meal when she appeared out of the cockpit. The only chance he had was if Misty was going solo and had not brought along a cast of thousands. Given the history, she might well be solo. Misty was a sport.

He drove down Route 1 for twenty minutes until he came to the entrance to Fort Belvoir, where he turned in. Belvoir was an open post, the home of the Army Corps of Engineers School, so there were no gates or guards. But it was still a military reservation, and it seemed safer to stop there than out on the street. He drove around the campuslike facility for a few minutes before parking the van in front of the main post exchange complex. He shut the van down and closed his eyes, commanding his brain to organize and think about his situation.

Misty was coming. She'd used Janet Carter as her messenger, which meant that Janet was having a bad evening. Daniella Morganavicz was her real name. Her parents had supposedly emigrated from Serbia, and she had clearly inherited the ruthless faculties of that bloody-minded tribe. Somebody at Langley must be really worried if Misty had been put in play.

Then the pager went off again.

He looked down at the little device and thought about throwing it out the window. The first page had been the warning; was this one Misty making a tracking call? He looked at the number in the window. It was the Roanoke area code and a number he didn't recognize. Carter again? He had rented a cell phone with the van, but wanted to save using that for when he was certain someone was hunting him. How certain do you want it? he thought, remembering the warning. He looked around for a phone booth and finally saw a bank of them by the exchange entrance. He looked at the number again and then turned the pager off without acknowledging the call. He got out, threw the pager into a concrete flower planter, and walked over to the bank of pay phones. He dialed the number, entered his credit-card number, and waited. The credit card would tie him to this place, but he hadn't really begun to run and hide yet, so that shouldn't matter. Emphasis on the *shouldn't*. It was Carter who answered.

"Sorry about being rude," she said. "That goddamned woman was here. Do you know whom I mean?"

"Oh yes," he said. "Tallish? Black eyes? Absorbs ambient light?"

"That's the one. Said you would understand that message to mean she was coming for you."

"Clear as a bell. Why are you calling me?"

"I'm on a pay phone. My phone is being tapped, I think. I called because I need to talk to you, first about your daughter, and second about what's going on."

He felt a clang of alarm when she mentioned Lynn. "What about Lynn?"

"She's awake. I was there when she came around. I think she's going to be fine—no apparent mental damage. We talked. She told me what happened out there at the arsenal. The other two kids apparently got caught in some kind of traps and were drowned by a flash flood."

"Yes, I found leg traps."

"Well, she also told me some stuff about the guy I think you're hunting. It involves a bomb, and I think I know what it is. I—"

"Hold on a minute, Carter. I'm not hunting anyone."

There was a moment's hesitation. "I think you are, or at least you were," she said. "I think you were hunting one Browne McGarand, because he kidnapped Lynn. I also think you did something to his grandson, Jared."

She stopped talking, but he decided to remain silent.

"This woman—is she a real threat?" Janet asked.

"What do you think?" When she didn't answer, he explained her nickname.

"Scared me just to look at her," Janet said. "I think she took it as a given that you'd be afraid of her, too."

"Which is why I have to go now, Carter."

"I've quit the Bureau," she said.

That surprised him. "What happened?"

"They wanted me to do something that I didn't want to do. They wanted me to page you for the Dragon Lady."

"But you did anyway."

"Because she showed up here at my house and dazzled me with her personality and some nasty little number you people call a 'retinal disrupter!' Then she trussed me up in some kind of sticky shit and told me that things would go poorly for me if I didn't do what she said. I elected to do what she said."

"That was the correct decision, Carter."

"Yeah, that's what I thought. Humiliating, maybe, but ultimately smart. But that was only the half of it. I quit because, originally, they wanted me to tell you they'd found Lynn but that she had *not* survived."

It was his turn to be silent for a moment. "Sweet," he said.

"Well, it kind of offended me, too. But I was able to talk Farnsworth out of that. Games like that—not my style. Then this shit with Dracula's daughter. Even Farnsworth wouldn't mess with her."

"Your boss knows the real thing when he sees it," he said, looking around at the darkening parking lot. If Misty had been in Roanoke at 6:00 P.M. he had a few hours before she could be here, but no more than that. Unless she had helpers, and of course she might. Time to go. And yet—he owed this woman.

"You really put a snake in a guy's car?" Janet asked, seemingly out of nowhere.

Ransom, he thought. "No, a tape of a snake. But you're asking about Misty? She likes things visual. She cut the rattles off a snake and stuffed the thing into the back pocket of a guy's bucket seat. He never heard it buzz, of course, but he did get to see it in his mirror just before it slid over his shoulder and dropped into his lap. What's this about a bomb?"

Janet filled him in on what she had been doing since Kreiss had pulled her out of the tunnels. She emphasized McGarand's ties to the Waco disaster. Kriess didn't say anything when she finished. The bureaucrats never change, he thought. He wondered if he should tell her about the propane truck.

"Are you still there?"

"I have to go," he said, cutting her off. "And I dumped your pager. It's in a flower planter in front of the main exchange at Fort Belvoir, if you're interested."

"Do you think that McGarand's taken a bomb to Washington?"

"It's possible. But that's not my problem anymore, Carter. You recovered my daughter, like you said you would. I thank you for that. I've got other problems right now."

"But—"

"Does that woman know about Lynn?"

"I don't know. It's possible. She was there in the Roanoke office when I got there. I don't know what Farnsworth told her. But why—oh."

"Yeah, oh."

Another silence. "Would you like me to go to the hospital? Stay with her until you can get back here?"

"I appreciate the offer, but in what capacity? You're not with the Bureau anymore."

"Everybody tells me I was a shitty agent. How about as just a human, perhaps?"

He laughed but hesitated. If he went back to Blacksburg, he might walk directly into a trap. But if he didn't, and Misty took Lynn, then he'd have no choices at all. Carter was no match for Misty, but she might be better than no one at all. And Misty would never take Carter seriously, so Carter, suitably warned, might have a chance to do something.

"I'll tell you what," he said. "I have a neighbor out there near my cabin. Name's Micah Wall. He has a phone. And he's got lots of kinfolk, as they call them. They're mountain people. They're pretty decent people, although they don't look it. If Lynn can be moved, maybe you could get her out of that hospital and into Micah's hands."

"I can sure as hell try," Janet said. "If they'll release her into my custody."

"Lynn's over twenty-one. Technically, I think she can release herself, as long as there's no medical issue. Take her to my cabin, make sure you're not followed, and then call Micah. I think he'll know what to do, and I'm also pretty sure he and his boys can make it tough for Misty if she tries them on. But you'll have to move fast."

"I will. Now, how's about a quid pro quo: I seem to be the only person down here who thinks McGarand has gone to D.C. on a bombing mission. My bosses, my ex-bosses, are suddenly not interested in hearing that, based, I think, on guidance they're getting from Bureau headquarters. If you have something, some evidence, I can give to Farnsworth, and then maybe I can ask that *they* protect Lynn in return."

Kreiss shook his head slowly in the darkness. "You are depressingly naïve for an ex-special agent," he said with a sigh. "Your boss has been told to *assist* this woman who is coming after me, not get in her way. Those orders probably came from Bureau headquarters, if not Justice. At this juncture, I'll bet Farnsworth won't even take your calls."

"But that explosion at the arsenal was *huge*. If there's anything like that being planned for Washington, we have to do something!"

"Look, Carter. If there's a bomb here in Washington, that's your ex-employer's problem. Or actually, it's ATF's problem."

"But they won't even admit the possibility, or at least that's their official stance. They keep saying there's no direct evidence. Please, can't you tell me something?"

Kreiss thought about it. Carter sounded frantic, and she still cared, even if she had left the Bureau. And she was going to help him with Lynn.

"Okay. Tell 'em this: McGarand left Blacksburg driving a propane truck. I saw that truck at the arsenal, inside the power plant."

"*Propane* truck?"

"I've got to roll, Carter. Listen to me: If Misty needs a distraction to get Lynn out of that hospital, she's most likely to start a fire. So be prepared. Take a gun if you have one."

"I'll give it my best shot," Janet said.

Her best shot, he thought, giving a mental sigh. Right through her foot, probably. "Okay," he said. "And whatever happens with Lynn, thank you. Big-time."

"Can you stop McGarand?"

"Stop him? I can't even find him."

"But if you do, you can do better than revenge, Mr. Kreiss. You might prevent a tragedy. You say he has a propane truck. I think he has a truckload of hydrogen. That would make a helluva truck bomb."

"This what you really mean by quid pro quo, Carter? You get my daughter out of harm's way if I'll prevent a bombing?"

"I'll try to help your daughter regardless, Mr. Kreiss. But right now, the people who mean you harm are depending on your staying true to form: an eye for an eye, blood for blood, heads on pikes. Why don't you try doing a good deed for once? Think of how badly that would confound your enemies."

He didn't know what to say to that. Impudent goddamn woman.

"Now that you're a civilian, you're getting devious, Carter," he said.

"Hey?" she said.

"What?"

"You ever going to call me by my first name?"

"Don't know you well enough," he replied. "Gotta boogie."

He hung up the phone and strode back to the van, kicking an empty Coke can halfway across the parking lot. He got in and slammed the door shut.

Decision time. Ever since his termination, he had had some preplanned disappearance arrangements in place. But until he knew that Lynn was safe, he wasn't really free to move. The next twenty-four hours would be crucial. Misty was already in Roanoke, and he had not been exaggerating about her starting a fire. Even in a hospital, it was what he would have done. He hadn't given Carter anywhere near enough information to prepare herself for what Misty might do. He considered calling her back, then decided against it. His using the telephone credit card would bring someone here pretty quick. He had to move. The question of where didn't matter all that much right now.

But what to do about McGarand? He was not about to indulge in altruism at this late stage in his life. On the other hand, Carter was right from a tactical standpoint: Misty and company would expect him to bolt, to go to ground, possibly to a hidey-hole they already knew about. If instead he continued to hunt McGarand, that would be unexpected. He'd already spun his wheels looking for that truck. Maybe he was going about this the wrong way. Instead of looking for a rolling truck bomb, maybe he ought to look for the truck bomb's target. If this was about Waco, that left two possibilities, both of them easy targets for a determined truck bomber. He started up and drove out of the exchange parking lot, heading back to Route 1 and Washington. He thought about Carter. She'd do, for an amateur.

Janet hung up the phone and got back into her car. She was dressed in jeans and a sweater, having had to take a second shower to get all that sticky crap off once the woman had released her arms and hands. She drove back to her town house from the convenience store. Propane truck, she thought. Hydrogen bomb. She shivered at the thought. That ATF expert had said it had been a gas explosion. Okay: A propane truck was designed to carry gas, or at least she was pretty sure it was. Or was propane a liquid? Damn! But she'd been right: Kreiss *had* gone after McGarand, which, as far as she was concerned, confirmed that McGarand was already in Washington. With a propane truck full of—what? Propane? Or hydrogen? Either one, she thought. Either one would generate a real crowd-pleaser.

She got home, parked, and went in. She went through the house to make sure there was no one else there. Situational awareness of a tree—bitch had hurt her feelings. So what was the target? Lynn had said the bearded man claimed to be going after a "legitimate target." As in, I'm going after combatants, not innocent civilians. McGarand had lost his only son at Waco. Son of a bitch, she thought with a sudden cold certainty: He's going after Bureau headquarters. The FBI had been in charge at Waco, at least by the time the Mount Carmel compound had been torched. Aided and abetted by their smaller cousins, the BATF.

She looked at her watch: It was almost seven o'clock. She went into the kitchen and dialed into the Roanoke FBI office, got the after-hours tape, and hit the extension for the RA's office. There was no answer, then main voice mail. She hung up, remembered he'd given her his home number, but then couldn't find it. The number was in her case notebook, which was in her office. Her ex-office, she reminded herself. She looked Farnsworth up in the phone book for the Roanoke area. Not listed. She called the Roanoke office number back. When the tape came up, she hit three digits and her call was forwarded to the day's duty officer, an agent who worked in the felony fraud squad. His phone was in use, but she did get his voice mail. She groaned, then left a message that she needed to get an urgent message to the RA about a possible bomb threat against Bureau headquarters and gave her home number. Then she hung up and went to make a cup of coffee. The phone rang in five minutes, and it was the duty officer, Special Agent Jim Walker.

"Got your call," he said. "Called the boss, gave him your message and your phone number. But don't hold your breath. Is it true you resigned today?"

"Yes, I did, but I have new information."

"Well, um, what the boss said was, and I quote, 'Janet Carter no longer works for the Bureau, and one of the reasons is that she's become obsessed with this notion of a bomb threat to Washington. I may call her and I may not.' Okay?"

His tone was faintly patronizing, with none of the familiar agent-to-agent courtesy. It pissed her off, but she held her anger in check. "No, not okay," she said quickly. "Please, would you make one more call?"

"Hey, Carter—"

"Please! I know you think you're dealing with a hysterical female. But look, if there *is* a bombing, do you want to be the one link in the chain of precursor events that did not pass on vital information? When some independent prosecutor comes investigating? Remember Waco? This involves Waco."

Walker didn't say anything, and she knew she'd touched a nerve. These days everyone in the Bureau considered his or her every action in light of what might happen later if the case, investigation, or operation recoiled on them. She pressed him. "Just call Farnsworth back and tell him that Browne McGarand, that's Browne with an *e*, went to Washington with a propane truck. That the hydrogen bomb isn't a nuclear device—it's hydrogen gas, which is what probably did the arsenal power plant. Got all that?"

"That explosion at the arsenal? *Hydrogen bomb?* Are you fucking serious?"

"Please, Jim, just make the call. Please? Tell him exactly what I just told you." She repeated it. "If he chews your ass for bothering him, tell him you're so sorry, hang up, log the call, and go back to watching TV. But then if something happens, it's on him, not you, right?"

Walker reluctantly agreed to make the call and hung up. Janet let out a long sigh: She had done the best she could. If they chose to ignore this, then it would indeed be on their heads. She wondered if she shouldn't put a call into Bureau headquarters operations, but then she realized she didn't have the number. It was in her official phone book at her office, at her ex-office, she realized again. She'd get what any civilian who called the Bureau headquarters would get: a polite tape recording introducing the caller to a menu labyrinth. Life was going to be very different now that she wasn't part of the most powerful law-enforcement organization in the country. Those FBI credentials had given her almost automatic entrée into any place or situation. Now she was just Janet Carter, unemployed civilian. She almost felt a bit naked. But at least now Kreiss would have to stop calling her "Special Agent."

She went into the kitchen, wanting a drink, not coffee, but satisfied herself with the coffee. She was hoping the phone would ring again, with Farnsworth on the other end this time. But he didn't call. That damned Kreiss. She started pacing her kitchen floor. How long should she wait? Kreiss had been pretty specific about her moving quickly to protect his daughter. That might end up being a tough play, especially now that she no longer had any standing as a law-enforcement official. On the other hand, Lynn had seemed pretty strong, and stashing the girl with a bunch of mountain hillbillies might be the perfect answer, especially if they were his friends.

She got out the area phone book and found a number for an M. Wall on Kreiss's road. The phone rang, but there was no answer. She wrote down the number on a scrap of paper, put it in her pocket, finished her coffee, and went back upstairs to her bedroom. She took out the Detective's Special hidden in her sock drawer and then rooted around in the closet until she found the waist holster for it. She checked to make sure it was loaded, then clipped it on her jeans waistband in the small of her back, pulling the sweater down over it. She checked the dial tone of her phone to make sure she hadn't missed a call, grabbed her car keys, and left for Blacksburg.

Forty minutes later, she checked in with the main reception desk at the Montgomery County Hospital and learned that Lynn had been moved from ICU to a semiprivate room on the fourth floor. She took the elevator upstairs and was relieved to see that there was no longer a police officer stationed outside the girl's door. Lynn's door was open, and she appeared to be dozing in the semidarkened room. It was after visiting hours, but the nurse who had been in ICU the day before remembered Janet and waved her by. The girl woke up when Janet came into the room and gently shut the door.

"Hey," Janet said. "How are you feeling?"

"Better," Lynn said. "The deputy got me some real food before he left. Made a big improvement over Jell-O."

"Do you feel up to moving?"

"Moving? As in out of here?"

"Yes. As in checking out and coming with me. Per your father's urgent instructions. There's someone after him, and that someone may try to take you in order to trap your father."

"*What!*" Lynn exclaimed, sitting up in the bed. "But he's retired. Who's after him? And why?"

"Lynn, I'll tell you everything once we're in the car. But your old man gave me the impression we have minutes, not hours. Do you have clothes here?"

The girl looked around the room with a bewildered expression. "I don't know—check that closet."

Janet got up and looked in the closet, where there were a pair of battered jeans, a shirt, a jacket, and some hiking shoes. There was no underwear or socks. She brought it all out and then turned away to give Lynn some privacy. The girl got dressed, but it was obvious that she was still pretty weak. Janet had to help her tie the laces on her hiking shoes. She explained quickly about the Agency woman, and she also told Lynn she had resigned from the FBI over the handling of the bombing case. Lynn put her hand on Janet's forearm.

"Describe the woman," she said. Janet did, emphasizing the extraordinary black eyes, pale white face, and the detached, almost lifeless expression.

"Shit," Lynn said. "I think she's been here. But she was dressed like a doctor. She stopped by my door about, oh, I don't know, an hour ago? I was dozing, but I remember that face. There'd been docs coming and going all afternoon. But I distinctly remember that face."

"What did she do?"

"Nothing. She stood in the doorway. I was kind of tired of being poked and prodded all day, so I didn't really open my eyes. But when she looked at me, I had the feeling she knew I was watching her. It was creepy." Lynn looked pale and drawn, and her clothes appeared to be too big for her. She sat on the edge of the bed and held herself upright with rigid arms.

"She's apparently pretty dangerous," Janet said. "I'll tell you more in the car. But first we have to get you out of here and not spend three hours doing paperwork. I—"

Just then, from outside the room, came the jarring blare of an alarm system, which emitted five obnoxious Klaxon noises, followed by an announcement that there was an electrical fire on the second floor and that all floors were to begin evacuation procedures. Then came five more blats, with the announcement repeated. There was an immediate bustle of people and gurneys out in the hallway.

"Quick," Janet said, going to the door, cracking it, and looking out into the corridor. "Your father said this is how she'd do it—start a fire and grab you in the confusion." Two nurses went hurrying by, one pushing two wheelchairs in front of her, while the other consulted a metal clipboard and talked on a cell phone. There was another wheelchair parked across the corridor from Lynn's door. Janet stepped out, grabbed the wheelchair, and pulled it back into Lynn's room. The fire alarm sounded again, repeating the fire announcement. We got it, we got it, Janet found herself thinking. "Okay, let's go," she said.

Lynn sat down in the wheelchair. Janet folded a blanket over Lynn's legs and rolled her out into the corridor. Janet knew the elevators would have gone out of service, which meant that everyone would head for the stairs. They joined a procession of nurses and patients, some ambulatory, some in wheelchairs, and a couple of frightened patients being pushed on gurneys. The movement was orderly toward the end of the corridor, where Janet could see red exit signs. But suddenly, the overhead lights went out and there was a wave of concerned noises up and down the corridor. Small emergency lights along the edge of the ceiling came on, which helped until a sudden and very distinct smell of acrid smoke broke into the hallway from the ventilation ducts. Janet couldn't see smoke, but she could sure as hell smell it, and it was getting stronger. The parade of wheelchairs and patients surged forward. If the noise was any indication, the level of anxiety had gone way up. She could also hear the sounds of angry congestion down at the end of the corridor near the exit doors.

That did it. Janet turned Lynn around and pushed her rapidly back up the darkened hallway, away from the growing traffic jam at the other end. She went past Lynn's room and came to a cross-corridor intersection. She looked both ways but saw no exit doors. The smell of smoke was getting stronger, and now there was a gray pall building along the ceiling. Janet turned around to look back at the original route. There appeared to be one large elevator still working, and everyone appeared to be trying to get in it or into the stairwell. It was genuine bedlam down there, with both patients and hospital staff shouting at one another.

"There has to be another exit, at least a stairwell," Janet said. "But I sure as hell don't see it."

"Try the passenger elevators?" Lynn suggested. Her face was still pale, and she was clutching the blanket as if she was cold.

"They won't work once the fire alarm's gone off. Not until the fire trucks get here. That's probably what's happened down the hall there."

The smoke was getting strong enough to sting Janet's eyes, but the evacuation effort at the other end of the hall sounded as if it was rapidly turning into a disaster as sixty or so people tried to get patients and wheel-chairs into the single elevator or down four flights of stairs. Janet decided to look one more time, but after two more minutes of trotting the full length of the cross corridors, she gave up. There really was only one exit down. As she wheeled Lynn back to the intersection, the smoke was thick enough that she could no longer see what was going on down at the exit stairwell. But she could hear it, and it was not a pleasant sound. The smoke stung her eyes and smelled of burning plastic.

"We're going to have to find a room with an exterior window and wait this thing out," she said. "The fire department will have a ladder truck."

She took Lynn all the way back to the end of the right-hand cross corridor and began looking into every door that wasn't locked. She finally found a small lab room of some sort that had windows, through which the lights in the parking lot were visible. She wheeled Lynn backward into the room and shut the door. There was a stink of smoke in the room, but it was not as strong as out in the corridor. Sirens were audible outside, although she couldn't see fire trucks.

"You okay?" she asked Lynn as she searched for towels or rags to stuff under the door.

"Yeah, I'm good. I'd help, but my head is spinning a little."

"Sit tight. They said the fire was on the second floor. We have one floor between us and the fire. They'll have it out pretty damn quick. If it's electrical, they turn off the power, and that usually stops it."

As if the building were listening, they heard the sound of big vent fans winding down, and then even the emergency lighting system out in the corridor expired in a clatter of relays as the battery-operated lights came on. Janet saw that Lynn was frightened by this. She tried to reassure her. "That's good, actually. I think the vent system was spreading the smoke. We should be okay up here. This building is mostly concrete."

"I'm glad we're not down there in that corridor. That sounded pretty ugly."

"Amen. As soon as I seal the door cracks, we'll check out the windows."

There were three large windows along the back wall of the lab. Enough light came through these from the streetlights in the parking lot for them to move around the lab benches without running into things. Janet found some paper towels and stuffed them along the bottom crack of the door. With the ventilation system off, the smoke didn't seem to be getting any stronger, so she didn't bother with the rest of the door. She found a fire extinguisher and set it out on a lab table. Then red strobe lights lit up the ceiling as a fire engine came around the building, stopped, and began setting up in the parking lot. She tried to open the windows but could not budge them.

"See? They'll have this mess under control pretty quick. I think we'll just wait until we hear firemen out in the hall."

"What about that woman?"

Janet stopped what she was doing. She'd forgotten all about the Terminatrix. Kreiss had said she might do something like this to cause maximum distraction. She'd forgotten that Lynn thought she'd already seen her in the building. Shit.

She went over to the door and looked for a lock, but it took a key to lock this door. She put her ear to the opaque glass panel in the upper section of the door and listened, but all she could hear were the sounds of fire-fighting commands over the loudspeakers on the truck outside. There were more strobe lights out in the parking lot now. She looked around for a way to block the door, and found a lab table that could be moved. She slid it across the floor, but its top edge was two inches too tall to fit under the knob.

"Lift it and wedge it," Lynn said. She pushed the blanket aside and got out of the wheelchair. She came over to where Janet was standing, steadying herself on the edge of the lab table. The table, which was six feet long and two feet wide, was made of heavy wood, with a zinc top. The two women lifted the far end and slid the end nearest the door under the doorknob, then gently let the table back down. It wedged under the knob, its back legs off the floor about half an inch. Janet went around and tried the knob, which was now jammed.

"That'll at least make it feel like it's locked," Lynn said. Then she wobbled back to the wheelchair and sat down heavily. Janet saw a sheen of perspiration on the girl's forehead.

"Good thinking," Janet said, a little embarrassed that she hadn't thought of it herself.

"You got a gun?" Lynn asked.

"Yes," Janet said, patting the lump at the small of her back.

"Good," Lynn said. "After all this, if that woman shows up, you better use it. She's not coming as the fucking welcome wagon, and I'm not going to be abducted again. Had enough of that."

"We'll wait until we hear firemen out there, then open the door."

"Lots of firemen, okay? That creature looked pretty competent to me."

"Let's move to the back of the room. If she opens that door, we might still fool her."

"Not with that table there," Lynn said. "You go find a good shooting position. I'll be at the other end of the room. Give her two directions to cover."

Janet nodded. The room wasn't that big, but the girl was making tactical sense. "Your father give you lessons?" she asked.

"He taught me about situational awareness," Lynn said. "I used to go deer hunting with him. You should see him in the woods. He could whack a deer on the ass with a stick before it knew he was there." Lynn gave her a studied look. "Can you do it?" she asked. "Shoot someone? Shoot a woman?"

Janet hesitated. She wanted to say, Of course I can. I'm a big FBI agent now. But she knew that it wasn't a done deal until she pulled that trigger.

"Because if you can't, give me the gun. I'm the one she wants. And I'm not going to be taken again, by anybody." Lynn's face was set in a mask of determination. Definitely her father's daughter, Janet thought.

"I can do it if I have to," she said. "But I'm not going to just start shooting the moment someone comes through that door, okay? There are rules about that."

"According to my old man, Agent Carter, the only rule those people have is that there are no rules. If you've got reservations, give me the gun."

Janet wished Kreiss were here right now. She assessed the room from a tactical standpoint, trying to remember her training at Quantico. The room had four large lab stands, the single table now wedged against the door, several glass-fronted cabinets against the side walls, the window wall overlooking the parking lot, and two desks with PCs. The corridor outside was still darkened, and the room had lots of shadow zones. Lynn had backed her wheelchair into a shadowed corner next to a lab stand. She was doing something with her blanket. Janet moved to the opposite corner, pulled over a trash can, upended it, and sat down behind a bench. She pulled over a stack of notebooks. If she leaned down, her head would be barely visible from the doorway, and she would have the lab bench on which to steady her gun.

"You're closer," Janet said. "She shows up, comes in, shout or say something, talk to her. I'll keep down. If she has a gun, use the word *surprise*. And if you see something small and shiny in her hand, close your eyes immediately."

"You said you'd tell me what this is all about?"

In low tones, Janet explained about the bombing incident out at the arsenal, the palace games going on among the agencies involved, and what little she knew about the woman pursuing Kreiss. Lynn took it all in without saying anything, leading Janet to wonder just how much the girl knew about her father's former professional life.

The noise level from outside the building was rising as more fire units came into the parking lot. The sounds of tactical radios could be heard above the steady roar of diesel engines. Janet wondered if the fire was indeed out, and, if so, why there were so many more fire units out there. The air in the room wasn't clear, but it wasn't getting any smokier, either.

"Maybe we ought to get someone's attention out there," she said to Lynn. "Break a window or something. Except I don't think they'd hear us."

But Lynn was pointing urgently at the door. Janet turned and saw a dark silhouette on the other side of the cloudy white glass. She got down on one knee, then realized she couldn't see what was going on with the door handle. She got back up in time to see the table tremble ever so slightly as whoever was out there tried the handle. She reached behind her and drew the .38, checked the loads, and waited, staying upright enough to watch the door handle. The shadow withdrew and she relaxed fractionally, only to yell in surprise when all the glass in the door shattered and a fully masked fireman thrust a hose nozzle through the broken-out window. Janet stood up to get his attention, but she was stunned when he fired a stream of water full force into her face. Her head snapped back and she went flying back into the corner, her gun skittering across the floor into the opposite corner. She tried to get up, but the stream of high-pressure water kept coming, rolling her around in the corner of the room like a dog under a truck, until all she could do was curl into a ball while yelling at the guy to stop it. Until she realized that a fireman wouldn't have done that.

When the stream stopped, she tried frantically to get up, but her eyes were totally out of focus, the eyeballs bruised and stinging from the hard stream of water. By the time she got onto all fours, all she could make out were shapes and shadows, so she couldn't find her gun. Then she heard Lynn scream, followed by a rocket sound from the other side of the room. In another moment, Lynn was at her side, grabbing at her, pulling her upright, yelling, "C'mon, c'mon, we gotta move." She stood up, staggered, and then went with Lynn, blindly banging into the lab stands until they got to the door. Janet felt her foot kick the gun, and she reached down to retrieve it. The table had been shoved aside, so they spilled out into the corridor, which now was murky with smoke. A single portable floodlight stood on the floor, illuminating the doorway. Janet grabbed it and they struggled down the cross corridor through the smoke, keeping low, getting away from the lab room.

"What did you do?" Janet asked.

"Got her with the damn fire extinguisher," Lynn said. "Had it under my blanket. She took her mask off and grinned at me, and I shot her right in the face, and then I threw the damn thing at her. Jesus, I can't breathe in this shit."

"Stay low," Janet said. "There's more air down here."

They stumbled over something on the floor—a fireman who appeared to be unconscious, his rubberized coat, breathing rig, and helmet missing. In the distance was a vertical rectangle of light on the wall.

"The elevator," Janet shouted. "The fireman brought a passenger elevator up. Go! Go!"

Lynn staggered through the smoke toward the elevator. Janet grabbed the fireman under his armpits and pulled him backward toward the rectangle of light. Lynn helped her pull the man into the elevator, and then Janet was smacking the buttons to close the door, but nothing was happening.

"Use the key," Lynn said. "The fireman's key—I think it controls the door."

Janet peered down at the console, saw the black cylinder sticking out of the control panel, but she was barely able to read the instructions on operating the elevator with a fire key. Finally, she succeeded in keying the door shut and punching the button for the ground floor. The elevator started down. She slipped down the wall to a sitting position, where she faced Lynn over the prostrate body of the fireman. He looked far too young to be a fireman. She blew a long breath out of her lungs, glad for the marginally fresher air in the elevator.

"Is he breathing?"

"Yes," Lynn said. "What do we do now?" She was still pale-faced, but her eyes were bright with excitement.

"We get off at the ground floor and get out to the parking lot. Tell someone about him."

"What about her?" Lynn said, indicating upstairs.

"I hope she fucking cooks up there. But somehow, I doubt it. And she probably has helpers in the building." The elevator slowed as it neared the ground floor. She got back up. "We're two hysterical women who got trapped upstairs," she said to Lynn. "And now we want out and we don't want to be seen to by EMTs, grief counselors, priests, or anybody else, okay?"

Lynn grinned at her. "I can do hysterical," she said as the door opened. There was a pack of firemen standing right there and Lynn screamed when she saw them. Janet grabbed her and pushed through them. "One of your guys was down on the fourth floor," she shouted. "We got him in and came down. How do we get out of here?"

There wasn't as much smoke on the ground floor and there were more portable lights stabbing through the gloom. The biggest fireman pointed her in the direction of the front doors as the rest lunged into the cab to tend to their downed mate. Janet heard one of them ask, "Where's his fucking air rig?" before she and Lynn bolted out the front door and into the blessed coolness of clean, fresh night air. Janet's eyes were just about back to normal, except that she couldn't stop blinking. She realized they were on the wrong side of the building: Her car was parked out back of the hospital. It had probably been visible from the lab windows. She told Lynn to wait and said she would go get her car. Lynn said, "no way in hell," and went right along with Janet.

Ten minutes later, they were out on the main drag and headed south to intersect Highway 460. She asked Lynn if she knew the number for Micah Wall, but Lynn did not. Then she remembered she'd written it down, and she went fishing for the scrap of paper. It was soaked but still legible. She dialed the number on her cell phone, but there was still no answer.

She explained her plan, and Lynn nodded. "We'll be as safe with Micah's clan as with anyone," she said. "But we have to tell him that she's a revenuer."

"We? The idea is to protect you, Lynn. I promised your father I'd keep you out of the clutches of that creature back there." She kept an eye on her rearview mirror.

Lynn was grinning again. "And who's going to protect you? Excuse me for saying so, but you're not very good at this shit, are you?"

Janet felt a spike of irritation, but then she grinned back. Kreiss had said the same thing. "Believe it or not, I'm getting better," she said. "You have no idea. But I wouldn't mind knowing where your father keeps that fifty-caliber rifle."

Kreiss drove the van across the Fourteenth Street Bridge into the downtown District of Columbia. Leaving the bridge, he went straight, past the U.S. Mint and toward the Washington Monument grounds, until he cut Independence Avenue, then went right until he came to Tenth Street. A sign on Tenth Street said NO LEFT TURN, but he ignored that and went up to within one block of Constitution Avenue, where he found a parking place. It was just after 10:30, and what traffic there was consisted mostly of cabs and the occasional long black limousine streaking through the nearly empty streets. A Washington Metro cop car was parked across the street; two cops inside appeared to be reading newspapers. They paid him zero attention when he got out of the van, put on a windbreaker, and walked up the street toward Constitution. It was a cloudy night, with a hint of spring rain in the air. He stopped when he got to the corner.

Constitution Avenue was eight lanes wide, in keeping with its ceremonial use, and pedestrians crossed it at night at their considerable peril. By day, the traffic was usually dense enough that it was almost possible for a pedestrian to walk *over* the cars with impunity. One block away, diagonally to his right, was the FBI headquarters building, the J. Edgar Hoover Building. It was on Constitution Avenue, between Ninth and Tenth streets, and bounded on the north by Pennsylvania Avenue, which went off at an angle from Constitution. Architecturally, it was an oddity, which

Kreiss thought lent a certain historical consistency to the design, given some of the stories that had surfaced about Hoover after his demise. From overhead, the building was shaped like a hollow rectangle, with the top of the rectangle cut back at an angle to accommodate the diagonal run of Pennsylvania Avenue as it diverged from Constitution. The upper floors were cantilevered out over the streets below, which made the building look top-heavy. Kreiss wondered if the architect had been having some fun with the Bureau's design committee. The windows were slightly casemated, giving the building's facade a fortresslike character. Most of the windows were still illuminated, although Kreiss could not see people from where he stood. But one thing was for sure: The building was absolutely made for a truck bomb, because that cantilevered overhang would trap any street-level blast and focus its full force directly into the structure.

McGarand had come up here in a propane truck. His son had been killed at Waco. His grandson, who had apparently been helping him in whatever nastiness they'd been doing out there at the arsenal, was now dead. Given the appearance of feds at the arsenal and the subsequent explosion of the power plant, McGarand would surely link the feds to Jared's death. In a manner of speaking, he'd be right. He looked around. There were no street barriers to prevent McGarand from driving that truck right up alongside the building and throwing a switch, as long as he was willing to die along with everyone in the building. Suppose they'd been brewing some powerful explosive out there at the ammunition plant. That truck could probably carry eight, ten thousand gallons of propane. Having been a chemical explosives engineer, McGarand was surely qualified to construct a truck bomb. Look what McVeigh and company had done in OK City. If they had filled a propane truck with that much C-4 or even dynamite, it would be enough to put the Hoover Building out onto the Beltway.

Even from half a block away, he could see the array of security cameras on the building's corners, and there were probably others right over his head. Most of downtown Washington was covered by surveillance cameras, and the Bureau's headquarters was undoubtedly well covered. Some steely-eyed agent in the security control room could probably see him even now, standing out here on a street corner at 10:30 at night, looking at the headquarters. He started walking down the block toward Ninth Street, trying to act like a tourist, out from his hotel, taking a walk, getting some fresh air. He looked mostly straight ahead, but he was able to scan the Constitution Avenue side of the Hoover Building without being too obvious about it. When he got to Ninth Street, he dutifully waited for the crosswalk signal. If anyone was watching him, that simple act would brand him as a definite out-of-towner. He kept going east, leaving the building behind him, passing the huge National Gallery of Art on his right, until he reached Fourth Street, at which point, he sprinted across Constitution and Pennsylvania avenues and then walked back northwest up Pennsylvania. This would take him along the diagonal segment of the headquarters building, where once again the pronounced overhang of the upper floors made the place look like a fort. But it was a fort with the same terrible vulnerability to a large truck bomb, and McGarand probably knew this. The question was, Did McGarand plan to make this a suicide bombing, or was he going to try to survive the operation?

He kept going up Pennsylvania, assuming he had been tracked along the sidewalk by the television cameras, until he was out of sight of the building. Then he cut back down along Fifteenth Street, walking by the White House and the Treasury Building, where the security forces were very visible. All the immediately adjacent streets near the White House were blocked off with large concrete objects in all directions, in celebration, no doubt, of the president's popularity among the lunatic fringe. He kept his hands in his pockets and walked briskly down to Constitution, where once again he waited for the crossing signal.

He had seen dozens of NO TRUCKS signs on the bridges and along the main downtown streets, but he had also seen a large heating-oil tanker truck, bearing the logo of the Fannon Heating Oil Company, maneuvering into an alley behind the Smithsonian Building institution, across the Mall. So the propane truck would not have been an automatic stop for the local cops. McGarand must have known this, too. But getting a heating-oil truck up next to the Hoover Building would require a ton of paperwork and advanced scheduling. Then a cop car swung in alongside the curb, going the wrong way. The driver's window rolled down.

"Help you, sir?" the cop asked.

"Nope," he said. "Out for a walk. Got a big presentation tomorrow and I'm nervous as hell about it. This area's okay, isn't it?"

"If it isn't, we're all in big trouble," the cop said, nodding his head back toward the White House. "You have a good evening."

The light changed and Kreiss crossed Constitution and headed back to the van. The Hoover Building might be the target, but, based on what those cops had just done, it was also within the security envelope of the White House. A thought had occurred to him: Given that McGarand's motive might be Waco, there was another possible target.

Janet drove carefully down the darkened mountain road, alert for deer on the road and lights in her rearview mirror. She had seen neither since turning off 460, and she hoped to keep it that way. Lynn was dozing in the passenger seat, the hospital blanket wrapped around her, despite the car's heater being on. Janet's clothes were just about dry, and she had the .38 out on the seat beside her. The girl had saved them both with that fire extinguisher trick, and perhaps had disabled their pursuer, at least for the night. It would depend on what kind of extinguisher that had been. A blast of CO_2 in the eyes ought to do some damage.

She glanced into the rearview mirror again, but it was still dark. She woke Lynn.

"Do you recognize where we are?" she asked.

Lynn blinked and watched the headlights for a minute. They descended a steep hill and crossed a creek. Green eyes blazed at them from the creek bed and Janet tapped the brake. "Yes, we're about ten minutes from Dad's cabin. Micah's is a half a mile beyond. Nobody following us?"

"Not so far," Janet said, looking in the mirror again. It would have been pretty damned obvious if there had been a vehicle back there. The night around Pearl's Mountain was clear, but there was no moon, and the surrounding forest was dense and dark. She would not have liked to have driven that road without headlights.

"We'll have to be careful going up to Micah's," Lynn said. "That's sometimes a crowd that shoots first, asks questions later."

"What are they so sensitive about?"

Lynn laughed. "They're Appalachian mountain people. They distrust anyone who spends more than an hour a day walking on flat ground. They make their own clothes, grow most of their own food, and hunt down the meat they eat. They also make their own whiskey, grow their own dope, and operate a pretty interesting black economy of barter and trade, for which they pay no taxes."

"Sounds pretty good."

"Well. It does, until you get a close look at sanitary conditions, pediatric health, the death rate from cancers caused by chewing tobacco, the infant mortality rate, the prevalence of incest and other self-destructive practices. Paradise it is not. But they hew to their way of life, and treat outsiders poorly."

"How did your father come to fit in?"

"Think about it, Agent Carter. Dad was a professional hunter. He's a loner. He's more than a little scary to be around. I think they recognized one of their own. Plus, he saved Micah Wall's youngest son from a bad situation, literally the day he moved into the cabin."

Janet braked hard to allow three small deer to bound across the road. "What this guy Wall like?"

"Micah Wall is a damned hoot. He's got this dog—it's like a Jack Russell terrier mix? The dog's idea of fun is when Micah brings out this huge old western-style Colt .45 and sits on his back porch. The dog takes off and Micah shoots right in front of it, and the dog chases the bullets when they go ricocheting around the back sheds and all the junk out there. He calls the dog Whizbang."

They went down a long, dark hill, crossed another creek, and began to climb again. As they rounded the hairpin turn that came up just before the entrance to Kreiss's cabin, Janet swore and braked hard again, this time to avoid a large white Suburban that was parked partially across the road, with only its parking lights on. There was barely enough room for her to pass the larger vehicle, and she would have to stop first to manage it. As she got her car stopped, two men got out of the Suburban. They were wearing windbreakers with ATF emblazoned in reflective tape, khaki pants, and ball caps with the ATF logo. She could see a third man inside the vehicle when they opened their doors. There were several aerials on the top of the Suburban, but no police lights.

"Shit," Janet murmured.

"What do we do?" Lynn asked, gathering the blanket around her.

"Hold on to this," Janet said, passing the .38 to Lynn as she rolled the window down. Lynn reached under the blanket and put it in her lap. Then Janet reached back into the seat-back pouch and pulled out her own ball cap, which had FBI emblazoned on it. The men came up on either side of Janet's car, but Janet told Lynn not to roll her window down.

"What's going on?" she said to the man who came up to the driver's side. He was a large black man, who kept one hand in his coat pocket. She put both hands on the top of the steering wheel so he could see them.

"Evening, ma'am. We're with the Bureau of Alcohol, Tobacco and

Firearms." He glanced nervously at Lynn's hands resting beneath the blanket. Then he saw Janet's ball cap. "You're Bureau?"

"That's right. Special Agent Janet Carter, Roanoke office." She normally would have asked for his identification, but since she no longer had her own credentials, she had to finesse it. "What's going on?"

"We're on orders to apprehend one Edwin Kreiss. Subject's wanted in connection with a federal homicide warrant. Who is this with you, Agent Carter?"

"She's my niece, visiting me from Washington." The second man was standing three feet back from the right side of her car, in position to handle any sudden emergencies. Lynn was keeping her mouth shut and her hands were still beneath the blanket.

"And you're going where?"

"I'm going to my uncle's house; that's a mile beyond the Kreiss cabin."

"That . . . place? With all the junk? That's your uncle?"

"Micah Wall. Her father, my father's sister's brother. We're not necessarily proud of him, but, well, what I can I tell you? Now you know why I'm assigned to the Roanoke office."

He nodded, obviously trying to sort through the father-brother-sister lineage. "Would you mind waiting right here, please, Agent Carter? I have orders to call in anyone who comes down this road. There's a pretty big manhunt up for this Kreiss guy."

Janet shrugged. "Sure, but can we make it quick? We're late, and I'm tired of dancing through the damned deer on these mountain roads."

He promised that he'd be right back and walked over to the Suburban, taking down her license plate number as he did so. The other man kept his station on the edge of the road, slightly behind her line of vision. She couldn't see the third man inside the Suburban until the black man opened the door on the driver's side.

"Hand me the cell phone," she said quietly, "and hit the recall button and then the one for send when you do it. Move slowly."

Lynn did as Janet asked, and Janet put the phone up to her ear. The man outside shifted his position when he saw Janet's hand leave the steering wheel. The phone rang. C'mon, she thought urgently. C'mon. I need you to answer this time.

"Micah Wall," a gnarly voice spoke into her ear.

"Mr. Wall, this is Janet Carter. You don't know me, but I'm a friend of Edwin Kreiss. I have Lynn Kreiss in the car with me and we're in trouble with the local law. We're about a mile south of your place, and we need somewhere to hide. And we may have some company on our tail when we get there."

"Lynn Kreiss? She gone missin'," Wall said. Janet handed the phone to Lynn, then leaned over to listen to what he said. "Micah, it's me. Dad's in trouble and I need a place to hide."

"How'n I know it's you?"

"Lions, Micah. Dad's cabin has lions in it."

"Yeah, it does. C'mon, then. You got cops on your tail?"

"ATF."

There was a short laugh. "The revenuers? Bring 'em bastids *on*."

The connection was broken and Janet put the phone down. The black man was half in, half out of the Suburban, talking on either a radio or a phone. She could see him better now because there was suddenly more light, and then she realized there must be a vehicle coming up behind them, and coming fast. Really fast. She saw the man silhouetted in the right mirror moving back, his hands waving, and decided this was the moment. She slammed the car into drive and accelerated right at the Suburban. The black man looked back and then dived into the front seat as she clipped his door and roared past, fishtailing all over the place. She thought she heard a gunshot but it was hard to tell with all the gravel flying everywhere. She rounded the next curve as the other vehicle's lights flooded her mirror, but then the hillside obscured them.

She took her foot off the gas momentarily to keep control of the car as she pushed it up the winding road.

"How far?" she asked Lynn, but Lynn didn't answer. She glanced over and saw that Lynn was sagging against the opposite door, a confused look on her face. "I think I've been shot," she said in a weak voice. She pulled her right hand out from under the blanket and it was shiny with blood.

Janet swore and accelerated. "Where are you hit?"

"I don't know," Lynn said in a dreamy voice. "Back, I think. Side, maybe? It's not too bad. Feels like I got kicked by a small horse."

There was a brief flare of bright lights behind her, but then she rounded the next curve and hurtled past Kreiss's driveway. The next turn again blocked out the pursuing headlights. Another half a mile. She took it up as fast as she could. She couldn't believe it—one of those ATF agents had fired at an FBI agent's car? Even if they had found out she'd quit, they shouldn't have been shooting. Unless—

The bright headlights came up again in her mirror, and she realized the

ATF agents could not have gotten that big Suburban turned around and headed after her that quickly. This was the other car, and she had a sinking feeling she knew exactly who this was. She nearly lost it on the next curve, again shooting gravel and other roadside debris out into the woods.

"Hang in there, Lynn. Can you reach the spot? Can you feel where you're hit?"

"No. I can't—can't move my right arm all that well anymore." Her voice was drifting. "Right side. My side is hurting real bad now."

A straightaway opened up and Janet accelerated, trying to think of something she could do to slow down her pursuer. But then she came into the next turn, too fast, spinning the wheel, hitting the brakes, anything to get control, but the car spun out and actually rolled backward for a moment, tires squealing, before shooting ahead again back *down* the way they had come. She was about to slam on the brakes, but then she had an idea. She doused her headlights and braked to slow down. The sharp curve was dead ahead, behind which the loom of bright white lights was rising. She got it stopped right at her side of the curve, found her .38, and rolled the window back down. Holding one hand on the brights switch, she reached out with her left hand, extending the pistol and resting her wrist on the little metal valley formed by the mirror housing. In the next instant, the pursuing vehicle came sweeping around the curve. Janet flipped on her bright lights and opened fire with the .38, deliberately aiming low, right between the approaching headlights, letting off five rounds before diving down behind the steering wheel. There was a screech of brakes, an instant of silence, and then the roar of the other vehicle's engine racing as it went crashing down into the scrub woods, smashing into rocks and small trees and then flipping partially over on its side in a hail of gravel and a spray of window glass.

Janet raised her head to look. The other car was a hundred feet down the embankment. Its headlights were still on, pointing up into the pine trees. Its left front wheel was spinning furiously. Janet did not hesitate. She turned her car around and sped up the hill as fast as she could go, aware that Lynn wasn't making any noise at all.

Browne McGarand got back to the propane truck at 11:30, after spending the afternoon and early evening asleep in a motel room. He was dressed in a set of dark coveralls that had lots of pockets. All of the equipment he would need was in the cab of the truck. He had made a detailed map of his approach routes to the ATF building, and he had laid out a couple of possible escape routes once he'd abandoned the truck. The fake delivery manifest was on a clipboard by his side.

The night was cloudy, and the lights on the Pentagon building were fuzzy in the mist blowing in from the river. There had been no traffic in the approach roads to the Pentagon when he had walked over from Crystal City. He looked around the deserted parking lot and sighed. This was the moment he had been working toward all these months. Now there was nothing more to do than to get going. He got in, started up the truck, backed it across the parking area, and drove out onto the approach road, turning right to go under the elevated highway, then taking the tight ramp up to get on the Fourteenth Street Bridge. Big trucks were generally not allowed into the District, but fuel trucks were an exception. He was hoping not to be stopped. The manifest should get him by a cursory police inspection, as long as the cop didn't ask him for the exemption certificate, which he did not have. Shift change for the Metro Police came at midnight, which was why he had chosen this time to make his approach to the target. Most of the District's patrol cars would be in station house parking lots, refueling for the next shift, all the cops inside.

In the event, he didn't see a single cop car. He made it onto Massachusetts Avenue, where there was zero traffic. The ATF headquarters building loomed to his left as he turned into the ramp gate for the parking garage next door. It was a tight fit and his rear bumper tagged a concrete abutment, but he just made it. There was an attendant's booth at the bottom of the ramp, but it was dark and unoccupied. He had to get out of the cab to extract the ticket from a dispenser. The side ramp was a two-way ramp, and a sign said to give way to vehicles coming down. The gate dutifully opened when he took the ticket, and up he went in first gear, making a lot more noise than he wanted to. At the top of the ramp, he turned right and headed for the back corner nearest the ATF building. There were some SUVs and a couple of pickup trucks up on the roof deck, more than he had expected. He backed the truck into the corner space along the wall and shut it down. First exposure successfully completed, he thought. He looked over at the ATF building. Only a few of the windows facing him were lighted on his side of the building, but the interiors were above his line of sight. He scanned the side face and corners of the building again for video cameras, but the only one he could see was pointed down onto Massachusetts Avenue. He took out a small pair of binoculars and scanned the top edges of the buildings across the street from the ATF building. As he had suspected, there was one camera jutting out of the middle of the office building directly opposite, but it, too, was pointed down onto Massachusetts Avenue. It might conceivably look into the alley, but the back of the alley was in deep shadow. He cracked his window, then nodded his head when he heard the sound of the vent fans down in the alley below.

He looked at his watch. It was just after midnight. He sat back in the lumpy seat, listening to the ticking sounds of his diesel engine cooling down. The windows of the cars parked around him were already glistening with nighttime dew. There was a flare of yellow light as the stairwell door opened up at the front of the roof deck and a couple stepped out, arm in arm. They appeared to be wine-happy from an evening in one of the local restaurants. They got into a Toyota Land Cruiser and left, going down the exit ramp. Neither of them had given the big truck parked back in the dark corner a second look. Good.

Now he waited. He wanted to begin dropping the hose sometime around 2:30, when most humans were at their low ebb of performance, and then go down to attach it to the air-intake vent screens in the back of the alley between 3:00 and 4:00 A.M. Originally, he had planned to shinny down the hose itself, but he might just walk down the interior exit ramps and see if he could hop a wall at the back of the ground-level parking deck, out of sight of any cameras, of course. In the meantime, he would watch the ATF building for any signs of walking patrols or other security features he might have missed. But he didn't expect any: Above all else, these people were bureaucrats. They would pay close attention to the size of their office and whether or not they got a parking space, but he was pretty sure they weren't too concerned about someone attacking them in their own building. If he could permeate that entire building with hydrogen, the explosion would certainly be memorable. Even if he only got a partial ignition, it would still create a two-thousand-degree fireball in every cubic inch of the affected office spaces. Quicker and somewhat more merciful than what these goons had done to those people at Mount Carmel, who had cooked for a while as the burning building melted down around them, helped along by *tanks*, for God's sake. Maybe next time they'd be a little more careful, those who survived what he was about to do. He settled back against the seat to watch and wait. He wished he could have done the FBI building, but, short of a suicide attack with something like a truckload of Ampho, there were no good approaches that would let him walk away from it. Not like this one. It was wide open.

13

Edwin Kreiss sat in a locked interview room at the Seventh Street police station, wondering how he was going to get out of this one. He had been standing on the corner of Twelfth Street and Massachusetts Avenue, looking at the ATF headquarters building, when the same cops who had seen him down by the White House drove by, on their way into shift change. The cop car had slowed and then stopped. Kreiss had briefly considered bolting, but he didn't know the streets and alleys around this area of office buildings. They would have had him in a heartbeat for taking off. The car had backed up, and this time the cop's partner got out, one hand on his nightstick, the other parking his hat on his head. The cop driving, who had apparently recognized him, stayed in the car but watched over his shoulder. The cop had asked him politely enough what he was doing up there, and Kreiss literally had no answer. Fortunately, he had left the gun in the van, which he had parked in an all-night parking garage right next door to the ATF building. They'd cuffed him, pat-searched him, and put him in the backseat. They brought him into the police station, presumably on a loitering beef. They had not booked him, however, and he had been in the interview room for what he estimated was almost three hours now. He was no longer cuffed, but they had taken his wallet, watch, and his keys. He would have appreciated some coffee.

He had not had enough time to do a complete reconnaissance of the ATF building, but it had been pretty clear that it was a softer target than the FBI headquarters. The building was much smaller, and though there were surveillance cameras, the approach to the front of the building was a lot more straightforward than driving down Constitution and dealing with all the traffic islands where the major avenues met. Yes, they would see the propane truck pulling up in front of the building, but, by then, it would be too late. In fact, McGarand would probably have time to park it, set a fuse, and run before the security people in the building could really react. He smiled grimly to himself as he thought of the options facing a guy at the security desk when he saw a big truck pull up in front of the building and a guy get out and run. Now what? Who goes down to see what's in the truck, and who goes out the back door at the speed of heat?

In the meantime, he was stuck in here, and he had a pretty good idea of what was going to happen. And who was going to come through that door next.

The door finally opened and the desk sergeant admitted two men in suits into the room. Kreiss looked up at them and congratulated himself on being right. One of the men, the larger of the two, sat down across the table from him. The other remained standing. The big man was in his forties. He had a round face that needed a shave, impatient blue eyes, and thinning black hair. He produced a credentials wallet and flashed it at Kreiss.

"Sam Johnstone, FBI," he said. "And you're Edwin Kreiss. The notorious Edwin Kreiss."

Kreiss said nothing. Johnstone leaned back in his chair.

"We've been looking for you, Mr. Kreiss. Or rather, the Roanoke RA has. Seems there're some questions they want to ask you about a homicide down in Blacksburg."

Kreiss maintained his silence. Johnstone looked over at his partner.

"You not going to speak to me, Mr. Kreiss?" he asked.

"You haven't asked me a question yet," Kreiss said.

"Okay, here's one: Why were you loitering around the ATF headquarters building tonight? After being seen loitering around the White House? I guess that's two questions. Well. And you were also seen on our cameras at Bureau headquarters. You got something going tonight, Mr. Kreiss? You're not still mad at us, are you?"

"Nope."

Johnstone continued to stare at him as if he was an interesting specimen. Then his partner spoke. "I hear you used to be a spooky guy, Kreiss. That you used to go around hunting people down with your pals out in Langley. That true? You a spooky guy?"

Kreiss turned slowly to look at the partner, who was a medium everything: height, weight, build. Even his soft white face was totally unremarkable. He would make a very good surveillance asset, Kreiss thought. Then he turned back to face Johnstone.

"He gave me the look, Sam," the second agent said. "Definitely spooky. I think I'm supposed to be scared now."

"Better watch your ass, Lanny. I've heard that Mr. Kreiss here was responsible for a guy shooting his wife and his kids and then himself. He must be really persuasive. That was before the Bureau shit-canned you, right, Mr. Kreiss?"

Kreiss smiled at him but said nothing.

"Damn, there he goes again, Lanny. Won't talk to me. I think I've hurt his feelings. Of course, here *he* is, in the local pokey, picked up for loitering in downtown Washington. What do you suppose he was looking for, Lanny? A white guy walking the streets at midnight in the District? Looking for some female companionship, maybe? Or maybe some sympathetic *male* companionship? Is that it, Mr. Kreiss? All those years of playing games with those Agency weirdos, maybe you got a little bent?"

Kreiss relaxed in his chair and looked past Johnstone as if he didn't exist. They had either planned their little act in advance in some effort to provoke him or they were pissed off at having to come over here at all, just because a routine name check had triggered the federal want and detain order. Or both. But so far, they weren't talking about a bomb. Apparently, Janet's attempt to warn them about a bomb threat had gone right into the bureaucratic equivalent of the Grand Canyon. He looked at his wrist, then remembered they'd taken his watch.

"Got somewhere to go, Mr. Kreiss?"

"Am I being charged?"

"Nope. You're being *held*. As a material witness to a homicide in Virginia. But before you go back down to Blacksburg, we've been informed that the commissars out in Langley want to have a word."

Shit, shit, *shit*, Kreiss thought while keeping a studiously indifferent expression on his face. He had managed to evade the best sweeper in the business, and now he had handed himself over to them on a loitering beef. Johnstone was looking at his watch.

"Anyway, now you're going to come with us, Mr. Kreiss. First we're going to escort you out to Langley, where some people in their Counterespionage Division want to talk to you. Then you'll be brought back to our Washington field office for further transport down to Roanoke. Cuff him, Lanny."

Kreiss sighed and stood up, putting his two hands out in front of him. He was much bigger than the agent called Lanny, and he almost enjoyed the sudden wary look Lanny had in his eyes when he approached Kreiss to put plastic handcuffs on his wrists.

"He looked at me again, Sam," Lanny said, trying to keep it going, but Kreiss could hear the note of fear in Lanny's voice. The man was physically afraid of him. That was good. They'd already made their first mistake, cuffing his hands in front of him. Now, as long as they had a car and not a van, and as long as they put him in the backseat and they both rode in front, he was as good as free. He'd do it on the G.W. Parkway, with all those lovely cliffs. He looked down at the floor, putting a despondent expression on his face. He let his shoulders slump and his head hang down a little. Defeated. Captured. Resigned to his fate. He heard Johnstone make kissing noises behind him, and both agents laughed contemptuously. Kreiss sincerely hoped that Johnstone would drive.

Janet was afraid of missing the turn into Micah Wall's place, but when she saw all the junked cars, rusting refrigerators, tire piles, and pallets of assorted junk on both sides of a wide dirt road, she knew she'd found it. She turned the car into the driveway and drove through more junk up toward the lights of a long, low cabin on the hillside. Halfway up the hill, her headlights revealed a telephone pole barring the drive. She slowed and then stopped. Several figures came out of the dark, walking toward her car with rifles and shotguns in their hands. She opened the door and got out, leaving it open.

"That's Lynn Kreiss," she said, pointing into the car. "I think she's been shot. We need some help."

"Who done it?" an authoritative voice asked from the darkness.

"A federal agent who was chasing us. I forced her off the road about a half a mile back there. But if she isn't seriously injured, she'll be here very soon."

"*She?*" The voice sounded incredulous.

"That's right. Please? We need to see to Lynn. She's bleeding."

Micah Wall materialized out of the darkness and introduced himself while three men went to the other side of the car and lifted Lynn out. Janet told him her name, shook his hand, and then went around the front of the car. The girl groaned but did not resist when they laid her out on the ground on her uninjured side, illuminated by the wedge of light coming from the car's interior. One of them lifted the back of Lynn's shirt, revealing an entrance wound on the lower-right side of her back. A second man grunted and leaned forward, a long knife suddenly glistening in his hand. Before Janet could object, he probed the wound and then lifted out a spent bullet. The bleeding increased immediately, as if blood had been dammed up behind the bullet, but Janet realized that the wound was not significant. The bullet's passage through the car's metal body and the upholstery must have slowed it down.

"Less'n there's another one, this ain't too bad," the man with the knife said. He had a full black beard and a face like a hatchet. He pulled out a handkerchief, folded it, and pressed it against the wound. Janet hoped it was cleaner than the surroundings.

"Take her up to the house, Big John," Wall said. "Tommy, Marsh, y'all help him. Git some sulfa dust and a real bandage on that. Rest of us, we gotta git ready to met this lady badass, supposed to be comin' round the mountain any minute now."

Janet told him about the fire in the hospital, and her suspicion that the woman had started it deliberately. Micah nodded slowly, looking around at the dark woods. "Yonder girl's daddy, he kept some interesting company. Why'n't you leave your car here, go on up to the house. See to the girl. Boys'n me, we'll wait and see what comes along."

"Be careful," Janet said over her shoulder as she stepped past the telephone pole. "This woman was Edwin Kreiss's instructor."

"That so," Micah muttered. "Well, then, I wish I had me some of her daddy's lions. Or maybe that there Barrett. Spread out, boys."

Browne McGarand awoke at just before 2:00 A.M. and sat up in the seat. The truck's windows were all opaque with dew. He leaned forward and hit the wiper switch for one cycle to clear the windshield, then rolled down his window. The same windows that had been showing lights before in the ATF building were still lighted, which meant that they had simply left the lights on. He reached up and picked the lens cover off the interior cabin light and took out the bulb. Then he opened the door and got out. The temperature had dropped noticeably, and the night was now clearing. There were no traffic sounds coming from Massachusetts Avenue below, and the remaining cars on the roof deck had fully opaque windows.

He walked to the back of the truck, stretching his knees, and then to the very back corner of the parking deck. He put his head over the low concrete wall and listened. The sound of vent fans coming from the HVAC building in the alley was much reduced. Good, he thought. They had put the system on low speed for the night. Blocking one of the intake screens wouldn't raise any system alarms at that fan speed. He checked the time again and then went back to the truck. The hose reel on the back unrolled in the direction of the ATF building. There was a modified brass connector nozzle on the end he was going to lower. At the truck end, the hose was not connected at all, leaving it open to the atmosphere.

He began pulling hose off the reel, being very careful not to damage the modified brass connector nozzle. He hefted it over the concrete wall and let it down into the darkness. After a few minutes, the weight of the hose began to pull itself off the reel and he had to go back to the reel and set the brake halfway to keep it from running away. When a white blaze of paint on the hose showed up, he set the reel brake all the way and then checked the hose. The gleaming brass connector was hanging just a few feet above the surface of the alley. He resumed letting it out until a second blaze of paint marked the length he needed to get the nozzle over to the intake screens. He reset the brake.

He knew that he was entering the period of greatest exposure, because now he would have to go down, enter the alley, attach the plastic tarp to the one screen to blank it off, and then attach a second tarp, with a nozzle-receiver fitting sewn into its center, to the second screen. At that point, all the intake air for the ventilation system would be sucked through that one fitting. If it wasn't big enough, he should see a lot of strain on both tarps. If he had to, he could peel back two or three corners to keep sufficient air moving. Then he would attach the end of the tanker's hose to the fitting on the tarp and trip the discharge lever. As long as the two tarps and the receiver nozzle let in just enough air, he could go on back up. After that, it would be a matter of choosing the best time to begin sending in the hydrogen gas. He wanted as many of those bastards in the building as possible when the hydrogen reached critical volume, but the more people that were around, the higher were the chances of someone discovering the rig.

Ideally, he wanted the blast to take place as close as possible to 8:00 A.M. Based on his calculations it would take around ninety minutes to fill the building with an explosive mixture, so gas injection had to begin no later than 6:30. It would still be dark at 6:30, but not for long. He wished now he had some way to spark the mixture from outside the building, if for some reason it didn't ignite, but they had not been able to devise anything that would do that. Besides, he did not plan to hang around. He checked his watch again: 2:35. The minutes were passing slowly. He wanted to get going, but he knew that he would have to be patient and flexible. Hooking up the hose would be relatively easy: If they hadn't spotted the hose coming down into the alley, they probably would not spot him. Then it would all depend on the whole lash-up remaining invisible until 8:00 A.M. He made sure the hose brake was secured, then unstrapped the five-gallon gasoline can he'd mounted on the back step of the truck. He took it to the cab, set it down in the middle of the bench seat, and taped on the ignition device, setting it for 8:00 A.M. That would take care of the truck if the building explosion didn't. Then he closed the doors, locked them, walked over to the interior exit ramp, and started down into the darkness of the parking garage.

It was just after 4:00 A.M. when the two agents finally signed Kreiss out of Metro Police custody. After retrieving the envelope with his wallet, watch, and keys, they escorted him out of the building. Then the agents put him into the backseat of their four-door government sedan, which was parked in the lot for patrol cars at the side of the station. They made him sit right in the middle of the backseat, and they kept him cuffed. Lanny buckled both rear seat belts around him, so that if he tried to move, there would be two latches he would have to undo. Kreiss was perfectly happy with this arrangement, and even happier that there had been no hookup wire to which he could have been cuffed in the backseat. While Lanny waited in the car with Kreiss, Johnstone went back into the precinct station and came back out with two coffees. The two G-men sat in the car with their coffee for a few minutes, making a point of enjoying it while Kreiss went without. Then Lanny called into their operations center on the car's radio and reported that they were transporting the subject to Langley, as per previous direction. The ops center acknowledged and told them to report when delivery had been made. Lanny rogered and hung up.

Johnstone drove while Lanny rode shotgun, turned partially in his seat to keep an eye on Kreiss. It was Johnstone who kept peppering Kreiss with mildly insulting questions about why he was in town, what he had done that made the Agency people so anxious to see him, and what his part in the Blacksburg homicide had been. Lanny seemed to enjoy it all, but he didn't say anything. Kreiss remained silent, his eyes closed, as if he were trying to sleep. Johnstone gave up after a while and concentrated on his driving. He took Constitution Avenue down to Twenty-third Street, drove past the Lincoln Memorial, and then went over the Memorial Bridge into Arlington. Kreiss kept track of where they were while he made his mental preparations.

When Johnstone turned down the ramp that led to the northbound George Washington Parkway, Kreiss began to reposition himself, adjusting his body in tiny increments. By now, Lanny had turned back around and was bitching to Johnstone about duty schedules back at FBI headquarters. Kreiss, who had driven the G.W. Parkway a few thousand times during his career, needed only an occasional glance out of slitted eyes to know precisely where they were. The G.W. was a four-lane divided parkway, climbing up through the Potomac palisades toward McLean and Langley in northern Virginia. Because they were going northwest up the Potomac River, they were on the river side of the parkway. To the left was the low, stone-walled median and the eastbound roadway, bordered by a band of large trees. To his right were more trees, through which the Potomac was clearly visible, initially right alongside, and then increasingly below them as the parkway climbed some two hundred feet above the river's rocky gorge.

Kreiss was not going to allow himself to be taken into the Agency headquarters. He knew what could happen there, and where he might be taken from there. Someone pretty senior in the Bureau must have reached an understanding with the Agency hierarchy. Or perhaps higher, he thought, like maybe someone at Justice. This little trip to Langley wasn't about any bomb plot. This was about payback for Ephraim Glower. It took real juice to launch Misty, so until he knew that Lynn was truly safe, he was going to do whatever it took to remain free and operational. If he could prevent whatever Browne McGarand was planning in the District, fine, although he hadn't actually promised Carter anything. But she promised you something pretty important, he reminded himself. Either way, he would *not* allow these bozos just to hand him over like a lamb to the slaughter to a government agency that had every motive to make him disappear. He had personally delivered one individual to the federal maximum-security prison in Lewisburg, someone he knew for a fact had never seen the inside of any courtroom, or the outside world, ever again.

When they passed the first scenic overlook turnout, he got ready. There was another overlook in exactly one mile, right below the Civil War park where the president's lawyer had been found shot to death in a supposed suicide. Lanny was complaining about getting stuck on midnight-to-eight shifts twice a month when other, more junior agents were getting tagged only once a month, especially if they were female. Johnstone appeared to be tuning out Lanny's monologue, but he kept up a steady stream of uh-huhs while he drove and sipped his coffee. Kreiss could see that he was doing an even sixty-five, ten miles over the posted speed limit, but entirely normal for the parkway, especially at 2:30 A.M. Any Park Police cruiser sitting out there would recognize the sedan as a government car. Johnstone had his left hand on the wheel and his right hand down in his lap, holding the paper coffee cup.

Kreiss began surreptitiously tugging on the seat belts, taking out all the slack until they were almost painfully tight around him, the two shoulder straps cutting into his chest in an X configuration. When he saw the sign for the next scenic overlook, he sat way back in the seat and tensed his legs. When he saw the actual turnout coming up on the right, he raised his right leg and, pivoting on his left buttock, leaned left and kicked up to strike Johnstone under his right ear as hard as he could. Johnstone gave a grunt and pitched to the left, against the door, which had the effect of turning the car to the left, directly toward the stone wall in the median. Lanny dropped his coffee, raised both hands, and yelled, "Look out!" to the stunned Johnstone, and then grabbed the wheel, yanking it hard right. The car swerved back across the two lanes, tires screeching, until the left-front tire failed and the car whip-rolled three times down the outer north-bound lane in a hail of glass and road dust. Then it hit a small tree, spun around the tree on its side, and slid down the embankment and into the scenic-overlook parking lot fifty feet below the level of the roadway. It righted itself as it slalomed into the parking lot and then crunched par-tially through the low stone wall overlooking a sheer cliff that fell all the way to the Potomac.

Kreiss, who had been prepared for the crash and was double-belted, was unhurt. He popped the latches on the seat belts and lunged forward to grab Lanny around the throat with his cuff chain. Lanny, stunned by the violence of the crash and entangled in his deflated air bag, did not resist as Kreiss hauled him back over the seat and stuffed him down into the space between the backseat and the floor. He checked on Johnstone, who appeared to be unconscious and pinned beneath the headliner of the car, which had been smashed down on him in the crash. His face was obscured by his deflated air bag. The front windshield was gone, as were all the windows, and there was a strong smell of gasoline in the car.

Kreiss fished in Lanny's suit pockets for the cuff key. When the agent stirred, Kreiss hit him once in the temple with a raised-knuckle fist, and the man sagged. Kreiss got the key, unlocked the cuffs, threw them out the window, and climbed over the front seat to retrieve the envelope with his own wallet and keys from the floor. He reached into Johnstone's suit jacket pocket and took his credentials. He left their guns alone. He turned off the ignition and threw the car's keys over the wall. He tried the right rear door, but it was jammed. He climbed out the right-front window and dropped to the pavement, shaking off bits of glass from his clothes. He found himself standing in a spreading stain of gasoline. He swore and then spent the next five minutes dragging the two unconscious agents out of the car and fifty feet back away from the wreck. Both had been wearing seat belts and neither one appeared to be bleeding or otherwise seriously injured. They are assholes, he told himself, but they are essentially just working stiffs doing their jobs. There is no reason for them to die for their incompetence. He retrieved the handcuffs from the ground and cuffed their wrists together through the iron rail of a park bench that was cemented to the ground. He took their guns and threw them onto the floor of the car's backseat.

He went back into the car one more time and ripped out the radio handset, throwing it over the cliff. He saw their car phone dangling by its floor-mount wire. The light was still on in the dial. He hesitated and then punched in Janet Carter's number in Blacksburg. The phone rang several times but then hit voice mail. He hung up, ripped out the handset, and threw it over the cliff. Then he brushed himself off again, suddenly aware that there really was a hell of a lot of gasoline on the ground. He started up the overlook exit ramp. He hoped the car would not burn, because that would attract immediate attention, and he needed some time to get back down to the vicinity of Key Bridge. There was a hotel right near the parkway ramps at the bridge, and hopefully he could get a cab back into the District. The good news was that it was all downhill.

He got up to the parkway and started jogging back down the northbound lane. He would have plenty of time to duck down behind the stone walls if he saw approaching headlights. He would try to get a call through to Carter again from his van. Right now, everything would depend on how long it took for the Park Police to find the wreck. He watched for signs of a fire as he jogged back down the empty roadway, but the woods behind him remained dark.

Janet Carter came out of the tiny bedroom where Lynn lay, relieved that the bleeding had stopped. An elderly woman who smelled of lilacs had cleaned the wound with soap and water, then applied some yellow powder and a clean bandage. There was a large bruise around the wound, but the bullet had apparently hit a rib and stopped. Lynn had remained awake and had gasped when the soap and water hit, but the old woman had given her some hot herbal tea, and now she was asleep.

To Janet's surprise, the interior of the log house was spotlessly clean, in sharp contrast to all the junk piled around the front entrance and out behind the cabin. She couldn't tell how many people actually lived in the cabin, which appeared to be a central log house with a conglomeration of additions and extensions. It was much bigger than it had appeared from the road. The woman, who had not spoken since Janet had followed the men carrying Lynn into the house, led her back to a kitchen and family room area. The kitchen smelled of coffee and baking bread, and Janet saw three more loaves of bread rising in an oven next to the stove. There was another small bedroom and bath behind the kitchen, and the woman indicated Janet could go in there and clean up. She closed the wooden door behind her and went into the bathroom to wash her hands and face. She had some bloodstains on her hands and her face was sooty. She cleaned up as best she could and then went back into the kitchen. Micah Wall was there, taking off his jacket. A semiautomatic shotgun was parked on the wall next to an ancient-looking refrigerator.

"What happened?" Janet asked.

"Took the pickup down the road, and they was a bunch of mean-lookin' gov'mint boys and some cars pulled up where the other one went into the woods. One of 'em told me to turn around, take my boys, and git outta there. He had him a Steyr machine pistol, so we done like he said. They friends of your's?"

"Nope," Janet said, surprised to hear this old mountain man talking about Steyr machine pistols. "How many of them were there and how were they dressed?"

"Couldn't rightly tell. They was lotsa of headlights, so most of 'em was in shadow. The one doin' the talkin' was wearin' sunglasses. Big fella."

"But not uniforms? Not deputies?"

"No, hell no. We know all the deputies in these parts. No, these boys wasn't from round here. Now your car's got five bullet holes in it. Here's a coupla the rounds we dug out. How's about you tell me what's goin' on here with that girl yonder."

Janet explained who she was, and how she came to be flying through the night with federal agents in hot pursuit. The old woman brought them both a cup of coffee and then sliced some fresh bread, which she put on the table with a crock of butter and another one with preserves. Micah indicated Janet should eat something, and she ate three slices of the fresh bread before stopping short of eating all of it. Micah took it all in, nodding his head a couple of times when Janet described Ransom and his partner and told about the incident with the Bronco. When she was finished, he just sat there, staring down at the table, as if lost in thought. Then the phone rang. He looked at Janet with raised eyebrows, but Janet just shook her head. He went over to the wall-mounted phone, answered, and listened for a moment. Then he handed the phone to Janet with an amused expression in his eyes.

"Yes?" she said.

The woman's voice was as cold as she remembered it. "Not bad for an amateur," she said. "But you can't shoot for shit."

"I was aiming low, between the headlights," Janet said. "Otherwise, you'd be dead."

"You put them all through my windshield. Like I said, you can't shoot for shit. I have some news for you."

"You shot Kreiss's daughter," Janet interrupted. There was a second of silence on the line.

"No, I didn't," the woman said. "I'm not carrying."

Janet didn't know what to say. "Then who—"

"Did you recover a bullet?"

"Yes."

"Good. Keep it. It might give you some leverage later. But in the meantime, I thought you'd want to know. We have Kreiss. The Bureau picked him up in Washington and is delivering him to Langley. So I don't need the daughter anymore. You can relax."

"Relax. Right," Janet said.

"Suit yourself, Carter, I no longer care. But the ATF people whose roadblock you ran might."

"The ones who shot at my car and hit a kid?"

"That's why I told you to keep the bullet. If you get your tail feathers in a crack over it, find a reporter, tell your tale. The ATF hates that. And don't let your famous Bureau lab get the bullet; their ballistics work goes to the highest bidder these days. But you probably knew that."

The dial tone came on and the woman was gone. Janet, her face a bit red, slowly hung up the phone.

"Friend of yourn?" Micah asked.

"No," Janet said. "She was the one who set the hospital on fire and then chased us up here. But she says she didn't do any shooting. That it was a bunch of ATF guys who did that."

"Now, that'll please brother Edwin no end," Micah said. "Revenuers shootin' at his little girl." He shook his head slowly. "Mama says the girl's goin' to be all right; we don't have to get a doctor into it, less'n we see proud flesh."

"Shouldn't we do that anyway?"

"Doc sees a bullet wound, he's obliged to call local law," Micah said. "Might want to wait on that."

Janet sat back down at the table. She was aware that there were other men in the cabin, out in the front rooms. She was suddenly very tired. "They, the feds, already know it was me in that car. They may or may not know who Lynn was." She stopped, and then it penetrated—what the woman had said about Kreiss. "Oh, *hell*," she said. "She said they had Kreiss. Up in Washington. She said the FBI had him and was taking him to Langley. Where *she's* from."

Micah obviously didn't know what she meant by Langley, but then the phone rang again. "Grand Central Station," Micah muttered, reaching for it. He said his name, then smiled. "She's right here." He handed her the phone. This time, it was Kreiss.

"Where are you?" she said in a rush.

"I'm in a pay phone. I don't have much time. Where's Lynn?"

"She's here and we're safe, for the moment anyway." She saw Micah shaking his head slowly. He was warning her not to tell him his daughter had been shot. She nodded. "A lot's happened, but we're safe. But that woman just called, said the Bureau had you."

"They had me, and then I had them. Look, I've got to get back to my vehicle, and then I'm coming down there. I don't know where McGarand is. He and his truck have disappeared."

"That woman said she was no longer interested in Lynn because the FBI was bringing you in—to Langley. When she finds out—"

"Yeah, that's why I'm leaving here. Soon."

"And there's no sign that McGarand is going to bomb something up there? Like Bureau headquarters?"

"I looked. I looked for his truck at all the Washington truck terminals. Then I went over into town and looked around the Hoover Building, and then I went up to the ATF headquarters building. There was no sign of the propane truck."

Janet gnawed her lip. The warnings. All for nothing, apparently.

"Let me talk to Micah," Kreiss said.

Janet handed the phone back to Micah, who listened for a long minute. "I can do that," he said. "Keep your powder dry." Then he hung up.

"What?" Janet asked.

"We need to clear on outta here," Micah said, getting up. "First, we need to git you and the girl in there some warm clothes."

"Can she be moved?"

"Seein' that's just a flesh wound, yes. Even if it wasn't, old Ed says we gotta move. Now. Come with me."

Kreiss had the cab let him out at an all-night café one block up from Constitution Avenue, and four blocks away from the parking garage where he'd put the van. It was 5:45 when a yawning waitress brought him black coffee and a stale-looking Danish. He had taken a corner booth back from the door and was yawning himself. Outside, the first headlights of Washington's morning rush hour were starting to appear, and he could see even more vehicles down on Constitution. It didn't surprise him: Washington's traffic was so bad that many office workers went to work in the early-morning darkness just to avoid it. By 7:30 most mornings, a large majority of government workers were already in the office, stalking the coffee pot. His plan was to eat his fat pill, get some caffeine in him, and then go retrieve the rental van. Given the fact of rush hour, his best plan was to sleep in the van until the traffic crush was over, then hit the road south for Blacksburg. He would simply take the van, and leave his pickup truck at the motel. If they were looking for him, the cash-rental van would buy him an extra day, whereas his own truck might be picked up pretty quick.

He thought about driving down by the Hoover Building and waving to the cameras. Then he thought about Misty getting the word that he'd escaped again. Micah and his boys would provide as much safety as anyone could, especially on their home ground on the slopes and crags of Pearl's Mountain. Misty and her associates were pretty damned lethal in a city, but Micah might be a good match for them in the Appalachian woods, especially once he got them to one of the caves. He decided to get going, before those same two cops came in for morning coffee and busted him again.

He paid up and went out onto the sidewalk. There were no pedestrians, but definitely a lot more traffic. He walked up three blocks to Massachusetts Avenue and then over one to the parking garage. There was a line of cars turning in to both the street-level entrance and the ramp, probably desk-bound revenuers from the ATF building right next door. A bearded and turbaned Sikh carrying a rolled-up *Washington Post* and a paper cup of coffee was unlocking the ticket booth as Kreiss walked into the garage, but the man ignored him. Kreiss climbed the stairs and came out on the level just beneath the roof. His van was parked in the back-right corner, mostly out of habit. His level wasn't full yet, but it was getting that way. It was 6:50; in another thirty minutes, the Sikh would be putting a GARAGE FULL sign out in front. He unlocked the door, climbed in, and set the locks again. The rear seat folded down, so he was able to create a good-enough sleeping pad back there. The left windows of his van were right up against the outside wall, so incoming vehicles could park only on his right side. He draped a jacket up over that side's window and stretched out. The first light of dawn was coming through the apertures between the concrete support columns, and he could see people moving around in the ATF building right next door. Their offices looked like every other government hive: computer cubes, plants in corners, conference rooms, pacifying pastel dividers, vision-impairing fluorescent lights, and all the coat-and-tie drones, moving slow until their morning caffeine fix took hold. He had spent many, many hours in similar circumstances between operational missions, and he did not miss it.

He was just closing his eyes when he caught sight of something odd in the space of daylight next to the window. It looked like a hose, a big black reinforced rubber hose, and it was just barely moving from side to side in some invisible updraft. He closed his eyes anyway, then opened them again. What the hell was a hose doing there? He stared at it again, trying to see if he had imagined movement, but it did move, as if it were dangling down from the deck above him. He sat up and looked at it again. There was something familiar about it, but he couldn't place it. Just then a vehicle came by in front of the van, stopped, and then laboriously backed in alongside his vehicle. He lay back down instinctively, but the jacket blocked the view of the people getting out. Obviously a car pool; the men were finishing up an argument about the Washington Redskins, or Deadskins, as one of the men called them. They extracted briefcases, closed and locked the doors, and then disappeared toward the exit stairs. Kreiss sat back up again when they were clear. His eyes were stinging and he was dead tired, but there was something about that hose that bothered him.

He slid into the front seat, looked around at the nearly full parking deck, and then got out on the driver's side. The hose came straight down from above, within easy hand reach across the low concrete wall. He reached out and touched it, surprised at how cold it was. There was a sheen of moisture on the rubber, and a shiny metal collar just out of reach had a definite rime of white frost on it. When he stretched out to look up, he saw that the hose went up one more level to the roof deck, then disappeared. He looked down. The hose went straight down, then across a small, still, dark alley, and disappeared behind what looked like a small utility building at the back of the alley. The utility building appeared to be connected to the ATF building. As he listened, he heard the low whistling noise of vent fans rising from the alley.

He leaned back into the garage and looked across the space between the ATF building and the garage. He could see right into a bank of offices. He watched office workers arrive in their cubes, stash lunch bags in office refrigerators, and stand around with cups of coffee, talking to their cell mates. He saw one middle-aged woman come into what was obviously an executive corner office, turn on the lights, close the door, and sit down in her chair, where she proceeded to hike up her skirt and make a major adjustment to her panty hose. None of them so much as glanced out their windows, even though it was now getting light all around. Great situational awareness, he thought. He saw no more vehicles coming up into his parking level, so he went over to the exit stairs and climbed up to the roof. Once out on the roof, he looked around and then remembered where he had seen that hose before: on the green-and-white propane truck driven by Browne McGarand, which was now parked in the corner of the roof deck.

He didn't bother even going over there. He could see that there was no one in the truck, and he knew instinctively that whatever had been in that truck was probably now inside that office building next door. He ran back to the exit stair on the roof and started down, two steps at a time. He hadn't really figured out what he was going to do when he got down to the street: run like hell, or warn them? And would they listen?

He was slowed by morning commuters on the stairs as he neared the ground level, and he rudely pushed past them to a chorus of "Hey, watch it" from the people he jostled. He kept saying, "Sorry, sorry," but he also kept going. When he got outside to the street level, he stopped. The main entrance to the ATF building was a glass-walled lobby, and he could see the security people at their counter, next to X-ray machines and metal detectors. One of the men whom he had pushed by in the stairwell came abreast and gave him an angry look, but Kreiss ignored him. They were all in coats and ties; he was in slacks, a shirt, and a windbreaker. In about a minute, one of those angry ATF agents was going to ask him what he was doing out here. He looked into the alley. The hose was still there, barely distinguishable from the morning shadows. He wanted to go back there, make sure it had been routed into the ventilation building before calling a warning. But there might not be time.

He turned around to face the stream of people coming from the garage to the building. When one of the approaching men, who looked like a midgrade bureaucrat, gave him a quizzical look, he put up his hand to stop him and then flashed Johnstone's FBI credentials.

"Johnstone, FBI," he announced to the startled man. "Would you please ask one of the security guards to come out here? I think there's a problem in that alley."

The man looked into the alley and then back at Kreiss, and then he said, "Sure, wait here." Kreiss stepped out of the flow of pedestrian traffic and watched through the glass as the man went inside and talked to the security people at the counter, who all looked back through the glass at Kreiss. One of them, a young black man, put on his hat and started around the counter while the guard next to him picked up a phone and began talking. Kreiss's messenger put his briefcase on the X-ray machine's belt and stepped through the metal detector, taking one last look at Kreiss before disappearing into the building. The security guard came through the front door and walked over to him, carrying a small radio in one hand and keeping his other hand near the butt of his gun. Kreiss made sure his hands were visible, and he held open the credentials so that the approaching guard could see the big black FBI letters. He closed it before the guard could get a close look at Johnstone's picture, which wasn't even a passing match for Kreiss's face.

"Back there, in the alley. We've had a report of a possible bomb attack on your building. See that hose?"

The guard, who wanted another look at those credentials, locked on to the *b* word. "Say what? A bomb? Where?"

"See that hose—there, all the way at the back of the alley? Look up— it's coming down from the top deck of the parking garage. There's a truck up there on the top deck. A propane truck. That hose looks like it's going into your building's ventilation system—see it?"

The guard looked, frowned, and then nodded. "Yeah, I see it. But wait a minute. Propane? That shit stinks. We're not smelling anything inside."

"There's a tanker truck on the roof of that garage that's pumping something into your building. It might not be propane. Don't you think you ought to check that out?"

Kreiss stood there while the bewildered guard spoke on his radio to someone inside. As he held the radio up to his ear for a reply, three more guards came running out of the lobby with guns drawn, headed straight for Kreiss. They were not smiling.

Janet held on to Lynn's hand as Micah led them through the rising dawn up into the woods behind the cabin. The forested slopes of Pearl's Mountain rose above them like some brooding dark green mass. The rock face that overlooked Kreiss's place was only partially visible from this angle. Lynn was walking better than Janet had expected. Micah was following a path that led diagonally across the slope into the nearest trees, a kerosene lantern in his hand.

"Where are we going?" Janet asked.

"This here's Pearl's Mountain," he replied over his shoulder. "Limestone. Full of caves. We got us a hidey-hole up there."

"But if we can walk to it, so can anyone coming after us," she protested.

"They can, but then they gotta find the right one. Harder'n it looks."

They entered the trees, and the path diverged in three directions. Micah stopped. "Y'all take that left one there. Follow it 'til it hits the bare rock. Then wait there. I'll be along directly."

They did as he said, arriving at a sheer rock wall fifteen minutes later. Janet looked around for a cave entrance but found nothing. There was a broken segment of dead tree trunk propped against the rock, and they sat down on the log to rest. The climb had been steep, and Janet was a little winded. Lynn was taking deep breaths and holding her side.

Micah showed up five minutes later, dragging his jacket behind him by one of its sleeves. He put the jacket on the ground and grinned at them.

"See it?" he asked.

Janet and Lynn looked around but saw nothing that looked like a cave entrance. Janet shook her head.

"Mebbe that's cuz y'all are sittin' on it," he said, pointing at the log. They got up and Micah rolled the log sideways, revealing a narrow storm-cellar door laid flat into the ground. He tugged on a rope handle, and the door opened, exposing steps cut into the dirt. Holding the lantern high, he went down into the hole. Janet let Lynn go next and then followed. Micah told her to leave the door open.

The steps ended eight feet underground in a narrow passage of what felt like packed earth. Janet, less than thrilled to be underground, hurried to keep up with Micah's lantern. The air in the passage was dank and still.

Kreiss folded his arms across his chest as the three guards hurried over. One of them appeared to be older and in charge.

"You the guy claiming to be Special Agent Johnstone of the FBI?"

"That's what he said to me, Sarge," the man with the radio said. He had backed away from Kreiss.

The sergeant pointed his gun at Kreiss. "We called the Bureau ops center," he announced. "And they said Agents Johnstone and West had been involved in a vehicle accident this morning while transporting a prisoner. That would be you, am I right?"

Kreiss nodded but said nothing. The flow of pedestrian traffic parted visibly around the scene on the sidewalk. The sergeant had everybody go into the lobby to get this scene off the street. Once inside the lobby, he directed one of the guards to search Kreiss for weapons.

"Sarge, he says there's some shit going down in the building. Like a bomb. Says that hose back there is pumping gas into the building."

"What fucking hose?" the sergeant demanded. The guard took him over to a window and pointed back into the alley. A second guard told Kreiss to raise 'em while he patted him down for weapons. Kreiss obliged, trying to remain oblivious to all the stares from people going through the security checkpoint. He could hear the guard telling the sergeant about the propane truck.

The sergeant consulted by radio with the main security office upstairs. Kreiss put his hands back down while the guard who searched him examined Johnstone's credentials.

"Roger that," the sergeant said into his radio. He looked at Kreiss. "Central says there *is* a tanker truck up on the garage. What do you know about this?"

"I told the guard here: I think that truck is pumping an explosive gas into your building's vent supply, via that utility building back there. In a nonzero amount of time your building here is going to vaporize when some idiot lights up a cigarette in a bathroom. Don't you think you ought to clear the building?"

"Not on your say-so, bub; you're the one impersonating a feeb."

A large gray-headed man stepped out of the gathering crowd and approached the guards. "What's happening here, Sergeant?" he asked. The guards all appeared to recognize the man, and people had let him through quickly. The sergeant told him what was going down, including what Kreiss had said about a possible bomb in the building.

"Not *in* the building," Kreiss said. "Your building *is* the bomb. I believe that truck up there is pumping some kind of explosive vapor into your vent system. While we stand here and talk."

"Who are you?" the man asked. He spoke with the authority of someone who was used to getting immediate answers.

"My name is Edwin Kreiss, and I'm a civilian. Who are you?"

"I'm Lionel Kroner, deputy associate director. I've heard your name."

"Perhaps in connection with an explosion investigation down in Ramsey, in southwest Virginia. The power plant? The hydrogen bomb?"

Kroner's eyes widened at the mention of a hydrogen bomb. Some of the people who heard Kreiss use that term were obviously shocked, and a murmur swept the crowd. "Yes, we sent an NRT on that," Kroner said. "Your name came up in a briefing. What was your involvement?"

"Nothing direct, but I know about it. And the guy who did that is probably trying to duplicate what happened down there in your building here. While we stand here and talk."

The sergeant, who had been on the radio some more, said he had asked Central to get the lab people on the fourth floor to turn on an explosimeter to see if there was anything present in the building. "Nobody smells anything," he added.

"They won't, if he's using hydrogen," Kreiss said. "It's odorless, tasteless, and completely invisible. Mr. Kroner, do you have a public-address system in this building?"

"Yes, Central does."

"Can you get everyone to open their windows?"

Kroner blinked but then shook his head. "We can't," he said. "None of the windows in this building open."

"Then clear the building. Now. And tell people to run like hell once they're out of the building, because there's going to be lots of flying glass. And if you won't clear the building, I'm going to leave."

"Bull*shit*!" the sergeant said. The other guards still had their weapons drawn; they spread out a little, looking to their sergeant for instructions.

"Sarge, Sarge!" the black guard said urgently, pointing to his radio. "Lab says there's an explosive vapor in the building. They recommend an immediate evacuation."

"You going to pop a cap in here, Sergeant?" Kreiss asked. "Make a little flame?"

He turned to leave. Some of the guards went into shooting stance, but Kroner waved them down. The sergeant started to protest, but Kroner ordered him to be quiet and get him a microphone patch into the building's PA system. "Mr. Kreiss," he called, as Kreiss neared the doors. He stopped and turned around. "Thanks for the warning," Kroner said. "But we *will* see you later. That's a promise."

"If any of you are still alive," Kreiss said, which shut everyone up for the moment.

Kreiss nodded at him and stepped through the door. See me later? Not if I can help it, he thought. It was all he could do not to run like hell. Behind him, he heard Kroner's voice identifying himself on the building's PA system and ordering an immediate evacuation of the building, instructing people to walk to the nearest stairs and to do nothing—repeat, *nothing*—that might generate a spark. Kreiss hurried back into the parking garage to retrieve his van. When he reached the street level, the turbaned attendant was out on the sidewalk, trying to figure out what was happening next door. Kreiss told him there was a bomb in the ATF building. The attendant looked at Kreiss, back at the ATF building, and then took off smartly down the street. Kreiss swore, opened his door, and reached into the attendant's booth to trip the gate.

It took him ten minutes in morning traffic to get three blocks away from the ATF building, at which time he heard the first sirens. Three Metro cop cars with their blue lights flashing came racing past him into Massachusetts Avenue to block off the side streets. He pulled over toward the curb to let them go by. Pedestrians on the sidewalk paused to stare at all the cop cars, wondering if the president was coming. Fucking McGarand, Kreiss thought as he tried to pull back out into traffic, but now everything was stopped. He had damn near pulled it off, and had done so even after Carter had sent in a very specific warning. What the hell was it about Washington bureaucrats that made them think they knew everything, that no one could tell them a single goddamn thing?

He felt somebody or something bang hard on the back windows of the van, and he looked in the mirror to see if a vehicle had rear-ended his van. Instead, he saw an enormous orange fireball rising with a shuddering roar into the sky over the buildings behind him. The glare was strong enough to be seen through the windows of office buildings that were between him and the blast. Looking a lot like an atomic cloud, the fireball turned to a boiling red color and then was enveloped by a bolus of oily black smoke pulsing up into the early-morning sky over downtown. He heard a woman on the sidewalk scream right beside the van, and moments later, debris began to rain down on the sidewalks and the streets. He put the van in gear and pulled onto the sidewalk as people ran for cover into nearby buildings. Ignoring the sudden hail of metal and concrete bits rattling on the roof of the van, he drove down the sidewalk until he reached the next corner, then pulled past the huddled pedestrians and accelerated down toward the river.

Correction, correction, he thought. Not damn near. Score one for the clan McGarand. And he knew that as soon as the dust settled, there would be a host of feds hunting one Edwin Kreiss. A regular fugitive hat trick, he thought. He would now have the ATF, FBI, *and* the fucking Agency on his trail. Good job, Kreiss.

He turned right when he got to Constitution and headed toward the Memorial Bridge and northern Virginia. He would have to stay off the interstates once he got clear of the Washington area. He probably had twenty, thirty minutes to get out of town, and then someone would remember the speeding van on the sidewalk. The bigger problem would come when he got close to Blacksburg, because there were only so many ways into the foothills west of the town. He thanked God that Micah had Lynn, because Misty would undoubtedly take another shot, and very soon. Behind him, the big black cloud had tipped over in the morning air, casting a pall over the entire downtown area and blocking out the rising sun.

Browne McGarand felt a wave of deep satisfaction when he heard the monstrous thump and turned to see the black cloud erupting over the federal district. He had walked down Massachusetts Avenue after starting the hydrogen flow, trying to remain inconspicuous until he was able to cross Constitution Avenue and walk out onto the Mall, the wide expanse of trees and lawns fronting the Capitol grounds. Even at that hour of the morning, there was a surprising number of people out and about: joggers, power-walkers, and a tai chi exercise group of elderly people striking exotic attitudes out on the damp grass. He had rested on a park bench for a while, thinking back to 1993 and the similarly dramatic scenes created by the government's immolation of David Koresh and Browne's son, William, at Waco. Both the ATF and the FBI had conspired to cover up the truth of what had happened there, just as they had at Ruby Ridge. Murder will out, he thought, and the government had flat out murdered those deluded people. Then they lied about it, falsified testimony, concealed evidence, and otherwise acted more like Hitler's SS than agents of a democracy. Goddamned people burned babies for the crime of being different and delusional, while the president of the United States perjured himself with impunity and released bomb-throwing foreign terrorists for his wife's political advantage.

Watching the mushroom cloud, he wished he could have managed two bombs, because the FBI had blood on its hands from Waco, too. But it had been the ATF who set the stage for the ultimate carnage with their pigheaded assault. He didn't hate the agents who had bled and died on the roof of the compound. He blamed the coldhearted bastards here in Washington who had ordered it, and then pretended that they hadn't. Well, that black cloud rising above the federal office buildings would bring the message home right here to those same people: If the government won't hold agencies accountable, then, by God, an avenger will come out of the hills and teach the lesson. When the moral standards disappeared, it was time for the Old Testament rules: eye for an eye, tooth for a tooth, fire for fire.

He watched the smoke cloud collapse into itself as the rumble of the explosion died away over the Virginia hills. A wail of sirens and the astonished cries of the people out on the Mall followed. He got up and resumed walking, heading casually but purposefully down the Mall, past the Reflecting Pool, toward the Lincoln Memorial and the Memorial Bridge. His goal was to cross the river and walk to the Arlington Cemetery Metro station. From there, he would take the subway over to Reagan National Airport. He had enough cash to rent a car, and he didn't see any problem with using his own driver's license—all that would prove was that he had been in Washington. Then he was going to drive like hell back down to the Ramsey Arsenal, where he had everything pre-positioned for his imminent disappearance. He rubbed his bare face. He had shaved off his beard in the motel and his face felt naked. He averted his face as he passed by Lincoln's somber statue. He searched his soul for a sign of remorse and found nothing of the kind.

Janet and Lynn were huddled in a tiny wooden hut that had been built into the entrance passage, fifty feet back from the actual entrance. The hut consisted of a single room, containing two bunks, a tiny table, two straight-backed chairs, and a rack where six kerosene lanterns hung on one wall. Micah returned in the early afternoon, calling softly from the tunnel as he approached. He brought some sandwiches and a thermos of hot soup. Lynn was sitting up by now and feeling much better. She said her back and ribs hurt, but Janet was able to report that, thankfully, no infection was showing. Janet had slept like a log on one of the cots for three hours. They were both very grateful for the food.

"They's a ton of revenuers out there along the road," Micah announced as they ate. There was a single railroad-style kerosene lamp on the table, and the light in the tiny wooden room made his skin look like parchment. Janet wondered how old he was. "Had a passel of 'em come up to the cabin, askin' what we'd seen or heard."

"Which was nothing at all, right?" Lynn said.

Micah smiled. "Maybe heard some shootin' last night, heard some vee-hicles rammin' around on the county road. Buncha kids out a West Virginia, playin' thunder road, most like. But otherwise . . ."

"They search your place?"

"I reckon they will, soon's they git them a warrant," Micah said. "The boss man asked if they could look around. I told 'im no. Told 'im four of my fightin' pit bulls was holed up somewhere's in all that junk. Wouldn't be safe for no strangers to be pokin' around. Boss man said fightin' dogs was illegal; I told 'im they could tell them dogs that, they wanted to go take their chances."

"They'll find my vehicle," Janet said.

"No, ma'am, I don't b'lieve they will," Micah said solemnly. Janet just nodded. "Was there a woman with them?" she asked.

"No, ma'am, no women, just a mess a revenuers we've never seen before. They surely ain't from around here, way they talkin'."

Janet nodded again. Micah probably called any kind of federal law enforcement a revenuer. These people had probably been ATF, with maybe some FBI and possibly even some of that horrible woman's crew sprinkled in.

"They been to your daddy's cabin," Micah said to Lynn. "Had one a my boys watching the place from the ridge. Buncha ve-hicles, people goin' every which a way. They had some dogs with 'em, too, so they may do some trackin'. If 'n they do, they might could find the entrance to this here cave."

"Is there another way out?"

Micah smiled. "Three ways, one sorta easy, two real hard. Meantime, I got one a the boys paintin' some bear fat on that log near the entrance y'all used. Ain't no city dog gonna like that. But if there's a ruckus, that'll be the sign for y'all to move back into the mountain. Whatever y'all do, don't come out the way we come in. We gonna lay down a little trap in that passage. Now, this here's a map."

He unrolled a piece of brown paper cut out of a grocery bag and showed Janet where the hut was. The map showed three passages that led from the hut to various other chambers and passages back into the mountain, and, eventually, to the woods on the west slope. He pointed out the lanterns on the back wall and showed her where extra lanterns were cached along the passages. The way out of the hut was through a concealed door in the back wall. Each of the passages on the map was marked by a number.

"Number one here, it's the easiest goin'," he said. " 'Bout a mile all told, maybe mile and a half. Goes down maybe a hundred feet before climbin' back up and out. Comes out by a dirt road, through a flat door like we came in. You come out thataway, you pile on a buncha rocks on that door once you out if someone's behind you."

"And the others?"

"Two and three are longer and deeper, and they's some tight-assed narrow-downs. Three's got a lake. You gotta hand-over-hand along a ledge over on the left side to make it across. That there ledge is 'bout six, eight inches underwater. You don't even want to fall in, 'cause it's deep and cold as hell."

"But if they bring dogs into the cave?"

"Then three's the one you want. Be careful when you git to Dawson's Pit."

"Why is it called that?" Lynn asked.

" 'Cause Dawnson's still in it. They's a long, real narrow passage just before the lake; you women will have to be sideways to git through it. A man's gotta hold his breath and grease his ass *and* his belly to git through it. But you could kill a dog easy, he comes after you in that crack. Here. I brought your wheel gun."

"I'm afraid I ran it out of ammo, out there on the road."

Micah grinned. "Got you a refill. Ammo's somethin' we keep aplenty of up here. But looka here: Take one a them hickory sticks over there in the corner. Don't shoot the gun less'n you have to, 'cause you never know what the cave'll do. You follow?"

"You mean, as in cave-in?"

"Somethin' like that. Specially around that lake. It don't got a bottom, best as we can find out, and the ceiling in the lake cave is way up there. Lots a them stone icicles up there, I reckon. Lantern won't light it. Use the sticks on any dogs; that's why they got points."

Janet took a deep breath and thanked him. "Let's pray for no dogs," she said. "Tell me: When her father comes back, will he contact you?"

"I reckon," Micah said. "Them ain't no friends a his at his cabin just now. But we got ways."

Janet took the .38 and put it on the table. It didn't seem like much, compared to some of the weapons she had seen in the past twenty-four hours. "You've saved our skins a couple of times, Mr. Wall," she said. "I surely appreciate it. I don't even know who half the people chasing us are anymore."

Micah looked over at Lynn and nodded in the yellow light. "Ed Kreiss, he did me a real big favor, back when he first moved up here on the mountain. Didn't even know me or none of my kin, and he saved one a my boys. His name's Ben. He's a big'un, but Ben, he's a mite simple. Three old boys from the Craggit bunch over on Moultrie Mountain took it into their rock heads to whup Ben's ass. They caught up with him out on the county road and was fixin' to flat bust his head with some tire irons. Don't rightly know why. Old Ed, he come up on it. Said Ben was rolled up in a ball under his truck, and them bastids was yankin' on him. Old Ed said they was fixin' to kill him, most like. Old Ed, he went after them bastids with his truck, knocked two of 'em clean off the road and down into Hangman's Creek. Third one run off. Then he brung Ben home."

"Tell her about the Craggits," Lynn said.

Micah grinned again. "Oh, yeah, them Craggits came around, goin' to git 'em some ree-venge on Ed Kreiss. He heard 'em comin' somehow, turned that big fifty-cal loose on the Craggits' pickup trucks. They went a-howlin' and a-yellin' out into the woods, and then old Ed, he cut loose with them lion sounds into them woods. Them Craggits laid a trail a loose shit all the way back over to Moultrie Mountain. Time since, goin' on four years now, old Ed'n me become pretty good neighbors."

"I'm probably being impolite," Janet said, "but I have to ask: What do you and all these people do up here, Mr. Wall?"

"We git by," he said, revealing just a hint of a smile. Janet smiled back, understanding that was all she was going to learn.

"Well, look, there's probably a warrant out for my arrest right now," she said. "I ran a federal roadblock last night. And I shot at—well, I'm not sure who the hell she was. But I suppose she's federal, after a fashion."

Micah spat onto the dirt floor of the hut. "Them folks out there, they's all gov-mint. Got the smell and the look about 'em. Them people don't belong up here. Never have, never will. One day, they gonna learn that. These the same bastids shot down that woman and chile up on Ruby Ridge. Too many of 'em just killers with badges is all. They chasin' that boy Rudolph down in Carolina?" He spat again. "Shee-it. They ain't never gonna find that boy. Mountain folk got 'im hid and hid good."

The agent in Janet got the better of her. "That guy Rudolph set bombs that killed and maimed some people," she said.

"Yeah, that's what *they* say. But you willin' to bet they gonna take him alive?"

"Well, if they catch up with him, he'll certainly get that option," she said.

"You reckon? Them folks at Waco, they didn't git that option," Wall said. "How's a man gonna git his day in court, when them revenuers come a-shootin' first an' askin' questions later?"

Janet had no answer for that one. Lynn was looking down at the dirt floor of the hut. "Now I'm sorry we put you in this fix, Mr. Wall," Janet said. "They might try to arrest all of you, take you off the mountain for obstruction of justice."

Micah nodded. "I reckon we'll do the best we can, they come for us." He straightened up. "Meantime, y'all lay low in here, till old Ed comes for you. And, like I said, keep an ear peeled for any dog ruckus up at the front. Trap'll slow 'em down, but y'all gotta go if they hit it."

"What kind of trap is it?"

"When I leave, my boys'll take a hornet nest we sacked last night. Set it up in the passage. Them hornets, they gonna go for the lights."

"Big nest?"

"'Bout a miyun," Micah said, eyes twinkling.

Janet grinned in spite of herself. She could just see it.

He gathered up the bag. "Now, lemme show you somethin' else. Them people out there—if they come in a-shootin'? That's different. You open that trapdoor, grab you some lanterns; then you light this fuse right there—you see it? There's the matches. Light it; then pull that trapdoor down. Then y'all git on down that passage till you get to the first turn. They's a dead-end branch passage, goes to the right. Git in that, git down, and stop up your ears."

Lynn, who had been listening to all this, was nodding her head. Micah checked to see that the lanterns had fuel, then stepped back out the front door of the hut and disappeared into the front passage. Janet examined the fuse, but she wasn't so sure about doing what the old man had recommended. Just last week, she could have been one of the people coming in here. On the other hand, somebody seemed to be rewriting all the rules when it came to Edwin Kreiss and his daughter. Just like they did at Waco, she thought. That fire in the hospital, for instance. That had been *way* out there. And that guy Browne McGarand, going up to Washington with a truckload of hydrogen to blow something up. This old man could crack wise about it, but these people up here were obviously convinced that the government and all its works could not be trusted. If they came in with tracking dogs, looking, they ran into bear grease and hornets. If they came in with snipers, flash-bangs, and tear gas, as they had proved they could from time to time, they'd get the cave dynamited down on their heads.

Lynn said she was going to explore the trapdoor at the back and make sure they could get it open. Janet sat down at the tiny wooden table and put her head in her hands. Her people had to know she was up here in the mountains with Lynn Kreiss. They're not your people anymore, are they? a little voice in her head reminded her. Micah Wall and his people were protecting her until—what? Until Kreiss could get back? She felt as if she were out on the moon somewhere. Last week, she had been a federal agent; now, in the space of a day and a night, she was a federal fugitive. She began to understand the meaning of the phrase "out in the cold." She wondered what Farnsworth and her coworkers at the Roanoke office were doing right now: Combing the hills for the two of them? Sitting back and pretending that she did not exist? Waiting for instructions and the spin d'jour from the bosses in Washington? The same bosses who wouldn't listen to warnings of a bomb plot, and who were apparently more interested in embarrassing another government agency than in protecting peoples' lives?

What she instinctively wanted to do was call into the Roanoke office and check in, talk to somebody, see what the hell was going on. But whom could she call? Not RA Farnsworth. And not Larry Talbot, who would be too scared to take her call. Not Keenan. She didn't know anybody in the ATF. And not Edwin Kreiss, who was God knew where, and who had at least the Bureau hunting for him, if not the ATF. And the Agency, don't forget the blessed Agency.

Lynn, who had gone through the trapdoor, squeezed back into the hut. "I left a couple of lanterns and some matches in the passageway. He wasn't kidding about narrow."

"Make sure we have that map," Janet said. "If we have to escape that way, I want to be able to find my way back out of this mountain."

"I've got it right here, next to the door. You suppose this fuse goes to dynamite or something?"

"Yes. It will probably bring this part of the cave down."

Lynn came over to the table and sat down, wincing when her ribs touched the table. "I wish I knew where my father was," she said. "And what the hell was going on."

"That makes nine of us," Janet said. "I'm almost tempted to go back out front, see if I can find a phone."

"Whom would you call?"

"That's the problem. I don't exactly know who my friends are right now. Or who's chasing us. Where the hell does that woman get off, anyway—starting a fire in a fucking hospital! Those Agency people aren't even supposed to be operating within the United States."

Lynn nodded slowly. "I'm not so sure about that," she said. "When my father was working with them, he sometimes went overseas to do what he did. But he also worked here, in the States, too. It kind of depended on whom he was pursuing and what they'd done."

"But if a wrong guy needs pursuing in the States, that's the Bureau's job, not the Agency's."

Lynn smiled. "I think that's why the Agency let him stay: he was technically a Bureau man, not an Agency man."

"Ah," Janet said. "So if some part of an operation broached, he could flash Bureau creds and people would back off."

"Something like that. He never gave me details of what he did, but I think that the people they went after had overstepped the bounds. A lot. The big boys just wanted the problem taken care of, and I don't think they really wanted to know too much about how it was taken care of."

"You mean they'd go after some guy and just cap him?"

"I don't think so, actually," Lynn said. "Dad says there are some federal prisons where they can put people into the federal corrections system and bury the file. Lewisburg, Fort Leavenworth, for instance; they have lifetime solitary-confinement facilities there. Who's going to go up to a place like that and ask to see the dungeons?"

"The ACLU maybe?"

"The ACLU would have to know the guy existed in the first place."

"Jesus, you make it sound like Russia."

Lynn laughed. "I met a Russian graduate student at Tech last year. He was in the advanced physics program. We got to talking politics—God, how those Russians love to talk politics! He laughs at the proposition that we live in a 'free' country. He told me to go find out how many government police there are now, compared with ten years ago."

Janet just looked at her.

"Well, I tried. Like, do you know how big the Bureau is?"

"Well, it's big, I know that. Ten, fifteen thousand people, maybe."

Lynn shook her head. "Try twenty-seven thousand employees in the FBI. Ten years ago, it was sixteen thousand. I tried to find out how many federal government police there are, the total number, and do you know I couldn't really do it? Maybe you could."

"There are more cops because there is more crime, and a hundred new mutations of crime every day. Internet crime. Serial killers. Hannibal the Cannibal types. Chat rooms where pedophiles buy and sell children for snuff flicks. Sixty-two thousand bombing incidents in the past five years."

"Yeah, but look at that Waco thing: Sure, those people were a doomsday cult, and they had some weird people there. Koresh and all his 'wives'; all of them waiting around for Judgment Day, praying for it to come, probably, the end of the millennium, the Second Coming. But for that, the government burned them alive? Jesus Christ. Burning people for their beliefs went out with the Inquisition. Supposedly."

"Koresh burned them," Janet said. "Our people didn't do that."

"Maybe," Lynn said. "But your people gave Koresh the pretext when they drove tanks into the building. Hell, why didn't they just cut the power and the phones and the water and wait for a few months? But no, some cowboy—or maybe cowgirl, huh?—in Washington decides to send *tanks* in? And then, afterward, they all do the armadillo and try to cover it all up? I mean, the Bureau and the ATF could be telling the absolute truth, but when shit comes out like that business with the incendiary rounds? Nobody believes them anymore. For that matter, how many women and babies did David Koresh ever burn alive before the tanks showed up?"

"But we're the good guys," Janet said. "Koresh started those fires. Koresh killed those people. He was wounded and he was dying, and he had nothing more to lose!"

Lynn just looked at her. "That may be true," she said. "But America is a democracy in the full bloom of the information age. If agencies like the Bureau and the ATF aren't squeaky fucking clean, it will come out. In the past, maybe not, but now? It *will* come out. And then there's no more trust. If it's perceived to be a cover-up, then it *is* a cover-up."

Janet sighed and looked away. Lynn put her hand on Janet's arm. "Look," she said. "You're risking your ass to save my ass from some claw of the government we can't even name. Don't think I'm not grateful. But four or five years ago, my father found out something about some very high-level people in the government, a secret bad enough that a senior Agency guy shot himself *and* his whole family to protect it. I think the only reason they didn't 'disappear' my father is that he was a pretty resourceful operative who might have caused a train wreck or two in the process. When he was quote-unquote 'retired,' it was all done over a pay phone, okay?"

"You think that's what this is all about?"

"You know, I think it is," Lynn said. "Dad and I have talked about this before. There's been a lot that's come out about the Chinese spy case since then. I think he was afraid he was becoming more and more of a major loose end. He knew firsthand what can happen to a loose end, especially these days."

The kerosene lamp guttered, and Janet got up to light a second one to replace it. "How do you know all this?" she asked.

Lynn drew her sweater closer about her. "Dad and I talked a lot after my mom was killed and he was forced out. I sort of made it a condition of our reconciliation. I told him I had to know about him and what he did, not operational details, of course, but why my mother had been so afraid. Why she said some of the things she said."

"Which weren't true."

Lynn looked up at her. She had Kreiss's intense gray-green eyes, Janet suddenly realized. Eyes that knew too much and had seen too much. "But that's the point, Agent Carter," Lynn said. "Most of it *was* true."

Janet remembered the hunting woman's face, with eyes like those on a great white shark. Play "Misty" for me. She shivered. Then they heard the dogs.

Browne McGarand rubbed the itchy new stubble rising on his clean-shaven face again as he drove the rental down the back side of the arsenal. It was nearly sundown, and he was looking for the entrance to an old logging road that led back to the western perimeter fence. He planned to drive the little car up the logging road as far as he could and then hide it. Then he would walk to the perimeter fence and go north along the fence until he got to the point where the creek entered the federal reservation. Unlike the creek's exit point, it wasn't very big, and they had just run the fence atop of it, laying down some concrete culverts. Once inside the two fences, it was a mile's walk to the bunker farm and to bunker 887.

He had prepared his bolt-hole in the bunker field early in the project. It was in the remotest part of the ammunition-storage area. They had cut the rusty series padlock and unsealed the air-circulating ventilator fixture at the back of the bunker, converting the ventilator trunk into an escape hatch. Halfway down the bunker's empty length, he and Jared had constructed a fake partition of studs and plywood, creating a smooth wooden surface that ran from top to bottom. Jared, an able carpenter, had done most of the work, including building in a single flush-mounted door. They then painted the side of the barrier facing the bunker doors a flat black. The idea was to make it look to anyone shining a flashlight quickly into the partially buried bunker that it was as empty as all the rest. He had taken this precaution after watching the security patrols for a few weeks and seeing them occasionally pick a bunker at random, unlock the heavy steel doors, and poke their flashlights in for a moment. The barrier wouldn't stand a thorough search, of course, especially if someone restored electricity to the bunker farm and turned on each bunker's main lights.

Jared had then taken the old padlock to a swap meet up in Harpers Ferry, to a guy who claimed to be able to find a key for any lock. Since the Army's padlock was part of a series, the locksmith had been able to produce a master key. Then all they had to do was to lift a padlock from another bunker, well removed, and put it on their hideout. That way, they could keep it locked but not raise flags when security encountered a lock not of the series. If the security patrols ever came upon the bunker that no longer had its lock, they would go in and have a look. But there would be nothing there and then they would simply replace it.

He had listened to an all-news radio station on the way down from Washington. The ATF headquarters bombing was the center of attention, of course, with excited reports of hundreds killed and major damage to the entire downtown area. Reporters on the scene gave breathless accounts of the shattered building, streets full of glass and office debris, and five fire companies and their EMTs working isolated bloody vignettes up and down Massachusetts Avenue. Spokespersons for the Treasury Department, Justice Department, FBI, and belatedly, the ATF had all made grave pronouncements about the growing threat of domestic terrorists, the need for increased resources, expressions of condolence for the victims, and determination to hunt down the perpetrators. One interview had been most revealing, when a reporter put a microphone in front of the bleeding face of an ATF agent who had been injured up on the roof deck of the parking garage. He had sworn a bloody oath to find the son of a bitch who had done this and blow his—word bleeped—head right off, an hysterical comment his supervisors would undoubtedly regret.

Over the course of the day, however, the reports were toned down significantly. It was revealed that most of the building had been evacuated before the blast. Apparently, there had been a last-minute warning. There were indeed dozens of people injured, but most of these had been hurt in the street, or had not moved far enough away from the building when the top half was blown off. When he finally got to the logging road, they were reporting three civilian security men killed on the roof of the parking garage, twenty-six injured within the vicinity of the building, and the top four floors of the ATF building destroyed. By the time he switched off, speculation as to the source of the bomb and the motives behind it was driving any hard, factual news off the story.

He was sorry that he had not been able to kill them all, to drive an explosive stake into the heart of that agency and to immolate the Washington policy makers he held responsible for Waco once and for all else. But there had been no disguising the sense of outrage and, behind the outrage, palpable fear in the voices of all those federal law-enforcement agency spokespersons. They probably all thought they had paid for Waco in the Oklahoma City bombing. Now they would know that there were people out there who felt otherwise. He got to the end of the logging road and parked the car as far back into the trees as he could maneuver it. He sat in the darkened vehicle for a moment. If there had been ATF building security people injured in the parking garage, they must have known about the propane truck. In any event, the truck would have survived, but they would trace it back to West Virginia, not here to the Blacksburg area. The gasoline incendiary he'd left behind in the cab should have taken care of any fingerprints. He was taking a mixed chance coming back here to the arsenal, but he still believed in the old rule about hiding things under people's noses. Especially these people.

By the time the first dog hit the front wall of the hut, Lynn had the back door open and two lanterns lighted and ready to go. She waited in the narrow passage behind the hut while Janet wedged the little table against the front door. They both heard a man shout, "In here!" from the front passage, and then there was a huge commotion of dogs and shouting voices as someone brought a light into the passage and the hornets finally had a target. As the voices and screaming dogs withdrew, Janet stepped through the narrow back door and shut it tightly. She had the .38 stuffed into her waistband holster and was struggling into her jacket. She looked for some way to block the back door, but there wasn't one.

"Let's go," she whispered, picking up a lantern. "They'll be right behind us."

"Not until they figure out a way to get past those hornets," Lynn said.

Lynn led the way down the narrow passage behind the hut. The passage was seven or eight feet high, and the rock on either side was cold and damp. The trail beneath their feet was hard-packed dirt. Janet had pulled the fuse in the hut out into full view, hoping that whoever was hunting them would see it and slow down to check for booby traps. The passage went straight for fifty feet and then there was a cross passage, with two more caverns opening into the intersection. Lynn consulted the map and chose the left branch. The noise behind them had subsided, but Janet knew the dogs would be coming soon, even if the men did not.

The passage they were in now was even narrower, and the roof came down the farther they went. The floor had turned to loose gravel, and they had to slow down to keep from turning an ankle. At one point, Janet lost her footing and sat down heavily, sliding on her backside for a yard or so before stopping. She managed to put her lantern out in the process.

"Leave it out," Lynn said. "We may need the fuel later."

Janet got back up and hurried after the girl, who seemed to be doing just fine. She wondered if Lynn had been in the caves before. There was still no sign of pursuit behind them, for which she was very grateful. The air remained dank and oppressive. Janet was not exactly claustrophobic, but she was certainly aware of the mass of the mountain above their heads.

"Can you follow the map?" she asked.

"Yes, it's pretty clear. There's a pit coming up. Not sure what that means."

They rounded a dogleg turn in the cave, the lone lantern throwing weird shadows along the ceiling, and Lynn stopped suddenly. They had entered a round chamber, which was about twenty feet wide. The ceiling domed up a similar distance. The path ahead skirted a perfectly smooth conical hole, which disappeared into the depths of the mountain. The top of the hole was almost as wide as the chamber. Lynn kicked a small rock off the trail. It slid down over the smooth edge of the hole and then disappeared without a sound. The bobbing lantern made the walls look like they were moving.

"That's what *pit* means," Janet whispered. "Damn thing goes to China."

"And we go that way," Lynn said. She pointed with the lantern to the left side of the pit, where an eighteen-inch-wide ledge led around the lip of the hole and into another passage on the far side. The walls of the chamber curved up toward the top of the dome.

"Shit," Janet said. "Look at that curving wall. What do we hold on to?"

Behind them came the sounds of something moving down the passageway.

"Duck-walk," Lynn said. "Now."

She led the way, holding the lantern extended in her left hand to move her center of gravity closer to the wall. She squatted down, facing the hole so as to maximize the room between the side wall and the lip of the pit, then duck-walked sideways out onto the ledge. Janet followed, willing her eyes to look at Lynn's bobbing back and not into the pit. They were halfway across the ledge when they distinctly heard a dog coming, its unmistakable snuffling sounds amplified by the narrow tunnel. There was nothing they could do; they couldn't move any faster, and the dog would be on them in seconds. Suddenly, the lantern went out, and Janet gasped. She froze in place, her left hand scrabbling against the damp rock, searching for something to hold on to. The darkness was absolute, and she was terrified.

"Don't move," Lynn hissed.

The dog, hearing her voice, barked once and kept coming. Judging by the size of that bark, it had to be a pretty big dog, and Janet could feel its presence when it launched into the chamber, accelerating down the path as it hunted the sound of Lynn's voice and their fresh scent. Then there was an instant of complete silence, followed by a plaintive yelp as the dog sailed over the smooth edge of the pit and fell away into nothingness. Janet heard a scratching sound, and then Lynn had a match going, relighting the lantern. She realized she had been holding her breath and now let it out in a small sob, and then Lynn was moving again, duck-walking across the remainder of the ledge into a small antechamber beyond. Janet followed, her knees and hips hurting. Her mouth was dry as dust and her heart was pounding.

When they got to the other side, Lynn stood up and grinned at her. "Pretty good, huh?" she said, her eyes alight. Christ on a crutch, Janet thought as she carefully stood up, she's enjoying this. But there was no getting around it: Lynn had done the one thing that eliminated the pursuing dog problem. There were two passages leading out of the chamber, and Lynn consulted the map. "Left," she said. "We're going on trail three."

"Any more pits on that trail?" Janet asked in a strained voice. But Lynn was already moving into the smaller of the two passages, ducking her head to get through. Janet took one last look at the pit chamber as Lynn's lantern bobbed away: she shivered, then followed.

They tried to keep quiet as they pressed into the narrowing passage. It went level for a while, then dipped precipitously. The footing was now slippery clay, and they really had to slow down to keep from pitching headlong down the passage. Janet banged her lantern against the rock wall and thought she heard the glass crack. Lynn, six feet ahead of her, kept going for another fifteen minutes and then stopped and swore.

"What?" Janet asked, dreading another pit.

"No trail," Lynn said, consulting the map. "But I don't see any other way to go."

Janet came up alongside her. Lynn lifted her lantern. The passage had opened onto the edge of what looked like a very steep slope that disappeared down into the darkness. There was a faint movement of cold, wet air against her face, and then she realized they had come into a very large cavern, whose vaulted ceiling rose up out of the range of the lantern light.

"Jesus, this is huge," Janet said. Her voice echoed out into space. They stood there for a minute, taking it all in, when they again heard sounds behind them, men's voices and the excited yelping of dogs. They weren't close, but they were certainly back there.

"That pit will slow them down," Lynn said softly. "But I don't see any other way to do this."

Janet looked down. They had forgotten to bring the sticks. The surface of the slope was loose rock and what looked like shale. "You mean slide?"

"Yeah. This has to be the way. It's been a straight shot so far. So it's probably safe. I'll go first. Hold this."

She gave the lantern to Janet, turned around, and let herself out onto the slope. Her feet precipitated a small avalanche of stones and dirt, but she was able to maintain position on the slope. She reached for the lantern. "You got matches?" she asked.

"Yes," Janet said.

"Okay, light your lantern. I'm going to put this one out while I go down."

Janet lit her lantern, and she saw that she had indeed cracked the glass. The flame burned unevenly until she adjusted the wick. Lynn doused her own lantern, then started down the slope, moving carefully to keep from starting a big slide and going with it. Janet held her lantern out as far as she could, while listening for sounds of pursuit. She could just barely hear the men back there, but the cave distorted the sounds and she had no idea of how far back they were. She was more worried about dogs ranging ahead of the men. Then she heard a noise below her. Lynn swore as she lost control of her climb down the slope and began to slide. Janet leaned way out but could no longer see her down the slope. Based on all the noise, Lynn was going for a ride. After a minute or so, the rattling noise of falling stones died out.

"Lynn?" Janet called, trying not to make too much noise.

"Yeah, I'm all right. Lemme get this lantern going. Then you come down. Douse yours before you try it."

There was a flare of light below, and Janet could see that the slope ended about two hundred feet down. There was a glint of water at the base of the cliff. She could see Lynn's light but not Lynn. She doused her own lantern and then listened again. The men's voices were getting louder, but she still had no idea of how close they were. It sounded as if there were lots of them back there. Then she heard a dog barking eagerly, and the dog sounded a whole lot closer. She went backward over the edge and started down, getting into the rhythm of a controlled slide while she protected the lantern. Lynn must have taken the loose stuff with her, because Janet got down to the bottom without going into an uncontrolled slide. She dusted off her hands and knees and got up. She stepped away from the slope and then turned around. In front of her was a vast lake, whose size she could only feel. The lantern light reflected only about fifty feet out onto its surface. She could get no sense of walls or the ceiling.

"Man, look at that," she said.

"Yeah, it's huge," Lynn said. "We go this way."

She turned to their left and began picking her way along the shore of the lake, which was made up of small round stones, some larger boulders, and loose gravel. The mass of the shale cliff rose into total darkness to their left. The shoreline curved around slowly to the right, and they had to go slowly to keep from slipping into the water. Janet listened for sounds of pursuit, but now she heard nothing. They climbed over the treacherous footing for five minutes before arriving at a sheer rock face. The gravel beach disappeared at the foot of the cliff. The water stretched out into darkness on their right, and the shale cliff rose on their left.

"Now what?" Janet asked.

Lynn studied the map. "I think this must be the submerged ledge Micah was talking about."

Suddenly, from way above and behind them, a dog barked once and then again, excitedly. Lynn took Janet's lantern and raised it as high as she could to see how far across it was, but there was only the black water and the glimmering reflection of the lantern. The cavern wall rose on their left, black and sheer. The dog kept barking, and Janet realized there was no echo down here. This cavern must be really huge.

"Shouldn't we douse the light?" Janet whispered urgently.

"We have to find the ledge," Lynn said.

"We'll find that with our feet. Douse the light. They can't see us without it, not until they come down the slope. We need time to get across this thing and out of range of any guns."

Lynn complied, and the dog stopped barking. Janet led the way, stepping down into the icy water, her left hand held out on the rock wall. Her feet found the ledge, which was about a foot underwater. She explored with her toe to see how wide it was; not very, she decided. She was wearing sneakers with a hiking tread, which gave her pretty good traction. She started forward, keeping her hand on the wall, leaning into it actually, while trying not to think of what a full-body plunge into that water would feel like. She sensed Lynn was behind her, but she did not turn around. She slid her feet forward, rather than taking steps, to make sure the ledge didn't end suddenly.

The dog barked once more from the top of the slope, tentatively now that there was nothing to see. Then Janet heard a familiar sound, that of a tactical radio. The sound seemed to be coming from ahead of them, and she hoped that it was just the tricky acoustics of the cavern. If their pursuers had managed to get ahead of them here, they were screwed. She heard Lynn's lantern tap the rock wall.

"Okay?" she said softly.

"Yeah," Lynn whispered. "Cold."

The water was extremely cold, and Janet's ankles were getting numb. She had no idea of how far they had gone, when, from way above and behind them, beams of white light shot out. She looked up out of the corner of her eye but kept going. She thought she could see the ceiling of the cavern, but there was something odd about the shape of it. The dog started barking again, and then there were two dogs, getting excited now. The light beams came down onto the lake and played about, and she could hear men's voices, and more radio noises. Inevitably, one of the light beams found them.

"Halt!" a man shouted from up on the slope. "Halt or I'll shoot."

"Fuck you," Lynn said matter-of-factly, her voice carrying clearly over the water. Janet squinted her eyes against the reflection of the flashlight in the water and kept going.

"Send the goddamn dogs," a man ordered.

"It's straight down," protested a second voice.

Janet and Lynn were a good fifty yards off the rock beach by now, but Janet had no idea of how far they had to go. She dared not light a lantern. The men argued, and then there was a yip from one of the dogs, which was followed by the sounds of a small-scale avalanche. Janet realized someone had pushed one of the dogs over the cliff, and it was coming down the slope. There was a loud splash, more yelping, and then the dog was out and casting about on the rock beach. A second dog came crashing down the slope. Janet kept going, taking bigger sliding steps now, determined to get off this ledge. She didn't think the dog could follow them out here, but there was no telling. Then the flashlights came back to them, illuminating them both. Whether the dogs saw them or picked up their scent, they gave cry and came bounding down the gravel beach to the spot where the women had gone into the water.

"Git 'em, Tiger," a third man yelled. "Go on, boy, git 'em!"

From the sounds of it, the dogs were unwilling to plunge into the water and were milling about on the beach behind them, barking excitedly. Not small dogs, Janet thought as she pressed on. Her front foot slid out onto nothing and she barely got stopped in time. The ledge had ended.

"What?" Lynn asked as she came right up on Janet. The man up on the top of the slope was still urging the dogs to go after them. Their lights were weaker now that the women had progressed farther out into the lake.

"No more ledge," Janet whispered. "I think we're fucked."

"Are you sure?" Lynn asked. "I'll hold your hand. Reach way out."

Janet leaned against the rock wall and extended her foot as far as she could. She thought she felt something, but she couldn't quite reach. The flashlights were still on them. There was more light reflecting off the black water than shining directly on them.

"It's a giant step," she told Lynn. "If it's not the ledge, I'll fall in."

There was more noise from up on top of the cliff. And more lights. "You have to try," Lynn said. "I can't get past you."

"I can't do it with the lantern," Janet said. Then she had an idea. "Give me a match."

Lynn passed her a match and asked what she was doing.

"I'm going to light this and set it afloat. That might distract them. It'll look like we're not getting anywhere. I have to ditch it anyway to make this step, so what the hell, okay?"

She struck a match and lit the lantern. Immediately, there was more noise up on the cliff, with another voice telling them to halt or he would shoot. Janet set the lantern into the water; the weight of the base kept it upright, the wick assembly just out of the water. She gave it a gentle shove, took a deep breath, and stepped way out. Her foot hit ledge and she took a giant step across the gap. She moved forward one step and then told Lynn to pass her lantern over. The lantern in the water bobbed gently from side to side in the ripples coming from the dogs, who were splashing in and out of the water somewhere behind them. Lynn stepped across the gap, and they hurried on, getting farther from their pursuers and the bobbing lantern. The ledge actually began to get wider, and Janet, greatly relieved, was able to step normally now instead of slide. Lynn picked right up on it, and they made better progress.

Then they heard the sounds of men coming down the slope, accompanied by several avalanches of rocks, sand, and gravel and lots of shouting. It sounded like at least half a dozen men were coming. The dogs stepped up their own noise, eager to continue the hunt but not sure how. Janet bent low after bumping her forehead on an overhang of rock that had appeared out of nowhere. She warned Lynn, but Lynn bumped her head anyway and swore.

"There's a ledge!" a voice shouted. "C'mon. We can follow them."

Someone else back on the gravel beach punched on a much more powerful flashlight, which just reached the two women, and once again warned them to halt or he would shoot. Janet tied to ignore the noises behind them, but it sounded like both men and dogs were coming, the dogs swimming now and the men coming out along the ledge. Then a second light found and pinned them in its beam; at least one of them had remained back on the beach. There was a great splash and some excited yelling behind them as one of the men fell in, swearing furiously about how cold it was. Janet had to duck even farther under the overhang, which now stuck out almost three feet. There were more splashes, and it sounded like most of their pursuers were now in the water, thrashing about, trying to find the ledge in the darkness. The two bright white beams stayed on them, however, and the big voice warned them one more time.

"Halt or I'll shoot. I mean it, goddamn it. Stop right there!"

"Keep going," Janet whispered. "Unless they have rifles, we're too far."

She was wrong, she realized, as a gun boomed behind them and a heavy round spanged off the rock face above them and slashed into the water. The booming sound reverberated in the cavern. The powerful lights never wavered. Janet took two more steps and then a second round came, hitting between them and causing Lynn to cry out in fright. Janet stopped and turned around, blinded now by the bright light. Some of the men were still in the water behind them, apparently thrashing back toward the stone beach. Whoever had the lights on them was definitely down on the beach at the foot of the cliff. The sound of the shot reverberated in the cavern.

"Now what?" Lynn whispered.

Janet was about to answer, when there was a sudden noise in the water, about ten feet off. Then another, and another. Janet recognized it as the sound of something heavy and sharp hitting the water like a champion diver, a wicked slashing noise that was instantly covered over in a small boil of foam. Janet flattened herself against the rock wall under the overhang, pulling Lynn back with her. Then it was raining heavy objects, and a man screamed way behind them. A second man screamed, and the lights suddenly went out as a hail of stalactites came down from the ceiling of the cavern like a shower of stone knives. A dog made a horrible noise as it went under, still screaming. The rain of stone intensified for a few seconds, seemingly covering every inch of the lake before it stopped, leaving only an occasional cutting splash way out in the lake. Behind them, all was silent. Janet strained to see in the sudden silence, and she thought she saw a single flashlight pointing out into the water, but it was not moving. Nothing appeared to be moving behind them anymore.

"Son of a bitch," Lynn murmured. She lit her lantern.

"Micah said not to shoot off a gun down here," Janet said. "Let's get going before they regroup."

As they started forward along the ledge, one last immense stalactite came down, way out in the darkness. Lynn raised her lantern, but the ceiling was still too high to see. Moments later, actual waves washed against their feet. The silence behind them was absolute; Janet didn't think they would be regrouping anytime soon. She pressed forward, shivering, and soon they were at the other side of the lake. Behind them, there were no further signs of pursuit.

When Kreiss saw the first road signs for Blacksburg, he pulled into the parking lot of the next convenience store that came along on Route 11 and placed a call to Micah Wall. He used the rented cell phone this time: They could get a number off a tap, but it should trace back to the Washington calling area. He looked at his watch while the phone was ringing: It was 8:30. He had taken back roads all the way down from Washington, and it had nearly doubled the time for the trip. But there were too many people hunting for him now. The Bureau would be after him for what he done to Johnstone and Lanny boy. The ATF would want to question him further in connection with the bombing of their headquarters building. He had listened to news reports of the blast on Massachusetts Avenue. They had apparently listened to his warning, but McGarand's bomb had done its job. The attack would really shock them, he thought. The ATF was a tiny organization compared to the Bureau, but they had been a pretty high-profile group lately. The field agents he had known were competent people who were sincerely trying to make the country a safer place. But their policy people in Washington were another story, especially when a "situation" developed. Then too many of them wanted to play John Wayne.

And the Agency? That posed a trickier question. He suspected that some senior devils in Main Justice and Langley had decided to eliminate their Edwin Kreiss problem once and for all. If so, his maneuvering room was shrinking fast. Right now, he needed to know where Lynn was. And his favorite ex–special agent, for that matter. Someone picked up the phone at the other end and he asked for Micah.

"Who's callin'?"

"The lion keeper," he answered. The man told him to hold on, and he could hear the sounds of an urgent discussion in the background. Then the man came back.

"Pap's done gone. Buncha damn revenuers into them caves under Pearl's Mountain. Pap says they's huntin' kin o'yourn. Pap's up on the back ridge, with some a the boys, waitin' on 'em. Ain't had no word back yet."

Revenuers? He wondered what the ATF was doing going after Lynn. Unless they were trying what Misty had tried—take the daughter, bag the father. "Was Janet Carter with her? When they went in?"

"Don't rightly know. They was two wimmen, all's I know."

"Did these people show any identification? Warrants?"

"Don't know who they was. Pap said they didn't bring no warrants. They was wantin' to come in here, search the whole damn place, but Pap and Uncle Jed took the ten-gauges out, tole 'em to git on out a here. They went on back down to the road. Then they come back, with 'em dogs. It was 'em dogs took 'em to the cave. Ain't seen hide nor hair of 'em since."

Micah had shown Kreiss the cave hideout up behind the cabin and the junkyard. He had implied there were passages leading back from the tiny hut, but he hadn't volunteered any further information, and Kreiss hadn't wanted to pry. Now he needed to tell Micah where he would be hiding, but he knew the government people would have put a tap on Micah's line.

"All right. I appreciate it. Tell Micah I'm back, and that there's a bunch of revenuers after me, too. Tell him I'm going to lay up in that place he and I talked about, last time he heard the lions."

"Awright."

"And one more thing—the government is probably listening to this conversation. Tell your Pap to stay shy."

There was a soft, contemptuous guffaw on the phone, and then the man hung up.

Kreiss pressed the button to end the call and turned the phone off. He had to assume there was a government signals intelligence van some-where, listening to that entire conversation. What had they learned? Kreiss was in the area. He was working with Micah Wall. He was going to lay up somewhere that Micah would recognize. Ergo, they would want to talk to Micah, who would tell them zip-point shit, assuming they could even find him at all. Right now, there was a probably a lanky, bearded figure with a rifle humping it up the ridge to find Micah and deliver the warning.

He leaned back in the driver's seat and rubbed his eyes. He needed some coffee, but the convenience store was shut for the night, its doors and windows barred, security lights burning, and the gas pumps locked. The Virginia countryside and backwoods were apparently no longer places of safety and sociable trust. And the hills were alive with the sounds of—what? Federal agents, with dogs. Hunting two women, one of them an ex–federal agent. Which government law-enforcement agency was it? The Bureau? The ATF? Or could it even be the Langley crowd? He still wanted to settle accounts with Browne McGarand for what he had done to those kids, but McGarand was probably long gone, or being hunted by the feds himself.

He took a deep breath, let it out, and started the van. First, he needed to make sure Lynn was safe. For that, he would have to get in touch with Micah. He couldn't exactly go home, and he couldn't go to Micah's. If the feds had real coverage of the Blacksburg-Christiansburg area, he couldn't go to a motel, either. He had stashed the essentials of a base camp at the arsenal the first time he'd gone in. He had his crawl suit in the bag, his sound equipment, and this time he had a gun. He decided to make one stop for a meal and some extra drinking water, and then he'd go to ground in the last place anyone would expect him to go: back to the Ramsey Arsenal.

Janet and Lynn flopped down on the cave floor when they finally reached the flat wooden door. The rising passage had been covered in smelly, slippery clay, and they were both filthy with it. They were also very thirsty, having taken no water with them. The lantern was guttering, which meant it was nearly out of fuel.

"What time is it?" Lynn asked.

Janet looked at her watch. She could feel the moisture in the clay seeping into her clothes, but she was so tired, she didn't care. She was already covered in mud from head to toe anyway. The passage up from the subterranean lake had climbed forever, through some incredibly narrow cracks, and one scary part where the ceiling had come down to within two feet of the floor, an area that they'd done on their backs. She blanked that part out of her mind with a shiver. "Ten-thirty. At night, I think."

"So what do we do now?" Lynn asked, holding her side. She sounded as exhausted as Janet was. "Just go out there and see who's waiting?"

Janet looked over at the girl. She looked like she had been camouflaged for hunting, but there was also some pain showing in her face. "That wound hurting?"

"Ribs, mostly," Lynn said. "Plus, I wasn't a hundred percent when we left that hospital."

"You've done amazingly well. I want to open that door and get out of here, but I have this nightmare that goddamned woman will be sitting on a stump out there, looking at her watch as if we're late."

Lynn grinned. "Then you cap her ass, Special Agent. I need a shower and a hot meal."

Janet patted the .38 that was still strapped into her waist holster. "She'd probably catch it in her teeth and spit it back at me," Janet said. "But actually, it should be Mr. Wall out there. Presumably, no one else knows where this cave comes out."

"They discovered where we went in," Lynn pointed out.

"They had dogs; the dogs followed our trail to the cave."

"Where's my father, I wonder," Lynn said, rolling over on her side.

"Last time I talked to him, he was still in Washington, looking for

McGarand. But he said he was coming back down here. Apparently, the Bureau picked him up in Washington, but he got away from them. Which is why I'm worried about that woman being out there when we open the door."

"She doesn't want me—she wants him?"

"Yes. But don't ask me why. Whatever it is, my boss got some pretty high-level guidance, because at one point, he wasn't willing to cooperate in moving against your father, and then all of a sudden, he was."

"And that's why you quit?"

"Partially. They wanted me to do some things that I thought were wrong. It involved that woman. When Farnsworth—that's my boss in Roanoke—couldn't or wouldn't explain why, I quit."

"What will you do now?"

"I have a Ph.D. in forensic sciences from Johns Hopkins. I can do anything with that."

"Wow, I guess you can. The Bureau won't queer the deal for you, will they? Because you quit?"

"You mean when I go looking for a job? No, I don't think so. I have pretty damn good performance evaluations, and I also have worked inside the laboratory. I don't think the Bureau would want any more publicity about its laboratory just now."

"Meaning what?"

"Meaning the Bureau has a basic problem in its laboratory: The lab rats work for the prosecutors. Sometimes their evidentiary conclusions aren't exactly unbiased. That's where I got into trouble in the first place, and it's the real reason I was sent to Roanoke."

Lynn thought about that, turned again, and winced. Janet checked her bandage for signs of bleeding, but there was nothing significant. "You know," she said, "that woman said she didn't shoot you; she said it was the ATF doing that roadblock, that *they* shot you."

"The ATF? But why? Why were they even doing a roadblock? And, besides, they thought you were FBI. They wouldn't shoot at an FBI agent, would they?"

"Some of them would probably like to, actually," Janet said. "But no, I wouldn't have expected that."

"Well, somebody sure as hell did," Lynn said, rubbing her side.

"I have two bullets," Janet said, patting her own pocket. "We'll have to look into that when we get clear of this mess."

"Speaking of which . . ."

"Yeah," Janet said, getting up. "I guess it's time to open sesame."

Lynn dragged herself off the floor of the cave, and together they examined the wooden door. It was horizontal and appeared to be seated in the ceiling of the small chamber they had reached. It was not quite six feet off the floor of the chamber, but Janet couldn't see how they could get it open more than a few inches without something to stand on. There did not appear to be any hinges or connection point. There was a handle on one end.

"You suppose it's pull instead of push?" Lynn asked.

Then the lantern went out. "Your guess is as good as mine," Janet said. "We'll try to do this quietly." She pulled down on the handle. The door, which was hinged on the other end, pulled grudgingly down into the chamber, accompanied by a rockfall of dirt and small stones from above. The other side of the door had a set of small boards nailed onto its surface, which they could feel but not see. A draft of cool, clean air filled with the scent of pine trees blew down into their faces. "All right!" Janet whispered. "Up we go."

They clambered up, using the boards as steps, Janet leading, gun in hand. They crawled out onto the forest floor, staying low. The night was clear and moonlit now. They could see that they were on the side of a steep slope covered in tall pines. As soon as Lynn came off the door, it rose from the chamber below and settled back onto the level of the hillside. They sat there for a few minutes, getting their night vision. There was a small breeze blowing up the mountain. It was enough to stir the pines, which, in turn, made it impossible to hear if anyone was moving around them. The ground was covered in a thick bed of pine straw, adding to the sound insulation. Above them, an outcropping of rock rose straight up, gleaming gray-white in the darkness. It looked like the bow of an enormous ship towering above them.

Janet moved closer to Lynn so that she could whisper softly. "You live here. Where do you think we are?" she asked.

"My father lives here. I live in Blacksburg. But we're probably on the back side of Pearl's Mountain. That's the west side. Dad's cabin and Micah's place are on the east side. So now what?"

Janet put the gun back in its holster. Her damp clothes made her cold. If anybody was waiting out there in the woods, he or she would be able to smell all this cave mud, she thought. "We need to get to Micah or some of his people," she whispered. "The question is, Up and over, or walk around?"

"Up and over is out of the question," Lynn said. "I'm not sure I can even walk around. And the east side has a sheer rock face. I don't know how high we are, but . . ."

"We're going to have to do something," Janet said. "We stay out here in these wet clothes, we're going to get hypothermia. We know they had people at your father's cabin. Let's go the other way, north, around the mountain. Micah has to have some scouts out on the mountain. Hopefully, we'll run into one."

Lynn groaned but got to her feet. Janet wished they had brought along those sticks Micah had pointed out. She had gone hiking several times up on the Appalachian Trail and knew the value of a good stick. The bigger problem was to keep from going in aimless circles in the darkness of the pine forest. They would have to pay attention and keep the top of the mountain to their right. And watch for timber rattlers, stump holes, wait-a-minute vines, deadfalls, loose rocks, and whatever else the mountain slope had in store for them. She tripped over a long stick, picked it up, broke it down to a useful length, and told Lynn to find one, too. Then they set out into the trees.

Kreiss established his hideout up behind the wrecked industrial area of the arsenal. He picked a heavily wooded spot upstream of the logjam and near the top of a hill on the opposite bank of the creek. Come daylight, he should be able to look down into most of the industrial area where the power plant had been, and also into the beginning rows of the vast bunker farm. He had driven north on Route 11 past the entrance to the arsenal. The signal lights had still been out, but the barrels were gone and there were floodlights up on the hill where the entrance gates were, which told him that the investigation into the explosion was still going on. He'd driven on into Ramsey, stopped to eat at a drive-through burger joint, and then retraced his route past the arsenal entrance to the place where the rail spur turned off to go into the arsenal. A half a mile beyond was a small shopping mall, where he had parked the van. He then walked back along the highway, carrying one bag of equipment, until he came to the railroad line, and then he turned off to get into the arsenal.

His plan was to get some sleep and then call into Micah's around midnight. By then, hopefully, there would be news of Lynn. After that, he would have some decisions to make. The only way he could prove his own innocence with respect to the Washington bombing was to bring in McGarand, and that would be tough to do with everybody hunting him.

Plus, he had no idea where McGarand was. What he might have to do would be go into permanent hiding for a few years and maybe tell his story through the public press. But that would leave Lynn unprotected. He wasn't worried about the Bureau or even the ATF doing anything to Lynn, but what Misty would do was a very different question.

Headlights flared down in the industrial area. As he watched from the trees, he could see and then hear a security truck prowling through the littered streets. So there was active security now, he thought. He'd been lucky to get over the fence. The truck turned away and went down a road behind the blank concrete slabs that had been the power plant, then headed into the bunker fields. The headlights disappeared.

He knew he wasn't thinking clearly. Focus, he told himself. Get some rest. Find out what's happened to Lynn. Then decide.

Janet stepped across the trail before recognizing what it was. Lynn did see it, and she said, "Hey." They examined the trail, which was not much more than a footpath, but it ran up and down the mountain, not across it. It looked to Janet like it was maybe five, six hundred feet to the summit. "If this goes all the way to the top," Janet said, "we could cut our little hike here in half."

Lynn groaned and then sat down on a log. "I'm sorry. You go ahead, and I'll hole up somewhere. I can't make that climb."

Janet sat down next to her. "I'm not going to leave you out here," she said. "Let's rest a while and then see what we can do."

"I know what I *can't* do," Lynn said. "I can't climb this frigging mountain."

Janet said nothing, just sat there in the darkness. She had regained her night vision, and she could see amazingly well. The sky was full of bright stars and a partial moon. Light-colored objects stood out with sudden clarity against the dark pines. Like the man standing there by that tree, watching them.

"*Shit!*" she shouted, jumping up and fumbling to get her gun out. Lynn saw where Janet was staring and got up slowly, backing in the direction they had come. The man didn't move, but just continued to stand there, motionless. He was very tall, bearded, and was wearing a slouch hat and carrying a long rifle with a scope in the crook of his arm. Finally, he advanced one step and raised the rifle into the air. A single shot blasted out against the night air, followed by two more as he worked the bolt so fast, Janet couldn't see his hands move. The final gunshot reverberated across the rock face of the mountain like an insult against all nature. Back in the forest, a night bird squawked its disapproval. The man put the rifle back into the crook of his arm and stepped forward. Janet kept her own gun ready, but pointed it at the ground. The man approached, his footfalls silent on the pine straw. He was even taller than she had thought. She could smell the gun smoke rising from the barrel of his rifle.

"Y'all cold?" he asked in an old man's voice. Janet couldn't really see his face.

"Yes," she said. Had he signaled Micah? Or someone else?

"Them rocks yonder? They still warm. Y'all stay here. Pap's a-comin'."

Then he stepped back into the forest and disappeared right in front of their eyes.

"That mean what I think it means?" Lynn asked in a low whisper.

"I sure hope so," Janet said. "Scared the shit out of me. Let's go see if he's right about those rocks."

Half an hour later, they were sitting with their backs up against a smooth wall of rock, which had indeed still been warm from the afternoon sun. They saw a lantern approaching through the trees, and then Micah and the tall man came across the path. The man was still carrying the big rifle, and Micah was carrying what looked like a stubby double-barreled shotgun in one hand, the lantern in the other. He greeted them and then put a finger to his lips, signaling for silence.

"We're goin' down," he began.

"Thank God," Lynn murmured.

"Cain't talk," he said, dousing the lantern. "They's revenuers aplenty out on the mountain."

"Where are you taking us?" Janet asked, wondering why the revenuers wouldn't have heard the shots.

"To ole Ed's cabin. Ain't no one there right now. Where's them folks what came after you in the cave?"

Janet told him about what had happened on the subterranean lake, and Micah nodded. He put a finger to his lips again and then started down the trail. Janet and Lynn followed, Lynn limping a little. The tall man followed for a while, but then, on Micah's signal, he stepped sideways into the forest and disappeared again.

It took them forty minutes to get down to the level of the big meadow behind Kreiss's cabin. Micah signaled for them to rest while he went forward to the edge of the woods. He watched for a few minutes. Then he walked carefully out into the meadow until he reached the rock where

Kreiss hid his Barrett. He lit the lantern, cropped the flame down to a minimum, and then extended it beyond the side of the huge boulder. As Janet strained to see, an answering flicker of light appeared down among the trees at the cabin. What is this? she thought. He had said there was no one at the cabin. Micah turned around and waved them out of the trees. Had to be some of Micah's people, she concluded. She had to help Lynn get to her feet, and the girl staggered when she first started to walk. All in, Janet thought, giving her an arm for support. "We're almost there," she said.

"Almost where?" Lynn asked, which is when Janet noticed Lynn's eyes were closed.

"Your dad's cabin. Micah got a signal that it was all clear."

They walked across the meadow, going slow to accommodate Lynn's halting footsteps. Janet felt terribly exposed out in the broad expanse of grass between the woods up above and the dark cabin, but Micah proceeded ahead confidently. When they stepped into the shadows of the trees around the cabin, Lynn was stunned to see Farnsworth and five of the Roanoke agents, including Billy Smith, step out of the darkness. They converged on Micah. She was reaching instinctively for her weapon, when she realized from the way he was acting that Micah had known they were there. Farnsworth came over, took one look at Lynn, and instructed two agents to help her into the cabin. Janet just stood there with her mouth hanging open until she saw Farnsworth smile. He had something in his hands, but she couldn't see what it was.

"Hey, Janet," he said. "Feel like a cup of coffee?"

Janet looked at Micah, who was standing to one side, looking considerably embarrassed. He had led them directly into the government's hands. "Mr. Wall, what have you done?" she asked.

"Don't blame him, Janet," Farnsworth said. "He's doing what he had to do. Let's get a cup of coffee. I've got some things to tell you."

Forty-five minutes later, after a hot shower and some dry clothes borrowed from Lynn's closet, Janet sat with Farnsworth in the kitchen, having a cup of coffee. Lynn had been seen by some county EMTs and then had collapsed on her father's bed, where she was now fast asleep. The rest of the Roanoke agents, except for Billy, were outside. Farnsworth put Janet's credentials and her Sig down on the kitchen table. Billy sat at the dining room table, facing a laptop computer that was used for secure communications from the field.

"First, I want to ask you to take these back," Farnsworth said, pointing to them. "I never sent in any paperwork, and the circumstances surrounding your resignation have changed. A lot."

She looked at the credentials, pulled them toward her, but then she left them on the table between them. "Tell me about those changes," she said. She was physically tired, but the caffeine was working and her mind was alert. She decided that she wasn't going back to the federal fold until she heard Farnsworth's explanation. Billy pulled on a set of headphones and started talking to someone.

Farnsworth sat back in his chair and rubbed his fingers across his chin in his characteristic gesture. "You were dead right about a second bomb. Somebody went to Washington and parked a propane truck next to the ATF headquarters building and managed to pump several thousand cubic feet of hydrogen gas into the building. Right at the start of the working day."

"Oh my God! The *ATF* building? Not the Hoover Building?"

"Right. The results were very similar to what happened down at the Ramsey Arsenal. Obliterated the top floors of the building, and burned the rest."

"Damn!" she whispered. "How many—"

"Almost none. They had some warning and got all the people out before it let go. Guess who provided the warning?"

"Kreiss."

He cocked his head to one side. "And you knew that how?"

"We've been in touch. As you know, I've been protecting his daughter."

"Yes. Well, Kreiss appeared in front of the building to deliver said warning after having been picked up earlier by two Washington beat cops for loitering in the White House security zone. There'd been a security alert downtown ever since the Ramsey thing. Then—and this is the interesting part—he was transferred to Bureau custody, from which he escaped by causing a car crash out on the G.W. Parkway at oh-dark-thirty in the morning, leaving two agents handcuffed to a park bench to watch their Bu car marinate in gasoline."

"Oh my," Janet said, working hard to keep a serious expression on her face. They had me and then I had them. "Why was he transferred to Bureau custody?"

"Because the local cops did a wants and warrants check, and the next thing they knew, here came two crackerjacks from the Hoover Building, saying they had instructions to take subject Edwin Kreiss into custody in connection with a homicide down here in Blacksburg. District cops said,

Be our guest. Got him off their blotter. But in the meantime, these two superstars took him, on instructions from the Foreign Counter Intelligence Division duty officer, for a midnight ride to Langley, Virginia, where certain people out there wanted to have a word."

"Did *you* file an apprehend-and-detain order on Kreiss?"

"No, I did not. We're all looking into that little mystery."

"This has to involve that horrible woman."

He got up to get more coffee. "Beats the shit out of me," he said. "I discovered all of this after the fact. The last thing I did before the ATF building changed shape was to call in your warning that FBI headquarters was a possible target, and that that hydrogen bomb business referred to gaseous hydrogen, not nuclear hydrogen."

"What was their reaction?"

Farnsworth grinned. "Building security thanked me for my interest in federal law enforcement, than wished me a good night. Several hours later, the world ended up on Mass Avenue. By the way, what did you tell Agent Walker, about forwarding the report?"

"I asked him if he wanted to be the one link in the chain that failed to forward warning of a bombing up the line, in the event that there was a bombing."

Farnsworth nodded. "I want you to know that he was very, very insistent. Said he was logging and date-stamping his call to me."

Janet smiled. "We never change, do we?" she said.

"CYA forever. Anyway, back to Kreiss: He shows up at ATF headquarters at daybreak, flashing the creds of one of the agents he stranded out on the parkway. While he was warning them, one of the guards checked with our headquarters, and then *they* apprehended him at gunpoint. This was about the time their gas monitors detected the hydrogen. Kreiss starts to walk away. They give him the usual warning. So Kreiss, cool as a cucumber, asks the guards if they really want to pop a cap in a hydrogen atmosphere. Instant hoo-ha. Fortunately, one of their ADs was there; he let Kreiss walk. But now, of course, they want to have a word, as well."

"Why the trip to Langley? What's up with that, boss?"

Farnsworth tugged at his shirt collar. "That's a great deal more complicated, and it's why I'm here with five agents, and why they're outside in tactical gear. And it's also why I leaned on those Hatfields and McCoys to make them bring you and Kreiss's daughter to me."

"How did you know they even had us?" she asked.

"That Agency woman? We got word to her that Kreiss had been

picked up. She said she had tracked you and the girl in there to the Wall clan, but now that they had Kreiss up in D.C., she was backing out. End of story. Good-bye. That was before Kreiss did his thing on the parkway and got away again, of course."

"And Mr. Wall? He's not a fan of things federal."

"That old man was here when we got here, sitting on the damned porch like he owned the place. I think he had some of his 'boys' out there in the woods. Probably still does. All we got out of him initially was tobacco spit."

"What changed his mind?"

Farnsworth moved his coffee cup around on the table in a small circle for a moment. "Well," he said, "Mr. Wall out there is a realist. I told him who I was and that I was not one of his regular revenuers. I told him I'd bring the full weight of every government law-enforcement agency—FBI, DEA, ATF, DCIS, IRS, and even the Secret fucking Service in here and hound him and all the fruits of his two-branch family tree until the end of time. I told him we'd freeze his bank accounts, audit everybody's tax returns, cut off their Social Security and Medicaid, intercept his mail, tap his phones, tail his pickup truck, haul him and everyone he knew into court on a weekly basis, and force him to consort with lots and lots of lawyers. I think the thought of lots and lots of lawyers did it, actually."

"Micah Wall doesn't strike me as a heavy-duty crook," she said.

"Oh, hell, all these hillbillies are fringe, at worst. They make a big deal of being fierce mountain men and the last of the Mohicans, that kind of stuff. But what they really are is a bunch of poor, undereducated white trash making a subsistence living up here in the hills. They work on-again, off-again minimum-wage jobs while making side money salvaging parts out of junked cars and appliances, distilling a little 'shine, fighting their roosters and their dogs, or poaching illegal furs. It's more lifestyle than crime."

"He didn't strike me as someone who scares easily."

"Mostly I convinced him that there are no more refuges from the government, not even for hillbillies. Then, I told him something else."

"Which was?"

"That you'd be safer with us than with him, because the person hunting both of you worried even us."

Janet put her coffee cup down on the table. "Last time I checked, you were on her side."

"Because I had specific instructions to that effect. From the executive assistant director over FCI, no less. That was before I went and checked with *my* SAC in Richmond, and he with our assistant director. Like I said, we now have significantly changed circumstances. Remember that DCB deal?"

"That Domestic Counterintelligence Board that Bellhouser was being so coy about?"

"Right. Best we can tell, there isn't any such board. Nobody in our chain of command can put a line on it, and the question's been asked at the director's level at headquarters."

"Son of a bitch," Janet said. "That means Bellhouser and Foster had their own agenda. That business about a bomb cell was bullshit."

"Except, as things turned out, it wasn't exactly bullshit, was it? As the ATF found out the hard way. But here's the thing: My boss says AD Marchand was personally involved in Kreiss's termination. What he can't find out is what that was really all about. The Office of Professional Responsibility has the files, and they're not only all sealed but physically over at Main Justice. Now, tell me something. You think Kreiss had a part in that bombing?"

"Absolutely not," she said. "Kreiss was not involved in that bombing. He was up in Washington hunting that McGarand guy because of what he did to Lynn."

Farnsworth considered that and then nodded. "Yeah, I buy that."

"Okay. Now, that Agency woman—let me tell you about that piece of work." She began with Misty's appearing in her house, then told him what had happened at the hospital and her breaking through the roadblock on the way to Micah's. When she said that they were ATF people, Farnsworth interrupted her. "We've had no report of that," he said. "And their SAC would have been in my office with his hair on fire if they thought one of my people did that. They *shot* at your *car*?"

"Yes, they did. That's how Lynn was wounded. Then that damned woman came over the hill." She told him how she had driven the woman off the road and then made it to Micah's, and then she described the cave expedition that followed. He was shaking his head in amazement when she was done.

"You think those people were all killed down there?" he asked. "In the lake?"

"Don't know," she said. "But it got real quiet when the stalactites stopped falling. No dogs, no more lights or voices. I don't know how many men there were back there. But we were not pursued after that."

"Son of a bitch," Farnsworth muttered. "This just doesn't sound right. We'd have been *avalanched* with calls if the ATF thought they were chasing one of our agents and there was shooting."

"Maybe we're making assumptions," she said. "Maybe this wasn't ATF. Maybe that damned woman just said it was, to throw some shit in the game."

"You're assuming they were her people?"

"I'm beginning to think so."

Farnsworth got up and paced around the kitchen. One of the agents stepped in through the back door and reported all was secure outside. Farnsworth acknowledged and the man stepped back out. Farnsworth asked Billy to crank up a fresh pot of coffee and get it to the men outside. Billy signed off from the communications terminal and started hunting for coffee makings. The agent, whom Janet knew only slightly, had nodded politely to her before he'd stepped back outside. Back in the fold, she thought.

"Now I *know* we need to pick up Edwin Kreiss," Farnsworth said finally. "I mean, headquarters wants his ass for what he did to those two agents, and local law wants him for the Jared McGarand thing. I think we need to bring him in for his own protection. Damn, I think I got snookered here."

"That woman knew all along that it would be damned difficult to trap Kreiss. Once Lynn was recovered, though, she saw her opportunity. She came after his daughter, knowing Kreiss would come in to protect Lynn."

"Right, right, I can see that."

"Once she knew that Kreiss had been picked up in Washington, just before the bombing, she backed off, left us alone at Micah's. Until, of course, she found out that Kreiss had managed to escape."

"Which means she has a source inside the Bureau," Farnsworth said. "I've been making reports up my chain of command since this shit started. Maybe the leak's in Richmond."

"Well, then," she said. "we have to move. We need to get Lynn to a safer place, and we need to find Kreiss. Actually, I think I know how to do that."

"How?"

"Let me talk to Micah. Do you have one of your cards? He's still outside?"

"You going to take those with you?" he asked, indicating the credentials and the Sig. When she hesitated, he added, "How 'bout if I say I'm sorry?"

She smiled wearily. "This wasn't you, boss. This is something slimy and corrupt oozing back out of the ground in Washington. You need to get Lynn to tell you what she knows about her father's termination."

Then she picked up the credentials and the gun, her badges of office. He passed her one of his cards, and she went outside.

Micah was sitting in the front seat of one of the Bureau cars, his hat on his lap, his face a mask of shame. Janet opened the driver's door and got in.

Seeing his expression, she said immediately, "You did the right thing."

"Not in my book, I didn't," he said. "Your car's over there." He wouldn't look at her. Without the mountain man hat on his head, he looked old and much diminished.

"Look, Mr. Wall. First, you saved Lynn and me from some seriously bad people. Second, nobody in this country can fight the government anymore, not if they decide to come after you the way Mr. Farnsworth said they would. Everyone knows that."

"Ain't everyone up here knows that," he said.

She sighed and then she saw a way to let him save face. "I didn't tell you the whole truth, Mr. Wall. Look."

He looked over at her, and she showed him her credentials. "I'm the government, too, Mr. Wall. I'm one of them. You didn't betray anyone."

His chin rose slightly, and his face cleared. "I was assigned to protect Lynn Kreiss," she continued. "And that's what I did. With your help. But now we must get in contact with her father. The last he knew, *you* had Lynn, so we think he's going to call."

He started to shake his head. "He ain't told me nothin'," he said. "And I ain't gonna—"

"No, no," she interrupted. "We're not asking you to turn him in to us. But you must tell him that we have Lynn now, and that *I* said she's safe with us. I need him to contact me. Not anyone else. Just me." She turned Farnsworth's card over and wrote her home phone number on the back of it. "Here's my number."

"What about them revenuers in the cave?" he asked, taking the card. "Wasn't they gov'mint?"

Janet got out of the car. "What people in the cave, Mr. Wall?" She looked at him for a moment to make sure he understood, and then she went back into Kreiss's cabin.

"I don't think he knows where Kreiss is," she told Farnsworth. "But I think he'll put Kreiss in touch with us. For Lynn's sake."

"Good," Farnsworth said. "We'll be safer in Roanoke, I think. Get the girl up and let's get the hell out of these mountains."

"Why don't I take her to my place? Micah has my car right over there. We both need some sleep."

Farnsworth thought about it. "Okay," he said. "And I'll put some agents on your house. Then I think we're going to have to call in the ATF people in the morning; we've got to sort this out."

"Get them to explain the bullet holes in my car, for starters," Janet said. "Goddamn cowboys." Billy grinned at her from the kitchen. Then she went to get Lynn up.

Kreiss awoke and took a moment to remember where he was, which was in his sleeping bag in a one-man tent on the Ramsey Arsenal. He rubbed his face, looked at his watch, and realized he'd overslept. He had wanted to talk to Micah before 2:30 A.M. He listened to the sounds of night outside. Everything sounded pretty normal. He slipped out of the warm bag and struggled into the crawl suit. He slithered out of the tent, listened again, and then pulled on his boots. It was almost cold, with a clear atmosphere and enough moonlight to define individual trees. There was a steady background noise of crickets and tree frogs. He could barely hear the creek making its way down toward the logjam. He took several deep breaths and watched his exhalations make vapor clouds.

He had to think carefully about what he would say when he called Micah. He had to assume that someone, and possibly more than one someone, would have Micah's phone line tapped at the local telephone central office. He needed to find out what had happened to Lynn without giving away his current location. Unless the Bureau had set up a very elaborate radio triangulation net, the closest they should be able to get was that he was operating off a Blacksburg or Christiansburg cell-phone tower. That would tell them he was in the area, but not where. He switched the phone on and saw that the battery wasn't at full power. He swore; the damn thing was dependent on being plugged into the rental van. He dialed Micah's number and got a rejection tone because he hadn't used the area code first. He exhaled, tried again, and the phone was picked up on the second ring. It sounded like Micah.

"It's me," he said.

"Yeah, good. Them federals from Roanoke, they done got your daughter."

Kreiss felt a surge of alarm. "Which federals?"

"FBI. That woman what was with her? Said she was with the FBI. She done left a message. Says to call her in Roanoke. Says Lynn is safe with her, but you gotta call, and only to her."

He gave Kreiss the number and then there was a moment of silence. Then he asked if Kreiss needed anything. Micah didn't sound quite right, and Kreiss thought that he might be trying to tell him to get off the line. He told him no, thanked him, and hung up abruptly. He got a pen out and wrote down Janet's phone number. He looked at his watch: It was almost 3:00 A.M. Not a terrific time to call anyone, he thought. But Lynn was with Carter, which should keep her safe from Misty, especially if they had her at the federal building in Roanoke.

He was fully awake now, so he decided to scout his immediate area, and perhaps lay in a few approach-warning devices. He went to the edge of the little grove where he had pitched his camp and looked down at the wrecked industrial area, which was about three-quarters of a mile away. There was no sign of the security patrol vehicle, but there were portable lights rigged to run off a trailer generator around the remains of the power plant. The wreckage of the other buildings looked like a scene from World War II in the dim moonlight.

To his left was the edge of the vast ammunition bunker field, arrayed in rows and lanes to the visible horizon, secure behind their own double fence line. A single road led from the industrial area to a double gate, which was closed and presumably locked. Each of the bunkers was topped by two galvanized-steel helical ventilator cowls, all of which were motionless in the still night air. The hundreds of partially buried bunkers made the place look like one vast graveyard. Two thousand acres of canned death, Kreiss thought. It was a fitting symbol for what they had once contained. He wondered where McGarand had gone to ground. He set about rigging some motion detectors. He'd call Carter just before daybreak. Between now and then, he'd try to figure out what his next moves were, assuming he had any left.

14

Janet sat straight up in her bed with the worst headache she had ever had, a blinding, throbbing pain behind her eyes and lancing down both sides of her neck. Her mouth was dry as parchment and her skin felt hot all over. She tried to clear her throat, but there was no moisture; even her eyes were sticky and dry. The room was hot, unnaturally hot. There was daylight outside, but not sunlight. She looked at her watch: It was 6:45 on Wednesday morning. Then she realized the heater must be running.

The heater? She didn't remember turning on the heater. She tried to clear her throat again, but it hurt even to try. She got out of bed, slower than she wanted to, and went into the bathroom. She looked in the mirror and saw that her face was bright red. She blinked her eyes to make sure, then splashed some cold water on her face. It felt wonderful, but the headache hammered away at her temples and she felt a wave of nausea. What the hell is the matter with me? she wondered. And why is the damned heater going full blast?

She put on her bathrobe and went back into the bedroom to open a window. The cool air from outside felt like she was breathing pure oxygen, and she stood there for a moment taking deep breaths. Then she stopped: blinding headache. Hot, dry skin. Bright red face. She knew what this was: carbon monoxide.

The heater.

She bolted from the bedroom and ran down the hall to Lynn's room, trying not to breathe. To her horror, Lynn's door was wide open, and Lynn was gone.

Maybe she had awakened and gone out of the house. She ran to the stairs and called for one of the agents who had been downstairs. Her voice came out in a dry squeak. Dear God, let her be downstairs, she prayed. She went down, holding on to the banister, her breathing strangely ineffective. She realized she had made a mistake going downstairs, but she was committed now; no way she was going to make it back up those stairs. She focused on the front door and made it, her lungs bursting from holding her breath. She threw open the door and stumbled outside. Then she realized what she had seen out of the corners of her eyes as she ran for the door: the two agents, down on the floor in the living room.

She took three deep breaths and ran back inside, grabbing the first one she came to and dragging him roughshod over the front threshold and out onto the landing. His face was bright red and he didn't appear to be breathing. She ran back inside and got the other man, dropping him almost on top of the first. Then she fell down to her knees, gagging, as her lungs screamed for oxygen from the exertion of getting them out. After a minute of this, she got up and staggered over to her car, opened the door, and got on the car phone, calling 911. Then she called the Roanoke office and asked the duty officer for backup, agents down. Then she rolled out of the car onto the wet grass and fought off a siege of the dry heaves while she desperately tried to get more oxygen into her damaged lungs. A car drove past. She caught a glimpse of a man's white face gaping at the scene on her lawn, but he didn't stop. Thanks, pal, she thought.

Lynn was gone.

Jesus, Mary, and Joseph, what would she tell Kreiss?

She opened her eyes and saw the two agents still lying motionless on the front porch, their red faces looking like grotesque Halloween masks. She forced herself to get up and go back over to the porch, where she checked for heartbeats and then began giving mouth-to-mouth resuscitation to the first agent.

That goddamned woman had done this. She was certain of it.

She thought she heard her phone ringing inside, but she ignored it and moved to the other man, alternating between them now, trying to get some oxygen into both of them while waiting for the ambulance to get there. It seemed forever before the sound of sirens rose in the distance.

Deep in the ammunition bunker, McGarand was cold. The whole damn structure is cold as a tomb, he thought as he shivered under two blankets. He had food, water, a cot, blankets, flashlights, several lanterns, and a tiny cookstove, but no way of heating the seventy-five-foot-long portion of the bunker they had closed off. He put a hand out and touched the concrete floor. It was cold as ice. Probably stays that way all year round, he thought.

There was a faint glow of light at the top of the ladder leading up to the ventilator shaft. Must be coming daylight out there, he thought as he groped for the light on his watch. He had climbed out the ventilator shaft last night to lock the front steel door again after getting set up in the back half of the bunker. He wished they had rigged some way to take the front door's hinges down from inside, but they were much too heavy. The bad news was that there was only one way out; the good news was that there would be no indication outside that this bunker was any different from any other bunker.

He stretched, wondering what he was going to do to pass the time. He hadn't thought to bring any books or magazines, not even a Bible. He sighed. That had been stupid of him. He realized he must never have really believed he would need this place. He shivered again. There was plenty of kerosene. Maybe if he lit all the lanterns and put them close to his cot, they might warm the place up. The ventilator above his head should take care of any problems with the fumes. He decided to try it.

Janet sat in the back of a Roanoke EMS ambulance, sucking on an oxygen mask while the EMTs worked on the two agents behind privacy screens in the yard. Farnsworth and two more agents had shown up right behind the ambulance and were now in the house. All the windows in her house were open. Out on the street, two county deputies kept traffic moving and curious neighbors from getting too close. Her headache was abating very slowly, and she had downed two bottles of water and wanted another one. Farnsworth came out of the house, his face grim. She put down the oxygen mask.

"They came in through the basement; through that half window at ground level. Connected the damned furnace exhaust line to the house-supply vents."

"Not they," Janet said. "She."

"We don't know that," he said, looking over at the EMTs huddled inside their screens. They'd been there a long time.

"Yes, we do," Janet said, hopping down from the back of the ambulance. "She took Lynn. You know it's her."

Farnsworth kicked an empty water bottle across the yard.

"How are they doing?" she asked, indicating the downed agents.

"Not so good," he said. "They were downstairs, I take it?"

"Yes, sir. Lynn and I were sleeping upstairs. They were supposed to keep each other awake and make sure no one got in or upstairs."

"Well, apparently nobody heard a thing," he said.

"I wouldn't have heard a bomb go off, I'm afraid. Once I realized there was something wrong, I checked on Lynn. She was gone. Then I ran downstairs."

"They were already unconscious?"

"Yes. I got the front door open and then pulled them out. I gave them mouth-to-mouth until the EMTs got here, but there were two of them. I didn't do a very good job, I'm afraid."

He fixed the scene with an angry glare. "Goddamned woman disabled all of you with gas. She didn't have to leave it on once she had the girl."

"I think maybe those *were* her people in the cavern," Janet said.

He looked at her, then nodded slowly. His cell phone went off in his pocket. He snapped it open and answered it. After a minute, he said they would be back shortly.

"That was my secretary. Abel Mecklen from the ATF is in my office. He was Whittaker's boss. Judy says he's going ballistic. I better get over there."

"Do you need me to come along?"

He thought about it. "No, not at this time. You've had a bad experience, and we've got a lot of things to sort out. One of them involves you and that roadblock. Kreiss hasn't contacted the office; has he contacted you?"

"No, sir."

"Damn. We just about had a handle on this mess. Tell Kreiss we have his daughter, get him to come in, tell us what he knows about McGarand's little expedition."

"Uh, sir? After what happened up in D.C.? He might not be so willing just to come in and talk. Plus, there's the little matter of the Jared McGarand homicide. Although, Lynn told me some things that might mitigate what happened there."

Farnsworth looked across the lawn again at the EMTs. "I'll tell you what," he said. "I'm willing to deal on the G.W. Parkway caper and the McGarand homicide, in exchange for what he knows about the ATF headquarters bombing and his help in catching whoever did this. Because *this*"—he pointed with his chin at the EMTs—"this is personal. Plus, I think there might be something going on at headquarters that's bigger than both of those other two items."

"Can I tell him that if he calls me?"

"Janet, you tell him whatever it takes to get him to come in. The trick is going to be to talk to him *before* that Agency creature does. Because we know the trade she's going to offer."

Janet pulled her bathrobe tighter around her. "I can tell you right now," she said. "He'll focus on that above all else. None of this other stuff matters to him. Everything he's done has been in pursuit of getting his daughter back. That won't change now. Especially now."

"Not if he still thinks she's safe with us," he said.

Janet gave him a look and he raised his hands. "Okay, okay, it was just a thought. You do the best you can, and then notify me the moment he makes contact. Tell him we'll help him get his daughter back—anything he wants. He's all alone now. He's going to need help, and I think he'll realize that."

"Why can't we get our bosses in Washington to go to the Agency and just get this shit stopped?" Janet asked. "Why are *we* dealing with it?"

"Because the people at headquarters who are authorized to deal with the Agency are Marchand's people. Fortunately, you and I work for a different directorate. I have very specific orders to leave those people alone until *our* AD—that's Mr. Greer—finds out who authorized Bellhouser and Foster to start this shit in the first place. If it's Marchand, that's going to be pretty significant. If it's someone in Main Justice, like maybe Bellhouser's boss, that's doubly significant. Right now, everybody's still spun up over the bombing of the ATF headquarters."

"I can just imagine," she said.

"You probably can't, actually. But Greer, and also the director, I'm told, are very interested in why the Agency is targeting a retired FBI agent, and why that effort is being aided and abetted by someone senior in the FBI and possibly over at Justice."

Janet rubbed her eyes. The other reason, as she well knew, was that there was no proof that anyone from the Agency had been in her house last night. Or in the cave, now that she thought about it. By now, Micah Wall and his people would have removed any evidence left on the shores by the subterranean lake. Probably into that pit.

Across the yard, the EMTs were getting ready to transport the two agents. Farnsworth went over there and talked about the agents' condition. His face was grim when he came back over.

"You need to go to the hospital?"

She thought back about that night and her encounter with Misty in the hospital. "No, sir. No more hospitals just now."

"Okay, then get some rest, if that's possible. And stay here until you hear from Kreiss. He trusts you, I think. Try hard to get him in."

She thought about that for a moment. "I don't think I want to stay here right now," she said. "Let me get dressed, and then I'll go down to the office. My head hurts too much for me to sleep. We can call-forward my phone line."

He agreed, and she went into the house. A Crime Scene Unit was coming up from the lower level as she went in. The agent in charge told her it was pretty straightforward: They cut the glass out of the window, let themselves into the lower level. They took the hose off the dryer in the utility room, unbolted a section of the smoke pipe from the gas furnace, and then taped the hose to route exhaust gas to the heated-air-supply vent for the whole house.

"How did they get Lynn out of the house?" she asked.

"Through the front door, it looks like. You said in your statement that you yanked it open, but you didn't say anything about unlocking it. I assume it was locked last night?"

"Yes, locked and dead-bolted."

"Yeah, well, you might want to invest in a dead-bolt that uses a key instead of a knob. The furnace room had a lot of dust on the floor. We found traces of that up here on the hallway rug and also upstairs. They probably had a respirator mask on, waited for twenty minutes or so for everyone in the house to start flopping around on the floor, and then made their move."

She nodded dejectedly. *She*, Janet thought. Not they. *She* had come into Janet's house like it was nothing, right under the noses of two agents, grabbed what she wanted, and then left. Hell, she probably had a key from the last time.

The CSU leader escorted his team out and then stepped back in. "We're finished up here," he said. "Good moves on getting Williams and Jackson out, by the way. EMTs said they're breathing on their own. They said that was your doing. Glad to have you back, Carter."

She smiled weakly and went upstairs to get dressed. As she was washing her face, she remembered that the phone had rung while she was getting the agents out. Kreiss? She went to her bedside, got a pen and pad out, and then dialed star 69. The robot quoted her a phone number. She hung up and looked at it. It had a 703 area code. Northern Virginia. Shit, she thought. Is Kreiss still up in the Washington area? She started to dial it, then thought better of that. She'd take it to the office, where they could run the number and see what and who it was.

Kreiss moved out of his camp at daylight. He'd decided to have a look around the arsenal, mostly to see what kind of activity was going on down in the industrial area, and to walk the fence perimeter to identify alternative ways out in case he had to run for it. He figured the van would be safe for two, maybe three days in that shopping center parking lot before someone noticed it or stole it. He'd walk out and move it before then.

He was dressed out in the camo-pattern crawl suit, and he had some water, one MRE, the gun, and the cell phone. His call to Carter had not been answered, and he wanted to try again later in the morning. He wasn't sure if the number Micah had given him was her home or office, but she might have call forwarding on it. He went back through the woods in the direction of the railway cut to get to a point high enough to see down into the industrial area. There did not seem to be anyone down there, although there was what appeared to be a tan-colored van parked by the first intact building along the main street. The blast at the power plant had been powerful enough to knock down all the wooden structures in the low areas, as well as badly damage several of the big concrete buildings. He concluded that the van was an ATF Crime Scene Unit still working the site for evidence. As long as he stayed out of sight and sound, he should be free to move about the rest of the installation.

An hour later, he was in the bunker farm, which looked to be every bit as big as the overhead photos indicated. He'd gone over the fence rather than fool with the gates, especially with police and ATF people around. The ground inside the bunker farm was rolling, with narrow gravel roads defining the lanes and rows of the partially buried round-topped bunkers. From his vantage point on top of a bunker, he could see perhaps five hundred of the structures, interspersed with clumps of pines. There were no telephone poles, so power and monitoring circuits going to the structures must be underground. He fished the binoculars out of the chest pack and sat down to take a careful look at everything. He knew there were at least that many bunkers, if not more, over the far ridge, and behind that was the section of the perimeter fence he wanted to explore. The day was turning hazy with weak sunlight.

As he scanned the bunkers to the right of the main road, carefully studying the stands of trees and occasionally turning the glasses back onto the gates to make sure no one was coming, he worried about Lynn. The thought of Misty hunting Lynn had been very much on his mind. Even if she was with Carter, it didn't mean she was safe. Inexperienced as she was, Carter was no match for someone like Misty. Hell, most of the Bureau was no match for Misty. It wasn't just all the gizmos and special toys that made the sweepers so effective; it was their willingness to do very unconventional and dangerous things that made them so lethal, like starting that fire in the hospital. That plus the use of disabling weapons like the retinal disrupter, or psychological measures, like his own use of sounds.

He could still remember his first training session with Misty: "If you're going to hunt someone," she said, "there are two ways to go about it. You can hunt your target in secret and attempt to take him by surprise. But, by definition, you'll get only one chance doing it that way; if you fail, the element of surprise is lost. Considering that we are normally dealing with trained operatives when we go hunting, a miss can be permanent. On the other hand, if you subtly let the quarry know you're hunting him, you add the element of fear to all the other weapons at your disposal. The people we hunt are highly trained to pay attention to situational awareness, which is another way of saying they're permanently paranoid. If you choose the second method, you can amplify that existing paranoia with lots of nonlethal means, to the point where you can make the quarry bolt. Once he bolts, his situational awareness is gone, and he's yours for the taking."

After the first month, he'd realized that Misty truly enjoyed her work. And so, if he thought about it honestly, had he. It hadn't been at all like the Bureau, which tended to throw a wide net of resources around a subject and then slowly, if often not very efficiently, pull it tight. His first boss in the Bureau had explained it well: The Bureau was first and foremost a bureaucracy. The word had two roots: *bureau*, meaning "administrative unit," and *cracy*, from the Greek *kratos*, meaning "strength" or "power." We strangle the bad guys with paperwork—research, evidence, legal maneuvers, surveillance, wire-taps, warrants, and laws—while trying not to drown in our own internal paperwork. His work with the sweepers had been the absolute antithesis of the Bureau's approach: Tracking down and retrieving an Agency operative who had gone bad was an intensely personal mission. It was one-on-one ball, an exciting match of professional wits, stamina, cunning, mechanical skills, and, ultimately, the direct psychological engagement of the target. He hadn't liked it; he had *loved* it.

He shifted his position on the top of the bunker and scanned the other half of the bunker field, starting from the road and working to his left, looking for anything out of place or different from all the other bunkers. He also scanned the fence line; nothing there except some plastic bags and other windblown trash hung up at the base of the wire. The bunkers all looked much the same: old grayish green concrete, rusting steel doors facing a ramp that had been cut down into the ground, and two motionless rusting helical ventilators on each structure, looking like little frozen smokestacks.

Except one was moving. Right there, almost on the visible horizon, to the right of a large stand of trees. A bunker like all the rest, except that the helical cylinder on the back end of the bunker was turning very slowly. Now why is that? he wondered.

He knew that the helical cowls could provide ventilation two ways. If there was a breeze, it would spin the helix, which in turn would draw warm air out of the bunker. But if there was no breeze, as was the case today, it had to mean there was warm air inside the bunker, rising through the shaft to turn the helix. But the bunkers were supposedly all empty. Empty, cold, man-made tombs.

He walked carefully down the full length of the bunker roof he was standing on to examine the distant cowl from a slightly different angle. It was definitely moving. It was nearly half a mile away; perhaps there was a breeze over there. But then both cowls ought to be moving. He swung around to scan the fence and the gates behind him, but there was still no one there, and no sound of any vehicles coming. He took a mental bearing on the distant bunker, slid down from the one he had climbed, and headed for the ridge, trotting purposefully down one of the lanes. It was full daylight now, so he tried to keep a line of bunkers between him and the main gate to the bunker farm. He was almost there, crossing into a line of trees from the gravel lane, when the tiny cellular phone in his backpack went off. He moved sideways into the tree line, stood with his back against a tree, opened the phone, and hit the send button.

"You called me," he announced quietly.

"This is Janet Carter; where are you?"

"At the other end of this phone circuit, Special Agent," he replied. She sounded upset. "Where are you?"

"I'm in the office. In Roanoke. That woman—Misty, you called her? She's taken Lynn."

He sat down abruptly, his back to the pine tree. A cold wave settled over his chest.

"Tell me," he said.

She gave him a brief rundown of everything since the hospital, up to and including Misty's attack with the carbon monoxide. "My boss wants you to come in, preferably down here to Roanoke. He's—wait a minute."

Kreiss sat there with his eyes closed, trying not to think of anything. He'd had Lynn, but now he didn't. A man's voice came on the phone.

"Mr. Kreiss, this is Ted Farnsworth, RA Roanoke. We have a warrant for your apprehension as a material witness regarding a homicide over in Montgomery County. We have a federal warrant for you regarding the little diversion you ran in Washington. The ATF wants to talk to you about the bombing of their headquarters. And a certain Agency apparently just plain wants your ass."

"It's nice to be wanted," Kreiss said. "But not very."

"Yeah, well, you were in the business. You know the drill. There's one more want, actually. My AD—that's Mr. Greer, over at Criminal Investigations—wants to know why another AD—that's Mr. Marchand, over FCI—got someone very senior at Main Justice to activate the person who snatched your daughter and damn near killed two of my agents this morning. Three, if Janet hadn't awakened and realized something was wrong."

"Good question," Kreiss said. He would have to figure out how to contact Misty. There was no sense in delaying the inevitable. Talking to the FBI was now a waste of time. He knew what Misty wanted: a straight trade. Himself for Lynn.

"Mr. Kreiss? Are you there?"

"Yes, but I don't think we have anything to talk about, Mr. Farnsworth." He could just see the ventilator cowl. It was still moving.

"That's not quite so, Mr. Kreiss. I have authority to deal on the Jared McGarand matter and what happened up on the G.W. Parkway. My chain of command feels that what Bellhouser and Foster set in motion is a hell of a lot more important than anything going on down here in Roanoke. They also feel that this is all connected to something you know."

More than you would ever understand, he thought as he focused on what Farnsworth was saying. And here he was again, facing the same choice he had been given five years ago: "your silence or your daughter."

"Mr. Kreiss?"

"You can't help me do the one thing I must do, Mr. Farnsworth," Kreiss said. "I need to free my daughter. And I don't believe you or your boss or even *his* boss can fight what's behind all this."

"My SAC is telling me the director's into this one, Mr. Kreiss."

"I rest my case."

"AD Greer says this is about the Chinese espionage case in the nuclear labs. Is he right?"

Kreiss was surprised, very surprised. He forced himself to focus. Nobody knew this. Except *them.*

"Mr. Kreiss? Greer says you came back from your Agency assignment and the Glower incident with information that connects Chinese government campaign contributions to the way the nuclear labs investigations got derailed."

"We are speaking on an open radio circuit," Kreiss warned. He was aghast. Nobody could know this.

"They're telling me you agreed to forced retirement and a vow of silence. What he doesn't know or understand is why. The publicly stated reason was your role in the Glower mass suicides. But now he thinks it was something else."

Kreiss sat on the ground in the pine straw, his mind reeling. He had kept his end of the bargain. He had not said a word. He had not done anything but come down here to be with and support his daughter while she finished school. If it hadn't been for that total wild card, that lunatic McGarand and his mission of revenge, he'd still be sitting in his cabin watching the trees grow. *They* had broken the agreement. Unless . . .

"Mr. Kreiss? My chain of command desperately wants to know what you know, and what you can prove. They are willing to drop all the rest, all of it, in return for that. We think we can help you get your daughter back from those people, but only if we can apply the appropriate pressure at the seat of government. Agency to agency, director to director, if need be."

"You don't know her," Kreiss said. A bird started up with a racket way up in the trees above his head.

"What's that, Mr. Kreiss? Don't know who?"

"You don't know the woman who's holding Lynn. Ask Carter; she knows her. This is personal now, between me and her. The only way I *know* I can get Lynn back safely is to trade myself for my daughter. You and the rest of the Bureau would only get in the way."

"Not true, Mr. Kreiss. If you give my bosses what they need, they can get *her* controllers to turn your daughter over. Ephraim Glower's dead, so the Agency can admit what he was doing now and shrug their shoulders: He's beyond prosecution, dead five years now. They won't be the ones who'll have the problem. It will be the people at Justice, and whomever they suborned here at the Bureau. The Agency will play ball when they realize our director is going to reveal the connection."

Kreiss thought about it. Could he take on Misty? Could he even *find* Misty? And what would happen to Lynn if he did?

"You were a special agent of the FBI, Mr. Kreiss. You know how we do things. We're the G. We're big. We're huge. We overwhelm. So do they. If the Agency sets its mind to it, they can and will find you and grind you up. If you let them capture you, you'll end up in solitary confinement in a federal pen somewhere, and not necessarily in this country."

Then Janet Carter came on the line. "The last time, when you went along, it was strictly about your daughter, wasn't it?"

Kreiss didn't answer. He didn't have to.

"Well, this time you have some leverage you didn't have before. Last time, you traded her security for your silence. They broke the deal. So why not use what you've got?"

"Because, Special Agent, she might kill my daughter."

"Might? Mr. Kreiss, she already set fire to a *hospital.* What makes you think she won't hurt Lynn now? I told you what happened in the cave, remember?"

"Yes."

"Well, we're pretty sure now those were her people. They were not ATF assets. In fact, the local head of the ATF has been in here all morning, yelling at Mr. Farnsworth here to find you. ATF hasn't been conducting any operations down here other than out at that arsenal, after the McGarand thing. So those had to be her people in the cave."

He felt the world constrict. Misty had suffered losses. Would she take that out on Lynn? He had given his word. To leave the Bureau. To admit culpability for precipitating the Glower debacle. To maintain his silence. To submerge completely. In return, they would leave Lynn alone. Every fiber of his being was crying out for him to hunt that woman down, to destroy her. But he knew Carter and Farnsworth were right. The only realistic fix was in Washington, where the fix was the holy grail of modern government. It wasn't about tradecraft anymore, or personal competence. It was about information and evidence. The director had been demonized by his enemies at Justice ever since the campaign contributions scandal had erupted. Now he'd discovered that there might be a way to destroy those enemies. If he could believe Farnsworth, the director himself was willing to use what he, Kreiss, knew, to strike back. And, not coincidentally, to strike at the heart of the corruption that most people in the Bureau believed had consumed the Justice Department. These were monumental issues: How would one college student fare when federal law enforcement went to war with itself?

"If I do this, how can you guarantee that Lynn remains safe?"

"We can't," Farnsworth said. The words resounded down the phone line. "I want to say something different, but that's probably the truth of it."

Kreiss found himself nodding in agreement. At least Farnsworth was shooting straight.

"But you can't, either, Mr. Kreiss. From what Janet tells me, Lynn knows more about this than I think you would expect. If she reveals that to them, she becomes expendable, too. The only way this works is if we have information that *forces* them to let her go. She's a pawn, and that's how you want to keep it. You have to come in. You don't have any workable alternatives."

"All right," he said, almost whispering it. "I'm at the Ramsey Arsenal."

There was an instant of silence, as if Farnsworth was surprised by that. "Where, exactly?" Farnsworth asked.

Kreiss's eyes snapped open at that question. It didn't fit with everything else Farnsworth had been saying. It was too . . . tactical.

"Have Carter come alone to the industrial area," Kreiss said. "I'll find her."

There was another pause on the line. Then Farnsworth said, "Three hours. And not alone—she has to have backup."

"Distant backup."

"Agreed."

"Three hours," Kreiss repeated, and switched the phone off. He leaned sideways and let himself settle back into the pine straw, his eyes staring up into the treetops, unseeing. He did, in fact, have what the Bureau wanted. Much more than they needed. Direct corroborating evidence of a deliberate policy to suppress and impede the investigation at the nuclear labs. Not derived from any investigation, but from Ephraim Glower's safe, which he, Kreiss, had rifled after discovering the bodies. He had felt more than a little guilt when he beheld that bloodbath, but that guilt vanished when he read what was in Glower's safe. He smiled for the first time that day, or maybe even that week. They would be expecting him to take them to a safety-deposit box somewhere and produce an envelope. They would positively howl when they found out where it was. And what it was.

Then he remembered that ventilator, spinning quietly in the still air of morning. He looked at his watch. He had three hours. Why not go see?

Farnsworth took Janet with him down to the secure-communications area of the office. To her surprise, Billy Smith was manning the communication console. He winked at her as Farnsworth ordered him to get Assistant Director Greer's office on the line. The operator on the Washington end told him to stand by.

"This is the biggest thing that you'll ever be involved in," he told Janet. "If we can prove that the Chinese campaign contributions bought breathing room for their spies in the Energy Department, and that someone at Justice helped it happen, the Bureau will be invincible."

"But according to Lynn Kreiss, that 'someone' in Justice had some help in the Bureau," Janet pointed out. This comment elicited a gas-pain expression from Farnsworth. Then Assistant Director Greer himself was on the secure link.

Farnsworth briefed him on what had been agreed. Greer immediately overruled the RA's plan to send just Carter and some backup agents to pick Kreiss up. "You go yourself, and take along every swinging dick in the office," he ordered. "I want nothing going wrong here. The last time you sent people to that goddamned arsenal, it blew up in your faces, literally."

"Sir, Kreiss is nervous," Farnsworth said. "He sees a crowd, he may change his mind."

"Then make sure he doesn't *see* a goddamned crowd. Now, you think he has evidence? Real evidence? Not just opinions?"

"I think if all he had were opinions, he wouldn't have been hammered the way he was five years ago. I think he has something, and now that all that shit about the labs has resurfaced, those people are scared of it. But first and foremost, we must get the daughter back, or nothing good happens. Kreiss without the daughter is useless."

"Then make it happen. Pick him up and get him up here, *with* his evidence. Quickly, before our dear friends down at Justice figure out what's happening. Once the director evaluates the situation, we'll make the appropriate calls and get the daughter back."

"What if they won't?"

"Won't what?"

"Give the daughter back. What if they insist we give them Kreiss before they'll let the daughter go?"

"Once he gives us his evidence, I don't give a shit about what happens to Kreiss. He embarrassed the Bureau. The spooks can have him. Believe me, we don't have to go public with what we know to achieve the desired effect."

Farnsworth opened his mouth to say something but then closed it. Janet was staring at the secure phone in disbelief. Greer told them to get moving and hung up. Farnsworth put the phone down slowly, as if it were very fragile.

"Son of a bitch," he said softly.

"Amen to that," Janet said, sitting down in a chair by the phone console.

"I never agreed to anything like that with Kreiss," he said. "He shows his evidence, we send it up the line, and they force those people to recall their operative and get the girl back. That's the fucking deal. I never agreed to turn Kreiss over to anybody."

"But in a way, you just did," she pointed out.

"No, I did not," the RA said, his jaw jutting out. "Kreiss used to be one of us. It wasn't like *he* went dirty. I don't care what he knows or what he did up there in D.C.; I'm not going to be part of just handing him over to some bunch of out-of-control spooks."

"Let's take it one step at a time," she said. "Let's get to Kreiss. See his so-called evidence. I also want to know what happened with Jared McGarand; I think that his getting killed may have been an accident. And what he did up there in that car? Well, considering where they were taking him, I'd have tried the same thing, only I'd have probably screwed it up. But first, let's get Kreiss. Nothing happens until we have him."

Farnsworth nodded, staring down at the phone as if it smelled bad. "Okay," he said. "Find Keenan. We'll need everybody."

Kreiss approached the bunker from the front, along the gravel road that led between one row of bunkers and the next, staying close to the mounded structures in case a security patrol popped over the hill behind him. The bunker number was still visible, black lettering on a dirty white field: 887. The ramp leading down to the heavy steel doors showed no signs of recent human activity. There was a large rusty-looking padlock on the huge steel airtight door, just like all the rest of the bunkers had. The grass growing around the bunker was a foot deep, starting at the front face of the bunker and growing all the way around it, making it look like the bunker had grown naturally out of the ground. The building appeared to be 150 feet long.

Kreiss walked down the gravel and concrete ramp and examined the lock. It was securely made; there were no bright metal scratches to show evidence of any tampering. The steel door was blast-resistant, with heavy airtight seals overlapping its mounting. There was some Army nomenclature on the side of the lock, so it was probably part of a series set. He walked back up the ramp and around to the side of the bunker, climbing through the thick wet grass to stand at the bottom of the rounded top. The front ventilator was still; the rear one was just barely moving, making a repetitive pinging noise as a rusty bearing complained. But it was definitely moving. Stepping softly, he climbed up the rounded concrete top of the bunker, sliding his feet instead of stepping. That concrete was probably a foot thick, but if there was someone inside, he didn't want to be heard. When he got to the rear ventilator cowl, he smelled kerosene smoke. It was very faint, but recognizable. He put his nose to the cowl and the smell was stronger. Kerosene lantern or heater in there.

Someone was in the bunker. And since the front door was locked tight from the outside, there must be another way in. He slid back down the roof of the bunker and walked all the way around it. It was solid, with no other entrances or exits. He checked the boundary area where the grass met the sloping concrete of the structure, looking for a trapdoor, but it was all solid ground. He looked back up at the ventilator, then went to the front of the bunker and climbed to the front cowl. He sniffed that, but there was no smell of anything but the wet grass on his boots. He studied it, then went to the back cowl to see what was different, and he found it immediately.

The base of the rear ventilator cowl was hinged. The hinges had been tack-welded on and then painted flat black to match the tar that sealed the cowl flashing to the concrete. The tarred flashing, however, was gone. He put his fingers under the base of the cowling and lifted just a tiny bit. The whole structure moved. He went back to the front cowling and tried the same thing. Solid as a rock. He shuffled back to the rear cowling, looked on the side opposite the hinges, and saw a crude latch. The latch was made so that the ventilator cowling wouldn't move sideways if the turbine head really began to spin. He was willing to bet there was a ladder down there.

He squatted down on the roof of the bunker. Someone was hiding in there. Now who would be hiding out in the ammunition-storage area of an abandoned military facility? No, not military. Civilian. This place had been a GOCO installation—government-owned, commercially operated. McGarand had run this whole installation as the chief chemical engineer. He had set up his hydrogen laboratory in the most secure building on the site, the one that offered the most sound and physical insulation, the power plant. That must have taken months of effort. He had set up traps along the approach perimeter, and he had rigged the industrial area itself to destruct if anybody came around to take a serious look. Which meant he had had all the time in the world to prepare something like this, for the aftermath of his revenge bombing. If the kids hadn't come along, he would probably still be living in Blacksburg, watching the feds reel from another bombing that, somewhat like the OK City bombing, had no clear motivations. The bunker farm was a perfect place to hide, just like the industrial area had been the perfect place for a bomb factory. It was another case of hiding in almost plain sight: The one place no one would look for McGarand would be back in the damned arsenal. It had to be McGarand.

He stood up. McGarand had held his daughter prisoner for almost a month, after allowing the other two kids to die in a flash flood like bugs.

Then he had simply walked away, leaving Lynn in the nitro building to starve. This was an opportunity for justice such as rarely had come along in his previous life in law enforcement. He walked down the bunker roof and out to the gravel lane, looking along the ditches. He finally found what he was searching for, a piece of thin steel rod, about two feet long. It was rusted but still solid. He climbed back to the top of the bunker and quietly inserted the rod through the latch at the edge of the cowling base. Then he bent the two ends up to form a wide vee, so that the rod could not be shaken out. The hinges were solid steel and mounted on the outside. The cowling surrounding the turbine head was heavy steel, designed to allow a controlled release of combustion gases should the ammunition that had been stored there ever cook off. Rusty, covered in bird lime, but solid steel. Then he went down and found a stick, brought it back up, and jammed it roughly into the turbine housing, stopping the motion. No motion, no reason for anyone else to notice there was anything different about this bunker. And, best of all, McGarand had locked the front steel door from the outside before climbing back in through the ventilator.

He slid back down the concrete and examined his handiwork. Then he remembered the plastic bags out on the fence line. Even better. He trotted back out to the fence line, gathered up three of the largest plastic trash bags, and returned to the bunker. He climbed back up and hooded the front vent grill with one of the bags. Then he covered the immobilized vent with the other two. Before knotting on the final piece, he fished in his backpack and extracted Lynn's weather-beaten high school ball cap, which he had carried with him ever since recovering it from the logjam. He pushed it through the grill, dropping it into the bunker below, and then finished wrapping plastic over the vent grill. The bunker was now sealed. In twelve hours or so, there would be no more oxygen in there, even less time if McGarand kept a kerosene lamp going.

"Burn in hell, Browne McGarand," he said not so quietly.

At noon, Janet Carter checked through the arsenal's main gate in a Bureau car and drove down into what was left of the industrial area. The new civilian security guards reported that an ATF forensics team was going to be on the site today, although they had not signed in yet. She told him that there would be four more vehicles with FBI agents coming behind her. She parked her Bureau car near the windowless administrative building at the top of the hill, shut it down, and opened the car's windows. She could see what she assumed to be the ATF CSU van down near the rubble of the power plant, but not the technicians. The hole in the main street, into which she had driven her car, was still visible. Several of the overhead pipe frames had been blown down in the blast and remained where they had fallen, looking like piles of steel spaghetti in the now-cluttered street. The windows in the administrative building had been blown through the building and into the parking lot, which sparkled as if covered in new frost. There was a fifteen-foot-high ring of rubble surrounding the site of the power plant.

Farnsworth and Keenan had worked up a quick plan back in the Roanoke office. They would post two-man teams at the known incursion points, such as the rail spur, the back gates, and the creek penstock. The rest of the tactical squad would go through the main gate and then deploy on foot into the tree line overlooking the open meadow above the industrial area. Farnsworth had briefed Abel Mecklen, the SAC of the Roanoke ATF office, as to what they would be doing at the arsenal, and he had requested that the ATF launch one of their small surveillance planes. The aircraft would be tasked to orbit the arsenal perimeter at ten thousand feet with its engine muffled. A county hospital MedLift helicopter was put on short standby at the hospital pad; after their last exciting visit to the arsenal, Farnsworth was taking no chances.

The RA had taken AD Greer's direction literally and pulled everyone into the operation, even Billy Smith, who was again assigned to tactical communications. Janet, like the rest of the agents, had changed into tactical gear: jumpsuit, Kevlar vest, tactical equipment belt, and FBI ball cap. She had a portable radio with collar microphone and her SIG was holstered on her right hip. Her personal .38 revolver was in the glove compartment. She looked at her watch: The tactical radio circuit would be established in twenty minutes, after which the various elements of the team would check in on-station. After that, she would be cleared to do whatever she needed to do to find Kreiss. Which was probably nothing, she realized. Kreiss would probably just step out of one of these wrecked buildings and come over to the car. That's when it might get hard.

She still had a residual headache from the carbon monoxide, and she would have loved to have had a bottle of oxygen to suck on for a while. Goddamned woman. The frustrating thing was that once they had Kreiss and could get what he had into the right channels, they would then all have to wait some more, for the right pressure to be applied and the Agency's black widow to turn loose her hostage. The nagging question in the back of Janet's head hadn't changed: What if Misty wouldn't go along?

What if she had gone off the tracks and was now engaged in some personal vendetta against Kreiss? If this didn't work for some reason, and Kreiss didn't get Lynn back, there would be hell to pay. Coupled with the implied treachery in what AD Greer had said, she felt pretty uncomfortable about Kreiss's prospects.

She shook her head to clear her thoughts and focused on what was going on around her. Too many what if's could be very distracting. The ATF van hadn't moved and there was still no sign of their techs. She wondered where they might be working, since most of the structures at that end were demolished or too badly damaged even to be safe. For that matter, she thought they now pretty much knew what had caused the blast: a concentration of hydrogen. Then she remembered what the civilian gate guard had said: ATF forensics hadn't signed in on-site yet. Then what—

The radio squawked in her left ear as Keenan came up on channel one, establishing the tactical net. She acknowledged when he polled the various teams. He reported that the ATF's aircraft was still at the local airport, down temporarily with a parts problem, ETA one hour. Here we go, she thought, stuff going wrong before we even get going. She scanned the wrecked buildings down the hill for signs of Kreiss. She had parked the car in plain sight, and he could surely recognize a Bu car. She looked at her watch again: 12:20. They were now in the window.

Where are you, Kreiss? she thought, beginning to feel exposed out here in the sunlight. She thought of the stark contrast between what he'd been doing for all those years, on his own, and the way the rest of the Bureau did business. Dependent solely on his wits and cunning, with no partners, no backup, no base, and no rules. Every new mission coming with its own fresh hunting license. The silence around her was palpable.

C'mon, Kreiss. This is your only hope of getting Lynn back, this, or giving yourself up to those people. Now you need us. No more Lone Ranger. She drummed her fingers on the steering wheel. The sooner the better, Kreiss.

Kreiss was in the trees above the creek, flat on his belly, scanning the entire industrial area through his binoculars. He had seen Carter drive down the main access road and park near the admin building. He was waiting to see if he could detect how much backup there would be and where they would set up. And he was curious about that van down by the flattened power plant. It looked like a CSU van, except there was no lettering of any kind to identify whose CSU might be there. He couldn't see the license plate, either. He knew ATF would work a scene like this for weeks, even if they had already figured out what had happened. They liked to gather a ton of evidence, and bomb sites often yielded literally tons of evidence.

He scrunched around in the pine needles to get a better visual line on the van. Ford, full-sized, tan. It could be a piece of the FBI backup team, too. Except he was pretty sure he remembered seeing it earlier, when he had gone into the bunker farm. He studied it carefully. The windows facing into the morning sun were clear; the others, toward the back, still had dew on them. It had definitely been there awhile. He scanned up the street to Carter's Bu car; he couldn't make out the details of her face, but it looked like her, sitting alone in the driver's seat.

He continued to scan right, up into the tree line where the road from the main gate came out into the industrial area. That's where the bulk of the backup team would be, he figured. And probably at the other entrances to the arsenal. He rolled over on his back, looked into the sky, and listened. No airplanes, or not yet anyway. The empty bright sky made his eyes water. It was tempting to close his eyes and just relax there, safe in the pine needles among all these silent trees. The birds had quit worrying about him. So what was he waiting for? He rolled back over. Two things: Farnsworth's question about where he was, exactly, and that van. The RA had probably just been trying to figure out where to deploy his backup team. In any event, he couldn't do anything about Farnsworth. The van was something else. It might be FBI, ATF, or even local law.

Or it might be Misty.

Why would she be here at the arsenal? She could hide anywhere, and, unlike McGarand, she had not had that much time to prepare a place here. More likely, he thought, she had a source inside the Bureau and knew why Carter was here. Her mission was to bring him in. A straight retrieval. That was the only logical explanation for her taking Lynn hostage: They didn't want Lynn. They wanted him. And Misty would trade. If she was here, and watching, he would have to be very damned careful about getting to Carter's car. He began sliding back into the woods, and then he stopped as it hit him.

Ford, full-sized, tan. My God, he thought. Was that the van he'd rented in Washington and left at the strip mall? Wasn't that his van?

Janet acknowledged a second station poll on the tactical net, confirming again that she was in position. It was getting warm in the car, especially in the vest, and she was tempted to move into the tiny bit of shade of the admin building, on the other side from where she was parked now. But that would put the building between her and her backup, and her instincts told her not to do that. Farnsworth came up and asked if she saw anything going on. She reported that there was nothing moving. Then she asked if the ATF Crime Scene people had been backed out during the pickup window.

"What ATF Crime Scene people?" Farnsworth asked. She told him about the van down by the power plant. Farnsworth told her to stand by, then, a few minutes later, came back. "ATF does not have any people or vehicles on the installation. Describe the van."

Janet asked him to wait and then got out of the car. She put binoculars on the van and described it to the RA. She could not get a license plate. She asked if he wanted her to go down there. He told her to stand by. She knew that he didn't want to reveal the scope of the backup forces, in case Kreiss was watching and got spooked. She also didn't think he would want her to approach an unknown vehicle on her own. He came back on the net.

"Move your vehicle to a position where you can get a license plate on that van," he instructed. "Do not get out of your vehicle."

She acknowledged, got back in, and started the car. She rolled up the windows, switched on the AC, and then drove around the admin building and onto the main street. She had to go very slowly as she threaded her way through chunks of concrete and piles of other debris in the street. The toppled overhead pipe racks obstructed her way, so when she reached the first side street, she went left, down around the pushed-over remains of the wooden sheds, and then up a small rise where a water tower lay on its side like a smashed pumpkin. From this vantage, she could get the binocs on the van's back plate. She called it in to Farnsworth. He acknowledged and told her to hold her position and reiterated his instruction to stay in her car.

She looked around the area where she had parked. Behind her was the line of pine trees, and behind that, she was pretty sure, there was a creek, just over that hill. In front of her, the full scale of the blast was evident, highlighted by the bare concrete swath where the power plant had been, surrounded by a nearly perfect circle of rubble and boiler parts. The two enormous turbogenerators, wrecked and shifted off their foundations, leaned to one side in mute testimony to the force of the explosion. The shredded insulation and shattered flanges on the scattered steam pipes made them look like giant broken bones. Big black holes gaped beneath each turbogenerator, and she wondered if they led down into the water chamber at the end of the Ditch. She put the car in park, shut it down, and rolled her window down. A small building whose roof was gone provided a patch of shadow for the car, for which she was duly grateful.

"It's a rental," Farnsworth reported. "Rented two days ago in northern Virginia, along with a cell phone. We're waiting now for headquarters to get the info on the drivers license. The contract is in the name of a John Smith, who paid cash."

"I'll bet that's Kreiss's vehicle," she said.

"And you'd be right," a voice behind her said softly. She turned and found Kreiss crouching by her door, a finger to his lips. "Hold your position and report any movement," Farnsworth was saying.

She acknowledged, while Kreiss walked around the back to the other side and let himself into the front seat. He asked her to roll the window down on his side. He was dressed in a camo jumpsuit, head hood, a pack front and back, and a heavy equipment belt, not unlike her own, which was strapped around his waist. A large automatic, probably a .45, was slung under the left side of his chest pack, ready for a cross-draw. He smelled of pine needles and wet mud.

"Well, Special Agent," he said in a tired voice, "here we are."

She didn't say anything as he took off the hood. His face was gaunt with fatigue, and his normally well-trimmed beard was a little ragged around the edges. His eyes were red-rimmed, but alert, looking at her while keeping a watchful eye on their surroundings, as if he were expecting something dangerous to spring out of the rubble.

"Do you think she's here?" Janet asked. "Not Lynn. That woman?"

"It's possible," he said. "That van down there? I left it in a shopping center parking lot last night." He patted his front pack. "I still have the keys."

"So how did it get here?"

"Beats the shit out of me, but someone with the right resources could manage it. I thought maybe you guys had moved it here."

"Nope," she said.

"Bad sign," he said as he scanned the area again. "So what happens now?"

"I tell them you're here and then we leave," she said, getting a little anxious about the possible presence of Misty. "Sooner rather then later, okay?"

"What about Lynn?"

"You give headquarters what they need, they pressure the Agency to get that woman to release Lynn."

"And what if she doesn't?" he asked, echoing her own earlier question.

Then the vehicle's cell phone rang. Kreiss looked at her. She shook her head. "Moot point now, I suspect," he said with a wintry smile. Janet had no idea of who might be calling her vehicle's cell phone when there was a tactical radio net up. She picked it up. "Carter," she said. Her voice cracked and she cleared it.

"Let me talk to him," the woman's voice said.

"No," Janet said.

"Don't be an ass, Carter. How do you think I knew *when* to make this call?"

"I don't care," Janet said.

"Yes, you do. I'm looking at you through a sniper scope. Want proof?"

"Tell me what you want."

"You know exactly what I want. Kreiss."

Then Kreiss was reaching for the phone. Janet didn't want to hand it over, but something in his eyes made her yield. Then he slid across the seat so she could listen to both sides of the conversation. She was suddenly very aware of him as the front seat dipped under his weight. She hadn't realized how large he was.

"Speak," he said.

"I have your daughter. I will release her, now, as long as you get out of that car and go back into the woods until the feebs leave."

Kreiss was trying to scan the area outside the car without turning his head.

"I've had a better offer," he said. "I'm going to give these people something, and then they're going to make your people an offer they can't refuse."

"And then what happens to you?"

"What?"

"I said, what happens to you?"

"I get to live in peace."

"And you believe that?"

"Why not? They get the smoking gun and a lock on Justice that even Hoover would love. And your people basically shouldn't care. Your traitor blew his brains out five years ago up in Millwood."

"Palace games, Edwin," she said. "You've never cared for palace games.

And you think you can come in from the cold once you've done this, do you? A grateful Bureau welcoming the exiled hero back into the family, right? Listen to this."

There was a pause, and then, to Janet's shocked amazement, Farnsworth's conversation with Howell Greer was playing back to them. She cringed when she heard Greer's words about Kreiss being expendable. She stared rigidly out the windshield, holding her breath, unable to meet his eyes when it was over. That damned woman had someone *in* the Roanoke office. Someone who had had access to secure communications, *while* they were being transmitted. Oh shit, *Billy*?

Farnsworth's voice came over her collar radio. Kreiss, not letting go of the phone, ripped the mike off her shoulder and threw it out the window.

"Edwin," the woman said. "I've been sent to retrieve you. I'm not leaving until I do. Here's the real deal: You get out of that car and walk back up into the woods. If you don't, I'll drop your daughter down one of these deep holes I keep finding here."

Janet saw Kreiss's hand close on the phone handset so hard that it began to crack.

"Edwin," the woman continued. "You get out of the car and she gets to walk away. You have my word, which you now know is a lot more reliable than your precious Bureau's word, isn't it? Then I'll give you an hour or two. Let's wait until dark. Then we'll work it out, you and me. Sound and light, like old times. You can even try to stop me. But this way, what happens to your daughter is up to *you*, not some faceless bureaucrat in Washington."

Kreiss said nothing, staring straight ahead.

"It's a no-brainer, Edwin."

He hesitated, then said, "I need a minute."

"Take a lot. Take two. I know where to find you."

The phone subsided into a hissing noise. Janet was paralyzed: She absolutely did not know what to do. Kreiss closed his eyes and then the handset shattered in his white-knuckled grip. Janet tried to think of an argument, a reason, *any* reason for him not to take the woman's deal, but she knew there wasn't one. Not after what he'd heard Assistant Director Greer say. Son of a *bitch*!

"I'm trying to think of an argument not to do what she wants," she said. "For the life of me, I can't."

"There isn't one," he said, dropping the broken handset onto the seat and moving back to his side of the front seat, his hand opening and closing.

"Can you tell me what it is the bosses want so badly?" she asked.

"A graphic file. A picture of a letter. Signed by the deputy AG. Garrette himself. Sent to Ephraim Glower. Telling him that Justice was attaching one of his bank accounts."

Janet didn't understand. "Why is that important?"

He rubbed the sides of his face with his hands. Then he turned to look at her, his eyes hollow. His expression scared her. "Glower didn't kill himself and his family because he was going to be uncovered as a servant of the Chinese government. He killed himself because *they* took the money back."

"What money? And who is 'they'?"

"The money he'd been paid to derail the espionage investigation for all those years. He'd run through the family fortune, but this Chinese money was going to save his ass. When they got caught taking the illegal campaign contributions—you know, the Hong Kong connection money—the reelection committee opted to give it all back. Some of that, a couple of million, had been used to pay off Glower. So they used Justice to get the IRS to attach Glower's bank accounts. That meant Glower was now broke again. That's why he did it."

"The reelection committee knew about Glower? My God! That means—"

"Yeah," he said, scanning the area around the car again. "Anyone who has that letter can tie the Chinese campaign contributions to a quid pro quo: a fee paid for services rendered. Access to our nuclear weapons secrets in return for several millions in campaign contributions. Not directly, of course. Through the Hong Kong cutout. Basically, anyone who knows the case would recognize the letter as the smoking gun. Only problem was, the political side lost their nerve. What a surprise."

She took a deep breath and tried to get her mind around all this. "What was your deal?" she asked. "When you were terminated?"

"Glower called Agency security to have me thrown out of his house that day I went to confront him. But I went back a few hours later. Found him and his entire family slaughtered. Very obvious suicide. Maybe too obvious, now that I think about it. Like that White House lawyer? Anyhow, he had a wall safe. I broke into it, found the letter."

"They found the safe, they knew somebody knew too much."

"Something like that. Initially, they didn't know who, or what. Later, after the investigation, they began to figure it out. They knew it had to be me, so they threatened the only remaining thing of value I had: Lynn.

The threat was pretty clear. If I agreed to remain silent, they agreed to leave her alone."

"Why didn't they just move against you?"

"Because by then, I had a lock on them: AD Marchand was part of it. He'd been taking care of the FBI end. I let Marchand know that I had documentary evidence on the real reason Glower killed himself. Anything happened to me or Lynn, there was a mechanism in place that would guarantee that information would get to the appropriate congressional committee chairmen. When I told Marchand what it was, he just about fainted. Basically, I had a gun to the administration's head. They had a gun to Lynn's head. A lock."

"And it held until Lynn disappeared," she said. "Oh, *that's* why they came, not because of any phony bomb cell. With her gone, you had no more reason to keep quiet."

"Precisely, Special Agent." He sighed. "Only there *was* a bomb cell, wasn't there. That was the kicker. Browne McGarand and his merry band."

"What would happen if Greer and the director got their hands on this letter?"

"They'll burn Marchand and Garrette right down. After that, it's whatever deal the director wants to make with the attorney general herself. Based on all the friction these past five years, they'll have a lot to talk about, don't you think? Problem is, now I can't give it to you."

"*What!* Why not?"

"I've already explained that. Lynn."

She stared out the window for a moment. "You're wrong, you know," she said. "About the lock. They will have learned from all this. You get Lynn back this time, they'll just send someone else. There's an infinite supply of *them*. Even if you take that woman out there, they'll tap someone else. Someone maybe worse than she is. You have to turn loose of what you know. That's the only thing that'll put this thing to rest."

He started to say something, to argue with her, but then stopped. He was listening. She went for broke.

"The problem with your so-called lock is that you're just one individual," she said. "Okay, you're Edwin Kreiss. But the G's gotten too big. Too powerful. Trust me, I'm part of it—I know. One man? No chance. Lynn will never be safe until you give up what you have to another government agency. Let *them* get a lock. Hoover-style. Then everyone will leave you alone. Otherwise, you're condemned to a permanent hunting season."

She stopped. She was almost afraid to look at him. She could feel his anger. The clock on the dashboard advanced silently, each increment increasing the tension between them.

"You mean give the Bureau the lock."

"Exactly. The organization can make it stick. As a lone individual, you can't. No disrespect intended."

He took a deep breath and let it out in a prolonged sigh.

"What the hell," he said finally through clenched teeth. "I'm getting too old for this shit. I hid it in Marchand's own archives, FCI Division."

"Sweet Jesus," she whispered. "It's right there? In the fucking Hoover Building?"

"Right there. File name: Year of the Rat. Just like that book. Password: Amoral." He gave a cold smile. "Think they'll be embarrassed?"

Janet could just imagine. "What happens now?" she asked.

He looked at his watch. "I just made a deal, and now I need to ask another favor. I need you to cover Lynn for a while, once Misty releases her."

"And you?"

"She has orders to retrieve me," he said, pulling down his hood. "I have other plans. One of us will prevail. Will you take care of Lynn for me?"

"Yes, of course, but—"

He opened the door and got out. Then he leaned back in. "If I survive this, you'll eventually know about it. But I'm going to have to go under-ground for a while until the elephants sort things out in Washington."

Knowing she might not ever see him again, she felt she had to ask. "What was it like being on your own for all those years? Hunting people down, making up the rules as you went along?"

He stared down at her for a moment. "You mean without the FBI Manual? Without a squad supervisor, and the ASAC and the SAC, and a fistful of teletypes from some ad hoc committee in Washington telling you to go right, when to go left? What was that like?"

"Yes."

"It was amazing. It was every G-man's dream, Special Agent. Until I came up with the right answer to the wrong politicians."

"Come in with us," she said impulsively. "Once she lets Lynn go."

His weary eyes smiled at her. "Can't do that, Special Agent. You know how it is: You can fall in love with the Bureau, but the Bureau never falls in love with you. Take care of Lynn."

Then he was gone, loping up the hill and into the trees like some big cat.

"Wait," she tried to say, but the word died in her throat. She got out to look for the speaker microphone, found it, and stuck the jack back into the wiring harness on her left collar shoulder. Farnsworth was yelling. "Carter? What the hell's going on down there, Carter? *Carter!* Come in, damn it!"

"Kreiss was here; now he's gone," she said. Her chest felt constricted by her sense of failure. "I'm going to wait for Lynn Kreiss. I'm returning to the admin building position. Request you meet me there."

"Goddamn it, Carter, what the hell is going *on?*"

"Request you meet me at the admin building," she said again. "For what it's worth, I believe we have achieved AD Greer's objective."

Kreiss pushed into the tree line, hit the ground, rolled to the right, and then scurried through the underbrush for fifty feet before stopping. He then crawled back to a point from which he could see down into the industrial area. Carter's car was moving back toward the admin building, its tires crunching through gravel and broken glass. The van was still sitting there. He felt his pulse throbbing from the dash up the hill, during which he'd half-expected to hear a rifle shot. But maybe Misty had developed a sporting side. He, on the other hand, would have made that deal and then dropped his quarry as soon as he appeared.

Carter had stopped the car on the power plant side of the admin building. In the distance, he heard other vehicles coming as the Bureau's backup brigade closed in. Then he saw Lynn emerge from the wreckage of the turbo generator building beside the power plant's foundations, hesitantly at first, shielding her eyes against the sunlight, as if she had been blindfolded. She took three steps out into the debris field, stumbled over something, recovered, stopped, and looked around.

Move, goddamn it, *move*, Kreiss thought. The first of the backup cars reached Carter, spilling agents. Lynn had to see them, but she still wasn't moving and seemed disoriented. He needed to get Lynn out of there. He drew the big .45 from his chest holster and sighted down the stubby barrel at the nearest of the two ruined generators behind her. It was a distance of at least two hundred yards, so he elevated the barrel, pointing it at least a foot over the top of the generator, and fired once. The booming sound of the .45 echoed across all the wrecked buildings in the industrial area, dropping all the agents, including Carter, instantly to the ground. The bullet, partially spent, hit the base of the generator well behind Lynn, causing her to yelp and take off up the main street at a dead run toward the cars and the agents huddling behind them at the top of the street.

Kreiss backed away from the tree line. He had accomplished two things: made Lynn move, and told Misty that, for once, he had a gun. He was deciding what to do next when something blasted an entire branch off the tree under which he was hiding, followed by the distinctive *crack-boom* of a big rifle. Misty answering in kind: I know where you are, and I, too, have a gun.

The agents must be going nuts down there, he thought with a small smile. Then he squirmed farther back into the woods and began crawling, head down, as fast as he could go, east this time, away from the power plant. His objective was the patch of trees that projected down to the area where the wooden mixing sheds had been. It was about five hundred yards, line of sight, but longer the way he went through the woods. From there, maybe he could get back into the wreckage of the industrial area. Misty was down there somewhere, in among that ring of rubble surrounding the remains of the power plant. She would expect him to stay in the woods, where he was most proficient. He intended to travel in a large circle, staying literally on the ground, moving slow enough to keep the wildlife from revealing his position. He would creep for an hour, then dig in and rest, making his move back into the industrial area right after dark. He didn't think Misty would come out until after dark, either, especially if the Bureau people hung around.

He hoped they wouldn't linger after Carter told her boss about the archive. Farnsworth should see where his interests lay and invoke standard procedure: They had the hostage clear and a line to the evidence, which was all his bosses really wanted. What happened back at the arsenal after that shouldn't matter, especially to the big guns at Bureau headquarters, where life in the fast lane was probably about to get really interesting.

Janet didn't hesitate after getting Lynn into her car. She took off, turning the car in a screech of tires and gunning it up the hill toward where Farnsworth and the rest of the backup team were waiting. The other two cars followed, once they were sure she had the hostage out of harm's way. She made Lynn put her head down on the front seat until she thought they were well out of rifle range. Fucking Kreiss, letting off that cannon. But it had done the job.

"You okay?" she shouted as she maneuvered noisily around a pile of concrete blocks.

"Yes," Lynn said. "She had me blindfolded. I didn't see anything useful. Thanks for the rescue. Again."

"My pleasure, but it was your father who got you out, not me."

"Dad? Here? Where is he?"

"Up there in the woods somewhere. I think he's going to have it out with that woman, now that you're clear."

Lynn sat up, biting her lip as Janet pulled up alongside Farnsworth's car. He was sitting in the right-rear seat, with the window open, a radio mike in his hand. His driver had his gun out and was searching the industrial area with binoculars. Janet got out to explain what had happened, while Lynn laid her head back on the back of the front seat and closed her eyes.

"Goddamn it," he said. "We were supposed to bring him in."

"Begging your pardon, sir, we were supposed to bring in the evidence he has."

He gave her an exasperated look. "So? Where the hell is it?"

She leaned forward and whispered what Kreiss had told her. He blinked, then gave a slow whistle of surprise. "In Marchand's own archive system? Man!"

"I believe we can access that archive right here from Roanoke."

"But we're not going to," he said, shaking his head. "I'm gonna let AD Greer and his people go grab that little buzz saw."

"Don't you want to see it? After all this?"

"Hell no," he said. "And neither do you. Look what happened to Kreiss for knowing what he knows. Where is he anyway?"

"Out there in the weeds," she said. "And that woman is down there somewhere, in all that rubble around the power plant. That's where that second shot seemed to come from."

The other agents were gathering around, looking for orders. Farnsworth thought for a moment, then announced they were pulling out, that their mission was complete.

"I thought we were supposed to pick up some guy along with the girl," one of the squad supervisors said. Keenan, taking his cue from Farnsworth, gave him a signal to back off, and then Farnsworth told everyone to mount up and get back to Roanoke. He told one of the agents to drive Janet's car; Janet and Lynn Kreiss were to get in his car.

Lynn Kreiss stared out the back window of the car as they pulled out.

She shivered when she thought of what they'd be doing come nightfall. She could never do that. She wondered if Lynn knew what was going to happen back there. Of course she did.

Kreiss made his move an hour after sunset, before the chill air of night cooled the ground enough to provide too great an infrared contrast between his body and his surroundings. The sky had clouded over during the afternoon, rendering the darkness almost absolute once the sun went down. But Misty was an active sweeper. She would have a real IR surveillance device, maybe even an illuminator and receiver set, not just a nightscope. IR devices created images based on the contrast between warm objects and a cold background, or vice versa. The greater the contrast, the clearer the image. He crept out of the tree line on his belly and snaked down as fast as he could, hugging the bottom of a swale he had scouted earlier. He was also assuming that Misty was still down in the vicinity of the power plant's ruins. That van was still there, and there now seemed to be a bioluminescent glow emanating from the ring of rubble surrounding the flattened plant. She might have deployed a defensive light ring, which was a thin, flexible tube of clear plastic Lucite, the diameter of a straw, filled with the material contained in Chem-Lights. It created a faint green glow that could be used to illuminate a defensive perimeter for hours without degrading the defender's night vision. He had chosen his vantage point because it put several buildings between him and the rubble around the power plant.

His immediate objective was a valve pit where a dozen of the big overhead pipes came down into a walled enclosure, which was twenty feet square. There were mounds of rubble from collapsed buildings on three sides, and what looked like a storm drain coming out on the fourth side, pointing down into the swale. The swale, a shallow, grassy ditch, cut across a gentle slope of deep grass. He was able to crawl through it to the storm drainpipe, which was nearly three feet in diameter. He went through the drainpipe for ten feet, sweeping a stick ahead to rustle any lurking snakes out, and emerged out onto the concrete floor of the valve pit. There was a carpet of small rubble on the floor, and he had to sweep some of it out of the way with his forearm as he pulled himself across the floor between the huge steel valve stems. The pipes over his head were large, twelve to twenty inches in diameter. Some were lagged with insulation; others were bare metal. The ones that bent down into the floor of the valve pit pointed in the direction of the Ditch.

He had chosen the pit because it offered concealment, while remaining escapable. Going into one of the ruined buildings would have been risky; she could trap him in or on top of a building. The big pipes, being metal, would also offer some infrared masking, at least until the cool night air drained all the heat out of the metal. The valve pit was at the end of one of the shorter side streets. It was less than a city block from the main street, and the concrete buildings from that intersection on up the hill toward the admin building remained pretty much intact. All of the buildings below that intersection had been seriously damaged, having lost at least one wall. The four buildings nearest the power plant had been flattened into mounds of broken concrete, surrounded by tangled ropes of steel pipes. The shattered concrete was visible only as big blobs of gray in the near-total darkness.

He extracted his sound-cone apparatus and assembled it up on the lip of the concrete wall surrounding the pit. He pointed it between the nearest buildings, in the general direction of where the power plant had been. He reminded himself to keep thinking in terms of infrared contrast. He piled some pieces of rubble around the cone to ensure it would blend in with the rest of the structure's IR signature. Then he pulled out another plastic pouch and extracted two golf ball–sized cubes and a coil of very thin wire. He took one of the cubes and crawled along the pit wall, keeping the top of the wall between him and the power plant. He set the cube on the left corner of the pit, placing it between a pipe fragment and a broken concrete block. He connected some wire to it, then brought the other end of the wire back into the pit, burying the wire as best he could. He repeated this procedure with the second cube, taking it in the opposite direction. Once back down in the pit, he connected the two wire ends to a cigarette package–sized plastic box and set it down. Crouching down behind the pit wall, he extracted a small battery pack and attached it to the plastic box. Then he activated the box, illuminating a small red window. In the window was a scrolling menu of sounds stored digitally in the box. He could select a different sound for each of the two channels going out to the miniaturized speakers, or a stereo signal through both at once. He set the box down and turned the digital window down to minimum brightness. Then he took out a pair of silver-mirrored sunglasses and put them on. He couldn't see anything in the darkness anyway, and these would give him some protection in case she got close enough to pop a disrupter in his face. The coating on the glasses was keyed to the color frequency of the disrupter. Then he crawled as quietly as he could around the bottom of the pit, patting the floor with his gloved hands until he found a flat piece of metal about a foot square. He slid this into the back of his chest pack. Then he went back to the wall nearest the power plant, slipped the stethoscope on, crouched down behind the wall as comfortably as he could, and settled in to listen.

He was able to train the cone across an arc of about fifty degrees, which was sufficient if his assumptions were correct. She could, of course, come from any direction at all, but he had watched the industrial area for most of the afternoon and had seen no sign of her. The light ring meant either that she was there or it was a distraction. Since he couldn't know which, all he could do was make his assumptions. He tried to clear his mind and concentrate on the soundscape in front of him. The air was not moving, and neither was anything else, if the cone was working correctly. He reached up and trained the cone slowly from side to side, straining to detect any differences in the earphones. Nothing. He touched the butt of the .45 hanging in its shoulder holster. He didn't have any spare ammunition. He drank some water, closed his eyes, and listened. He wondered if McGarand was still alive. He hoped so.

He had no illusions that Misty was coming to talk to him or even to take him in. She was coming to kill him. Those had probably been her orders all along, once the Agency headquarters found out that Lynn was missing. They'd have known full well that if Lynn was dead, and that would have been the logical assumption when a kid had been missing for that long, then the lock was open. Kreiss would have had no incentive to keep quiet anymore. Worse, Kreiss might have thought the Agency had taken Lynn, which would have given him every incentive to reveal what he knew. The solution would have been the same either way they looked at it: This wasn't a retrieval operation. He had become the mother of all loose ends.

Something clicked in the stethoscope.

Janet stood looking out the window of their fourth-floor room in the Donaldson-Brown Center. Lynn was on the bed, fully dressed, staring at the muted TV screen. The remains of a room-service meal was sitting on the table. Janet could see the Virginia Tech campus stretching before her, a small city of crenellated academic buildings, barrackslike dorms, and streetlights. The sidewalks were surprisingly filled with students moving between the buildings like so many industrious ants. Typical engineering school, she thought. Labs all night. Computer time when you could get it.

The streetlights were crowned with fuzzy halos as the evening atmosphere thickened.

Farnsworth had set up a debriefing session with Lynn Kreiss upon return to the federal building and then closeted himself in the secure-communications pod, with no operator this time, for an hour and a half. When he finally came out, he had ordered them into the hotel as a protective measure. There were supposedly four agents downstairs in a loose perimeter.

Janet didn't think they were in any danger, because that woman would be busy. Kreiss was definitely in danger, however, based on the look on his face when he'd left the car. She had argued as vehemently as she could that they ought to go back out there, in force, and retrieve him. Farnsworth had given her a strange look when she used that particular word, but he remained adamant: Their mission was complete. AD Greer and a horde of executive assistants from the director's office were probably combing through the FCI archives as she stood looking out the window. Once they found the document, all hell would break loose, especially with a national election looming. Or, more likely, and as Kreiss had predicted, an extremely private deal would be made at the highest levels of the Justice Department, and the Bureau would enjoy a sudden degree of unprecedented operational freedom.

Lynn hadn't said three words since they'd left the federal building. Janet had explained what Kreiss had told her on the way to the hotel, and the girl had just nodded. She was obviously deeply disturbed that the Bureau had chosen to throw her father to whatever wolf was waiting in the ruins of the arsenal. She'd given Farnsworth a look of such reproach that he had actually blushed. Now they had orders to stay at the hotel and wait to see what, if anything, broke loose in Washington. The ATF was still hunting McGarand, but that particular mad bomber had simply disappeared. Janet wondered if he, too, was out there at the demolished arsenal. Probably not.

She had mixed emotions about what they'd done. It was 11:30, and Leno was doing his monologue. Somehow, none of it seemed very funny tonight. Yes, Kreiss had made this deal, and gotten his daughter out of that woman's clutches. Her own bosses were about to peel back a scab they thought would give them nearly unlimited leverage over their tormentors at Justice. That might or might not be true, she thought, given the fact that the current administration was in its final months, with not too much left to lose in terms of its already-odious legacy. Farnsworth said he was putting Janet in for an award, and he had told her to think about going back to a headquarters assignment in Washington. Janet wasn't so sure about that, either. "Palace games," the woman had said. Pretty fucking lethal palace games, Janet thought. And what Greer had done to Kreiss was just plain dishonorable. She might have made a mistake coming back to the fold.

She turned around, to find Lynn watching her. Something in the girl's expression reminded her of Kreiss. No drama, just a patient consideration of the situation and a hint, just a hint, of unexpected action if an opportunity presented itself. She and Lynn looked at each other. They had done the wrong thing.

"What would you think about going back out there?" Janet asked. "See if we can find your old man?"

Lynn sat up. "About fucking time, Special Agent," she said. "You got another gun?"

Kreiss carefully put his gloved hand on the cone to see which way it was pointing. To the right of the direct line between the valve pit and the power plant. He removed the stethoscope, closed his eyes behind the mirrored glasses, and listened hard to the bare susurrations of a night breeze filtering through the piles of debris all around him. The breeze was just enough to obscure the sounds of traffic out on Route 11. It had been three hours since he'd heard the last noise. He'd been dozing since then, which actually was part of his craft. Relax the body and concentrate the mind. Build energy reserves while that part of his brain that did the sound work listened with all the mysterious precision of the subconscious mind. He looked at his watch: 11:40. He shifted his body behind the wall, easing a cramp out of his knee. He put the stethoscope back to his ears.

Ten minutes later came another click, followed by what sounded like the rattle of a very small pebble. Something, or someone, moving out there. Misty? He pulled the glasses down again. Black night to the max. *Tenebrae factae sunt.* Darkness has fallen. Got that right.

He shifted position again, putting his left shoulder in touch with the cooling surface of the wall, his right hand now holding the .45 automatic. The tactical question was, How many people did Misty have with her? They'd sent a crew into the mountain after Janet and Lynn, but they hadn't come back out. Lost them all? That would put Misty in a rare mood, especially being defeated by a redheaded amateur. She wouldn't agree: The cave had done them in, not Janet Carter. But would she have had time to summon more backup? One-on-one against Misty was bad enough, but if she had help, this was probably hopeless.

Another click, not as loud. He reached up again and swung the cone to the right ten degrees. The faintest movement of air against his cheek told him that the weather might be changing. The night now smelled faintly of moisture against the backdrop of the pine forests surrounding the industrial area. He squeezed the stethoscope earphones harder into his ears. If Misty was moving, she'd be doing so while searching for some visual cue that he was out there. Some small patch of infrared contrast, a blob of green warmth where there shouldn't be one. He reached up again and moved the cone farther to the right. A minute passed, and then another. Then a new sound, a tiny scraping noise. Fabric over concrete? It had seemed marginally louder. He wondered if she'd done the same thing he had—parked herself in a corner and dozed for a few hours before starting the hunt. One thing about a sleeping human: If properly hidden and wedged the body didn't move. You took a chance, of course, of being caught sound asleep. It depended on how well your subconscious mind had been trained to listen. He took a deep breath, let it out quietly, and then decided it was time to get things under way.

He took out the piece of metal he had been warming inside his chest pack and placed it up on the top of the side wall. If what the cone had detected was Misty, she shouldn't be able to see the warm piece of metal until she had moved another hundred feet or so farther to his right, because of the buildings. Then he reached down for the control box and selected the third program and entered a fifteen-minute delay. He slipped off the stethoscope, brought the cone down off the wall, and buried them in loose gravel. Then he slithered silently into the big drainpipe. A minute later, he crawled out of the valve pit altogether, rounded the first street corner, and began inching toward the nearest concrete building rising above the side street that led back down to the valve pit. He crawled six feet and then stopped to listen. This was the dangerous bit: If she illuminated the area with the IR system, he was dead meat down here on the street. He repeated these movements until he reached the corner of the building. There he got up, flattened himself against the wall of the building, and went hand over hand until he felt the ladder.

This was the decision: There was only one ladder. If he went up it, he could not get down again if she detected him up there. But if this worked, and she closed in on the valve pit to investigate the infrared target he'd left for her, he'd be in a position to fire down at her. Especially if she reacted when the sound program let go. He considered the time: He had only a few more minutes to make his decision.

Did she have helpers? He decided that she didn't. Misty was supremely confident in her own abilities. She also knew that Kreiss wouldn't run very far into the woods to prolong this. He figured she was moving and scanning, crawling a few yards at a time and then sweeping the entire debris field with the IR scanner, looking for a point of contrast. Or she could have an illuminator up on some wreckage, bathing the whole debris field in invisible light. Probably had the scanner mounted on an AK-47, based on the sound of that single shot earlier this afternoon. Misty normally didn't carry a handgun, but she had always liked the heavy-duty Eastern Bloc weapons.

The wind blew in his face again, this time carrying the scent of old chemicals, overlaid with a residual whiff of nitric acid. That has to be coming from the main street, he thought. So she should be upwind of him, then, and, therefore, up-sound. He estimated the time remaining. He had to move, one way or the other, or she'd get close enough to hear him on the ladder. He started up.

Janet shut off her headlights as they coasted quietly down the hill on Route 11. The intersection marking the entrance to the arsenal was a quarter of a mile ahead, the dead traffic lights just visible before she shut off her lights. They had gone out a back fire door of the hotel and circled the block around the library to come into the parking lot from the town side, away from the front entrance. She'd called down to the lobby before they left and told one of the agents that they were going lights-out in the room. He told her to sleep tight. They'd waited a half hour before making their move. Then she and Lynn got into her Bureau car and headed for Ramsey.

Janet pulled the car into the exit lane for the arsenal. The barrels were still there, but they were no longer blocking the ramp. She drove slowly and quietly up the road toward the main gate, stopping just down the hill from the gate itself so as to minimize their engine noise. She parked to the side and shut it down. She rolled down her window and listened. She had been having second thoughts about this little caper ever since leaving downtown Blacksburg, but, given Lynn's enthusiasm, she couldn't think of a way to back out. When Farnsworth found out, she'd probably be a civilian again. Lynn had Janet's .38 in her lap and was rotating the cylinder, click by click.

"So," Janet said. "This seemed like a good idea at the time. Now I'm not so sure."

"I say we drive in there, lights and horn going," Lynn replied. "Go in there and make a shitload of noise until Dad pops out of the bushes and yells at us. Then grab him."

"Might not be that simple," Janet said. "If they were going to go after each other, that will be a free fire zone down there. Open season. We go down there, we might get ourselves killed. You heard that rifle this afternoon. Plus, if you show up, you'll distract your father. Maybe get him killed."

"If you're thinking of leaving me out here," Lynn said, "you can just forget that shit."

"I'm thinking we shouldn't go in there at all," Janet said, conscious now of the open window and how their voices might be carrying. She scanned the chain-link fences ahead of them. "Hell, it may be all over by now. But either way, we know nothing about the tactical situation. I'm saying we probably can't help, and we might even screw things up."

"Then let's call the police. The local cops, I mean. Make some hysterical phone call to nine one one; two women in trouble at the Ramsey Arsenal. Rape. Murder. Frenzied bikers. Bring a mob of cops out here and they'd have to stop it."

Janet was shaking her head. Coming out here had been a dumb idea. "They might stop it tonight, but then it would just go on. That woman and your father would melt away into the woods. I think after all that's happened—in that cave, and with the big explosion we had here—this has become personal now. The matter in Washington is being solved as we speak. I'm just afraid if we go in there now, we might do more harm than good."

"I think you're just plain afraid," Lynn said, turning away from Janet and staring through the darkened windshield.

Janet held her tongue. Of course she was afraid. Anyone who wasn't afraid of both those people down there would be an idiot. But the more she thought about it, the more she knew she was right. Of course Lynn was burning up with worry about her father, but that didn't solve the practical problem: They couldn't just drive down there. What would they do once they got inside? Offer mediation services? Counseling? She could just see herself climbing around the wreckage of the industrial area, calling for them to come out and talk things over. And if they called the local cops, they'd get one deputy sheriff. Whoopee. What they really needed here was an army of feds. No onesies and twosies, but ten Suburbans with federal SWAT troops, helicopters, dogs, tanks—

Tanks.

She picked up the car phone.

"Now what the hell are you doing?" Lynn asked.

"Getting some reinforcements," Janet said. She pulled her phone book out of her purse and looked up a number, then dialed it. The phone rang three times. She swore when she thought it was going to voice mail, but a man's voice finally answered.

"Bureau of Alcohol, Tobacco and Firearms, Special Agent Rogers speaking."

"This is Special Agent Janet Carter of the Roanoke office, FBI. I've got the gomer who blew up your Washington headquarters building cornered in the Ramsey Army Arsenal. I need some backup down here, and I need it right fucking now! My duty officer isn't picking up. You people interested?"

Kreiss reached the arched top of the ladder and, moving with excruciating care, stepped over the top rung and down—onto nothing at all. He felt himself falling and just barely managed to catch himself on the curved ladder edges. He deliberately let his hands slide down the rusty metal railings right to the mounting brackets in order to soften the noise he was making. It took all his strength just to hang there. He felt the cool night air between his legs and realized that the building's roof must have collapsed when the power plant blew up. What he had thought was a solid building was nothing more than just a side wall, with the rest of the building blown completely away. He couldn't see what was below him, but he was at least forty feet up in the air. He was entirely exposed, dangling in plain sight over the debris field below. If she happened to lift the scanner, she'd probably start laughing. He heard the metal in the railing creaking. But then the sound program saved him.

Back in the valve pit, the tape switched on. A tiny sound of a screwdriver tapping once, very gently against a steel pipe, clinked out into the night. Kreiss heard it, and he hoped like hell Misty heard it too. He tried a two-handed chin-up to pull himself back onto the ladder, but his feet did not connect with anything but air. He couldn't really use his feet without making scuffing noises against the concrete wall. Gripping tightly with his right hand, he shifted his left hand over to the right railing, lifted his left knee, and this time was able to use his knee to lever his upper body onto the parapet at the top, then over to the top outside rung of the ladder. He nearly lost the mirrored glasses off his face in the process. Bits of old concrete dust fell away into the rubble below, sounding to Kreiss like an avalanche.

Then came the sound of a metal buckle hitting the stock of a rifle, a muffled but distinct sound clear enough that he could classify it immediately. It sounded as if it was coming from in front of the valve pit, but he couldn't be sure, not way up here, dangling on the side of a building. He had to get down now, because there was nowhere else to go. If she saw him, she'd just blast him off the ladder like a fly off a window. Then the hair went up on the back of his neck.

She was here, or at least very near. Down there in the dark.

He froze on the ladder, willing himself to become invisible. With one finger, he pulled the glasses down his nose and peered down into the side street below. It was pitch-black, darker than dark, but he sensed there was something down there. Something moving.

The side street pointed directly at the valve pit, which was about twenty-five yards away. The sound program was set to make a noise every three minutes. He waited, dangling on the ladder, afraid even to breathe. Then from the valve pit came the sound of a human sniffing, one little noise, as if a man was clearing his nose while he waited for something. He pushed the glasses back up on his nose. Soon now.

A gust of wind came down the street, and he could feel it along the full length of his body. It was almost strong enough to ruffle his clothes. Was she down there right now, pressed against a building, *this* building, in the kneeling position, holding the assault rifle and sweeping the IR sight back and forth across the sector from which the tiny noises were coming? Seeing the barely visible fuzzy patch of green in the scope where the warm piece of metal, cooling fast now, would show up against all that cold concrete? Gripping the railing as hard as he could with his left hand, he drew the .45 across his chest and pointed it down into the black void beneath his feet. Virtually blind behind the glasses, he put his thumb on the hammer and then squeezed all thought and sensation out of his forebrain and focused every bit of his energy into listening.

The next sound came a minute later. This time, it was a barely audible squeak, like the sound a plastic egg carton makes when a human hand pushes down on it. Then something definitely moved down below him, not a whole body in motion, but something less, a human effort, the sound of cloth straining for just a second, and then a brilliant purple flash ignited over the valve pit. The glasses protected him from the full effect, but the soundless, dazzling blaze of light still almost blinded him. He caught a glimpse of a black figure bolting down the street, straight at the valve pit, and then there was a second purple explosion, followed by the thump of a thermite grenade erupting down in the pit, the explosion flaring into a brilliant white bolus of sparks and flame. Then the AK-47 opened up in a roar, blasting rounds directly down into the pit, sending red-and-yellow ricochets off into the night, the sound of the automatic weapon rebounding off the nearby concrete structures. The rifle hammered away on full auto until the magazine was empty. Misty with a gun, Kreiss marveled as he thumbed back the hammer, I'll be goddamned.

He flipped the glasses off his nose as the thermite fire hit its peak, throwing every feature of the wrecked buildings into searing black-and-white relief. He finally saw Misty silhouetted against the opposite wall, and he didn't hesitate. He twisted his body in midair, took a snap aim at the silhouetted figure, and emptied the .45, the big gun banging painfully back into his wrist with each round. Just as he realized that all the bullets had done nothing more than blast chunks of concrete off the opposite wall, a voice below him said, "Nice shooting, Edwin, but you just killed an illusion. Now come down from there."

Janet saw the familiar purple flare over the hill behind the main gates and instinctively closed her eyes, missing the second one. Then she heard Lynn gasp as an unearthly white glow lit up the trees in front of them, accompanied by the stuttering roar of an assault rifle. They looked at each other for an instant, and then she started the car, slammed it into gear, and punched it up the road, through the police barrier tapes, and right through the chain-link gate at the top of the drive. Accelerating too fast, she nearly lost it on the first curve. They topped the hill leading down into the industrial area, going fast enough to lift the car off its shocks and then bang it down on the concrete. She started braking when she saw the searing glare of burning phosphorus in the valve pit and heard the thumping reports as the .45 let go. The boiling thermite fire turned the wreckage of the arsenal into a vision of hell, throwing grotesque demonlike shadows onto the stark concrete shells of the buildings. She felt the car lose traction on all the loose gravel and concrete bits in the street, the tires scattering debris like shrapnel. She instinctively braked hard, too hard, whipping it around in a 360-degree spin, and then the next thing she saw was that big black hole that led down into the Ditch right in front of them. She started to scream, but then the car hit the pile of pipes, steel straws clattering along the sides of the car, and then it plunged through them and into the hole, slamming both of them into the windshield. Her last thought before she lost consciousness was that she really should have put on her seat belt.

Kreiss dropped the empty .45 down into the street and came down the ladder. Misty stood there in full field gear, with an IR goggle headset pushed back up over her hood. She held what looked like a miniature camcorder in her left hand and a Colt Woodsman .22 semiautomatic pistol in her right hand. As he reached the street and dropped onto all fours in the gravel, he saw that the camcorder was really a video projector. A green-lighted human silhouette was bouncing around the adjacent walls as Misty walked over to him.

"Put out your hands," she ordered.

"Let's just get it done, why don't we?" he said.

"Get what done? I'm not going to shoot you. This is a retrieval mission. Put out your hands. Fingers joined together."

He crouched there for a second, considering his options. Her expression confirmed what he already knew: He didn't have any options. He put out his hands. She dropped the projector and brought out a small cylinder, from which she sprayed capture curtain all over his joined hands. It felt cold and then warm. His hands disappeared into a glob of latex.

They both heard the car coming at the same time. Kreiss turned to look, hoping she would look also, but Misty never moved as she kept that Woodsman pointed at his face. The car sounded as if it were out of control coming down the main street, which was now out of sight behind Misty. They heard the brakes squeal and then the sound of tortured tires losing traction. The car hit something solid. The engine raced for a moment before stalling out. Then silence.

"Your cavalry?" she asked.

He shook his head. He desperately needed to distract her. His hands were globbed up, but he still had his feet. As if she sensed his intentions, she moved back a step. There was an ominous silence behind the building where the car had hit something.

"Well, it's not mine, either," she said. "So let's go see. Sounds to me like they fucked it up. You first."

He complied, holding his hands out in front of him to keep his arms free. He didn't want the sticky stuff enveloping his hands to touch any

other part of his body. He could see from the shadows thrown by the subsiding fire that Misty was behind him, but he could not determine how far
back she was. It smelled as if some wooden boards were burning back in
the valve pit. The wood smoke was a pleasant contrast to the poisonous
stink of burned phosphorus. He kept looking for an opening, but Misty
wasn't likely to give him one.

They came around the shattered front wall of the building and saw the
car. It looked to Kreiss like a Bu car, with those two whip antennas on the
trunk. It was nosed down into that same big hole Carter had driven into
before. Carter? Could Carter have come back here? And then he had a
really bad thought: Had she brought Lynn with her? No, she wouldn't
have been that dumb.

They approached the car carefully. He had the sense that Misty was
even farther behind him. Maybe he could jump past the car down into
the Ditch. But then he remembered how far down it was; he'd break both
his legs.

"Stop there," she ordered. He complied.

"Get down on your knees."

He didn't move. There was nothing moving in the car, which he could
see now was held in place by a lone steel pipe bent under its frame. The
nose of the car was below street level, kept from falling all the way
through into the Ditch by the pipe that was jammed up under its left-
front wheel well. No one was visible inside.

"Get down on your knees or I'll wrap you. Then you'll get to roll all
the way to the van."

He sighed and got down awkwardly onto his knees, his hands still held
out in front of him. His arms were getting tired, but he was determined
not to get his hands tack-welded to his body if he could help it. The fire-
light behind the building shell was dying out, and the street was slipping
back into darkness. Misty was moving around him, staying at least ten feet
away, the gun still pointed at his head while she examined the car. Then
he thought he heard distant sirens.

Janet awoke into a red haze with a splitting headache. Getting tired of all
these goddamned headaches, she thought irrelevantly, and then she tried
to open her eyes. They were stuck together by some warm sticky substance, which she finally realized was her own blood. Her forehead was
covered in blood, and she could feel it dripping down her chin and onto

her chest. She moved sideways and tried to wipe the blood out of her eyes. She wiped the blood off her hands and felt around for her Sig, then remembered it was in her holster. She looked over to see what had happened to Lynn, but the girl was not visible. Then she was, a crumpled white-faced form scrunched into the space between the dashboard and the front seat. No, not white-faced—red-faced. She, too, had hit the windshield and was bleeding profusely from a scalp cut. Janet swore softly and tried to untangle herself from between the front seat and the steering wheel. Then she heard something outside, sat up very carefully, raised her head, and looked through the shattered windshield. There was just enough light coming from the fire to reveal Kreiss on his knees in the street, and a tall black figure with a gun moving slowly toward the car. She recognized that figure, and she moved her hand behind her to draw the Sig. Lynn moaned from under the dashboard, but she did not move.

"It's your cavalry all right," Misty said. "She drives like she shoots, though. Nice going, Special Agent."

Janet shook some more blood out of her eyes as she struggled to get more upright in the seat. She glared at Misty through the open side window. She saw two Mistys, then three, then one, and blinked her eyes rapidly to clear her vision. She held the Sig just out of sight below the windowsill, her fingers sticky with blood. Misty was stepping closer, but her gun hand kept that Colt aimed right at Kreiss's head as if it had its own fire-control system. Janet looked over at Kreiss. He appeared to have a ball of fabric wrapped around his hands, which he held out in front of him as if praying.

"We've come for Kreiss," Janet said.

"We? *We?* Got a mouse in your pocket, there, Special Agent?" Misty was smiling wolfishly.

Janet swallowed to relieve the dryness in her throat. She thought she heard distant sirens, but she dismissed it as wishful thinking. Then she saw Misty's expression change. Damn it, she did hear sirens.

"Here's the deal," Misty said. "He's going with me. You try to interfere, I'll execute plan B."

"Plan B?" Janet repeated stupidly.

Misty gave her a patient look but said nothing. Janet figured it out.

Janet tried to think of something to say, a move to make, but she was staring at an impasse here and she knew it. God, her head hurt. Her teeth hurt and her eyes hurt and she was feeling a little nauseous. She felt the

Sig in her hands, and wondered when she'd managed to draw it. Misty smiled as if reading her mind.

"Whatcha got there, Special Agent?" she said in a taunting voice. "Got your gun, do you?" She stepped closer, her weapon still pointed unwaveringly at Kreiss. Janet definitely heard sirens now, but they were getting closer not nearly as fast as she wanted. Lynn groaned again behind her. Kreiss looked over at the car; he had heard his daughter.

"Want to try it out, Special Agent?" Misty asked. She took a fighting stance, extending her arms, crouching, and gripping her weapon with both hands, still keeping it pointed at Kreiss. She was maybe six feet from the car, her body facing Janet but her head turned to watch Kreiss. "Think you can actually shoot someone? Because I don't think you can. I think I can nail you and then him in the time it'll take you to work up your nerve, because you're just another fucking amateur and always will be. But, hey, Carter, I'm game if you are."

Kreiss moved then, struggling to his feet. Janet felt her heart start to pound. Her mouth was now absolutely dry and there was a chemical taste in her throat. The Sig suddenly seemed to weigh twenty pounds, and she gripped the butt even harder.

This was the moment she had dreaded the whole time she had been in the Bureau.

"Get back on your fucking knees, Kreiss," Misty hissed, steadying the gun on him but now watching Janet.

"No," he said, starting to walk toward her. Janet realized what he was doing. He was creating a diversion, forcing Misty to split her concentration. Giving Janet the shot. But only if she did it *right now*.

Time slowed down. A rivulet of blood ran into her right eye and she had to blink rapidly to clear her vision. Misty saw Janet blink and smiled. Kreiss kept coming.

"Watch this, baby face," Misty said, snapping her eyes back to Kreiss for a second and then back to Janet. "Let me show you how this is done."

Janet fired right through the car door. She didn't try to aim. She just stared at Misty and forced her hands to track that stare, willing the bullets to slash through the six feet of air between them and tear into that goddamned woman's body. She fired until the Sig wouldn't fire anymore, her fingers burning as the car's insulation caught fire, watching with grim satisfaction as Misty staggered back from the hail of bullets that were tearing into her, still trying to bring the Woodsman around and then dropping it with a wail that was cut off as the final round tore out her throat, spinning her around and down onto the concrete. Janet's last three rounds hit the concrete wall behind, sending two ricochets howling down the ruined street and one back into her own car, inches from her knee.

When the noise finally stopped, Janet tried to focus on the scene in front of her. Misty was motionless on the ground. Janet turned her head to locate Kreiss. Oh God, oh God, Kreiss was down, too, face flat on the concrete, not moving, his face buried in the rubble.

She dropped the Sig by her foot and tried to get the door open, but it wouldn't budge. Lynn was crying behind her now, making a whimpering little-girl sound that surprised Janet. She pushed herself sideways, getting more blood in her face, wiping it off on the seat back, and then started climbing through the window feetfirst. She felt the car move then, swaying as she changed position. She froze, then resumed her movements, forcing her legs and then her hips out the window, straining her back, and then dropping out of the car onto—nothing.

She yelped, grabbed the blood-slick windowsill, and hung there for a moment while the car rocked dangerously on the single pipe holding it over the hole. She heard the end of the pipe grinding ominously. She climbed partially back into the car, got another faceful of blood, and then blindly kicked out with her legs until her feet hit solid ground. She arched her back, making a bridge of her body between the rim of the hole and the car, and then stood up, windmilling her arms until she could get her balance. She sat down, then recoiled when she felt Misty's foot move against her back. She rolled away, wiping her eyes clear of blood, and came up on all fours. Misty was also on all fours. Her chest pack was a mass of black blood, and there were bloody holes in her right hand and throat. Her left eye was hanging partially out of its socket. Her face was twisted into a white mask of fury. The hole in her throat was pumping visibly, spattering the concrete and literally drowning out the words she was trying to speak. Janet crawled backward from this horrible apparition as the sweeper brought up a large stainless-steel syringe in her left hand. The needle dripped a fuming substance from its glittering tip, and then Janet, still moving backward, felt a searing lance of pain on her right shoulder as Misty pressed the plunger to fire a jet of acid across the concrete at Janet. Then Janet heard a single shot from her left and Misty's head jerked sideways and she dropped like a stone, the syringe clattering into the street.

Janet tried to get up, but her skin was screaming in pain as the acid melted through her shirt and burned her. She saw Lynn hanging partially out of the car window, her face white, blood streaming from her forehead, still clutching Janet's .38. The car shifted again, the steel pipe under the wheel well beginning to bend up at a dangerous angle. Janet yelled at Lynn to stop moving as she tore away the upper-right part of her smoking shirt and rubbed at her skin, trying to get the acid off her. Then Kreiss was there, telling her to stop moving, and then he was kneeling next to Misty's body and dissolving the capture curtain in the fountain of blood coming out of her throat until his hands came free, flailing away the ropes of the latex hanging off them like a bundle of snakes. He pulled Lynn all the way out of the car, getting her clear just as the steel pipe made a loud creaking noise and then viciously snapped, dropping the car nose-first down into the hole with a terrible crash. After that came a profound silence, into which the sounds of sirens finally penetrated. Kreiss put Lynn down gently, sitting her up against the building's wall.

Janet sat on the concrete, still batting at the skin on her shoulder while trying to keep the blood out of her eyes with her left arm. Kreiss squatted down next to her, rubbed his bloody hands against the jumpsuit, and took her hand.

"I wasn't sure you could do it," he said softly.

"I wasn't, either," she said, looking over at the Misty's shattered body, which was draining four distinct streams of blood across the concrete and into the Ditch. Lynn still held Janet's .38 in a virtual death grip while she stared at Misty's inert form. Janet realized she was clutching his hand like a lifeline. Her own legs were trembling.

"Look," he said. "You've both sustained head injuries. Your memory will be affected. I'm going to take . . . that . . . away. Here's your story: You got here, heard shooting, saw the thermite, and then fucked up and drove into the hole and got out by the skin of your teeth."

Janet blinked. The sirens were definitely closer now. "They'll certainly believe that," she said. "Still the fucking amateur."

"No, not anymore you're not," he said. He looked over at Lynn to make sure she was still conscious. "Who'd you call?"

"Would you believe the ATF?"

He smiled at that. "I've got to move," he said. "You remember the crash, but nothing else. Stay close to Lynn, if you can. I'll be in touch when things cool off."

"Will you?" she asked.

"Oh yes, Janet. But first I'll send you a sign. Now, lie back down, relax. That's just a cut on your head. Scalp wounds bleed. Looks worse than it is, but it will divert any questions for a while." He looked up and listened. "They're almost here."

"Farnsworth is going to be seriously pissed," she said, not letting go of his hand.

"Farnsworth is going to be too busy to be pissed," he replied. He squeezed her hand and then he moved to Lynn. She watched him gently put his daughter down on her back in the antishock position, head down, knees raised. He wiped her forehead, took the gun out of her hand, and then held her face in his hands for a moment. He kissed her forehead and stood up. He picked up Misty's gun, and then lifted her inert form, hunched into a fireman's carry, and then he was gone, bent over with the weight of her, like a lion off to hide his kill.

Janet relaxed onto the concrete, hearing the noise of vehicles up by the gate, knowing they'd be down here soon. She let the blood seep over her forehead now without trying to impede it; the bleeding actually seemed to help the headache. The skin along her upper arm and shoulder still burned, but it was more like a really bad sunburn now. She wondered if her shoulder would be scarred forever. She realized she didn't really care.

What had he called her? Janet? No more "Special Agent"? She smiled at that as headlights flooded the street. It began to rain.

15

Three weeks later, Janet Carter waited outside the RA's office for her final meeting with Farnsworth and Keenan before she formally checked out of the office. That morning, she had tentatively accepted a teaching and research position over at Virginia Tech in the materials forensics department of the civil engineering school. The school was developing a postincident forensics program to investigate and determine the cause of catastrophic failures in large structures, such as bridges, streets, or buildings. When the department chair, who had also headed up one of her Saturday seminars, found out she was looking, he had offered her the job immediately, subject, of course, to the appropriate due diligence on her academic degree and an FBI recommendation. Like many government employees leaving federal service, she'd been a bit surprised at how easy it had been.

As she sat there, she wondered, not for the first time, where Edwin Kreiss was. Based on the way Lynn had been acting lately, she was pretty sure they had been in touch. The past three weeks had been interesting times, in the Chinese sense of that expression. The ATF never did find McGarand, but they had found a vehicle in the woods that had been rented up in Washington at the Reagan Airport, and the driver's license used had been Browne McGarand's. A joint forensics team had spent some time at the scene where they found Janet and Lynn. It had taken a specially equipped fire truck to get the fire in the valve pit out because the thermite grenade had ignited some metal fittings. There had been no trace of human remains in or around the valve pit itself, but they had recovered an IR sight-equipped AK-47, along with evidence that it had been emptied almost indiscriminately into the valve pit. She wondered if anyone had tried to account for all the blood trails out on that street, but the rain had probably washed most of it away.

Farnsworth had had a lot of explaining to do to his bosses in Richmond and Washington, as well as to the ATF. He stonewalled the latter, while trying to explain what one of his agents had been doing there at the arsenal that night, with a civilian in tow. There had been endless meetings and lots of report writing to do over the whole incident. Janet had had time to prep Lynn in the ER, so their story remained fairly consistent: They had gone out there to help Kreiss and ended up crashing the car. End of story, as far as they knew. Never saw Kreiss. Never saw anyone else. Never saw a firefight. Janet's acid burns had come somehow from the hole into which they'd crashed the car. Didn't know how they got out, or how they got back up to the street. Both of them had taken a shot to the head, hadn't they? Everything after the crash was a blur. Didn't remember calling the ATF, but must have. Knew they'd come, wasn't sure the Bureau would. That last had hurt Farnsworth's feelings. No, never saw McGarand.

Billy Smith had been recalled to temporary duty in Washington the day after the incident. Janet had been prepared to pursue the theory that he had been an Agency plant all along, put in place to watch Kreiss. But he was gone, and Farnsworth had bigger fish to fry. Three days after the incident, all the hate mail from Washington had suddenly stopped. Word came down directly from the executive assistant director over Criminal Investigations that the incident was officially closed. It had been as if a giant hand had simply wiped all the postincident counterops and turned out the lights on the whole affair. One day, she was in the hot seat; the next day, everyone was suddenly all smiles and happiness and the office was back to business as usual. All she could figure was that larger issues, and one in particular, had finally hit the fan at the senior-executive service level.

Lynn Kreiss was back in school, after Janet had explained to the university's finance office why Lynn had been absent and, more important, why her tuition for that quarter ought not to be forfeited. The university's finance office had been incredibly unsympathetic, and it wasn't until Janet had threatened publicity that adult supervision was brought to bear. Lynn had agreed to go with Janet and Larry Talbot to one final meeting with the boys' parents, which had been tense initially and then extremely emotional. Now she was spending her weekends at her father's cabin, waiting and watching for her father to appear out of the woods one night. Janet had been spending her weekends there, too, just to keep an eye on things and to get out of her town house. In the back of her mind, she knew she also wanted to be there when, if, he showed up again, but there had been no sign of Edwin Kreiss.

She had also been assigned to work out a case-closure report with the Montgomery County detectives on the matter of Jared McGarand. She had written a Bureau memo outlining her theory that Jared McGarand's death had probably been accidental, occurring during the course of a confrontation between Edwin Kreiss and the subject. She appended an evidentiary statement provided by Lynn Kreiss as to the sexual abuse and near rape she had endured while a captive at the hands of the subject. The county people, slaves to the same closure statistics that drove their federal cousins, said they would have to keep the case open, but they allowed informally as to how nobody was going to put a lot of man-hours on a creep like that anytime soon. Because she had named Edwin Kreiss in her report, the paperwork was whisked off to Washington and never seen again.

She had spent a great deal of time doing some soul-searching about staying in the Bureau. The Roanoke people might all have been told to forget that anything had happened, but, of course, a hell of a lot had happened. The kicker came when Farnsworth put her in for a meritorious service award. The headquarters Professional Awards Division had come back disapproving the recommendation, citing an opinion from OPR that there had been several clear instances where Special Agent Janet Carter had either disobeyed direct operational orders or departed from approved procedures, causing the loss of a Bureau vehicle in two different instances. Farnsworth had loyally driven up to Richmond to raise hell about the disapproval, but when he returned, all he could say was that he had run into an absolute bureaucratic glacier. It apparently had nothing to do with Janet. It had everything to do with the fact that the Edwin Kreiss case was not only closed but positively entombed. "Chernobylized," the SAC in Richmond had said. Images of helicopters dumping concrete on the whole affair.

That was when Janet had made her decision to leave the Bureau. She could understand how the organization would want to pave over the Edwin Kreiss affair. She could not, however, forget what she had done out there in the arsenal. For that one instant, she had become an instinctive, rather than rational, human being. She could justify the shooting; she could not rationalize emptying the Sig, no matter how much she recited Bureau training about gunfights. She had looked Misty in the eye and emptied the Sig until her hands were on fire, and she would have come out of that car and strangled the woman if she'd been close enough. She could still remember the shock of triumph in her heart when she saw the look of surprise in Misty's face, even as her bullets took that face apart. As far as she was concerned, she'd met the beast, and the beast had looked a lot like her. Once was enough.

"Mr. Farnsworth will see you now, Special Agent Carter," the secretary said, a triumphant look in her eyes. Janet came back to the present and stared at the secretary long enough to make her look away. Then she went into the RA's office. Ben Keenan was already there, and they both appeared to be in an expansive mood. Janet sat down.

"So I guess this is good-bye," she said.

Farnsworth nodded. He had not attempted to talk her out of leaving the Bureau this time, which pretty much confirmed Janet's own suspicions that, careerwise, she had become radioactive. "Yes, I guess it is, Janet," he said. "I'm sorry it didn't work out better, but I think you understand by now that, knowing what you know about the Edwin Kreiss case, any subsequent assignments would always be . . . uncomfortable? I guess that's the right word. If it makes you feel any better, I'll be following you out the door by year's end."

"They didn't—"

"Oh, no, but these kind of cases always create a certain amount of fallout. If I go peacefully, the rest of the troops here get a second chance."

"The rest of the troops here just did their jobs," she said. "Why should they suffer over the Kreiss affair?"

"You know the answer to that, Janet," he said. "Kreiss was a Bureau man. He embarrassed the outfit. This whole thing reminded everybody of an old rule."

"What's that?"

"Once a deal is made at the executive level, always clean up any loose ends. Kreiss was a loose end with consequences, and look what happened."

"I would have thought that document would have made them somewhat more grateful," she said.

"What document was that?" Farnsworth asked. His expression was one of bland disinterest.

Janet cocked her head. "C'mon now," she said. "The document in AD Marchand's archives. The smoking gun. Which proved—"

"Never heard of it," Farnsworth said, giving Keenan a questioning look. Keenan shook his head. He'd never heard of it, either.

"*What!*" she exclaimed.

"Nothing of the sort ever happened," he repeated. "The resignation of the deputy attorney general of the United States was simply a case of a senior political appointee resigning as the administration ended its own term of office. Nothing more."

"And the recent retirement of Assistant Director Marchand and his senior deputy AD, and a certain red-faced EA . . . well, those were driven entirely by personal reasons," Keenan said. "Nothing more."

"And the reappointment of our beloved director for another full term of office had been in the works for, oh, quite a long time," Farnsworth said, folding his hands across his chest. "Don't you think so, Ben?"

"Oh, yes," Keenan chimed in. "Quite a long time indeed. Absolutely. At least according to the attorney general of the United States, who publicly expressed her continuing full faith and confidence in him."

"As did the president himself. Am I right, Ben?"

"He absolutely did," Keenan said, beaming. "Several times. And he loves his Bureau, too."

"Oh, positively. He *loves* his Bureau. Just like the AG loves her Bureau."

"They fucking better," Keenan said. They looked at Janet with straight faces for a moment, and then they all laughed.

Janet shook her head. In a way, it was kind of comforting. The ultimate lock was in place. The big fish could afford to smile about it. Small fry who might know something about the antecedents of such deals were, of course, an embarrassing annoyance. Any offer on said small fry's part to fold her tents and disappear quietly into the desert night would be gratefully and expeditiously accepted, as evidenced by the recommendation Farnsworth sent over to the university. It had been glowing in the extreme, and, just for good measure, it had been warmly endorsed by the same official at the laboratory who had been the proximate cause of her original exile to the Roanoke office. Wonders never ceased.

Farnsworth was about to say something else, when the secretary buzzed in on the intercom.

"What?" Farnsworth asked.

"An urgent telex for you, sir. From the VHP?"

"Yeah, go ahead."

The secretary read it over the intercom. It was plain from her tone of voice that she was upset. The Virginia Highway Patrol was reporting that they had found two partially mummified human heads impaled on stakes in the median of Interstate 81 outside of Christiansburg. They were requesting immediate FBI forensic assistance. They reported quite a commotion out on the interstate. Media interest was expected.

"*Mummified human heads!*" Keenan exclaimed. "On stakes? Christ!"

Janet turned her face away to conceal the smile she was struggling to control. "Close," she murmured.

She wondered when he'd call. He probably wouldn't. He'd come shambling down that hill behind the cabin. Maybe with Micah Wall and Whizbang. "Hey, Special Agent," he'd say. "So where's your bu-car?" She could just see it.